# HART OF THE NIGHT

## Bloodline

## M.C. Ruskuls

# CONTENTS

# COPYRIGHT

To my sister-in-law Erica, your unwavering encouragement and genuine interest in this story have been the guiding lights through its creation. Without your support, this book would have remained a dream. Thank you for believing in me and helping bring this tale to life.

# CHAPTER I

## ONCE UPON A TIME

The frosty grip of an Illinois September clung mercilessly to the air and seeped into every crevice of my room. As I lay ensconced in my cocoon of warmth, the thought of facing the bitter cold outside filled me with dread.

"Uggggh, why is it so cold? This can't be normal," I groaned aloud in a futile protest against the relentless grip of winter's way too early arrival.

Every morning was a battle against the relentless cold, but today felt somehow worse. Rather than face the cruel bite of cold, I decided to lay there staring at the ceiling and wait. It was just a matter of time before my mom would burst into my room, saying that it was a beautiful morning and reminding me it was time to get up. Like I needed to be reminded to wake up; the freezing weather already did that just fine.

In a desperate bid to avoid the daily subzero struggle, a mischievous idea crossed my mind. Maybe I could convince her that I was sick, then *maybe* I could snuggle into the warmth of my cozy bed all day. But before I could devise an intricate plan to deceive my mom, a tantalizing aroma wafted through the air and pierced through my frosty resistance.

I tilted my head to the right to concentrate better on the scent. *Mmmm, maple bacon and eggs.*

My dad always knew how to get me up on a cold morning. In a flurry of motion, I dressed hastily, throwing on my school uniform then pulling a black sweater and matching sweatpants over it.

I glanced in the mirror and sighed at the fact that my "year-round" tan was rapidly fading. I continued with my morning makeup ritual, brushing on some blush, mascara, and a little purple eyeshadow, which brought out my brown eyes. Finally, I added a dab of lip gloss.

I worked for a few moments on the tangled chaos that was my hair before deciding to throw my long dark locks into a ponytail then proceeded down the stairs.

"Zay, is Nina up yet?" I heard my dad ask my brother as I got to the bottom of the stairs.

"I have no idea," he responded absentmindedly.

"Well, you're going to have a tough time getting to school if she's not, huh?" my dad shot back.

"I'm here," I answered as I slid to the kitchen counter on my socked feet. I couldn't help but smile, grateful for the small comforts that thawed the icy grip of winter's embrace.

My dad was a handsome man. He had the same light skin I did, but, like a typical Irishman, he had blonde hair and blue eyes. His fit, 6'2" frame sported his typical suit, but since we had moved, he had added colorful ties. Today, his tie had little snowflakes on it—another attempt to get us to appreciate the snow alongside his almost daily reminders about how beautiful it was.

"I'm sorry, honey. It's just unseasonably cold right now," he said to me sympathetically.

"I know, Dad."

I had no right to be mad at him, considering the sacrifice he had made for our family. He had just started his new job at Osbourne-Palmer Memorial

Hospital about a month earlier. When we had lived in California, his job had paid him three times what he was making in this new position, but our parents had decided to move because my brother Ian and I had received full scholarships to Vanguard Preparatory, one of the most prestigious academies in the country.

Since it was privately owned, the school could bring on one scholarship student for each team every year. Of course, that took us out of some competitions against public schools, but not at the state level. As such, we played only privately funded academies in sports until we reached the state finals. Then we could play whichever was the best team.

Ian had always loved learning new things ever since he was young. He was a little nerdy in that sense. Instead of going out with one of his many friends when they asked him to, he would rather stay home and study or read. He had never been much for team sports, but our parents had had him try out for the National Academic League, the NAL, back in California. He had ended up loving it, and the NAL had given him the opportunity to join Vanguard on a full scholarship.

Although I loved to read and to get lost in the worlds of fantasy and romance authors, I was not as smart as Ian. I excelled in a completely different area and been admitted on a full scholarship for soccer.

My younger brother, Zay, wasn't yet at VP. Unlike other schools, ours only had Grades 10, 11, and 12. The school board believed that having only the last three years of high school available would benefit students all around the area. They thought it not only would help ground new students entering VP, but it would also give all students something to strive for. After attending public schools, applicants could see what it took to be admitted into a school like VP. That effort alone would help them get into any college they wanted even if they didn't get in to VP itself.

"You know, I'm cold, too, but I can get out of bed," Zay hissed at me, his tone laced with a mixture of annoyance and defiance.

Despite him being only 14, he looked very mature and could probably pass for a high school senior. With his rather striking resemblance to our dad, he shared the same piercing blue eyes, but he had brown hair like mine. Also like my dad, he always dressed very nicely. Today, he wore a blue button-down shirt and faded jeans.

"What about Ian? Has he made it out of bed yet this morning?" my dad asked me suspiciously.

"Ouch! Son of a— gawwww!" I heard my brother Ian shout as he tripped over a pair of shoes then lazily walked down the hall.

I turned toward him and giggled at his tired appearance. He was tall like my dad, standing just under six feet, and had only recently turned 17. We had been born only ten months apart—me on November 23 and him on the first day of the following September—which was a bit annoying because it meant we had ended up in the same grade with him just making the cutoff. We also looked similar, with the same brown hair and eyes, so many people thought we were twins.

Ian and I tended to like similar things, but our appearances were not one of those. His school uniform was completely wrinkled, and his shirt was only halfway tucked into his pants. As always, the same black sweater, which was entirely too big for him, was draped over his arm. If he hadn't just buzzed his hair off, I'm sure that would have been a mess as well.

"Why are you so happy today? It's freaking freezing!" he shouted at me.

The weather was one of the things Ian and I *did* see eye to eye on. We were usually grumpy together on a cold day and joined forces to devise plans to stay home.

Instead of frowning in agreement, I cheerfully pointed at the feast our dad had prepared for us then smiled again before shoving another piece of bacon in my mouth.

"Oh, yummy. Gimme."

I laughed at him as he sat down.

"Shush," he added quickly.

"Okay, Nikolina Ifigeneia Hart, time to get out of bed!" I heard my mother call up the stairs. She always called me by my full name when she was serious about something, and getting me out of bed on a freezing day was serious.

"We are all down here, my love!" my dad called up to her.

We all laughed and watched the shock on our mother's face when she entered the kitchen. She looked around then quickly realized what had gotten us all out of bed that morning.

My mother's exotic beauty came from her Spanish and Greek backgrounds. Like Ian and me, she had brown eyes and hair—hers was shiny and fell about three inches past her shoulders. However, while Ian and I had fair skin, hers had a beautiful olive complexion.

She worked in an elite law firm as the lead paralegal for all departments. In her position, it was very important to look professional, so she always perfectly curled her hair every day. Those loose curls now framed her face exquisitely and brought out her almond-shaped eyes.

"Ahh," she responded to my dad.

"Would you like a plate, darling?" he smiled.

"Of your famous winter day breakfast? I wouldn't dream of passing it up."

She smiled at him and kissed him before taking her seat between him and Zay.

My parents had the kind of relationship I could only dream of. They had met while still in college when my mom had been visiting relatives in Greece and my dad had been doing research for a class. Ever since, they had been inseparable. Both were very attractive, but I had never witnessed any type of jealousy from either one because they trusted each other fully.

"You guys should get a move on," my dad reminded us as he pointed his fork toward the door.

I glanced at the radio clock hanging to my right just above the phone. It was already 7:11 a.m., and I still had to drop off Zay at his high school near VP.

"Let's go," I said as I snuck one last piece of bacon before standing and grabbing my purse and bookbag from the empty chair beside me. I hurriedly ran to the hall closet and tossed my brothers their jackets before grabbing mine.

"Shotgun!" Zay yelled.

"No way, man," Ian replied before making a mad dash for the door and almost letting out one of our three cats in the process.

"Oh, no you don't, Chloe," I said to her as I grabbed her by the tail and chest then yanked her back inside.

I picked her up and took her up the stairs into my bedroom then reluctantly headed back toward the door. I shook my head and laughed as she looked at me with her "my plan has been foiled again" look.

As I walked toward the hallway, I saw Boy, one of our other cats, with his eyes fixed on the door as if ready to make his escape, too. I grabbed him and tossed him on my bed before he could make a move. I laughed at the two cats now staring back at me then ran down the stairs as I glanced out the window, where it was still dark, and tried to prepare myself for what was coming.

As I stepped outside, I couldn't help letting out a fierce shiver before seeking refuge in my nice, toasty warm 1996 Toyota Celica. I didn't mind that my car was from the Stone Age so long as it was warm. I was extremely happy my dad had installed a new remote start in it before the big move as a consolation prize for moving us somewhere with ten months of winter. We had complained about it for a while, but we all loved and respected our dad. If he said this move would benefit us, we believed him.

"Stupid cold!" I exclaimed as I sank into the driver's seat.

I turned to Ian, who was already sitting in the passenger seat and had covered his head with his hoodie. "You know, one day, Zay might be bigger and stronger than you," I told him. I glanced in the rearview mirror to catch Zay smiling at my theory.

"Maybe, but for now I'm bigger than him, and I say I get shotgun."

Before heading out, I turned on the radio to a station that was mostly '50s and '60s music. My taste wasn't what you would call typical teenager music, but I loved it.

I glanced again into the backseat where Zay was already putting on his headphones. Always open to new things, Zay had tried getting into my music, but he'd decided it wasn't for him. Ian liked all different types of music, including this, so he sang along to *Jailhouse Rock* with me and Elvis.

As expected, there was a traffic jam on Mystic Boulevard, which was the only route to our schools. Everyone blamed "us kids" for the "big mess," but that was far from the truth. The real problem were the adults going to work from the border cities who wove in and out of the traffic as if they were on a giant checkerboard.

"Jerk!" I exclaimed as a black late-model BMW pulled out right in front of me so close I had to slam on my brakes.

The windows of the car were tinted so dark I couldn't see inside, but, sure enough, the next second produced a big bang as its driver rear-ended the brand-new red Honda right in front of him.

To my surprise, when the BMW driver stepped out of his car, he began walking toward us.

"What is this guy doing?" I whispered nervously as he came closer and closer to our car. Curious, I opened my window despite the cold.

"Hi, I'm Alan," he declared.

His smile was punctuated by dimples that could make any girl's heart stop. His presence radiated a charm and unwavering confidence that felt straight out of a romance novel. Clad in a maroon leather jacket that exuded rugged sophistication and dark jeans that hugged his form with precision, he cut a striking figure against the backdrop of the dark sky. The jacket, casually unzipped, revealed a fitted plain white V-neck T-shirt that showed off sculpted contours of a tight physique.

Even with a quick glance, he looked about an inch taller than my dad and in his mid- to late 20s. His bleached-blonde hair was long and slicked-back on the top and short on the sides. He had a perfectly sculpted square jawline, which was lightly stubbled, adding a touch of masculinity to otherwise boyish features.

But it was his eyes—twin pools of azure that shimmered with a hypnotic intensity against his pale white skin—that held my attention for an extended moment.

"Hello," I responded belatedly, my voice betraying a hint of shyness after being caught in the magnetic pull of his presence.

"I'm sorry for cutting you off back there. I'm just extremely late for work," he explained, flashing me a perfect smile that momentarily stole my breath away.

Our gazes lingered on each other, creating a subtle yet distinct connection.

"Can we help you with something?" Ian shouted from his seat, looking confused but more annoyed than anything.

Alan did not take his eyes off me; it was as if he were trying to understand something.

I glanced out the windshield to see the driver of the damaged Honda standing between her car and Alan's. It was Amanda Underwood. She was in our school year, and her dad was the dean of Vanguard. She was a pretty, petite, 5'3" blonde girl whose green eyes always had way too much black eyeliner for a 17-year-old. In my head, I called her Bert because her thickly applied eye makeup reminded me of a raccoon. It was an inside joke from an old cartoon my dad had watched with us when we were young.

"Oh, umm... oh?" I stammered. "It's okay, but maybe you should talk to Amanda. She's probably a bit more upset than I am," I explained when I could finally speak again.

When he didn't change his focus, I smiled at him warmly and pointed in her direction.

He looked over at her for a second then looked back at me. "Amanda?" he asked me with a confused expression.

"Yeah, we go to Vanguard together."

Suddenly he looked a bit angry, like maybe he didn't care much for the school, or maybe it was something else entirely. Whatever it was, that flash sent a chill down my spine.

"Do you not like Vanguard Prep or something?" I giggled nervously, trying not to show how uncomfortable he was making me.

"Um... it's—"

"Hello... You hit *me*!" Amanda interrupted.

He whirled his head around, still looking confused, then reality appeared to hit him. "Oh, I'm sorry, Miss," he said as he flashed a perfect smile at her, too.

Amanda's voice faltered momentarily as her gaze lingered on the enigmatic stranger before her. I saw a subtle recognition flicker in her eyes. "Well..." she began, her words trailing off into an uneasy silence as if a veil of uncertainty had descended on her thoughts. "Oh, it's okay," she continued hastily, a nervous laugh punctuating her words. "It's my brother's car anyway. I have a much cooler car. It's a red BMW... just like yours. I'm just getting it repainted."

I watched on as she continued babbling while she batted her overly made-up eyelashes and twirled a lock of her short blonde hair with her finger.

"It's pretty warm out today, isn't it?" she asked as she started to unzip her white jean jacket just enough to reveal her overdeveloped chest under a white tank top—certainly not meant for this 30-degree weather—and the black leggings underneath her skirt.

A sudden wave of concern washed over me as I watched Amanda conversing with the handsome stranger. In the far reaches of my mind, a nagging sense of foreboding whispered about the dangers that lurked beyond a façade of charm and allure—not all who captivated the senses could be trusted.

But, I remembered, she was a very spoiled girl and believed that the whole world revolved around her. Unfortunately, I had to put up with her like everyone else did. Not only was her dad the dean of VP, but she was also one of those girls who could turn the whole school against you. Even though I didn't much care what people thought about me, my friends did, so I had to put up with her for them.

"Hey, Nina, can you please tell Mr. Conrad that I will be a little late getting to class?"

The exchange struck me as odd because she always called me Nikki, which I hated, or Nikolina, but never Nina. But, of course, she hadn't exactly asked me. She was telling me without even turning to look my way, so at least that part was normal.

"Oh, yeah, sure, of course." I bit my lip.

Amanda was not the type of girl I would usually be friends with. She wasn't a bad person; she was just entitled and was a bit narcissistic. I put up with her not only for my friends but also for Zay. He only had a few months left to find out if he would be admitted to the school. Although Amanda didn't really have the power to exclude Zay from the admissions process, she had her dad's ear. From what I'd heard, she had a whole lot of influence over him.

I glanced down at the dashboard to see that it was already 7:55 a.m. Zay's school started at 8:00, so either way he would be late. VP started at 8:20, so we were cutting it close there as well.

I turned to look at Alan to say goodbye, but he was now staring at Amanda with the most intense look. As his eyes turned toward me again, I noticed that they seemed to be darkening. It was as if the color were draining straight out of them and changing from the beautiful blue from before to a blazing crimson red.

He quickly put on sunglasses that had been hanging from his jacket pocket before turning back toward Amanda. I looked away just as quickly then blinked a few times and shook my head. *Holy crap!*

"Bye, Alan, it was nice to meet you," I said nervously.

Although it didn't feel right leaving Amanda alone with him, no matter how handsome he was, I knew she wouldn't listen to me even if I told her it wasn't a good idea.

I turned toward Ian who had a stunned look that matched what I was feeling, and I wondered if he had seen Alan's eyes change, too. I looked in the rearview mirror for Zay's reaction, but he was still listening to his headphones as if nothing had happened.

"Ian, are you okay?" I asked curiously.

"I know you saw that," he responded anxiously.

"I'm not sure what I saw." I sighed. "What should we do?"

"Um, drive far, far away," he whispered.

I studied him for a few moments then looked back over at Amanda.

"Bye Nikki," she hissed at me, as if I needed the hint to leave.

I rolled my eyes at her then put the car back into Drive. When I glanced at Alan again, I saw that he had removed his sunglasses. His eyes were no longer that unnatural red I had seen a moment before but the beautiful blue I'd noticed first. Maybe my eyes had been playing tricks on me or the light had hit his eyes in a weird way to produce that odd color.

I drove away, still feeling weird about leaving Amanda, but shrugged it off because nothing ever happened in the town of Hallowed Hills. I had never seen a safer town. The only thing the police had to patrol here were people speeding.

When we'd first moved to the town, I'd left my cellphone at the gas station, but I only realized I didn't have it a few hours later. I never thought for a moment that my phone would still be there, but I went back to the gas station anyway. When I asked the gas station attendant if a phone had been turned in, he told me that it was still sitting by the chips and dip, which is where I had been looking for a snack a few hours earlier. I had been astonished that not only no one had taken it, but no one had even touched it.

Ian and I didn't say another word about the creepy eye-changing phenomenon for the rest of the drive. I turned into the parking lot of Hallowed

Hills High about five minutes later and finally understood why the adults thought teenagers drove like maniacs. I had driven pretty fast trying to get to the school on time. Of course, Zay took his sweet time getting out of the car as usual.

"Come on, Zay, go go go!" Ian yelled at him.

"Yeah, yeah, don't get your panties in a twist. I'm moving," Zay replied as he closed the back door and waved goodbye.

"Nina, I cannot be late today. Crazy Mrs. Taylor is going to kill me," Ian explained.

I took a deep breath and pressed the gas pedal to the floor, which had us screeching out of the parking lot.

"Okay! I would like to make it to school in one piece!"

I giggled under my breath because I knew I had complete control of the car, but it was always fun to scare my brother who was now gripping the dashboard as if he could prevent it from smacking him in the face if something were to really happen.

Even so, we made the 20-minute drive to the school in about 14 minutes.

"Holy crap, woman!" Ian exclaimed as I stopped near the main entrance.

"You're going to be late," I said quickly, not wanting to argue with him about my driving skills.

He looked at the digital clock in the dashboard then ran out of the car, leaving his math notebook behind. I grabbed it and stuffed it into my bookbag along with my wallet then went to go find a parking space.

As I walked toward the entrance of the school, I saw the group known as "the popular crowd." We were a part of it just because we were the new kids in town.

I had gotten along with everyone back in California, so I'd had similar friends there, but this was very different. People here seemed to watch everything Ian and I did, even mimicking our mannerisms at times. Ian did not care for it at all, but it didn't really bother me. However, it did feel odd how we always seemed to capture their attention in some strange, magnetic way.

"Nina! Nina!" called Emily Estes, one of Amanda's friends, which, by default, made her one of my friends, too. She had blue eyes, blonde hair, and was way too tan for living in Antarctica. Emily was just as petite as Amanda but not as "developed" and nowhere near as spoiled. I had been told that Amanda had taken her under her wing to help "guide her" about a year before we'd moved to Hallowed Hills.

"Oh, hey, Emily. What's up?"

She was practically jumping out of her skin with excitement, and that meant only one thing: boys.

"Do you know where Amanda is? I have something really important to tell her, so I have to find her," she piped excitedly.

"Umm, actually she's running a little late. She was in a very small fender bender," I answered.

Emily looked at me as if someone had just told her that her grandmother had passed away.

"Oh no, don't worry. She's okay. They're just exchanging insurance information, that's all."

My words seemed to work quickly as she immediately calmed down. I thought that a little odd given how emotional she had been only five seconds before.

"Oh, okay," she said then jumped up and down again. "Well, do you know when she'll be back?"

"I'm not sure, but she did tell me to tell Mr. Conrad that she would be a little late. I'm sure she'll be here no later than the start of second period."

I was now looking forward to first period. Not only was history my favorite subject, but, with Amanda being late, I wouldn't have to hear her and Emily ramble on and on about what guys they think are the hottest and which ones are better boyfriend material—a conversation that often included my brother. Of course, neither of them cared how incredibly uncomfortable that made me feel.

Finally, I saw Jennifer Shah and Rebecca Clarke, my actual friends, my best friends really.

As I waved to them over Emily's shoulder, she turned to look then rolled her eyes at me. "I don't know why you still hang out with them. They are so not popular."

For a minute, I gave her a disapproving look, but I already knew it wouldn't do any good. I found it funny that she felt that way because the year before I'd moved to Hallowed Hills, they were her best friends. But as soon as Amanda had started paying attention to her, Jen and Becca were the "unpopular crowd," and she could no longer be seen with them.

"I'll catch up with you later," I said to Emily as I walked toward Jen and Becca.

Emily rolled her eyes one last time then scampered back to her little mini-blonde crowd while I walked toward Jen and Becca standing on the steps right before the main door of the school.

I still wasn't used to how breathtaking the building was. The large four-story building had been constructed in 1783 as a private school for the wealthy white males from the most powerful families in the country. The exterior, adorned with reddish-orange bricks, bore the weathered beauty of age, with patches of vibrant green moss adding a touch of natural splendor.

The front of the school boasted three castle-like peaks, inside each of which were clocks showing different times. The middle one had our local time and was slightly larger than the other two. The one to the right had Eastern time, and the one to the left had Pacific time. The distinctive architectural embellishments, though functional, added an air of mystique to the edifice.

The huge wooden doors that led to the main hallway faced East. Arching over the main entrance and around the windows were lush vines and delicate red roses.

Above the main doorway arch hung an enormous falcon, our school mascot, which stood with its feet on the arch while its wings draped around the opening of the door. It had been added years after the original construction when the school had begun to accept students who were female or from different races, but it fit the architecture so well that it looked like it had been built with it.

The first time I had walked into the school, I'd thought that the wings looked more like angel wings than those of a bird because the way the sun reflected off them seemed to cast an ethereal glow. Even though they were made of bronze, their divine beauty was exquisite. It almost felt like the magnificent creature might carry you away as you walked into the school.

When I finally came out of my daze, I saw that Jen wore her normal huge smile. She was a petite, very tan Indian girl with brown eyes set behind thick, black-rimmed glasses that were stylish and hip, not like the Buddy Holly ones. Her brown hair was short and choppy, cut to her shoulders and flared out. In contrast, Becca's straight blonde hair went a bit past her shoulders, and she had blue eyes.

Both girls were pretty and always wore chic accessories to accentuate their school uniforms. VP's uniform policy was a little less strict than other schools. As long as we wore our uniforms, we could dress them up any way we wanted.

Our school colors were green and silver, but we could also wear white. Girls wore green-and-gray plaid skirts with white shirts under green blazers, and the boys wore gray pants with white or green shirts under the same blazers. We could also wear gray vests instead of blazers if we preferred.

Today, Jen had accessorized her uniform with a beautiful black-and-gold purse, gold earrings, and a long gold necklace. Becca had almost the same purse, but in white and gold. She also wore a gray scarf around her neck and silver earrings.

Whereas Jen was quiet and shy, Becca was outgoing and loud, but they still got along well and had been friends for a long time before I had moved to Hallowed Hills.

"Hey guys, what's up?" I asked.

"Hi, Nina! How was your weekend?" Jen asked happily.

"Like a treadmill," I laughed.

It was what we always said when we had a boring weekend because we hadn't ended up anywhere. We were still giggling when I remembered I still needed to get to my locker.

"Oh no, I have to go. Mr. Conrad will kill me if I am late again," I whined.

"Mr. Conrad?" Becca asked. "He's one of the most lenient teachers at the school," she laughed. "Oh, and the cutest, too."

"Sure, he is. Maybe if it's opposite day," I responded with a giggle.

Becca looked at me with confusion then shrugged as she turned to walk away with Jen.

"I'll see you guys at lunch," I said as I ran off.

As I approached the entrance to the school, a glimmer in the morning sunlight caught my eye. Curious, I bent down to inspect it, only to find a sharp fragment of glass lying just beneath the grand archway. Looking up, I saw that the middle clock was conspicuously still, its hands frozen in time. I frowned, wondering what could have caused it to malfunction. The broken glass at my feet seemed to suggest a possible cause. I looked up at the clock again and noticed that the glass was cracked in the middle as if it had been struck by something or someone.

Before I could delve deeper into the mystery, the two-minute warning bell suddenly rang, jolting me back to reality. Cursing under my breath, I hurriedly made my way into the school, the enigma of the broken glass temporarily forgotten in the rush of the moment.

I pushed my way through the throng of students standing in the hallway. When I finally made it to my locker, I had less than a minute to get to class, and I still needed to stop in the bathroom to take off my sweats. I stuffed the books I didn't need into my locker then ran into the bathroom. I yanked my sweats off, stuffed them in my bookbag, and sprinted toward my class. I made it there about two minutes late, so I tried to sneak in as quietly as I could.

"Thank you for deciding to grace us with your presence, Miss Hart," Mr. Conrad snorted.

I looked down sheepishly and went straight for my desk.

Mr. Conrad looked to be in his mid-20s and would have been very handsome if he'd known how to present himself. Becca was right about that part at least. It didn't hurt that he smelled good, too, sort of like a blend of grapes and vanilla but manly.

His brown hair hung an inch or two above his shoulders. He attempted to keep it tied back, but most of it spilled out the sides and half covered his face. He always wore a turtleneck, an oversized cardigan, and pants that looked way too big for him, so I couldn't tell if he was overweight or skinny. Plus, the Harry Potter glasses he wore were entirely too large for his face.

I assumed he was tough on us because he was the newest and youngest teacher. All the other teachers had been on staff for more than 20 years and had earned the respect of all the students. I could see how a younger teacher might have to think he had to prove himself. Even so, all the other teachers were much nicer than he was.

"I'm sorry, Mr. Conrad. I was sort of involved in a car accident," I explained as I sat in my seat. "Amanda is actually still there, and she asked me to let you know she will be running a little late."

"Is everyone okay?" he asked.

"Yes, it wasn't a bad one. Some college guy just rear-ended Amanda."

Knowing Mr. Conrad, if I had said the person who'd hit her was an adult driving to work, he instantly would think I was lying because "teenagers were the bad drivers, not hardworking adults."

"I think they're just exchanging insurance information or something," I added and heard a couple of people giggle from the back of the class.

Mr. Conrad looked over my shoulder to see who it was, but by the time he'd looked up, everyone was quiet and looking down at their textbooks.

Everyone knew Amanda was a big flirt, so I'm sure they guessed what "exchanging insurance information" really meant.

After I quickly settled into my seat, Mr. Conrad started his lecture on the Salem witch trials. Before I'd even set down my bookbag, Noah, the boy who sat beside me, pushed his history book into the middle of our table so we could share.

"Thanks," I said to him with a warm smile.

"No problem," he replied shyly.

I loved all kinds of history, but the type of stuff we were learning here was my favorite. I wasn't sure if that made me weird, so I kept my outward excitement about the subject to a minimum.

Mr. Conrad seemed to be a superstitious man when it came to the supernatural, and that made things more interesting. Of course, he taught us the facts, but he also would tell us the myths and legends that the villagers would tell. He spoke about the old tales of mystic beings and demons from other worlds—things straight out of a science-fiction novel. Even though I knew they were all just stories, it still intrigued me.

"Everyone knows who the Putnams are, of course," Mr. Conrad began, "but what most people do not know is what some people back then thought to be the real story. According to legend, it wasn't Ann who was the witch, but that guess did hit close to home. The true witch was said to be a family member of hers. Ann wanted to be a witch so badly that she would do anything to make it happen. We all know the official story about when she decided to take their family secret public. Not only did they get ridiculed for what they were, but, because of her, every other supernatural being knew where a large coven of witches had been living. This made it very dangerous for those who lived in Salem. Witches have many enemies in the supernatural world, so anyone knowing the location of a large coven would be extremely dangerous for them." Mr. Conrad paused, as he always did, to make sure everyone was paying attention to his lecture. Unsurprisingly, all eyes were completely focused on him.

Satisfied, he continued, "Due to the spectacle Ann caused, the real witches had to prepare for what they already knew would end in war and chaos. The coven leader did the only thing she thought would prevent that from happening. She called a meeting with as many leaders of the mystical world as she could. This was done to stop unnecessary bloodshed, but also to prevent humans from knowing the truth. I can't say what different types of creatures came to this gathering, but I can say that every creature that attended was quite upset that the witches had revealed themselves to the humans and had suffered almost no penalty for it. If any other supernatural creature had done the same, they would have been executed by their own kind. It was an unwritten law among all creatures—those who could take human form as well as those who couldn't—that no human outside their family could know anything about their existence."

Mr. Conrad stopped to look at the clock. "All right, only a minute left until the end of class and, of course... homework!"

"Awwww," the whole class sighed simultaneously.

"It's not so bad. Come on, people, have a little imagination. I want you to write about a mystic being and why it could be logical that it exists, or, for those nonbelievers, why it could not exist."

At that exact moment, the bell rang. We all leapt out of our seats as Mr. Conrad continued, "This 1,000-word essay is due next Tuesday. Make sure you approve your topic and argument with me. You can email me or stop back in the classroom, but I want the topic no later than Monday morning!" he shouted as everyone left the classroom. "Witches, demons, vampires, zombies... anything," I could hear him still shouting as I walked out into the hallway.

The rest of the day was filled with mathematical statistics and the elements of the periodic table, pretty much the usual, routine boring stuff. It was times like these when I felt lucky my brother was in the same grade as me. I would get so bored that I'd forget I was in class and start drifting off into my own little world. Although we didn't have all the same classes, I knew Ian would be able to help me with any questions I had.

Of course, staying focused that day was especially difficult. I couldn't stop thinking about Amanda and the handsome stranger we'd met that morning. I wasn't even sure whether I had seen her the entire day and became so worried that I broke down and called her a few times. She didn't answer. Eventually, I convinced myself that I wasn't all that important to her, which was why I hadn't heard back, so I did my best to put it out of my mind for the rest of the school day.

When I made it home, I sat in my room contemplating the day. As much as I tried, I hadn't been able to stop thinking about Alan and that eye color–changing phenomenon. At first, I'd thought my eyes must have been playing tricks on me, but Ian had seen it, too. There had to be some sort of logical explanation.

Ian wasn't the type of person to just let things go, so I wondered if he had come up with any ideas. I went down to the living room where I found him and Zay sitting on the couch. However, Zay looked pale, even for him, and Ian was sitting as far as he could from him, holding a napkin over his mouth and nose.

"Zay, are you okay?" I asked.

"I don't feel so good."

"Why don't you go to bed then?"

"Yes, go far, far away," Ian added.

"Don't you think you're being a little ridiculous, Ian?" I asked.

Ian shook his head then covered it with his hoodie.

"Do you really think a napkin and a hoodie are going to prevent you from getting sick?" I asked sarcastically.

"Go upstairs, Zay. I can't get sick again!" Ian shouted.

"Fine."

I understood why Ian was afraid. The first week after we had moved to Hallowed Hills, I had gotten very sick and been just as pale as Zay was now. It had been like having the flu but ten times worse. It had been painful to move but just as painful to sit still. I had felt like my entire body was covered in bruises, so whichever way I laid, it hurt. I remember feeling so cold but like I was burning up at the same time. My skin was ice cold to the touch, but my temperature was 103°. I had been completely out of commission like that for about 24 hours, but then I was completely healthy again—no more pain and no explanation of what had caused it. Two weeks later, the same thing had happened to Ian.

"It's probably some kind of virus," I suggested, trying to reassure Ian.

"Yeah, the type of virus you get from living in an old, creepy town," he shot back. "I'm telling you, this town is weird."

"Speaking about creepy..." I trailed off.

"Oh, creepy Beemer guy?" he laughed. "Huh, yeah, just another one to add to the list. I honestly have no idea. And what happened to Amanda? Did you see her in school?"

"No, I didn't see her. Do you think we should be worried?"

"I've thought about the eye thing all day. There are reasons the sclera of the eye can turn red, like from injury or infection, but not the iris. His sclera was almost black though," he replied, immersed in the memory then snapped out of it and asked apprehensively, "Have you tried calling her?"

"Yes, several times and nothing. I'm not sure what else to do."

"Let's just wait until tomorrow. This town may be weird, but the crime rate is pretty much nonexistent," he reassured me then stood up. "I'm going to go take a shower and study for the test tomorrow. Good night."

"Okay, good luck on your test," I said as he made it to the stairs.

"Yep, you, too."

"Wait. For what?"

"Seriously? The literature test," he answered as he walked up the stairs shaking his head.

I was disappointed with Ian's thoughts about the crimson eyes, but there wasn't much I could do. I was sure Amanda would be at school tomorrow, and I would probably never see Alan again.

Strangely, that disappointed me. He was gorgeous, and I had never seen anyone who'd looked remotely like him before. I usually liked tan guys, but his pale skin had been so perfect that it had almost looked like porcelain. I vividly remembered it having no blemishes or discoloration and so smooth that the light from the streetlamps had reflected beautifully off him.

Sighing, I didn't want to think about him any longer, so I decided that the best thing to do was to follow my brother's lead and go study for the test. I fell asleep amid the words of Alexander Dumas.

# CHAPTER 2
## THE WOMAN IN BLACK

The next morning wasn't unlike any other; the same fight to get out of bed, the same cold to be resentful toward. I was happy I had been able to sleep a little longer since I didn't have to take Zay to school. I felt bad for him, but I figured that at least he didn't have to go out in the cold. I wouldn't want to switch places with him though.

When we got to school, everything seemed normal as well. I was thankful that Ian had told me about the literature test because as we walked into the classroom, it was "all books and notes away." I finished the test in record time, even before Ian. It felt odd turning in my test earlier than everyone else, so I read over my answers until I saw Ian turn his in first.

After class ended, Ian and I walked to the dining hall together. I started thinking about Amanda and the fact that I hadn't seen her in school today either. I figured that maybe she was just late, and that was the reason she hadn't been in first period. Or maybe she was just keeping a low profile. But I didn't have to speak those words out loud to know how idiotic that sounded. Amanda was way too self-centered for that to be true.

When we got to the dining hall, we sat down at our usual table, and everything seemed normal until I saw Emily talking to Lisa and Justin. It was odd because Lisa and Justin weren't part of what was considered the "popular crowd" with which Emily usually associated.

Even though I was clear across the cafeteria, I could hear Emily already planning a search party for Amanda. I had to admit I was worried, too, but she was going a little overboard.

"Nina, you're not even paying attention to me," Jen said.

"Oh, sorry," I responded absentmindedly. "It's just Emily. She's talking crazy."

Jen turned around to look at where Emily stood. "How can you even hear what she's saying?" she asked innocently.

"What do you mean? She is being really loud," I responded, confused, but Becca was now staring at me as well. "What?"

"Nina, they are like 100 miles away," Becca laughed playfully.

"Stop it. They are not," I giggled.

I looked at Ian who was laughing, too.

Alex Reeves and Matt Menzel, who were also sitting with us, had no idea what was going on. Two of Ian's best friends, the boys were in their own world talking about wrestling. Alex was Korean, had a slender frame, and stood about two inches shorter than Ian. Matt was almost Ian's height, maybe just half an inch shorter, and had neatly cut light brown hair and blue eyes. Huge fans of the Hart Foundation in the WWF, they had bonded with Ian over their interest in our last name. In fact, Matt and Alex had gotten Ian into watching wrestling, which he now watched every week, but even more he enjoyed the reruns of older episodes where he could root for Bret and Owen Hart.

Although Ian was brainier and they were sportier, they got along well. When I stopped to think about it, I guess I was sportier and Jen and Becca were brainier. I let out a short giggle at my realization.

"What's so funny?" Ian asked.

"Nothing," I replied, still laughing.

"Nina!" Emily shouted, making me almost jump out of my seat.

"Geez, Emily," Ian and I said simultaneously.

"You just took five years off my life," I added as I covered my heart.

"Hilarious," Emily said sarcastically. "Amanda is still not at school!"

"You shouldn't worry. I'm sure she just didn't want to come to school in a banged-up car. She is probably at the auto body shop right now," I said, trying to reassure her while also trying to ignore the fact that I was worried about Amanda, too.

"No! I think that something is wrong!" she screamed at me.

I wanted to try to calm her like I had before, but now she seemed truly scared, and I didn't know what else to say.

"Don't try to change my mind. I know what I'm talking about, and I'm going to go see the dean," she spouted sternly.

"Okay, that's fine. Do you want me to go with you?" I asked her sympathetically.

Although I had only known her for a short time, I had never seen Emily look so upset before. It was very out of character.

"Yes, let's go now!"

I looked at my brother and the others at the table. Everyone's faces showed complete shock. Even though they didn't get along with Amanda, or Emily for that matter, they also saw the fear in Emily's eyes.

"I'm going, too," Ian said, making Emily's face turn bright red. She was attracted to him just like most of the other girls in the school despite his daily disheveled look.

Apparently, I rose too slowly from my seat because Emily hooked her arm through mine and pulled me quickly to my feet. I didn't argue with her, vividly remembering the fear in her eyes. I wanted so badly to say something to calm her down, but I was afraid that whatever I said would just make things worse.

"I guess we're going now," I said to Ian, who was just getting to his feet as we were already halfway to the dining hall exit.

He began walking after us, but I held up my hand and gestured for him to wait. I wasn't sure whether Emily would be herself in front of him, so I wanted to get her alone to question her first.

"Why exactly are you so worried about Amanda?" I asked innocently.

"Do you know what today is?"

"Um, Friday?" I responded blandly.

"No. I mean, yes, but it's also our first home game," she said then looked at me for a second. When I didn't respond, she continued, "If Amanda doesn't come to school today, she will not be able to participate."

She stared at me again, puzzled by my apparent ignorance, but I was still baffled. I had no idea what she was getting at.

"She is our head cheerleader, and we are playing CWA," she snorted at me as she rolled her eyes.

I waved Ian toward us, finally understanding why she was so scared. Emily was right. Amanda would never miss that game. Not only was our football team playing one of the best teams in the country, the school was our biggest rival as well.

Charles Wright Academy was only about two hours away from our school, so I was told the stadium was always packed for those games. Since we had moved to town, everyone had been talking about this upcoming game. I learned that VP and CWA had been rivals for centuries, so every game we played against each other was a huge event that not only the whole town would be attending but people from the border towns as well.

"Can we go now?" she hissed at me.

"Yes, let's go."

As we walked up to the door of the dean's office, I already knew that Emily would be incredibly overdramatic about the situation.

"Where is Dean Underwood?" Emily nearly shouted as she flung open the double doors to the main office with both arms.

I could see Ian's reflection through the glass doors. He was smiling behind me and attempting to hide his laughter.

"Is she serious?" he asked me in a whisper.

"Unfortunately," I answered. "Emily, hang on a second. What if you're wrong, and she's just ditching or something? Do you really want to get her in trouble with her dad?" I suggested as I rushed to catch up to her.

However, even as the words flowed out, I found myself not believing them. I had no valid reason to think something bad had happened to her, or maybe I did. I was starting to confuse myself.

"I mean, the other driver was really good looking," I added quickly, not sure who I was trying to convince.

Emily cocked her head to one side and put her hands on my shoulders. "You haven't met her boyfriend, have you?"

"Well, no, but—"

"His name is Aaron, and he is probably the most beautiful guy I have ever met. Well, besides your brother," she giggled. "My point is that she's not going to flirt with some nobody when she has the starting quarterback from CWA," she finished.

I wanted to tell Emily that if she had seen the guy who hit her car, she might feel differently, but I didn't want to argue with her.

"Miss, may I help you?" Mrs. Farnsworth asked politely.

Mrs. Farnsworth was a sweet elderly lady who was maybe in her 70s. She had white hair that she always wore in a perfect bun, and she always looked very elegant. She also always wore the same necklace with a pendant made of gold. It had an ivory circle in the middle with blue liquid in it and some strange symbols. I didn't understand them, but it was still pretty.

"I need to speak to Dean Underwood," Emily insisted.

"Of course, my dear, just sign in, and he'll be with you as soon as possible," Mrs. Farnsworth said politely.

"His daughter is missing. Are you really going to make me wait?" Emily shouted.

I felt so bad for Mrs. Farnsworth. She was such a nice lady, and there was no reason for Emily to shout at her like that. In addition, if Amanda had been gone since yesterday, her dad had to already know about it. Of course, Emily didn't care about that. The whole world revolved around her and her friends.

"What do you mean that she's missing, sweetheart?" Mrs. Farnsworth asked innocently.

"I mean she is not in school," Emily hissed back.

Mrs. Farnsworth looked at me, probably for some kind of indication about whether Emily was being serious or not. All I could do was mouth the words, "I'm sorry."

"Why are you looking at *her*?" Emily yelled when she realized that the woman's attention was no longer on her.

"I'm sorry, Miss. Let me tell the dean you are here, and he'll be out as soon as possible. He was just pulled into a conference call. It could be about 30 minutes until he is finished, dear."

"Fine, just tell him I'm here," Emily countered under her breath.

I looked over at the waiting area and saw Ian almost asleep in one of the overpriced, oversized loveseats the school had. Only he could sleep through all this drama. I wanted to throw a pen at him or something, but before I could, Emily plopped down right beside him, making him jump several inches out of his seat.

"Geez!" Ian yelled, holding onto the armrest to catch his balance.

Emily didn't say anything to Ian. She just stared at him. *What a creep. I mean, I could see how girls could think he's attractive, but again she was going a little overboard.*

As I giggled to myself, I began to look around. Two guys in the waiting area were giving me the same look Emily was giving Ian. The only word I could use to describe it was "enchanted." *Wow, this is a strange town.*

I knew what I looked like. I did consider myself attractive, and I knew my brother was attractive as well, but it wasn't like we were the best-looking people in the world. Yet somehow everyone in the town seemed to be utterly infatuated with us. I wondered whether Ian felt as awkward as I did about it or if he enjoyed the attention.

"What's going on, Emily?" Dean Underwood asked from behind the front desk. When he didn't get a response, he began to walk around the counter toward her.

Emily was still staring at Ian as if he were a priceless painting or a rare artifact in some museum.

Of course, Ian was completely oblivious to any of it and just continued reading his book while Emily sat beside him, not taking her eyes off him.

"Dean Underwood!" Emily shouted when she awoke from her trance.

The dean looked very militaristic—tall and intimidating, with a dark brown toothbrush mustache and a flat-top haircut. His hair was mostly gray, but it still had a little bit of brown on the sides. His suits were always nicely pressed, and his shoes were shiny. He definitely looked like a man you shouldn't mess with.

"Emily, where is Amanda? What is going on?" he asked.

By that time, the dean was just a few feet away from her, the worry in his voice becoming obvious. Of course, he would be worried. I couldn't even imagine what my dad would think if my best friend pulled him out of work to tell him I was missing.

"Amanda is not in school, and tonight is the big game. I've called and texted her a million times since yesterday. Nina said she was in an accident yesterday morning," she added when he was right in front of her.

"Accident? What accident?" the dean interrupted then turned to me. "Nikolina, please explain to me. What accident? Did it happen yesterday? Why is this the first time I'm hearing about it?"

"Umm, well, on the way to school yesterday, Amanda was rear ended by another driver," I explained nervously.

I looked up at the dean who looked like he wanted more information, but there wasn't much else I could tell him. I thought about telling him the truth, but I wasn't sure I could. *Oh yeah, by the way, it creeped me out when I saw the guy's eyes turn blood red.* I didn't think that would work out so well, so, instead, I just stared back at him, waiting for him to ask any questions he wanted.

"Was she hurt?" he asked.

"No, no, nothing like that. She only stayed to exchange insurance information."

"Either you're here to let me know my daughter is skipping school, or you know something else and truly think something is wrong. One of you needs to tell me now what is going on."

"Well, you see..." Emily began.

The dean cut Emily off. "Nikolina, please tell me what is going on. Why do you think there's a problem?"

*Why does he always have to ask me?*

Emily was more than willing to explain why she was worried. I was supposed to be an innocent bystander. If I told him the truth, he wouldn't believe me, but what else could I tell him? I didn't know Amanda that well, so I didn't know what her behavior was really like. All I knew was that she often became head over heels for any good-looking guy, but that wouldn't really be a problem. I wondered whether I should mention that the guy was good looking or that he was older.

Instead of making myself look insane, I went with my gut. I lied, "She said she would be only a few minutes late to class. When I left, they were parting ways. Emily mentioned that Amanda couldn't be part of the rally tonight if she missed more than a half day of school today, and, well, the day is nearly over now. It's just a bit concerning."

The dean looked at me for a moment. He seemed worried but also frustrated as well. He reached into his jacket pocket and pulled out his phone.

"Let me try to give her a call. One moment please," he said to us as he turned away to quickly dial the phone. "This can't be right. Barb would have said something to me," he whispered as he walked away.

He let the phone ring until it went to voicemail three times before coming back to us. "I'm sure she's fine. You two just go back to class and let me handle this," he said calmly but with a noticeable undercurrent of worry.

"Let's say that she *is* okay. Will she be able to be part of the rally tonight?" Emily asked.

"Rules are rules, Emily," the dean answered, clearly annoyed as he walked away.

Was the rally all Emily was worried about? Or was I just being paranoid? I thought she had been worried about Amanda. Then I remembered Ian. Why had *he* come with us? Was he worried as well? It wasn't like him to skip class, but he had been in the car with me the morning of the accident.

"You have to fill in for her," Emily yelled while I was still mid-thought.

I could hear Ian begin to chuckle when he finally looked up from his book. I shot him an evil glance then looked back at Emily. "What are you talking about, Emily? Are you crazy?" I hissed.

I had helped their squad with the new routine, so I knew almost all the moves. I loved to choreograph, so coming up with a cheer routine was fun for me. I had done the same for my old school's squad as well, but I had never cheered. I was happy to go to the rally but only as a spectator. I didn't have anything against cheerleaders, but I wasn't one, and I didn't want to be.

"All you have to do are some kicks and jumps, nothing fancy. How bad would it look if we were down a cheerleader for tonight's game of all nights? I bet it would look really good on a certain little brother's transcripts for his sister to help out our school," she said suggestively.

Of course, the entire school knew my family wasn't made of money like most of the rest of the students, and they also knew Zay still had yet to be admitted here.

I could hear Ian laughing; he wasn't even trying to hide it any longer. "You should do it, sis. It will be fun, and I'll be there to cheer you on," he added with a smug smile.

"Oh, be quiet. Male cheerleaders are allowed, too, you know!" I yelled over to him, which quickly shut him up.

*Who does Emily think she is anyway? If I don't cheer, would it prevent my little brother from getting into the school?* I didn't think so. "Emily, it's not going to happen. Sorry."

"Fine. Anyways, my boyfriend is out of town tonight, so I need a date to take me," she said as she turned to look at Ian.

*Haha, it's his turn*, I thought as I grinned wickedly at him.

"Oh, Emily, I'd love to, but you know our parents don't want us dating. Nina and I are going together tonight," he explained.

I quickly interrupted. "I'm sure Mom and Dad will be okay with it. I mean, it would only be date-*like*, seeing as she has a boyfriend, you know," I added smugly.

Ian looked at me like I had betrayed him, but I just gave him a cheeky smile.

"Great! I'll see you both at the bonfire tonight," Emily said before starting toward the door.

"Youlian, can you please stay for a bit? I wanted to speak to you in private," Dean Underwood said as he walked back out of his office. "Just give me ten minutes to get off this call."

"Who is Youlian?" Emily asked.

"That's Ian's full name," I responded with a smile, knowing how annoying having a long name could be. I added, "I'm going to wait for Ian."

Emily nodded then scampered down the hall.

It took another 20 minutes before Ian finally came out. "What was that about?" I quickly asked him.

"Ridiculousness that I don't want to talk about."

"Well, now I need to know," I said and jumped right in front of him.

He looked at me in annoyance. "No. First, get me out of the Emily thing, then we will talk."

"You were the one being a butthead with the cheerleading thing. That's what you get," I laughed.

"Yeah, funny is funny. Now, how are you going to get me out of it?"

"Get you out of what? She's cute and popular."

"Oh, yeah, two of the most important traits to me. Come on, don't be a jerk."

"Okay, I'll get you out of it," I conceded.

"Wait, we should talk about it. I mean about Amanda. We both know there's more to this story than you told the dean."

"Is there? I mean, okay, the eye thing. I admit that was strange, but honestly, maybe it was the light."

"Come on, how could someone's eyes change colors like that?" he asked.

"Well, even if they did, does it mean something happened to her? Maybe he just has some weird medical condition or something."

"Not any kind of medical condition I've ever heard of," he muttered under his breath. "We just don't know. That's the problem," Ian muttered worriedly.

My brother was a nice guy, but I had never seen him so worried about someone he hardly even knew.

"You were there, too. You could have said something. Can we talk about this in the car, please? I don't want people to think we are the crazy new kids," I suggested quietly.

Ian nodded in agreement.

Since there was only about 30 minutes left in the day, we decided to just go home. The halls were dead silent as we walked down them. I felt like if I dropped a pin, heads would poke out of the classrooms and tell us to shush with forefingers in the middle of their lips like in cartoons when someone was trying to sneak away.

We did our best not to make any noise, and soon I was unlocking the door to my old lady car. I quickly turned it on and slowly drove out of the parking lot since I didn't want to get stopped by a truant officer.

Even though it was just before 3:00 p.m., it was so dark it looked closer to 9:00.

"A storm must be coming," I commented.

"Yeah, it looks like it's going to be bad," Ian agreed.

After that thrilling exchange, we sat in silence for a while. I could feel Ian staring at me, waiting for me to begin the conversation, which I didn't want to do. I continued to drive, and we continued to sit in silence.

"This is weird," he finally said.

"I know, but what is there to say? How about you tell me what you and the dean were talking about?"

"I told you: ridiculousness," he responded with annoyance.

"Very specific," I said as I rolled my eyes. "I hope you and Emily have a good time tonight," I added smugly.

"You wouldn't."

"Wouldn't I?" I smirked.

He looked at me for a minute, then, realizing I was serious, he continued, "Like I said, it was ridiculous. Apparently, some people told the dean that Amanda and I had been seeing each other, so he wanted to know if I had more information."

I started to laugh even before he finished his sentence. Amanda and Ian were complete opposites, so it was hard to imagine them together.

"Shut up," he grumbled. "I don't know why anyone would say that. Everyone at VP knows she has a boyfriend."

"I'm sorry," I said, still laughing. "Strange. What did you tell him?" I asked, trying to be serious.

"I told him the truth. I said I had no idea what he was talking about, but I think he thought I was lying."

He looked at me again while I continued to try not to laugh.

"Stop it," he said as he lightly punched my arm.

"Ouch," I reacted as I turned to look at him, still unable to stop laughing.

"Nina! Look out!" Ian screamed as a huge, black, shadowy creature darted in front of the car.

I turned the wheel so quickly that the car made a 180-degree turn before ending up in a ditch on the side of the road.

"Oh my god! What was that?" I shouted.

I quickly realized I had to change my "what *was* that" to "what *is* that" as the shadow continued to lurk outside the passenger window, staring inside at us.

Now seeing it up close, it didn't look like a shadow at all. It was an entity that seemed made up entirely of black smoke.

Ian stared ahead, looking petrified. He didn't want to turn toward whatever creature was next to him with only a thin piece of glass between him and it.

But I couldn't take my eyes off it. It was wearing what looked like a robe with its hood up but made entirely out of smoke. Its arms were smoke as well, and it had no legs. The floating body was scary enough, but its face was even worse. It was black and skull-like and had the same demonic red eyes I knew I could never forget—the ones that had replaced the beautiful blue eyes of the man we had met the previous day.

"Oh, my g—" I said as I quickly put my hands over my eyes as if that would prevent whatever it was from seeing me.

Then, out of nowhere came a loud screeching noise that made it impossible to keep my eyes covered because I needed my hands to cover my ears. It was like nails on a chalkboard mixed with metal dragging on metal. I glanced over at Ian and saw he was doing the same. As I looked over to him, I saw that the smoke creature was gone.

"Ian!" I yelled, trying to shake him back to reality.

"What the hell was that?" he asked, visibly shaken.

"I have no clue. What are we going to do?"

"I have no idea, but it kind of looked like it had that guy's eyes from yesterday. This can't be a coincidence. It's just too weird. There has to be some information online about this."

"Ian, you do realize that we're stuck in a ditch, don't you?" I said while I tried to kick my door open.

"Oh, yeah, right. Well, let's see if we can push."

He opened his door easily, of course. His side wasn't right next to a huge dirt mound. I gave up on my door after a few more kicks, deciding to just use the passenger door.

"Hello there," a soft-spoken voice whispered.

Ian and I were already on edge, so, of course, the voice made us both scream out loud.

"My apologies for startling you. May I be of some assistance?" she continued as she stepped closer.

The girl had blonde hair, blue eyes, and pale skin and was extremely beautiful. Perhaps in her late teens or early 20s, she was petite but didn't look frail. She wore a black double-breasted peacoat that came to just below her knees on legs that sported black leather pants and knee-high boots. I hadn't seen anyone around here dressed like that before, so I assumed she must have been from out of town.

"Oh, yeah. I'm Nina, and this is my brother, Ian."

"Good to meet you. My name is Lavinia. I was just driving by and saw your vehicle spin out of control and end up in the ditch."

"Oh, thank you for stopping. Some sort of animal ran into the road, and I was trying to avoid killing the thing. I guess I underestimated the width of the street," I explained quickly, realizing after that I was getting good at lying.

"I see. Well, I parked my car just up the road. May I give you both a ride somewhere?" Lavinia asked.

"That's very nice of you to offer, but I'm not sure—"

"I promise I will not bite," she cut me off with a warm smile.

I really didn't think she was much of a threat, but just the thought of getting into her car instantly gave me "stranger danger" vibes. It might be a better idea to call Jen or Becca.

"Thank you, but I'm supposed to meet a couple of my friends in a little bit, so I'll just call them to come pick us up from here."

When I turned around, I noticed Ian just ending a call on his phone. "Jen is on her way now. I just have to call Dad, so he can get the car out of here," he answered before I could ask him who he was talking to.

"I already took the liberty of calling a tow truck," Lavinia said as she started to walk toward her car. "It's run by my brother, so it won't cost you a penny, I promise." She stopped and turned around with another thought. "And don't worry. My brother is a genius when it comes to cars. You will not even be able to tell you were in an accident," she added as she came back toward us.

"Well, thanks," I said warily. While I was ecstatic that this strange, overly enthusiastic girl was helping us, I still found it odd. *Why is she being so nice to us when she doesn't even know us?*

"You know what?" she began again. "Why don't you just go get something to eat, and I'll call you when your car is done? My brother gets these kinds of issues all the time, so he works pretty quickly. He will have your car looking perfect in no time. Well, as perfect as an old lady car can get," she winked.

*How does she know I call it an old lady car? And where did she even come from? There were no other cars on the road.*

The day already had been filled with so many unanswered questions, and so many things were still left unexplained, that I decided not to mention Lavinia's comment to Ian. He was on the phone again with Jen anyway. She wasn't the best with directions, so I assumed she was having a hard time finding us.

Lavinia pulled out her cellphone and started dialing a number then quickly stopped. "Why don't you give me your phone number, and then I'll call you with mine, so when the car is ready, I can give you a call."

I gave her my number then pulled out my phone to save hers. "Don't forget anything you need from your car," she reminded helpfully.

"Oh, right," I answered dazedly as I turned around to walk back toward my car.

Although Ian and I were still stunned and a bit confused about the new turn of events, we began gathering our things. Soon we saw Jen driving up. Ian quickly opened the front passenger door of her brand-new white Lexus and sat down. That meant I would be the one sitting in the back. I gave him an evil glare before shuffling into the backseat.

"So, you completely spun out? Where were you off to anyway? See? That's what you get for ditching!" Jen giggled. "I'm just kidding. I'm glad you guys are okay."

"We were just on our way home from school," Ian answered. "We were at the dean's office for a while. When we left, the day was almost over, so there was no point in going to class and getting yelled at for being late."

"Okay, well, is that where you want me to take you guys? Home?"

"Um, we should probably do something about my car. Our dad is going to be pretty mad. The girl that stopped said she was going to get it towed and her bro—" I froze.

I realized then that she had never called me with her phone number. I had been distracted by making sure I had everything from my car.

*What if she runs some sort of chop shop? Wait, who would want my car?* I wondered quickly.

Most of the car was pretty old, including the brakes and anything else that could be salvaged. The body of the car was full of scratches and dings because both Ian and I had learned how to drive in it, and it certainly showed.

"Crap," I said under my breath. "Hey, Ian, what do you think? Are you hungry?" I asked. I needed more time to figure out what I was going to tell my dad. I knew Ian's stomach was an endless pit, so that would take up a bunch of time. "Hey, at least you have your excuse now," I added to Ian with a giggle.

"What are you talking about?" he asked, confused.

"You crashed my car. There's no way you'll be allowed to go to the rally now," I supplied with a smirk.

He gave me a mean look then turned back to Jen. "Yeah, I could eat."

# CHAPTER 3
## STAR-CROSSED LOVERS

We decided to go to our favorite weekend hangout, a small restaurant in downtown Hallowed Hills called Luna's Bar and Grill. The owners were local historians, so there was a lot of town memorabilia displayed throughout the restaurant. Being new to the area, I appreciated learning about the town I had moved to. After we'd first moved, we came to Luna's every Sunday with our family, and the tradition had stuck.

We had only been living in town for about two months, but Luna's had made the move so much easier. It wasn't just the place itself. It was the people who worked there. Everybody was very friendly and helpful. Since the town was so close-knit, the staff knew pretty much everyone, so they'd introduced my family to many nice people in Hallowed Hills.

Founded by Thomas and Martha Carrier in 1693, the town had become a safe haven for people accused, or in danger of being accused, during the Salem witch trials. During the trials, many people had been afraid they would be accused of being witches, and that caused their families to flee.

Thomas and Martha had headed one such family. They'd had eight children; however, it had been Sarah, their youngest daughter, who had been pressured into saying she was a witch. After Sarah's confession, she was supposed to be arrested the next day. But before anyone could knock at their door, they left town.

"Hey, Nina! Is it Sunday already?" Kaskaskia asked with a sweet smile.

Kas for short, she was the head bartender at Luna's. She had lived in Hallowed Hills all her life, so she knew everything about the town and the people in it. Since arriving, we had gotten to know her really well. She was one of those people who always seemed to be working, so she was always at Lunas, making her a source of invaluable insight into the new town and its residents.

An indigenous woman from the Tamaroa tribe, Kas had taught us a bit about her ancestry when we first came, but the only thing I really remembered was that they had settled in Illinois in the 1700s and were deadly enemies of the Chickasaw and Shawnee. She was very beautiful, with brown eyes, long and straight black hair, and tan skin. She was about an inch shorter than me and was thin but also quite muscular, which she laughingly attributed to being a bartender.

"Hey. No, we just needed an extra caffeine fix this week," I replied with a smile as we slid into our usual table.

"Three peach iced teas coming right up!"

"Thanks, Kas. Can you add three burgers and fries to that order, please?"

"You got it," she replied with a wink.

"Make that four iced teas, please," a voice chimed in suddenly out of nowhere.

"Oh! Hi, Lavinia," I said with surprise as I turned to see the blonde girl regarding me with an innocent smile.

"Sorry to sneak up on you, but I just saw you walk in and thought I should probably give you my phone number in case you needed anything," she said warmly.

Although she seemed very nice, something about Lavinia made me feel flustered, sort of the way I felt when a boy I was crushing on spoke to me. But that was weird; she was beautiful, but I wasn't attracted to her. Yet there was something intriguing about her. The way she presented herself, the way she spoke, and even the way she smelled was... intoxicating.

"Four iced teas. Your burgers will be out in a few minutes," Kas said as she set down our drinks.

"Thanks, Kas," I said with a smile.

"My pleasure," she answered then quickly walked back to the bar where a new crowd was forming.

I turned to Ian and found all his attention focused on Lavinia. Usually, he was reading a book or trying to get one of his friends to come out so he wouldn't be surrounded by girls; however, right now, he didn't seem to care.

With a flourish, Lavinia passed a slip of paper across the table with her phone number on it. "There. Now that we have business taken care of, what are you guys up to tonight?"

No one said anything. I simply looked at Ian who sat there with a dumbfounded look and then at Jen who didn't look much different.

*What is going on here?*

"We are going to the bonfire tonight," I answered just so we weren't sitting in the awkward silence any longer.

"Oh, of course, the big game."

"Are you going?" I asked.

"Absolutely. Everyone around here goes to the VP vs. CWA football games," she replied with a smile. "Plus, those players are yummy," she whispered to me.

I wanted to ask her how old she was, but I thought that might be rude. She didn't look much older than us, but she was certainly older than any high school football player.

"I bet you're on the team," she directed at Ian. "What time will you be there?"

Ian continued to stare at her, but this time he looked as if he were trying to understand something.

"Ouch!" Ian shouted when I kicked him under the table. "What's wrong with you?"

"Someone is talking to you, weirdo," I whispered to him.

He looked around the table and then met Lavinia's eyes. She smiled at him tenderly. I could see red form in Ian's cheeks as he realized she was talking to him.

"Sorry, what was the question?" he asked nervously.

I shook my head and giggled. I had never seen my brother act that way with anyone, so it was odd to see him on this side of the awkwardness.

"Which position do you play?" she asked.

"Oh, I'm not on the team."

"Oh, really? Most guys with your physique are on the team," she said flirtatiously.

If Ian's cheeks hadn't been red enough before, they were now. He still didn't answer her. He just smiled and took a sip of his iced tea. It wasn't like this was the first time he'd heard that. The VP football coach had come up to him twice since we had arrived at the school to try to recruit him. But it *was* the first time he had heard it from such a beautiful girl.

Lavinia was right. Ian did have the physique of a football player. He had that typical quarterback body, muscular but not bulky. He was certainly the fittest nerd I had ever met. Not only did he have the physical form for playing football, but, because he was so smart, he also would have no trouble remembering all the plays and rules. If he had wanted to play football, he could have, but he had never seemed to have any interest in it or any other sport for that matter.

"Excuse him. He's just having a weird little brother moment," I giggled.

Ian looked at me like he was going to kill me, but I just smiled.

"Well, I don't think either of us will be going to the bonfire tonight, to be honest," I said to Lavinia. "Not after our dad finds out we crashed the car."

"*We* didn't crash anything. *You* crashed the car. I was just an innocent victim," Ian added with an evil smile.

I shot him back an equally evil glance then punched him in the shoulder.

"Your dad doesn't need to know," Lavinia said before Ian could hit me back. "The car should be done in less than an hour. All your dad needs to know is that you came to get something to eat after school."

"Wow, thank you," I said, completely stunned. "I don't know how we can repay you."

"Don't worry about it. I am happy to help," she replied with a reassuring smile. "I guess this will be your first major football game in our town, and it's against CWA. Of course, you have to root for the home team, but that CWA quarterback will make you think twice," she said as she smiled at me.

I smiled back as I recalled the conversation I'd had that morning with Emily. She had mentioned something about Amanda's boyfriend being the CWA quarterback. I wondered if it could be the same person.

That's when my phone started to ring.

"It's Dad," I told Ian as I held up the phone to show him the caller ID.

I turned it back around and stared at it, debating whether I should answer. I really didn't want to, but I knew I had to. But as I reluctantly reached to answer the phone, the front door swung open, and into the room sauntered the most attractive guy I had ever laid eyes on. My fingers froze in midair as I stared at him, my breath catching in my throat.

He was very tall, maybe an inch shorter than my dad. His light blonde hair was tousled in a way that spoke of carefree confidence and framed his face in a tantalizing manner. Those hypnotic blue eyes, twinkling with mischief, held me captive from across the room and drew me into their depths with an irresistible pull.

His diamond-shaped jawline, sculpted to near perfection, accentuated his features with a rugged appeal that sent my heart racing. His sun-kissed skin, glowing with a light golden tan made him look strong and healthy. A perfect balance of leanness and muscle made up his lithe frame, and his broad shoulders were accentuated by the blue and orange CWA football jersey he wore.

With every step, he exuded confidence and a self-assuredness that made it apparent that he was aware of his attractiveness.

"Speak of the devil," Lavinia said.

*This is him?*

He turned to look toward our table, and we locked eyes. I couldn't turn away even though I wanted to. As he looked back at me, his pink lips curved and cheeks glowed. His irresistible, tender, and enchanting smile put a spontaneous smile on my face, too.

He nodded his head to say hello then looked around the table until he saw Lavinia. I was surprised when he didn't exhibit the same reaction to her that everyone else had. Instead, he looked kind of annoyed to see her, and his beautiful smile vanished. He walked toward the bar and started talking and laughing with the large group of people sitting there.

*What just happened?*

"He doesn't care too much for me," Lavinia answered my unspoken question. "Family drama that goes way back."

I instantly wanted to know more about him, but I didn't want to seem pushy. And I especially wanted to know what Lavinia meant by family drama.

"I'm going to the washroom. You should call Dad back before he sends out a search party," Ian said, snapping me back to reality.

I had almost forgotten, and Ian wasn't exaggerating either. Our dad was the type that worried, especially since I had been in a train accident not too long before we moved. If he didn't see or hear from us 15 minutes after we should be home from school, he started calling us nonstop.

When I finished talking to my dad and reassuring him that we were okay, I looked up, and my heart skipped a beat. Ian was sitting at the bar with the handsome quarterback. I had only been on the phone for about ten minutes, but they were now talking like they were the closest of friends.

I looked at Lavinia, and she did not look happy. Her arms and legs were crossed as she stared at the floor. I wanted to ask her what was wrong, but something made me think that was a bad idea.

It felt like an eternity had passed by the time Ian finally came back to our table. I looked at him, trying to will him to tell me what had happened over at the bar.

"What?" he asked, annoyed by my scrutiny.

"Do you know him?"

"Who? Aaron? Sure, we're close friends. We hang out every weekend," he answered jokingly.

"Shu— st— why?" I stammered. "I mean, never mind," I said as I gave up trying to form an actual sentence.

"When you remember how to speak English again, let me know," he laughed.

I gave him an evil look, the one he knew all too well, the one I gave him before I spilled information that he didn't want spilled.

"Okay, okay. His family is originally from Hallowed Hills. When he didn't recognize us, he just wanted to introduce himself."

"I have to get going, but I will call you soon about the car," Lavinia said suddenly with a forced smile.

She stood up so quickly that the sound of the chair's legs scratching the floor startled me. It was a bit odd, her demeanor changing so fast. The only logical explanation I could come up with was that maybe she and Aaron had dated and it hadn't ended well. But I didn't quite understand how that could be considered "family drama."

I was beginning to get a headache from all the questions and unknowns today, so I excused myself from the table to go wash my hands.

When I walked out of the bathroom, a plaque on the wall caught my eye. It had on it a picture of the first building in the original town settlement with the founding date floating over the building. It was a memorial to all the people who had lost their lives in the Salem witch trials.

Right next to that was a plaque with the names of those who had been accused:

*Sarah Carrier – Evaded arrest*

*Andrew Carrier – Escaped prison*

It was common knowledge in town that Sarah had fled, but Andrew's name caught my attention. I'd had no idea that Andrew had been arrested. I wondered what had happened to him and if he had made it to Hallowed Hills.

I quickly scanned the rest of the list, but I didn't find any other Carriers. I thought about sitting in history class when Mr. Conrad had spoken about the witch trials. It seemed so long ago even though it really had only been the previous day.

I assumed that, given the town's history, most of my classmates were going to be writing about witches. Not only was it the easiest, but, because the town had ties to Salem, it made it the most interesting as well.

I wondered whether it was possible that the Carriers had fled Salem before being discovered. If I could speak to an ancestor of someone from the trials, it might set me apart from the rest of the class. Of course, I had no idea how I would do that. I knew the town still had living descendants, but I didn't know who they were. I hadn't come across anyone with the last name Carrier since we'd moved to Hallowed Hills.

Underneath the names was a painting of a woman handing out cookies from a tray and surrounded by children. She appeared to be in her mid- to late 30s and had long dark hair that lay in a ponytail over one shoulder. She looked happy to be there. I looked down to read the description of the painting.

Martha Carrier, Hallowed Hills, IL

First Founding Day Celebration, January 24, 1694

I was taken aback when I saw who it was. For a woman who'd already had eight children, she looked really good. I then reasoned that back then people started having children really young, but even if that were true, she must have had her first child in her early teens. I couldn't imagine having a child so young.

I thought the information might be helpful when I wrote my paper, so I took pictures of all the plaques. Suddenly, my head started to hurt, so I gently rubbed my temples.

"Hi. Nina, right?" an enchanting voice floated in from behind me and immediately swept away my senses in a whirlwind of excitement.

Though unfamiliar, his voice resonated deeply within me, and I knew without a doubt whose it was. I turned slowly to find Aaron standing before me.

I stood there in a moment suspended in time before I could find my voice. "Hi. Yes," I eventually replied while my heart danced to a rhythm he seemed to compose.

More than that, he smelled amazing. His scent was hard to explain; it was sweet but still masculine at the same time. It almost reminded me of Mr. Conrad, but it wasn't as strong.

While I stood there, every breath I took felt labored, but I didn't care. His full lips and subtle dimples were bewitching.

*Nina, snap out of it,* I silently scolded myself.

"I heard you and your family just moved to town. How do you like it so far?" he asked in my silence.

"It's cold," I blurted out, my words escaping before my thoughts could catch up. "But it's really nice. I like history," I added quickly, diverting my attention to the historical plaques that adorned the walls.

"Yeah. It's interesting, all right," he responded as his eyes scanned the names on the wall.

Something in his tone hinted at secrets he was hesitant to share. A sudden desire to unravel that mystery tugged at me, but I resisted the urge to pry. Ian had said his family was originally from Hallowed Hills, so I wondered whether he could be tied to the town's history, but I didn't even know his last name, so I couldn't easily find out on my own.

"Maybe you could tell me about it sometime?" I asked abruptly then bit my lip. "I mean, since I'm new in town. It would be me and my brother, not just me of course," I added nervously.

"Yeah, sure. Sometime soon," he answered with a playful smile. "You... and your brother of course."

"Will you be at the bonfire tonight?" I asked with a bit too much eagerness.

"Yeah, I kind of have to be there," he laughed.

*Stupid question. He's wearing his jersey. Of course, he's going to be there*, I thought to myself.

"I have to head out, but I hope to see you there," he said with a radiant smile.

I smiled shyly back at him as he turned and walked away. I couldn't help but watch him leave, and I was glad I had because his football jersey revealed the mystery of his last name as Andrews.

I looked toward our table and saw that our burgers had arrived. Ian was already stuffing his in his mouth. I walked back into the dining room and sat down next to him.

"What's wrong?" he asked, his words muffled around his mouthful of food.

"Nothing. Just eat your food," I answered. I couldn't quite hide my mild disgust at the sight of the chewed-up morsels in his mouth.

"Fine, whatever," he said then continued to devour his burger.

Ian was a typical guy. He couldn't care less if I didn't tell him something. He knew that if it was really important, I would tell him. Unlike him, I didn't care *what* it was, I just wanted to know right away.

I took a bite of my own burger, and it tasted really bland. I swallowed then took a sip of my drink. It lacked the strong peach flavor I was used to, tasting just as bland as the burger.

I glanced over at Ian. He was still eating and drinking like normal. I figured that if his food tasted funny, he would have said something, so I assumed I was getting sick again.

I let Ian and Jen finish their meals, but I had no interest in my food. On top of not being able to enjoy the taste, we still had not heard from Lavinia. I had no idea how I was going to explain the car to our dad.

"Do you guys just want me to take you home now?" Jen asked shyly when she finished her burger.

"Yes, please," I answered reluctantly. "Just remember my face how it is now because you will probably not see me again until I am old and gray."

"Don't be overdramatic, sis. She will see you in school," Ian laughed.

"Shut up, Ian," I snapped back. "Don't worry about the food, Jen. We'll get it."

"Actually," Ian said as he held up a $50 bill.

"Where did you get that?" I asked.

"Lavinia left it on the table," he answered.

"For an iced tea?" I asked in confusion.

"I guess. Unless she wanted to pay me for my company," he said then laughed at his own obnoxious joke.

"Whatever. Let's just go," I said, preoccupied about my car.

We walked out into a bright, sunny day with not a cloud in the sky. That was strange because it had been almost pitch black when we'd arrived. I hadn't heard any rain while we were inside either. It was almost like night had just changed into day for no reason at all.

The sun almost made the cold bearable. If it weren't for the clouds and wind that were around most days, the weather wouldn't be so bad. The sun on my face felt so good that it made me feel energized. I loved being out in it. Summer was my favorite season.

We started walking toward Jen's car, but before we could get even a few steps away from the door, we noticed my car sitting in a parking spot right in front of Luna's.

It looked great, even better than it had before, with no trace of the damage from the accident. Even the navy-blue paint had been freshened up, and the tires and lights looked new as well. This couldn't be my car; it was just one that looked like it.

I walked closer to get a better look inside. My CDs and my lunch bag were in the car but not the random papers and empty water bottles I'd had behind the passenger's seat.

"Is that..." Ian started to ask.

"I'm not sure," I answered as I took a chance and tried the driver's side door.

It opened, and I sat down inside and looked around. The interior had been detailed beautifully. It even had that new car smell. I pulled down the visor to see whether the picture of me and my grandpa was still there, and my keys fell into my lap. I looked at them and saw the soccer ball keychain he had given me when I was in junior high. And, inside the visor was our picture in the same spot it had always been.

"I guess it is my car," I answered Ian, who was already sitting in the passenger seat.

"Wow. They did a great job. Did they clean it, too?" Jen asked.

"Yeah, I think they did," I answered.

"You definitely have to give me the number of your guy," she said with a smile.

"Yeah, he's a miracle worker. I mean, this car was a mess," Ian laughed.

"So, I guess I will see you tonight then?" Jen asked.

"Yeah. We just have to pick up Zay from the house. We'll see you there. He wasn't feeling well last night, but I know he wanted to go," I answered.

We said goodbye to Jen and started our drive home.

# CHAPTER 4
## DISTURBIA

The drive back to the house was pretty quick. I wanted to ask Ian more about Aaron, but I didn't want to seem desperate. I knew I'd never live that down.

But as soon as we parked in the driveway, I couldn't take it any longer. "So, what did you think of Aaron?" I blurted out.

Ian looked at me with amusement and smirked.

"Shut up. Don't forget about how you acted around Lavinia," I added, which quickly wiped the grin off his face.

"Listen, this entire day has been weird. It was weird that Lavinia just popped up out of nowhere, and it was weird that Aaron just started talking to me. This town is just too friendly. It's kind of creepy. Let's just get ready to go to the bonfire," he said then got out of the car before I could ask anything else.

Our parents liked having a date night every Friday, so Zay was the only one home when we walked in the house. Per usual, he was sitting at the computer with his headphones on.

Like Ian and I before him, he was now completely healthy again. Maybe Ian had been right that it was the town that made us sick. But I'd never heard about anyone else getting sick like that; it was only the three of us who were affected.

I didn't want to think about it anymore, so I decided to get changed. I wasn't sure if I would get to see Aaron again, but I wanted to look at least decent in case I did. My hair was pretty long, sitting just above the small of my back when straight. I brushed it out as best as I could then added large, loose curls at the ends.

I quickly rummaged through my closet to find the best thing I could wear and ended up putting on a long, form-fitting, cream V-neck sweater shirt and three different lengths of silver necklaces. I coupled that with dark blue jeans and tan knee-high boots with a bit of a heel.

After putting on a bit of mascara and lip gloss, my look was complete. I was pretty satisfied with my appearance when I finally looked in the mirror.

The bonfire started at 6 p.m., so, when a glance at the clock told me we didn't have much time, I hustled down the stairs to find my brothers.

"Ian! Zay! Let's go!" I yelled back up the stairs when I didn't find them on the first floor.

Zay was the first one to come down. I knew he was excited about the bonfire even without him saying anything. As usual, he was dressed nicely in a black sweater and clean blue jeans. Ian sluggishly came down behind him.

"I think I'm just going to stay in tonight," Ian said before I could ask him what was wrong. "It's been a really weird day, and I'm just tired. Besides, I don't want to deal with the whole Emily thing. I've had enough craziness for the day."

"Okay. We won't stay long," I said to him.

"Sure, you won't. Nice outfit. Are you trying to impress someone?"

I glared at him and blushed, knowing he was right but hating that he could tell.

"Don't worry. Have fun," he chuckled then walked back up the stairs.

On the way to the bonfire, Zay told me about his day. It was nothing out of the ordinary, just him bragging about all the girls who had crushes on him. He was getting a bit conceited because of all the new attention he was receiving.

I debated telling him how my day had been but quickly decided against it. I didn't want to worry him for no reason.

When we arrived at the school, the parking lot was packed. I had never seen it so full; people were even parking on the baseball's outfield.

"Holy crap! There are so many people here!" Zay exclaimed.

"Yeah, this is a little nuts. I promised I would meet Jen and Becca, but neither one is texting me back. There's no way I'll find them in this."

"Good luck with that. I have a few friends I'm meeting up with, and I guess they like me better because they responded to me," he said dismissively.

"Just go," I said to him while practically shoving him out of the car.

I tried to call both Jen and Becca again, but they still didn't answer, so I decided to take a lap around the football field and attempt the nearly impossible feat of finding them in the enormous crowd.

As I walked, I could smell the smoke of the bonfire, so I knew it had already been lit. Since most people were in the stadium by then, getting through the line was pretty quick. Then I checked my phone again just in case I had missed a call, but I hadn't.

I soon noticed that players from both teams were mingling among the crowd. It was a much more friendly encounter than I was expecting.

And then I saw him: Aaron. To my complete and utter shock, he was standing with Amanda. My jaw dropped. She was all over him.

I didn't want to admit how jealous that made me feel, but it did. I'd known he had a girlfriend, so maybe the connection I thought I'd felt with him was all in my head. He hadn't really said anything to indicate he was interested in me, so he was probably just being polite. We were the new family in town, and maybe he was just welcoming us.

I looked back toward them, trying not to look at Aaron. Amanda was in her cheerleading outfit, but she wore a scarf around her neck that none of the other cheerleaders had. I wanted to pull her aside and ask her what the hell had happened to her, but I didn't want Aaron to think I was a crazy person.

For once, I was happy that wherever Amanda was, Emily wasn't far from her. I scanned the crowd around Amanda, and it didn't take me long to find her. I walked over to Emily and pulled her off to the side.

"What the hell?" I shrieked.

"What? What's wrong with you?" she asked cluelessly. "That hurt."

"Why? Who? I mean, that's Amanda! What the hell!"

"Oh, that. Yeah. It was all just one big misunderstanding. Amanda said her phone died, and this really hot guy gave her a ride to the body shop."

"What? For two days?"

"Yeah, well, she didn't want to come to school with a banged-up car, so she told her mom she wasn't feeling well so she could stay home."

"That's what I said!" I shouted, extremely annoyed.

"Calm down, girl. Amanda is fine. Even though she can't cheer, at least she'll be here to lead us from the sidelines," she said with a smile as she walked back to her friends. After a few steps, she turned back to ask, "By the way. Where is Ian?"

I looked at her with extreme annoyance, but all she did was stare right back at me, waiting for a response.

"He's not feeling well. But my other brother is around here somewhere," I added, giggling as I thought about how much she would annoy Zay.

"Hmm, I'm not interested in younger men," she responded quickly.

"Ian is younger," I snorted as she turned to walk away.

She stopped and turned back. "Yes, but he doesn't look younger," she said as she started walking again.

"Have you *seen* Xavier? He doesn't look younger either," I countered, amused by my evil plan.

"Hmmm. Well, where is he?"

"He's around here somewhere," I laughed. "Have at it," I said, gesturing at the thronging crowd.

She rolled her eyes at me before running back to her friends. I turned around and walked away, trying to fish my phone out of my purse at the same time.

I sent a text to Ian to let him know about Amanda, but as I hit the send button, I crashed straight into someone.

"Oops. I am so sorry," I said before even looking up.

When my eyes lifted and I saw who it was, I instantly felt like that cartoon character that sees a pretty girl and forgets how to speak. I was actually surprised my tongue wasn't laying on the floor.

"No worries," Aaron replied. "Hey, I'm glad you came," he said as I continued staring at him.

He looked even more handsome than he had before. Now he was all geared up for the game. I was speechless.

"Do you want to take a walk?" he asked.

Still unable to find any words, I just nodded as we started walking together in silence. I didn't know what was wrong with me. I had never acted this way before with any guy, but there was something I couldn't explain about him, something that made me feel nervous but excited at the same time.

"So, you're from LA. What was that like? What did you do for fun?" he asked.

"Well, for fun I played soccer. Wait, how did you know I was from LA?" I asked curiously.

"It's a friendly town. I asked the first person I saw," he admitted with a flirtatious smile.

Those words put an instant smile on my face. He actually had cared enough to ask around about me.

"As for what LA was like, I am not 100% sure," I said. I looked up at him to see the confusion on his face. "It's not really a fun story."

"Well, that sounds interesting."

I looked at him again for half a minute, not sure whether I wanted to reveal my life story to him.

He just looked back at me and smiled.

Those dimples were irresistible, so I couldn't help but continue. "As for soccer, I played with my grandpa since I was nine, but when it comes to living in LA, I was told that I liked it. I only lived there for a year and a half. Before that, we lived in Deerfield Beach. About a year ago, while in LA, I went on what was supposed to be a nice school field trip to the Los Angeles History Museum, but that didn't go as planned, to say the least."

I paused for half a second, not sure why I was telling him any of this, but seeing his rapt interest, I continued, "On our way to the museum, there was a huge thunderstorm, and our train collided with another train. The collision sent the second train flying off the bridge and stranded ours 300 feet above the ocean. Seventy-six people died that day, including all my classmates and teachers on the trip with me. I was the only person who survived the accident, but I was left with absolutely no memory of anything. All I remember is waking up in a hospital bed and not knowing anything or anyone around me. I was told I'd been found in the luggage area, which happened to be the only part of the train that stayed on the rails. The trains hit so hard that it sent that car flying back onto the hill beside the bridge we were crossing. The rest of the train was suspended above the ocean for a few minutes before the car I was in detached from the rest of the train."

I paused to look at him. Aaron looked at me as if asking for more information.

"It took a while, and it was very difficult learning again everything I had already learned, but my family never gave up on me. My grandpa helped me the most by making me feel normal. He didn't constantly remind me what my favorite color was or things like that. Instead, he retaught me all the ins and outs of soccer. I think focusing on that helped take the pressure off losing my memory, and gradually I was able to start remembering my life before the accident."

We continued walking, and he just listened to me very intently.

"I owe so much to my grandpa. He not only made me feel normal, but he gave me my entire life back. The more I forgot about losing my memory, the more I remembered. I still can't remember anything from the three months before the accident, but before that, I remember most things," I finished. He made me so nervous and confused. I had no idea why this handsome stranger was so interested in my life.

"Definitely interesting," Aaron said at last with a warm smile. "So, you still don't remember everything."

"Other than those three months before the accident, which are still a complete blank, I remember all the important things like my family, friends, and everything I learned in school, things like that. I also remember that it was warmer than here," I giggled then froze for a moment as I got lost in his ocean blue eyes.

"How does something like that happen? Didn't they have safety measures in place?"

"Umm, I was told that there was some sort of glitch in the system. They investigated after the accident, and it turned out that neither train was entered properly into the system. It was honestly just a freak accident."

I looked up at him. He continued to stare at me as if he had more questions but wasn't sure how to ask.

"And that's really it. Then we moved out here a little over a month ago," I added. "I've been talking so much. How about you. What's your story?"

"It's not that exciting. I was born in Hallowed Hills. I've just been here my whole life. I've been playing football since I was in grade school. Until recently, I went to VP, but my parents decided to pull me out at the end of last year," he said, clearly a bit annoyed at that.

"Did they tell you why?" I asked sheepishly.

"Not really. They've been really cryptic about it actually. We still have our house in Hallowed Hills. My uncle is staying there now, but my parents and I moved closer to CWA," he said as he looked toward the football field. "Hey, I probably should get out there," he said in a rush. "It was nice to see you again, Nina," he added with a smile. "Do you think you could give me your phone number? I would love to talk to you some more. And I did say I would teach you, oh, and your brother more about the town."

"I would like that," I responded with a gentle smile.

I looked through my purse. I didn't have much in it, but I did have a stick of gum. I unwrapped it, stuck the gum in my mouth, then wrote my phone number on the wrapper.

"Here," I said to him with a shy smile.

He smiled back then jogged onto the field where both teams were already lined up for their introductions.

I couldn't take my eyes off him as I watched his teammates pat him on the back, most of them seeming relieved to see him.

"Hey, Nina!" a voice yelled, making me almost jump out of my skin.

"Ahh! What is wrong with this town?" I said, trying to catch my breath, when I saw it was just Jen and Becca.

"Sorry," Jen said as she laughed.

"Where have you been?" I asked, clutching my heart as I continued to try to catch my breath. "Don't you two know how to answer your phones?" I asked when I was finally able to stand up straight again.

"My phone is dead," Becca replied.

"Mine, too. We were in the car trying to charge them, but then we saw you," Jen answered. "I'm glad, too, because that look on your face was priceless," she added as she began to laugh again.

"That wasn't funny. I swear, living in this town has taken ten years off my life," I said.

"Okay, I'm sorry," Jen responded as she continued to giggle. "Anyway. Was that Aaron we saw you talking to?"

"Yeah," Becca jumped in. "Jen told me you saw him at Luna's today. Wow, Jen, you didn't exaggerate. He is definitely hotter than he was last year. I think he got taller."

"Oh, yeah. His family is from Hallowed Hills, and he offered to teach me about it," I said, trying to make it sound like it was just like talking to anyone else. "I thought it might help with our history paper," I added, trying to hide the smile that just thinking about him put on my face.

Both girls looked at me, obviously not believing a word I was saying.

"Seriously," I added when they wouldn't stop staring at me.

"Yeah, okay. I wish he would teach *me* about the town," Becca said with a giggle.

"Becca, weren't you born in Hallowed Hills?" I asked pointedly.

"Yes, but that's beside the point," she giggled. "Anyway, he has to know so much more, of course, since he's a Carrier."

"He's a Carrier?" I asked in surprise. "But I thought his last name was Andrews."

"Yeah, but his mom's maiden name is Carrier. I'm sure their family has some crazy stories," she added as she began to daydream.

We noticed that the game was just about to start, so we began walking toward the bleachers. As we walked, we passed the lit bonfire. The red, yellow, and orange flames reaching up toward the night sky were hypnotizing, and the warm aroma from the cedar embers filled the air.

"Are you okay, Nina?" Jen asked.

I noticed then that I had stopped walking without realizing it. "Yeah. I just wanted to smell the bonfire."

"Pyro," Becca joked as she and Jen started laughing.

But that's not all it was. The smell of the fire had triggered a memory. I was sitting around a campfire with my entire family telling ghost stories and toasting marshmallows. I smiled at the new old memory. I was used to remembering things at weird times, but it hadn't happened in months.

When I snapped back to reality, I noticed a large, tall man looking at me from the other side of the bonfire. I glanced behind me to make sure he wasn't looking at someone else, but there didn't seem to be anyone else he could be looking at, so I turned back to look at him. He was still staring at me.

He had nearly black hair, dark eyes, and dark, weathered skin. He looked like he could have been a teacher or another kind of faculty member, but I had never seen him before.

Unnerved, I quickly turned to catch up with Jen and Becca, and we continued walking toward the bleachers.

"Hey, did you guys see that man?" I asked.

"What man?" Becca asked.

"The man that is over..." But when I turned to show them, he was gone. "Huh, never mind, I guess."

They both laughed at me, and we continued to walk toward the bleachers. When we made it there at last, the area was jam packed. I thought we would have to stand, but luckily Jen and Becca had left their coats in a spot, and there was just enough room for all three of us to sit down.

The game went by pretty quickly, and it was good. That, coming from a person who heavily preferred soccer over football, said a whole lot. CWA won the game by only one point when they kicked an extra point with only a few minutes left in the game after tying it with a touchdown. I felt bad our team had lost, but I was also excited Aaron's team had won.

We gathered our things as everyone started to leave their seats. I scanned what was left of the crowd to see if I could find Zay, but there were still so many people that it proved impossible.

I said goodbye to my friends and started walking toward my car, figuring that Zay would go there when he decided he needed a ride. I walked slowly, hoping I might see Aaron again, but I didn't. However, I did see three dark figures standing at the other end of the parking lot.

I couldn't really make them out, but I could tell they didn't look like teenagers. I wanted to get a better look, but when one of them turned around, glowing yellow eyes stared back at me. He had his hoodie up, so I couldn't see much other than hands covered with black gloves.

Then the one standing behind him put his hoodie down. It was the same man who had been staring at me earlier. I turned around and walked faster toward my car, looking back every few seconds to make sure none of them were behind me.

When I finally made it to my car, I was both surprised and not surprised by what I saw. Zay was sitting on the hood with his arms around the waist of a girl who was leaning into him. Their faces were practically touching, and they were flirting like no one else was around.

As I came closer, I saw that the girl was Emily, which annoyed me more than it should. When I had suggested she go find Zay, I didn't think it would actually happen.

He was certainly not like Ian when it came to the attention he received from girls. Zay embraced it while Ian didn't seem to care much about it at all.

"I see you found him," I said to Emily.

"What are you talking about?" she asked, confused by my presence. "Oh, this is Zay," she added quickly.

I squinted my eyes at her in disbelief. I wasn't sure whether she was being serious. "Emily, do you not see the car you're sitting on? Doesn't it look a little bit familiar?"

She looked down at the car Zay was leaning on then looked back at me. "It's blue. Zay said it was his sister's but that he has a much faster one at home."

"Oh, did he?" I asked as I fixed Zay with narrowed eyes. "Emily, you've seen that car like a hundred times. It's my car!" I exclaimed, now fully annoyed.

"Why would we be on your car? That's just silly."

"You are. Ugh, that's my brother."

"No, your brother's name is Xavier."

I lifted one eyebrow and looked at Zay. I thought she had to be joking, but I wasn't sure anymore. "Emily, 'Zay' is short for 'Xavier.' Ex-*zay*-vee-er," I emphasized to her phonetically.

She looked at me then looked back at Zay then looked at the car. "You told me you were in high school!" she yelled at him with a flirtatious punch to the shoulder.

"Ouch," Zay laughed as he unnecessarily rubbed his shoulder. "I *am* in high school. I just never said what grade I was in," he laughed.

Emily pulled away from him, clearly trying to remember something, then shook her head. "Never mind. I have to go anyway," she said then gave Zay a kiss on the cheek and skipped away.

"You are... something special," I said to Zay. "You know she has a boyfriend, right?"

"Meh. It doesn't matter."

"Ugh, you are gross," I said, letting out a shiver. "So, it seems you had some fun tonight. Other than messing with Emily's head, what did you do?"

"Mess with other girls' heads," he chuckled.

He turned to see my disapproving face. "Chill. It was a joke. I watched the game. Unlike you and Ian, I actually like football. I think I might try out for the team."

"Yeah, good luck with that. People from all over the country try to get on the team," I said to him.

"Well, how hard could it be? I mean, look at me. Just think, next year I will be even bigger."

"When did you get so cocky?"

"It's not cocky. I'm serious. Even if I do get into VP, Mom and Dad won't be able to afford the tuition, so I have to do something."

I looked at him. Apart from him being overly confident, he was right. He needed some activity to get a scholarship to Vanguard. "True, but most of the kids on the team have been playing since they were in grade school. I think that's the last time you played," I said sarcastically.

"Shut up. Just because I don't play on a team doesn't mean I don't play."

"Zay, it's going to be way different, you know."

"I know," he replied sheepishly.

I hated seeing my little brother this way, but soccer was my sport, not football.

"Maybe I could get Aaron to help you."

"Aaron? As in double A?" he asked, looking at me for a response.

I gave him a puzzled look.

"Aaron Andrews, Double A, the quarterback from CWA," he said leadingly.

"Why do you call him 'Double A?'" I asked, ignoring his question.

"That's his nickname. I mean, who cares. Is that who you're talking about?" he asked again.

"Yes. He's going to teach Ian and me more about the town. I can ask him then."

"Hell yeah! When? Can you do it soon?"

When he asked the question, I realized I couldn't give him a timeframe. I didn't have his phone number. He only had mine.

"Soon," I said, trying not to give anything away.

"Sooner than soon. Please, Nina, I will owe you big time."

"Yes, you will," I laughed.

He frowned at me, probably wondering what he would have to do as a favor.

When we got home, I was exhausted, but I still couldn't get the memory of the three men at the bonfire out of my mind.

I went to get a glass of water from the sink and looked out the window. It was already pretty dark, so I couldn't see much, but then I saw movement. Peering closer through the window, I dropped my glass, and it shattered in the sink, as the same three figures from the bonfire glided past the side of our house. Their movements were so smooth that it looked like they were floating.

"What happened?" Zay asked as he ran into the kitchen.

I looked back through the window, but the three men were gone. "Umm, the glass just slipped," I lied.

Zay rolled his eyes and went back into the living room to watch TV.

I went to the sliding glass door to see if I could see anyone, but I didn't dare open it. When I didn't see anything, I thought maybe it had just been my mind playing tricks on me, so I went upstairs.

With my exhaustion, I figured maybe I just needed some sleep. Without even changing my clothes, I just jumped into my bed and fell asleep quickly.

# CHAPTER 5
## THE WITCHING HOUR

The next day I woke up pretty early for a Saturday. It was only about 7 a.m. when I dragged myself out of bed. It seemed even colder than usual, but I was happy to see that it was a nice, sunny day.

I peeked out of my room and didn't hear anything, so I assumed everyone was still sleeping. I went downstairs and made myself a quick bowl of cereal, but again the food had no taste.

I checked my phone, but there were no missed calls or new text messages. I was disappointed but realized that it had only been a few hours since I had given Aaron my phone number. Even with that logical thought at the forefront, I still sighed as I put my phone down.

The rest of my family woke up within the hour, and we all did our own things for the rest of the day. By the end of the day, I still hadn't heard from Aaron, but I tried not to think about it as I got ready for bed. I checked my phone one last time, but there was nothing.

I reluctantly climbed into bed, but I couldn't fall asleep, so I decided to watch some TV. I picked *Buffy the Vampire Slayer* because Becca and I watched it a every time I spent the night at her house, or she spent the night at mine, so I didn't even need to focus on it anymore. I just listened with my eyes closed as I eventually drifted off to sleep.

I slept in the next day, but when I woke up, I still felt sort of tired. By the time I went downstairs, Zay and Ian had already finished their breakfasts. I sat down lazily next to them.

"Rough night?" Zay asked.

"Shut up," I shot back as I poured myself a cup of coffee. I didn't care that the coffee didn't taste like anything. I was starting to get used to that reality. I was just hoping the caffeine would make me feel less blah. After a few sips, I did start feeling energized, so I was thankful for that. I felt fine overall, but my taste buds hadn't been working for a few days now.

"Ian, are you feeling any better today?" I asked.

"Yes, much, now that I'm not around the weird people of this town."

I wasn't really sure what Ian was referring to. Yes, we'd met a few odd characters in the last few days, but it wasn't like it was the entire town. He seemed really annoyed by it all, so I didn't want to ask him anything else, knowing that he would tell me if it was important.

After breakfast, I decided to try to do some research on the town myself. I had given up on Aaron calling me that weekend, and I needed my paper topic by the next morning.

I started with the obvious: history of the town settlement. I went directly to the town's website, which had a lot of information about that. There I read that the Carriers were the original founding family, but four other families had settled here shortly after. These families—Osbourne, Walker, Hunter, and Palmer—were also considered founders in addition to the Carriers. I easily assumed that the Osbourne-Palmer Memorial Hospital was named after these families.

The town website listed lineages of all five families. For the Carriers, it started with the original Thomas and Martha and went all the way down to Aaron Andrews.

I closed my laptop harder than I should have. Aaron again. I had finally been able to get him out of my head, but then here he was in big, bold letters.

I decided to go another route and began an internet search on the Salem witch trials. Of course, this gave me a massive amount of information, including links to hundreds of other sites. Overwhelmed, I had no idea where to go from there, so I clicked on and read through a few random websites. Then I tried searching for just the Carriers, but there was still too much information on the family.

Ian was so much better at this stuff than I was, but I was determined to do it on my own. I finally decided to narrow the search to Sarah Carrier, 1692. Again, that yielded numerous links, but one in particular caught my eye because it looked like the website had been updated recently, and it was linked directly from the History of Massachusetts website.

This one had information about everyone who had been accused and included what had happened to them. I read through the rest of the information, and everything seemed pretty similar to what I had read at Luna's in the last month.

I was ready to call it a night when I noticed an asterisk next to one of the references. It was a journal from 1692. When I clicked on the link, it gave me the same information as on the previous website, but it also had another link to a scanned copy of the original journal.

I clicked on the link, and that opened an attachment of the entire thing. Whomever had kept the journal appeared to have been a family member of an accused person, but it never mentioned their name. However, that didn't matter because what I found—the one huge difference between this journal and every other listing of the accused—changed everything.

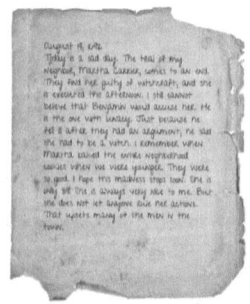

I read the paragraph over and over to make sure I had read it correctly. I was shocked. As I started looking up more information on Martha Carrier, everywhere else other than this source said Sarah Carrier had evaded arrest. The only mention of Martha was that she was Sarah's mother. Even the website that had brought me to this link had no mention of Martha.

I looked again through the pages of the uploaded journal, and it seemed authentic. The pages looked very old, and some were so worn that they were difficult to read. Others were impossible to read due to the discoloration of the paper.

I quickly clicked through the pages until I found some hand drawings of the town. Although they were just sketches, the illustrations were very detailed. The author also had drawn some of the people who had lost their lives, including Martha Carrier.

This drawing of Martha took up an entire page and was vividly colored. Martha looked like she was more in her mid-50s than 39. The artist had added wrinkles to her olive-toned face, which aged her even more. She had long brown hair tied back in a braid, which lay over her left shoulder. She wore a dark blue apron over a dark blue dress and was a bit on the chubby side.

Seeing her portrait made me think of the painting I had seen earlier at Luna's. I pulled out my phone to look at the pictures I had taken. The

Martha Carrier in this depiction looked extremely different. She looked more her age—maybe even younger—her skin was pale white, and she was in great shape. I examined this picture more closely. Although she looked different, it was definitely her. Unless Martha had some twin sister that no history books had recorded, this was the same person.

But the strangest thing about the picture was the year it was dated. How could Martha Carrier have been executed in 1692 and yet be alive in 1694? Could Martha be a vampire? No. There were only two years between the two portraits, so maybe one was just a mistake. With all the new information I had just read, I needed time to absorb it.

I hadn't noticed how late it was getting, and I was feeling hungry. It was already well past lunchtime but not quite time for dinner, so I went downstairs to find something to munch and see where everyone else was.

When I walked into the living room, Ian was sleeping on the couch. Feeling a little bit mischievous, I jumped onto the couch with him and sent him flying up into the air.

"Huh? What?" Ian asked sleepily.

"Good morning, sleepy head. Where is everyone?"

"I don't know. I was sleeping," Ian replied as he pulled the blanket back over himself.

"Fine. I guess I will just go to Luna's by myself," I said as I walked away.

"I'm up," he proclaimed as he rubbed his eyes. "Where is everyone?"

"I literally just asked you that."

I rolled my eyes then walked through the kitchen toward the garage to see if my dad's car was there, but before I made it, I noticed a note and some cash attached to the front of the refrigerator.

*Nina/Ian,*

*Here is some money for Luna's. Don't forget Mom and I are going to my company dinner tonight, and we will not be back until late.*

*Love,*

*Dad*

I had forgotten they had that dinner tonight. He had only told us about a hundred times.

"Oh yeah," I said out loud as Ian came into the kitchen.

"What?" he asked.

"Mom and Dad went to dinner for that work thing," I answered. "But where's Zay?"

"He went over to Jay's house. Jay's mom will drop him off around 8 o'clock," Ian answered.

"I just asked you a minute ago, and you said you had no idea where anyone was," I snorted.

"I was sleeping," he replied with a yawn.

I looked at the clock. It was a quarter to four. I couldn't find anything I wanted to munch on, so I figured it would be okay to eat dinner a bit early.

"Okay. Well, let's go then. I'm starving."

When we arrived at Luna's, it was packed. We didn't want to wait for a table, so we asked Kas if we could eat at the bar. She said we could, so we took our seats, and she poured us our usual iced teas without us even asking.

I didn't want to order my usual, a veggie cheeseburger with tater tots, because it had tasted like nothing the last time. I wasn't a vegetarian, but that burger was usually really tasty and flavorful. I asked Kas to have the kitchen make me something with a really strong taste, maybe something with garlic in it. I thought about telling Ian what I'd found in my research, but I wasn't sure if I should. He seemed so overwhelmed with all the weirdness going on lately that I didn't want to stress him out anymore.

"Did Zay tell you about Emily?" I asked.

"Yeah, he told me. I don't know what's gotten into that kid, but if that's what will make him happy then whatever."

Just as we were finishing our food, Lavinia walked in.

"Hey. May I join you?" she asked.

"Hi, Lavinia. Of course, you can," I answered.

I was happy to see that she seemed in a better mood than she had been the last time we'd seen her. "Thank you so much for fixing my car. I promise I will pay you back."

"Don't worry about it. My brother loves messing with cars. Believe me, he had so much fun fixing it up."

"Thank you, but I have to do something."

"Maybe I could take you out to dinner," Ian jumped in.

"That would be nice," Lavinia said shyly.

I was very surprised by Ian. He really wasn't the type to be so bold. I looked at him, and he looked confident, even sitting up straighter and smiling more than usual.

The three of us chatted for a while longer, and Lavinia told us a little about her life. Her parents and older brother had died during a family vacation in Venezuela when they were caught in a mudslide. After the tragedy, she and her younger brother had been sent to Hallowed Hills to live with her grandparents. We talked for another hour about our lives before realizing how late it was getting.

I was happy that I had been able to taste my food. It wasn't what I really liked, but at least it had tasted like something. Ian didn't hide the fact that he thought my meal smelled very strong. I knew it did because I could smell it, but when I tasted it, the flavor was very muted.

"I probably should get going. I ordered some food for Zay, and he'll be home any minute now," I said as I started to stand up, "but you guys stay. I'm sure Lavinia can give you a ride home," I added with a smile.

Lavinia and Ian both smiled. I could tell they were hitting it off. Just because I had no romance in my life didn't mean I wanted to get in anyone else's way.

"Of course, I can," she agreed.

"Thanks, Nina," Ian responded with a grateful smile. "I'll walk you out."

"Don't worry. You stay and have fun," I answered as I walked away.

"Wait!" he yelled. "Here," he added as he threw a piece of gum at me.

I scowled at him but popped it in my mouth anyway.

When I stepped outside, I let out a big shiver. "I hate the cold," I said a little too loudly to no one.

"So I hear," Aaron responded with a laugh.

I turned around quickly to see him just getting out of his car, a brand-new, sleek black Ford Mustang.

"Oh, hey Aaron."

"Are you leaving already?"

"Yeah, I have to take my brother some dinner."

"That's disappointing. I was hoping to spend some time with you," he said with a luminous smile.

I didn't want to seem desperate, but I really wanted to stay there with him. I felt a little lightheaded and dizzy again, but I didn't care.

"Maybe you can come over to my house for a bit," I suggested. "If that's okay with you," I added quickly.

"I think that sounds nice," he answered with a smile.

"Okay. Do you want to just follow me?"

"That works."

The drive seemed to be over way too quickly. My thoughts were all jumbled. I had so many questions, but I couldn't think of any I wanted to ask him.

As I parked in the driveway, I took a deep breath then opened my door. When I stepped out of the car, Aaron was only a few feet away. We walked in to find Zay watching TV on the couch. He looked stunned to see Aaron and me come in.

"Hey, man," Aaron said to Zay.

"Hi…" Zay answered, clearly surprised.

"Sorry. Aaron, this is my brother, Zay; Zay, this is Aaron," I said by way of introduction. They shook each other's hands. "Here's your food, Zay," I mentioned and put it on the end table next to him.

"Oh, thanks."

"Don't you have some homework to do?" I asked him, gesturing up the stairs with only my eyes.

"Yeah, I should get to that," he replied as he grabbed the bag of food.

I watched Zay walk up the stairs then waited to hear his bedroom door shut before moving again. I was still very nervous, and I wasn't sure what I was going to say. It was way too soon to ask him about Martha. I thought about how that might sound if I brought it up. *By the way, how was your ancestor alive two years after she was executed?* He would think I was nuts.

"You like mysteries, huh?" Aaron asked as he eyed the book sticking out of my purse.

I pulled out the book. It was *A Study in Scarlet* by Arthur Conan Doyle.

"It's my second time trying to read it," I said to him shyly.

He gave me a puzzled look. It wasn't really a hard book to read, so I understood his confusion.

"What do you mean?"

"Nothing. You'll think I'm weird," I answered shyly.

"What?"

"I always get to the part with the two pills. You know, the ones they find on Stragerson after he was murdered. I don't like that Holmes tests the pills on the dog."

"Really?" he asked with a smile.

"Yes. Don't make fun."

"I'm not laughing at you. My sister has turned off so many movies while we were watching them because an animal was hurt, so that just reminded me of her," he explained with a reassuring smile.

"You have a sister?" I asked.

"Yeah. She goes to Columbia."

"Wow! That's a great school."

"Yeah, my family would expect no less," he said with a weighty shrug.

"A ton of pressure being a Carrier, huh?" I smiled then immediately bit my lip because I wasn't sure whether he wanted me knowing he was a Carrier.

"Ah, so you know," he said with an awkward smile.

"It's a friendly town," I answered with a gentle smile.

"Don't get me wrong. I love being a Carrier. It's just... well... I love being an Andrews, too. And sometimes that part gets overlooked. My dad's family came from a small village in Scotland, and they did so much good there." He paused. "Sorry, a little deep."

"No, it's interesting. Tell me more," I said curiously.

"There's not much more to tell. I live in a town where my mom's family is pretty much royalty, so my dad's side doesn't really get recognized. It was actually a huge deal that my mom married my dad."

"Really? Why?"

"Well, he wasn't from around here, so he wasn't really trusted by the founding families."

"What do you mean? Oh, you don't have to tell me if you don't want to," I quickly retracted with a blush.

"It's okay. Remember how I said we just picked up and moved away?"

I nodded.

"I overheard my grandfather telling my mom that my dad wasn't like them, and if they had never gotten married, we wouldn't have had to pick up our lives and leave our home. It was really weird hearing my grandfather speak that way. He has always been so loving and accepting of others." He paused for a moment in thought. "It wasn't like we actually left our old life though. Since my uncle moved into our house in Hallowed Hills, he has been calling every week, and my mom has these private conversations with him. Some weeks it's okay for us to come home, but others it's not."

"What did he mean that your dad wasn't like them? Why wouldn't you be able to come home? Have you asked your mom about it?"

He paused as if saying that I had asked too much. "The Andrews aren't a founding family," he finally said. "And, no, my mom doesn't even know I listen to their phone calls. But sometimes that's the only way to find out what's going on."

I was just about to question him further when I heard the front door open. I could only hope it wasn't my parents. How would I explain Aaron being in the house without them being there? I wondered what time it was and held my breath as the door slowly crept open.

"Oh, hey," Ian murmured, appearing flustered at seeing Aaron.

"Hi, Ian," I said with relief. "How was the rest of your night?"

"Pretty good. We just talked at Luna's. I'm kind of tired, so I'm going to go take a shower and go to bed. Good night."

"Night," Aaron responded easily.

"Good night."

"He was out pretty late," Aaron noted.

"He was at Luna's with a friend of ours. Well, I think they may be more than friends, or at least they're getting there," I giggled.

"Ah, I see. Anyone I know?"

"Um, I'm not sure. Maybe? Her name is Lavinia. We just met her. Do you know her?"

I held my breath, not knowing if I wanted to know the reason it seemed he didn't like her. If they had dated, there would be no way I could compete with her.

He looked at me with concern but also seemed a little upset. "No, not really, but I know *of* her." He paused. "Her name just seems to come up a whole lot during those secret calls between my mom and uncle. Let's just say that my uncle knows her really well."

I smiled at him tenderly, relieved they had never been a couple, but I was also curious because there had to be more of a story there. I was determined to find out what it was, but it didn't seem like he wanted to keep talking about his family, so I quickly changed the subject, fully planning on getting more information later. "So, I have a favor to ask you," I said to him with a sweet smile.

"Sure," he answered right away.

"You know my brother, Zay, right?" I asked.

He nodded.

"Well, he's interested in trying out for the VP football team next year. And, well, he hasn't really played on a team in a while, so he could use some help," I finished with an innocent smile.

"I would love to help your brother," he answered before I'd really even asked.

"That's great! He'll be really happy to hear that. Thank you so much!"

"No problem. Have him give me a call. It's getting a little late, so I should probably get going. Thanks for having me over. Hopefully we can do it again soon," he said with a charming smile.

I looked at my phone and was surprised to see that it was almost 10 p.m.

As I walked him to the door, he stopped and turned back toward the living room. "Oh, hang on."

I watched as he grabbed the book from my purse.

"I'm going to take this and black out the part with the dog so you can finish reading it." He smiled warmly, and I smiled back. "The ending is good. I don't want you to miss out."

"You've read it?"

"Yes, it was my first mystery novel. It's what started my obsession," he laughed. "Bye, Nina," he said flirtatiously.

When he walked past me again, he brushed my hand. That one little touch made my heart flutter.

As soon as I closed the door, I smiled so widely that I had to bite my lip to stop. I ran up the stairs to my room and jumped into bed. What a great night it had been. He seemed like such a sweet guy. I was so happy that I wasn't even upset I hadn't asked him about Martha.

My head was swooning delightfully until I realized I still didn't have his phone number. "Ugh."

I tried to forget about that because I did not want to ruin the moment. Suddenly, my phone buzzed. I grabbed it eagerly and tapped the message icon then smiled when I realized it was from Aaron.

I had a really nice night, Nina. Good night and sweet dreams.

I threw my head back onto the pillow and put another pillow over my mouth so no one would hear me scream. I was over the moon! The boy I liked liked me back! I fell asleep fantasizing about the next time I would see him.

# CHAPTER 6
## PIED PIPER

The next morning, I jumped out of bed, ready to face the day and not let any amount of cold get to me. I knew my parents were both planning to sleep in because they had come home late the night before, so it was my job to feed everyone and make sure they got to school on time. I grabbed my soccer gear for practice, which I had Mondays and Wednesdays, and we began our drive to school. It was all normal until we dropped off Zay.

"There's something I want to tell you," Ian began once we were alone in the car. "The founders of this town keep many secrets, so you should be careful." He paused. "Even with the good-looking ones."

"That's funny, Aaron kind of said the same thing." I looked over at Ian, and he seemed confused, so I continued, "When we were talking last night, he told me that the founding families kept secrets, but he also said some of the secrets might have to do with Lavinia. Wait. What makes *you* think the founders keep secrets?"

"I read, and I ask questions. Do you like Aaron?"

"Do you like Lavinia?" I countered.

He frowned. "You know he's dating Amanda, don't you?"

"We're just friends," I answered nervously.

"Just be careful," he said, obviously not believing me for a second. "Besides we're still new in this town, and the people are a little weird."

"Does that include Lavinia?" I asked, relieved that he had slightly changed the subject.

"Yes... it does," he replied while looking out the window.

"Okay, little brother, but you have to be careful, too. You never know," I said, trying to lighten the mood.

"I think I could take Lavinia," he laughed.

"It's not always about physical strength," I teased back.

We were about to turn into the parking lot when we saw that the entrance was blocked off. Two cars made U-turns when a police officer standing next to the gate redirected them away from the school.

"What the hell is going on?" Ian asked.

"I have no clue."

I watched as, before turning around, the people in the cars in front of us spoke to the officer. I was too curious to just turn away, so I wanted to talk to the officer as well.

"Hi, officer, what's going on? We go to this school."

"Sorry, kids, no school today. Just turn around and go back home," she answered.

"What happened?" Ian asked again.

"Just go home and make sure you lock your doors," she responded blandly.

We made our U-turn and headed away from the school.

"Well, that was weird," I said.

"This entire town is weird. I swear we are living in a John Clancy novel."

"What are you doing?" I asked when Ian got out his phone.

"I'm going to text Alex and Matt. Maybe they know what's going on."

Alex texted Ian back first. That was great because his dad was an officer in the Hallowed Hills Police Department. For sure, he would have the best information.

Apparently two students somehow had ended up on the roof of the school sometime over the weekend and had fallen off. Alex said that it looked like they had been attacked by some kind of animal. I immediately wondered what kind of animal would follow someone up on a roof in the first place.

We didn't really see wild animals in the town since it wasn't really close to a forest or anything. The only thing we had were the hills, and the worst animal you might find was a coyote; certainly nothing that would chase a person three floors up and onto a roof. Besides, the hills were so far from here that there was no way a coyote could make it to the school without being noticed. And even if a coyote somehow was smart enough to do that, it would still be difficult for one to get on top of the roof of the school. Something wasn't right.

I wondered who the two students were, and my heart sank when I realized I hadn't spoken to Jen or Becca all weekend. Without even thinking, I reached for my purse in the back seat. As I did, I turned the wheel and almost swerved into oncoming traffic.

"Nina!" Ian screamed.

"Sorry, I have to find my phone."

"What's wrong?" Ian asked after seeing the panic in my eyes.

"Have you spoken to Jen or Becca this weekend?" I asked with a lump in my throat.

"Well, no, but..." he said then trailed off when he realized why I was so scared. "*You* just focus on the road; *I* will call both of them."

He tried calling both girls, but neither of them answered, so then I started to really panic.

"I know this is scary," Ian reassured me, "but let's not jump to any conclusions. Look, there's a gas station. Let's stop to get some junk food before heading home," he said, obviously trying to distract me.

"Okay, but just keep trying to call them."

"I will," he replied sympathetically.

By the time we'd parked, we still hadn't heard from either Jen or Becca. I tried them a few more times myself as I stood in front of the gas station. I debated whether to call their parents. If one of them had been on the roof and their parents still didn't know, I wasn't sure what I would say. After another few minutes, I couldn't take it anymore, so I called Becca's house.

"Oh, hi, Mrs. Clarke. This is Nina. Can I speak to Becca please?"

"Hi Nina! We didn't see you this weekend."

"I had so much homework," I deflected.

"Glad to hear you're focusing on your studies. One second, dear. I'll get her for you."

"Hello?" Becca answered sleepily.

"Becca! Thank God you're okay," I said in pure relief.

"Why wouldn't I be okay?" she asked through a yawn.

"Because of what happened at school."

"What are you talking about?" she asked, clearly confused.

"Didn't you hear?" I asked.

"Hear what?" she asked. "My mom just came in early this morning and told me I could sleep in because there was no school. I didn't ask her anything else. I just turned my alarm off and went back to sleep."

"Two students were attacked on the roof of the school over the weekend," I explained.

"What? How? By who?" she fired back at me.

I didn't want to tell her about the whole animal attack theory because that didn't make any sense to me. "I'm not sure. I don't have all the details. I'll call you back in a bit. I just wanted to make sure you were okay."

"Umm, okay. Well, keep me posted."

I didn't want to worry Becca anymore, especially because there was really nothing to worry about. At least not yet.

When I hung up with Becca, I called Jen's house, but no one answered. Determined to talk to someone, I tried two more times until someone finally answered.

"Hellos?" a man answered in broken English.

I didn't recognize the voice at all, so I was a bit startled when this stranger answered Jen's home phone.

"Hi, umm…" I trailed off. "This is Nina. Is Jen there?"

I heard the man put the phone down, then it sounded like he argued with someone in a different language. I heard some rustling and then more arguing.

"Hello?" someone finally said into the phone. It was a different man, but he also had a thick Indian accent.

"Hi, I was just looking for Jen."

"Jen no here. She go on vacation. Very fun!"

"Oh, okay—"

"Okay, goodbye," the man cut me off and hung up.

I looked at the phone, contemplating whether it was worth trying to call back, but I was getting cold standing outside. It was so windy and cloudy that it made the cold even worse.

I still needed to find out what was going on with my friend, but I became distracted when a large car with dark-tinted windows pulled up into the spot right in front of me. I examined the car from where I stood, and it looked like a Cadillac, but before I could really look at it, the driver turned on the car's brights, and I had to cover my eyes with my arm.

I began to walk away, but as I opened the door to the gas station store, I turned back to try to see who was in the car. Oddly, no one ever got out.

I quickly walked inside and looked around for Ian. Of course, I found him with five different snacks in his hands already.

"Are you getting anything?" he asked.

I shook my head but still went to see if there was anything I wanted. I walked down the aisles, but nothing seemed very appetizing, and the smell of the pork rinds and beef jerky were so strong that they gave me a headache.

Ian paid for his food, and we headed toward the door, but then Ian stopped to look at more snacks. I rolled my eyes and continued toward the door. I knew our mom would be calling us to find out where we were. I was sure they would have heard by now that there was no school.

Ian told me he had already called Lavinia, and she was going to meet us at our house later that night. I was surprised he had invited her to our house so soon after meeting her. It had to mean he was serious about getting to know her. I couldn't remember the last time he'd invited a girl over to meet our parents. As much as I wanted to tease him about it, I liked Lavinia, too, so I was excited to get to know her more as well.

When I stepped out of the store, I noticed a familiar girl sitting on a bench outside. She looked like she was cold and had been there for a while.

"Crystal?"

"Hi," she answered shyly.

Crystal Chery went to our school, but she was in the year below us. She was one of the first people we had met in Hallowed Hills because we went to the same church. She was originally from New Orleans, but she had lived in Hallowed Hills since she was nine. She was very petite, standing only about 5'1", and had very dark skin, dark brown eyes, and black hair she kept in box braids. She still had a slight southern accent, but it only popped up when she was nervous.

"What are you doing out here?" I asked as I sat down next to her.

"The school is closed."

"Honey, how long have you been sitting out here?"

"I stayed at my grandparents' house last night, so I had to take the bus. It dropped me off about 6:30 a.m., and I walked here from the school when they wouldn't let me in."

I immediately grabbed her and hugged her tightly. She didn't live that far from us, but her grandparents lived about 45 minutes from Hallowed Hills, so I knew the school bus would not go that far. As such, she had to take public transportation whenever she stayed with her grandparents.

"Why didn't you call me?"

"I didn't want to be no trouble. The next bus will be coming in a little while, but I had to use the washroom."

"Come on, let's go," I said as I pulled her up from the bench.

"I don't want to be no trouble."

"Crystal, sweetie, it's no trouble at all. Next time you call me. Do you hear me?" I said with an empathetic smile.

She nodded and walked with me back to the car. I turned it on while she settled into the back seat, and I went in to get Ian. When I found him, I saw he had picked up a few more snacks and was paying again for this new haul. I let him know about Crystal, and he said he would be right out.

When I went back outside, I saw that the mysterious black car was now parked right next to mine. Its engine was on, and the brights were still on, too. It was parked close to the driver's side, so I approached my car from the passenger side. Looking into my car, I saw that Crystal had her knees to her chest, and her face was buried in them.

I opened the passenger side door and stuck my head in. "Are you okay?"

"Yes," she replied as she rocked back and forth.

I didn't know what the person in the black car wanted, but whoever it was seemed to really scare Crystal. Feeling a little scared myself, I didn't want to walk toward the driver's side door, so I crawled in through the passenger side.

A few seconds later, I saw Ian walking toward us with bags full of food. When he got closer, the black car pulled back out of the spot to drive away. I looked back at Crystal who now had looked up and was watching the car drive away.

"Do you know them?"

She shook her head then put her feet back down on the floor. She seemed to be feeling better now, but when Ian opened the door, she almost jumped out of her skin.

"It's just Ian," I said, looking back at her.

I couldn't believe how terrified she was. I wanted to ask her more questions, but with the way she was acting, I thought that might make things worse.

"What happened?" Ian asked, oblivious to anything other than his snacks.

"I'm really not sure. There was a weird car, and... I really don't know. Let's just get out of here," I responded.

When we got to Crystal's house, I made sure her mom was home before we left. As soon as the front door opened, I could smell the aroma of the homemade gumbo she was cooking. I wasn't big on spicy food, but I loved her gumbo. Crystal had brought it to school once and let me try it. When I'd told her I liked it, her mom had always packed an extra serving for me every time she cooked it.

As I left, Mrs. Chery waved at me and smiled. She always had a smile on her face. Even if you were having a bad day, you couldn't help but smile after being around her.

When we got back to our house, Mom was hysterical. She had read the email from school and had been about to call us when we walked in.

"Mom, we're fine. Ian was just hungry," I responded, gesturing to the bags Ian was carrying.

"That food is simply terrible for you. I'll cut you up some vegetables," she responded as she started pulling ingredients from the refrigerator.

"Oh, before I forget, one of my friends will be coming over in a little bit. She's really nice. I think you'll like her," I said to her.

"That's so nice. I love meeting your friends."

I purposely didn't mention the burgeoning romance between her and Ian because Mom could be kind of nosy and would bombard Ian with so many questions that he would be stuck there all day. I knew that if she thought Lavinia was just my friend first, when Ian decided to tell Mom about their relationship, it would be easier on both him and Lavinia.

I was kind of glad, too. To make the story more realistic, I would be able to spend time with Lavinia alone, which would give me a chance to get to know her better.

Ian and I watched wrestling for the rest of the day.

After a few hours, I asked, "Can we watch something else?"

"What? This is a classic!" Ian explained. "This is 1997, Raw is War. It's when they reformed the Hart Foundation."

I looked at the screen where Owen Hart was facing off against The British Bulldog. Ian wasn't wrong; it was entertaining. I watched on with him as Brett Hart ran to the ring and started pleading with his family not to fight. I was just really getting into it when the alarm on my phone went off, reminding me that Zay needed to be picked up from school. Ian paused the recording and switched it back to live TV.

"I'll go," he said as he stood up.

"Thanks," I replied with a smile.

I continued flipping through the channels when the sound suddenly stopped, and the audio started beeping obnoxiously as a picture of a kid popped up and a message ran across the bottom of the screen:

***AMBER ALERT:*** *15-year-old Kenny Mahomes was discovered missing from his bedroom in Hallowed Hills early this morning. Kenny is described as a thin, African-American male with brown eyes and short black hair. If you have seen this child, please contact the Hallowed Hills Police Department immediately.*

I studied the boy's picture and realized that he went to our school.

*First, we couldn't find Jen, and now this?*

I was about to call Ian when the doorbell rang. It was Lavinia.

I was just introducing her to my mom when Ian and Zay came home. We spoke to them briefly, and then she and I went upstairs to my room while the rest of my family stayed downstairs. Lavinia and I watched a few episodes of *Buffy the Vampire Slayer* and talked about different things, mostly her school and family. She told me she was in college, but she studied from home, and she and her younger brother now looked after her grandparents since they had cared for them when they were younger.

She seemed like a good, genuine person, and I felt really comfortable around her. It was almost like I knew her.

I debated whether to tell her what I had found out about Martha Carrier. I really wanted to talk to someone about it, and she seemed like a person I could trust and wouldn't tease me about my belief in the supernatural. But before I did that, I wanted to start with something smaller, something that had been bothering me.

"What did you mean before when you mentioned Aaron and family drama?" I asked.

"Oh, that," she said, clearly reluctant to talk about it, but she conceded after a moment. "Well, my family isn't really from around here, and it was a big deal when I started to date his uncle. They have this weird thing about dating. Their dates have to be from a family approved of by the founding families. And, well, they didn't approve of my family."

What she said pretty much aligned with what Aaron had said about the families. However, based on the conversation we'd had the day before, I didn't think Aaron himself would judge anyone based on what family they were from.

What threw me off most was that she said she had dated Aaron's uncle. That made me even more curious to know how old she was. Even if he was Aaron's mom's younger brother, he would still have to be in his mid-30s. Even though I felt really comfortable with Lavinia, I didn't think it was time to ask about something like that.

"Why didn't they approve of your family?" I asked instead.

She regarded me as though she really wanted to tell me something but was afraid.

"Are you okay?" I asked when she said nothing.

"It's because our families were born differently," she responded self-consciously at last.

"What do you mean? Like class-wise?"

"No, not class-wise exactly. Umm... we are different... physically," she said cryptically.

Before I could ask her what she meant, there was a knock at the door, and my mom walked in with food and drinks. Of course, Mom stayed to talk to Lavinia as well.

"So, how did you two meet?" she asked lightly.

"We both have an obsession with peach iced tea," Lavinia answered with a sweet smile. "Nina and I both ordered it to go, but I accidently spilled mine, and she offered to share hers."

"That's my girl. You're always thinking of others," my mom responded as she brushed my hair back with her fingers.

"You girls have fun, but remember it's still a school night. I got another email from the school, and they said it would be open tomorrow," Mom said as she stood to walk out of the room.

"Your mom's right. It's getting late, and I should probably get going," Lavinia said as the door closed.

"Yeah, I can't believe how late it is, but I had fun. We should do it again sometime."

Lavinia turned back to me and smiled before walking out the door. I waited a few minutes before going downstairs. I was only halfway down when I found Ian waiting for me.

"What... are you doing?" I asked suspiciously.

"Hey, so I had to make up a story about how we met Lavinia. Mom didn't call me out on it, so I guess she didn't ask you guys."

"Actually, she did ask."

"She did? What did you say?" he asked nervously.

"Well, she asked Lavinia, and she told her we met at Luna's."

"Really? That's what I told her."

"Great," I replied with a shrug at his intensity. "So, is that why you're creeping around here like the Pink Panther?" I laughed.

"You know how Mom is. If she finds out we lied about one thing, she'll think we're hiding something big. Which is usually true, but that's beside the point."

"Take a breath, little brother."

"Well, what did you guys talk about?" he asked.

"You know, girl stuff," I answered flippantly as I walked past him.

I sat down with my mom on the couch before Ian could interrogate me further. He gave me an annoyed look but just sat down next to me. We watched a movie as a family and then went to bed afterward.

The next morning, the first thing I did was try to call Jen again, but there was no answer.

After we dropped off Zay at his school, I told Ian about the conversation I'd had with the men who had answered her phone the day before. I was really worried and starting to think Ian was right about the town. I also told him about the missing boy from our school, but he didn't think it was related.

"Even so, I keep trying to call Matt. He hasn't answered either," he confessed.

"Are you serious?" I asked nervously as I took in his panic-filled expression. "Do you think Alex would know anything more by now?"

"I called him last night. He told me that he hadn't heard from Matt either." He paused. "And he said... that the two students who were on the roof died. It was one guy and one girl."

"Who were they?!" I shouted.

"He doesn't know. And..." he trailed off.

"And what?" I asked with tears beginning in my eyes.

"Well, I tried to call Matt's house, and a man I didn't know answered. He sort of sounded like Matt's dad but a little younger. When I asked for Matt, the man said that he had gone on vacation."

I didn't say anything to him. I just watched the road.

"Did Alex say anything else?" I asked, not sure I wanted to know the answer.

"He said that the police department had no idea what could have caused the bite marks left on the bodies. And... the bodies were almost completely drained of blood."

"You're joking, right?" I asked with a smile. But when I turned to look at him, there was no humor on his face. "Ian, you can't be serious. The bodies were drained of blood?"

He shrugged. "I'm just telling you what he said."

I looked at him a bit longer then made a quick U-turn right in the middle of the street.

"Whoa! What are you doing?" Ian asked as he gripped the dashboard.

"We're going to the police station and finding out who was on that roof."

"How the hell do you think you are going to do that? Ask nicely?"

"Maybe," I replied.

"Be serious. They are not going to tell us anything."

"They will tell me," I insisted confidently.

When we arrived at the police station, Ian was still trying to convince me that coming here was a waste of time, but I was determined to get some information. By this point, I would have settled for any information at all about our friends.

"May I help you, Miss?" the officer asked right away.

"Yes, I want to file a missing person's report," I said quickly.

Ian looked at me puzzled but then seemed to understand. I knew I wouldn't be able to file a report, but I also knew nothing ever happened in Hallowed Hills, so if this officer knew something, he would react to the names I was going to give him.

"Okay.... Do you have a parent here or something?" he asked, needlessly looking behind us.

"No, the names of the missing people are Jennifer Shah and Matthew Menzel," I said before he could ask me any other questions.

The officer's eyes widened, and he regarded me nervously but didn't say anything for a few seconds. He cleared his throat then continued, "Listen, you need to have an adult here to file a missing person's report," he said after regaining his calm. "Officer Carol will make sure you get to school on time," he added as he waved another officer toward us. The officer promptly walked us to our car and told us he would follow us to VP... to make sure we got there safely.

"It's them, isn't it?" Ian asked hesitantly when we were alone in the car.

I didn't say anything as I put the car into drive and headed toward the school.

The parking lot was pretty quiet since we were already late for class. If it weren't for all the police presence, it would have been like any other day.

In addition to Officer Carol, two more officers were at the school. Apparently, they were being extra cautious because of what had happened. As far as the public knew, the students were still just missing, but there were already signs up that offered counseling for dealing with the loss of our classmates.

"I don't know why we're here right now," I said angrily under my breath to Ian.

"Well, for starters, we have a police officer following us like we're some sort of criminals, but, besides that, there's nothing else we can do."

"There's plenty we can do," I countered.

"Yeah? Like what?" he asked.

I thought about that, and even though I didn't want to admit it, he was right. What could we do? We were just high school students.

"Let's just go to class," I finally said, and we went our separate ways.

I was already 15 minutes late to history, but I didn't care. Mr. Conrad didn't even say anything to me; he just looked at me as I walked in then continued with his lecture. I didn't pay attention in class at all as I thought about ways to find out the truth about what had happened on the roof.

Before I knew it, everyone was picking up their books and leaving the class. That's when I realized I had spent the entire class daydreaming. I quickly grabbed my bookbag and headed toward the door, too.

"Nina, can I speak to you for a minute?" Mr. Conrad asked me as I passed his desk.

I didn't say anything and just walked toward him.

He gestured to the chair next to him, so I sat down. He straightened a stack of papers then folded his arms in front of him on the desk.

I immediately started to get a headache as a particular aroma reached my nose. Although the headache was painful, I was intrigued by the smell. The scent was sweet, like vanilla and grapes, but it also had a bold, earthiness to it.

I looked over at Mr. Conrad who was staring straight at me. The glasses he wore had a tint to them so I couldn't see his eyes very well.

"I know that the school is in a bit of a situation, so if you need to talk to someone, let me know," he said with concern as he pulled his sleeve up.

I was astonished at seeing his powerful forearm. On it was a black mark that went higher up his sleeve and looked like the tip of a tattoo. My eyes shifted up toward his face, but they stopped at his neck. His turtleneck was pushed down a bit, and I could see what looked like another tattoo.

I met his eyes then and noticed he was still staring at me. I instantly became nervous and shifted in my chair, which caused him to look away.

"If there is anything I can do to help you, let me know," he repeated the offer.

I wasn't entirely sure why, but I suddenly felt strangely connected to him. Mr. Conrad wasn't really my favorite teacher, but, in that moment, I felt like I could trust him. I thought about telling him everything that was going on, about the Carriers, about the strange things that were happening, and about my friends. Maybe it was because I knew he had an open mind, but I also thought he might be the best adult to tell.

"There have been some weird things happening, and now two people—wait, actually three people—are missing," I blurted out before I could stop.

"When something bad happens, it can be difficult not to jump to conclusions. But until we know what really happened and to whom it actually happened, sometimes it's best to stay optimistic. Just because Amanda wasn't in school doesn't mean something happened to her."

"Amanda?" I asked, confused. I wasn't sure why he was bringing her up again. I had seen her at the game on Friday, so I'd thought everything was fine.

"Yes, she was not in class again. That's the third day in a row. I thought it was a little odd."

"She wasn't in class?" I asked nervously while racking my memory to contradict his statement.

"No, she wasn't," he answered, equally confused. "Who were *you* talking about?"

"My friends, Jen and Matt. They both have you for fifth period. And there was this other kid on the news."

"Yes, I know them, and I heard about Kenny as well," he said gently.

"One of my friend's dads is with the HHPD, and he told us that the two kids who were on the roof died. I went there today, but they wouldn't tell me anything."

"It sounds like you've done some investigating already. I can see why you might think the two students could be Jen and Matt. I'll see if I can find anything out," he said sympathetically. "In the meantime, the best thing we can do is just wait for news. I know you're worried, but try to keep your mind busy until you know what actually happened," he advised then placed his hand on mine.

At his touch, I felt an electric shock, which made us both quickly pull our hands away from each other.

"Did you pick your topic for your paper yet?" he asked after clearing his throat.

Mr. Conrad had never been so nice to me before, and I had never been this close to him before either. He took off his glasses to wipe them and looked up at me. I noticed he had really nice green eyes and his facial features were very strong.

Before I could continue to study him, he cleared his throat again. "Nina?"

"Um, yes. I picked vampires," I said as I snapped back to reality.

When I told him why I had picked vampires, he seemed intrigued, but I also noticed that his body language changed.

He moved back in his chair and sat straight up. "I hope you have a good angle," he said with a bit of an attitude. "I don't want to read another paper about a girl falling in love with a vampire."

I wasn't sure what to say at his quick change in demeanor. It was so fast it had made my head spin, so I just sat there.

"Did you need something else?" he asked.

"No," I answered quickly and stood up to walk away.

"Miss Hart, I would suggest using a different surname for your paper. You never know with the Carriers; they are a very powerful family. Also, please send me the link to that journal you found. It sounds really interesting," he said then abruptly looked back down at the papers on his desk.

"Sure," I responded automatically.

It was strange that he suggested I use a pseudonym for the Carrier name. Why would anyone care about a high school paper?

"Miss Hart, wait. Here," he said as he handed me a little yellow piece of paper. "And you can have an extra day for your paper," he added then looked away again.

I looked at the paper in my hand and saw it was a hall pass that excused me from being late to my next class. I turned to go, but my mind lingered on what had happened. The entire exchange had been so weird. First, he had been really nice then a little rude then nice again; it reminded me of the commercial for Sour Patch Kids: "First they're sour, then they're sweet."

The rest of the day was pretty much more of the same, and I didn't pay any attention in any of my classes. On the way to pick up Zay after school, I told Ian about Amanda, but he didn't seem surprised. He said he'd heard she was visiting a college campus in Iowa. I thought it weird that the staff didn't know that, but Ian seemed okay with that explanation, so I tried not to overthink it.

While we were driving home, my phone started to ring. I saw it was Crystal and was happy she had taken my advice to call when she needed something.

"Hello?"

"Hi, Nina. Is Crystal with you?"

"Oh, hi, Mrs. Chery," I said when I realized it wasn't Crystal. "Um, no she's not..."

"Oh, okay. If you speak to her, can you please have her call me right away?"

"Yes, of course, I'll be sure to do that."

"What was that about?" Ian asked once I ended the call.

"Crystal didn't come home today."

"Great, now someone is stealing high school students," Ian said, thoroughly annoyed.

He seemed to be hiding something, but I wasn't sure what. I knew he would only do that if he thought it would hurt me in some way. I didn't know what it could be, but I knew he wouldn't tell me, and that made me frustrated with him.

*Why is he being so cryptic? Does it have to do with Aaron?*

The more I thought about it, the more annoyed I became, so I tried to distract myself by turning on the radio. I was singing along with the song when it was interrupted by a news broadcast.

**[Radio voice]** This is a special alert from the HHPD. Eighteen-year-old Johnathan Morales went missing early this morning after stopping at a gas station in downtown Hallowed Hills. Johnathan is described as a Hispanic male with a medium build, hazel eyes, and brown hair. He was last seen driving a silver 2007 Toyota Corolla. If anyone has any information on his whereabouts, please contact the Hallowed Hills Police Department immediately.

Ian and I looked at each other in disbelief.

# CHAPTER 7
## BEST BEACHES FOREVER

After we picked up Zay, we went straight home. We were surprised to find our parents sitting at the kitchen table waiting for us when we walked into the house.

They both looked up at us with concern. It was obviously bad news. I hoped we were just in trouble for going to the police station that morning, but I had a feeling that was not it.

"Kids, come sit down with us for a minute. There's something we have to tell you," Dad said to us gently.

We sat down in silence, expecting the worst.

"We received some information from your school today," he said then stopped to lean forward and rub my back. "It was about what happened over the weekend. I'm so sorry, but they have confirmed that it was Jen and Matt who fell off the roof. They were hurt very badly. The doctors did everything they could to save them, but... it wasn't enough. They didn't make it," he finished with tears forming in his eyes.

I looked at our mom, and she already had tears running down her cheeks.

My head started to spin, and my heart began beating so fast that I thought it was going to jump right out of my chest. My knees became so weak that, had I been standing, I would have fallen. As it was, I sagged against Ian. I couldn't believe it.

Mom stood up and walked around to our side of the table, hugging both of us as she cried. "I am so sorry," she said as she held us tightly.

"No! They are on vacation!" I cried out suddenly as I pulled myself out of the chair and away from her.

She looked at me sympathetically but didn't say anything.

I didn't even want to look at her. I didn't want to hear anymore. I ran past my brothers and straight up to my room, slamming the door behind me.

Why would those men say they had gone on vacation? It made no sense. There would be no reason to make that up if the school was just going to announce that they had died.

I picked up my phone and dialed Jen's house again. No answer. I tried her cell, but still no answer. Frustrated, I threw my phone onto my bed.

I sat down and put my face in my hands. I would not cry because it wasn't true. They were both alive; they were not dead.

My phone started buzzing, but I ignored it. It stopped but then started again right away.

I didn't want to talk to anyone, but I still wanted to check who it was. The caller ID said it was Lavinia. I watched her name blink on the screen until it stopped. I exited that screen and sent her a text message.

**Me:** I need your help. Can you pick me up?

Of course, but I'm not at home right now. Give me a few hours and I will be there.

**Me:** That's fine. Thank you, Lavinia.

**Lavinia:** Anytime.

**Me:** When you get here, park around the corner. I don't want anyone knowing I left.

**Lavinia:** No problem. I'll text you when I get there.

I knew my parents wouldn't want me going out, and Ian was keeping secrets from me, so I wasn't sure what he would do. I still had no idea what I was going to do, but I desperately wanted to prove that Jen and Matt were not dead.

A few hours later, as it was starting to get dark, I wondered whether Lavinia had forgotten or been held up with something else. As I began to write her another text, my phone buzzed again. It was Lavinia saying she was waiting for me around the corner.

Not wanting to be bothered by anyone, I threw my phone back on the bed, put my purse crosswise around my torso, and climbed down the tree outside my window. I'd noticed how close the tree was to the house when we'd first moved in, but I'd never thought I would have a use for it. I wasn't the type of girl to sneak out because I had a very open relationship with my parents and respected them and their rules, but not today.

I made it to Lavinia's car quickly but stopped a few feet from the vehicle. I hadn't noticed until now, but her windows were tinted so dark that it was impossible for me to see who was inside. That made me nervous, so I slowly walked closer to the car while squinting at the windows to try to see inside.

The car's headlights flashed, which startled me. I wasn't sure what to do and suddenly wished I hadn't left my phone behind so I could call to make sure it was her. Too late for that, I walked toward the passenger door, and the window started to open. I bent down to look in across to the driver's seat.

"Are you okay?" a familiar voice asked.

I let out a sigh of relief when I recognized Lavinia's voice. I quickly opened the door and got in.

"It's just been a long day," I said as she started to drive off.

I told her what had happened to Jen and Matt, and she was supportive. Unlike everyone else, she didn't try to convince me I was wrong.

"What do you want to do? Where should we start?" she asked.

"Jen's house."

When we arrived at Jen's house, it was pretty dark already. We got out of the car together and looked at the house. It was the same as when I'd seen it last, with one glaring difference: a For Sale sign on the front lawn.

"Is your friend moving?" Lavinia asked.

"No," I responded quickly with certainty.

We went up to the front door and knocked, but there was no answer. I peered into the window. Everything in the house was gone, and it looked like no one had been there for a while.

I looked at Lavinia who seemed just as confused as I did. I tried to turn the doorknob, but it wouldn't budge. Then I jumped down into the garden where I knew Jen kept an extra key; she was always forgetting hers at home.

I knew it was in a fake rock that was supposed to look real but looked more like a gray blob. I pushed the stones around with my feet but didn't see it, so I bent down to look closer. It wasn't there. The rock was always there no matter what since it was dug into the ground with a stake so it wouldn't move.

Lavinia then helped me look for it, but neither of us could find it. After a few more minutes, I gave up and sat on the porch steps.

Lavinia sat next to me and grabbed my hand. "Where to next?" she asked with a sympathetic smile.

After leaving Jen's house, we went to Matt's, but I wasn't surprised to find it just as empty as Jen's. Now at a dead end, I wasn't sure what else to do. Sure, families sometimes moved away after the loss of a child, but never this quickly.

Lavinia and I talked for a bit longer then headed back to my house. The more time I spent with her, the more I liked her. For one thing, she was a great listener, so I told her about everything that had happened since we'd arrived in Hallowed Hills.

After we looked around Matt's yard for a bit, Lavinia drove me home. Helpfully, she said she would try to find out what she could on her own as well.

I didn't want to get caught sneaking out, so I climbed back into my room. I had no issues; it seemed like no one had even noticed I was gone.

I checked my phone, and I had several messages. The first was from Lavinia asking if I was okay. I laughed as I imagined myself standing in front of her car looking so confused. The second was from Ian asking if I was sleeping. But the third was from a number I didn't recognize, and it was just a bunch of numbers.

*41.756816 -88.094443*

It was very strange and random. I texted the number back, but there was no response. I tried to search on the internet for the numbers in the text, but that just gave me a calculator.

Exhausted, I decided I would try to figure it out the next day. As soon as I laid my head on my pillow, I fell asleep.

I was awoken very early the next morning by a knock at my door. I opened my eyes slowly and looked at the clock. It was only 5 a.m., so why was someone waking me up so early? I moaned and turned over to go back to sleep. Then I heard my door open and someone walk in.

"Honey?" my mom whispered. "I know it's early, but I just wanted to let you know that you kids can stay home today. Just take some time. If you want to talk, I'm here, but if you want to be alone, that's okay, too," she said then just as quickly walked out of the room.

I sat up in my bed, realizing fully that the last few days hadn't been a dream. Jen and Matt were gone. I suddenly felt dizzy, so I closed my eyes and laid back down. When I started to feel better, I started drifting back to sleep.

I woke up a few hours later still feeling exhausted. I rubbed my eyes then looked for my phone. I was happy to see a new message from Lavinia. She said she was going to have a late lunch with Ian but wanted to meet me for coffee later.

I frowned at the thought of my brother. I was mad at him because he had never kept anything from me before. But now I knew he was for sure. It was so frustrating that I wanted to scream, but I knew if I did my mom would come running in and would not leave until I talked to her, so I controlled myself.

I needed to stop thinking about my brother and my friends, so I did what Mr. Conrad had suggested: I worked on my history essay.

The words seemed to type themselves because there was so much information from the last few days I wanted to include. I knew Mr. Conrad had an open mind, but I still wondered if he would think I was crazy if I did include it all.

I changed the Carrier name to Porter. I usually asked Ian to proofread my papers, but I wasn't going to do it this time. It wasn't just because he was keeping something from me; it was also because I wasn't sure if I believed any of it myself.

I had always considered myself a believer in the supernatural and that anything could be possible, but now that I was faced with it, I wasn't so sure. It just seemed improbable that vampires could be real.

I had just finished rereading my essay when my phone started buzzing. I looked at it, and the text made me smile. It was from Aaron. He was checking on me to see how I was and wanted to know if we could get together that weekend.

I was about to text him back when I started to think. First, he had a girlfriend. Second, even though I was mad at Ian, he was worried about me getting to know Aaron. That still counted for something. If Aaron's ancestor had been a vampire, maybe he was, too. But he couldn't be a vampire, but then again, everything I knew about vampires was from books and television, so I really didn't know what was true and what was not.

However, if I did, in fact, believe that Martha Carrier was a vampire, would it make any sense that Aaron was one, too? In appearance alone, the two were completely different. Aaron had beautifully golden tan skin, and it was warm to the touch. I smiled as I remembered when he had grazed my hand with his the other night.

I stared at my phone for a bit longer. I didn't want to be *that* girl, the girl who breaks up a couple, or worse, who ignores the fact that there is a couple in the first place. I had to admit it was a bit easier to think when Aaron wasn't in front of me. His presence somehow made me feel powerless and like nothing else mattered but being with him.

I put my phone down and turned back to the computer. Before I could type anymore, my stomach started to growl, and I realized how late it was getting. I looked out my window. It was really dark even though the clock said it was only 12 p.m. *What is with this weather?*

I went downstairs for a quick lunch. As I ate my tasteless sandwich, I wondered whether Lavinia had found out anything more after she had dropped me off. I still didn't believe Jen and Matt were dead, but I didn't know what else I cod do. There had to be funerals, but how could there be with both families gone?

I sighed as the frustration engulfed me then took my plate to the sink. While standing there, I stared out the window into the backyard. It was even darker outside than before, which made it difficult to see anything.

As I began to turn away, I noticed something strange. I turned back right away, but it was gone. For a moment, I thought I had seen the same glowing eyes of the man at the bonfire the other night.

"Ian!" I screamed up the stairs. As mad as I was at him, I wasn't going outside by myself.

He quickly came running down the stairs. "What's wrong?" he said frantically.

I told him what I had seen in the backyard and what I had seen the night of the bonfire. I was expecting him to be surprised or joke about it and say I was crazy, but he didn't. Instead, he grabbed a flashlight and started for the backyard. Thinking it wouldn't hurt to have two big strong guys with me, I called Zay down, too.

Of course, Zay thought I was crazy, but he still followed my lead. So, the three of us looked around the backyard until we heard Zay scream. Both Ian and I ran over to him.

"What? What's wrong?" Ian asked.

"Nope, nope, nope. I am going back inside," Zay said, completely ignoring Ian's question. We followed Zay back toward the house.

"What's wrong? What did you see?" I asked.

"It... it looked like there were red eyes staring at me from the bushes," he finally explained.

*Red eyes?* I had definitely seen yellow eyes earlier.

"It was probably just a rabbit or something," Ian said jokingly.

"No, they were human eyes, but they were red," he shot back.

Zay seemed pretty shaken up, and I knew we weren't going to get much more information from him, so we dropped the subject altogether and went back inside.

As for Ian, he didn't seem surprised. He had to have more information. I didn't want to scare Zay, but I needed to know what was going on. I didn't understand what was with all the different colored eyes.

I gestured to Ian to follow me to the living room while Zay was distracted with his phone. "Spill," I growled at him when we were finally alone.

He sighed and shook his head.

"Ian, do you know what's going on around here?"

He stayed quiet.

I was getting really tired of him acting so weird, but I knew getting mad at him would get me nowhere, so I did just the opposite. I told him everything I had been keeping from him. I told him about Martha Carrier and about what I had found at Jen's and Matt's houses.

"Vampires?" he asked. He seemed confused but not scared or even surprised.

"I know it sounds silly, but—"

"No, it's not that..." he trailed off.

"Then what is it?" I asked.

He looked at me, but again didn't say anything.

"What are you keeping from me?"

"You know, sometimes you have a secret, but the secret is not yours to tell. There's something I need to do right now," he said and ran out the door.

I was even more frustrated with him. What had he meant by that? What kind of secret could you not tell your own sister?

I went to see how Zay was doing, but he was already zoned into a video game, so I let him be. I wondered what was going on in his mind. Did he really just shake off things like this, or was he keeping something from me, too? What kind of person sees human red eyes then goes and plays a video game?

I was suddenly so annoyed that I took off my slipper and threw it at him.

"Hey! What's the matter with you?" he yelled.

He picked the slipper up and threw it back at me, but I ran up the stairs. That had felt oddly satisfying, so I laughed all the way back into my room. There the laughter ended.

I had so many questions, and I felt so alone. I had never felt like this before. I'd always had my brothers, especially Ian; he was always the one I could talk to about anything.

I needed a distraction, so I decided to study for a while. A few hours later, I was interrupted by a text from Lavinia letting me know she was on her way to pick me up.

When I walked outside, I noticed my car was missing. It wasn't so odd that it was gone because Ian used it all the time. What *was* odd was that Lavinia had said they were going to have lunch, so I'd thought they would be together.

I shrugged that off and got into Lavinia's car. We arrived at the local coffee shop, Once Upon a Bean, within minutes. If nothing else, Hallowed Hills had the best coffee in the country. Of course, I had only ever been to three states, but California was known for having the best of everything, even if they had to ship it in from somewhere else.

The coffee here had a smooth, rich flavor that was not too strong or too sweet. It had a vanilla scent but tasted a little like cherries, hazelnuts, and something else that was sweet but earthy. But the best thing about this coffee was that it would wake you up in the morning yet never kept you up at night, no matter what time of day you drank it.

Lavinia and I chatted more about Jen and Matt, and she mentioned that she'd spoken to a friend in the police department. "My friend told me that the attacked students were en route to the hospital, but the ambulance never made it there," Lavinia explained cautiously. She looked up at me, but I didn't know what to say, so she continued. "They searched for the missing ambulance, but it was like it had disappeared into thin air."

"How could an ambulance just go missing?" I asked.

"All I know is the GPS tracker on the ambulance stopped working when they crossed Weeping Willow Bridge."

"Okay... I don't... so, it was just gone?" I finally asked, still unable to make sense of that detail.

"The authorities searched in and around the river, but they didn't find any trace of the ambulance or the paramedics."

"So, how did they even know it was Jen and Matt?"

"They were identified at the scene by their student IDs, and they were pronounced dead based on the paramedics' report before transportation. According to my friend, the two students were definitely Jen and Matt. And..." she paused.

"What?" I said, urging her to continue.

"Well, neither paramedic has been seen or heard from since that night," she finished.

I knew something had been odd about the entire situation, and Lavinia had believed my suspicions enough to dig deeper. The more time I spent with her, the more I felt like she was the only one I could trust. I spent most of the rest of that day with her and told her about the situation with Aaron and Ian's desire that I not get too close to him.

In turn, she suggested that it might be because Aaron was the type of guy who would get a whole lot of attention from any girl. "But he's actually a nice guy. I know he's very big on family, and he's very protective of the people he cares about," she said with a warm smile.

"He has a girlfriend," I countered realistically.

"For now," she winked.

"Did you go out with Ian today?"

"No," she responded sheepishly, "he said he couldn't make it."

I frowned at the thought of my brother's actions. Ian was acting so strangely. I had never seen him act flustered with any other girl, so I knew he was interested in Lavinia. But why would he not want to hang out with her? I promised her I would talk to him about it.

It felt really good to have someone who understood me and didn't judge me. I knew at that moment that Lavinia and I would be close friends. I smiled at that thought as I stepped out of her car.

My car was now back in the driveway. Since I didn't really want to go into the house yet, I decided to go for a drive to clear my head. I ended up heading into downtown Hallowed Hills.

I felt so hungry, but I didn't have a taste for anything, so I thought I'd try the small grocery store. The store didn't even have a parking lot, so I had to park a few blocks away. As I exited my car, a huge gust of wind blew behind me.

"Hello?" I asked warily.

I started walking to the sidewalk then heard the sound behind me again. "Hello?" I repeated, but no one was there.

Unnerved, I walked quickly to the sidewalk where there was more light. As I walked along, I looked behind me every few seconds to make sure no one was following me.

When I made it safely into the store, I shook my head at my ridiculous paranoia. *Has this town made me become scared of wind?* I was still laughing at myself and browsing through the frozen food section when someone walked up and stood really close to me.

"Oh, hi," I said in surprise when I saw who it was.

It was Alan. He smiled then opened the door to the freezer and grabbed one of the frozen dinners. He was wearing the same jacket from the other day but a different shirt. He smelled so good—like lavender that was somehow masculine.

"Hello there," he responded with a cheeky smile.

Although he was very handsome, something about him made me uneasy. Thinking it best to let him be, I smiled weakly and started to walk away.

"Not hungry? I can give you some recommendations."

"Okay," I responded quietly and followed him back to the freezer. I felt strangely conflicted, like I knew I should leave, but something was keeping me there.

"Here," he said as he handed me a large frozen dinner.

I didn't see what it was. I was so distracted by his smell that I unconsciously stepped closer to him, making him move the meal to the side so I could get closer.

Toweringly tall, he loomed above me, his features striking yet veiled in an air of arrogance. With each breath, his essence enveloped me, casting a spell that momentarily clouded my judgment. I suddenly realized how weird I was being, so I pulled away.

"Umm, I have to go," I said as I ran off.

I left the store without getting anything to eat and drove home feeling really embarrassed about the encounter.

# CHAPTER 8

## PANDORA'S BOX

When I got home, I stepped up onto the porch and saw a large package sitting on the swing. Picking it up, I immediately noticed it was very heavy.

I read the name, and it was addressed to me. I turned it over, but it didn't have a return address anywhere. I thought that was odd because I hadn't been expecting anything, but I brought it inside anyway.

The house was quiet, so I went straight to my room with the package. I threw it on the bed and pulled out my phone.

I realized I hadn't yet ed Aaron back. After my talk with Lavinia, I felt more confident, so I sent him a text and told him I would like to see him that weekend as well.

After a brief exchange, we made plans to get dinner together in a neighboring city. I thought it a little odd that he didn't want to meet in town, but I just brushed it off, promising myself that if things still felt weird after the dinner, I wouldn't see him again. I bit my lip. I hoped I would be strong enough not to see him again.

Frustrated, I threw myself onto the bed and my head landed right on the package.

"Ow!" I exclaimed as I rubbed my head.

As I gingerly picked up the package, I couldn't help being captivated by the sender's elegant cursive handwriting. With an air of caution, I turned it over again and tore open the packaging to reveal a very large, thick tome. It exuded an ancient aura, its tough, reddish-brown leather cover hinted at both age and resilience.

Adorning the front cover were intricate designs—a large compass rose pierced through the center with a sword, a sun in the top left corner, and a moon in the top right. Unfamiliar symbols in the bottom corners resembled distorted versions of the common gender signs, but they both had triangles where the circles typically were. The female sign had a U shape embellished above it, and the male sign had the same underneath it. Flipping the book over, I discovered inscriptions in an unreadable language that further deepened the enigma.

Opening the book, the yellowed pages hinted at a storied past; their appearance felt weathered both by time and the elements.

The first page, possibly a title page, bore illegible writing as the ink had bled a bit. Among the indecipherable hieroglyphics, the words *Invisible Truth* emerged in English. Scanning further, I saw *La Verdad Invisible*. After reading that, I concluded that the page was indeed a title page with a multilingual translation.

Determined to unravel its secrets, I began flipping through the pages and discovered an intriguing collection. It seemed to be an encyclopedia of fictional characters and creatures from movies and fairy tales. Each featured vivid sketches and detailed descriptions. Some entries even delved into how to combat these fantastical creatures.

As I continued scanning through the pages, I noticed a bookmark stuck into a particular page. That seemed to invite me to further explore the mysteries of that entry. I began to read the page:

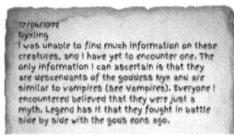

*The rest of the page and the following one were blank. I glanced back at the previous page and noticed the handwriting was different. I skipped around to look at some other pages. Some of the handwriting was the same, but some was different. It was definitely some sort of dictionary or encyclopedia but written as a journal.*

I returned to the first page and saw a date: 27/05/977.

*Could this book actually be from the year 977?*

I returned to the bookmarked page. I had never heard of a nyxling before and wondered why that specific page had been marked. I flipped through the book again, trying to find the entry on Vampires, but since there didn't seem to be any order to the entries, I couldn't find it.

As I continued my search, I saw many familiar storybook creatures as well as others I had never heard of. One I came across caught my eye:

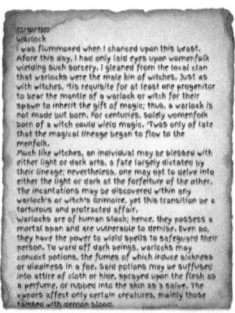

I was utterly immersed in the book when my phone started buzzing on my desk. Startled, I jumped up from my bed. As my heartbeat came back down to normal, I looked at the text. It was Lavinia letting me know she was in my driveway. I closed the book and hid it, along with the packaging it had come in, under my bed.

After we picked up coffee, we went to a nearby bookstore. I told Lavinia what I had seen in the backyard with my brothers and about the other bad things that had happened in the last few days. She seemed curious, and she wanted me to promise to check it out together later, which I reluctantly did.

She also talked about her feelings for Ian. I felt terrible because I had no idea what was wrong with him. He had a beautiful girl waiting for him, and he was out doing god knows what.

Maybe Zay was rubbing off on him. Usually, the younger brother followed in the older brother's footsteps, but not in our family. Ian had a mind of his own, of course, but Zay was very charming and always had the perfect argument for any subject. Maybe Zay had told him to keep his options open or something.

I had no answers for her, but I reassured her the best I could. She made me feel so comfortable that I shared what I had learned about the Carrier family.

When I told her, she was enthusiastic and wanted to know more. "I have always believed in all of that stuff," she said excitedly. "So, do you think they are a family of vampires?"

"No, I don't think so. I think their family was accused of witchcraft, and they found a way for Martha to avoid a death sentence. Well, sort of."

"What do you mean?" she asked.

"Well, I think that someone in the family knew a vampire, and when Martha died, she came back to life," I suggested cautiously, feeling embarrassed now that I was saying my thoughts out loud.

I looked at Lavinia who had an ear-to-ear smile on her face. "What are you smiling about?" I asked with a giggle.

"It's so cool!" she said as she threw her hands up in the air. "It has to be all connected though, right? I mean the different colored eyes, the shadow creature, everything!"

"Maybe, but I don't know how."

We were interrupted by a text from my dad. He seemed really mad and wanted me to get home right away. I wondered if he had found out that I had snuck out the other night. I let Lavinia know, and she took me home immediately.

When I got home, my dad was waiting at the kitchen table and looked furious.

"Come here and sit down. We have to talk," he snapped.

I went to sit at the table with him. I hadn't thought that my sneaking out would make him so mad. It wasn't like I had been out all night.

"Do you understand that people were killed?" he asked sternly. "Why would you go to the homes of Jen and Matt?"

I started to open my mouth to talk, but he cut me off.

"You could have gotten hurt. I understand that this is hard, but sometimes things happen in life that are not fair." He then continued calmly as he took my hand, "I can't lose any of you. Now, promise me you will drop this witch hunt."

I nodded in agreement simply because I didn't want to argue with him.

"Okay. I love you, kid," he finished.

"I love you, too, Dad."

I was baffled. He hadn't mentioned me sneaking out, only that I had gone to the houses. I didn't know why going to their houses mattered anyway. It wasn't like it was the first time I had been there.

"I have to finish my history paper," I said as I got up to leave the table.

He nodded and smiled warmly.

As I walked by the living room, I saw Ian. He looked up at me but then looked away quickly as if he were guilty about something. I wondered if he had told Dad I had gone to their houses. But I had never told him.

The only other person who knew was Lavinia. Maybe she had told him? Ian was her new crush, after all, so maybe she'd done it to try to gain his trust. I had to know, so I sent her a text asking about it.

Lavinia answered quickly, saying she hadn't said anything to Ian. I didn't know how else my dad would have found out, but I trusted Lavinia.

There was nothing I could do about it now, so I just printed out my history paper. As I pulled my history folder out of my bookbag, Ian's math notebook fell to the floor. I had forgotten about that; he had probably been looking everywhere for it.

When I picked it up, a piece of paper fell out. It was a flyer for a party the first week we had arrived in Hallowed Hills. I read over the flyer, and the location shocked me. The party had been at the Carrier estate, and it had been hosted by Aaron Andrews. I turned over the paper and found a handwritten note on it.

*2 PM this Saturday at my house*

*~AA*

I simply had no words. Why would Ian lie to me about knowing Aaron? I had had about enough of his secrets, so I went straight to his room. His door was open, and I walked in ready to yell at him, but he wasn't there. Then I remembered seeing him downstairs. I ran down, but he wasn't there when I got to the living room. I scrolled through my phone to send him a text to ask him where he was, but I stopped when I came across the unknown text with the odd numbers:

*41.756816 -88.094443*

It probably had been a wrong number, but it still bothered me. Why was there a negative number? Then it hit me. These numbers were latitude and longitude coordinates.

Forgetting all about Ian, I ran back upstairs and typed the coordinates into a browser. It pulled up a single-family home right here in Hallowed Hills. I scribbled down the address along with directions to the house then ran downstairs. As I was darting out the door, I yelled to my dad that I was going to get coffee. Luckily, my car was there this time. I drove to the address, not knowing what I was going to find or even what I was going to do when I got there.

When I arrived at the address, I gasped. It was not a house. It was a grand mansion, an architectural masterpiece from the 18th century. Its exterior of reddish-orange brick spoke of age, yet the mansion still stood tall and majestic, well-preserved in a way that offered an air of enchantment.

Its light gray roof, seemingly untouched by imperfections, crowned the structure with an almost otherworldly grace, and immaculate gardens and meticulously tended shrubbery surrounded the mansion.

Although there was no driveway, I drove onto a paved circular path that led directly to the imposing front entrance. As I parked, uncertainty gripped me and made me question the purpose of my being here. With a deep breath, I stepped out of my car and into the unknown.

Approaching the castle gate-like doors, I marveled at their sturdy, deep brown wood. It was devoid of a visible doorbell, but then I saw a hanging rope. Without thinking too long about it, I pulled on it. It produced a deep chime that gradually became higher pitched.

Minutes passed, but no one answered. My inquisitiveness overcame me, and I looked closer, noticing that the door was slightly ajar. Cautiously pushing it open, I peered into the darkness within. There was no sign of anyone, but my desire to uncover the sender of the cryptic text propelled me forward.

"Hello?" I called into the elegant abyss, but it was met only by the echo of my own voice.

I slowly walked farther down the long hallway. The interior was exquisite and filled with expensive-looking paintings and furniture. To my right was an enormous open room, so big that a small home could fit in it. I didn't want to go in, but I could see that the room was as well-decorated as the hall. It had a wall of books on the left in an antique wooden bookcase, and couches that looked like they were from the Victorian era.

I heard a door creak, so I turned toward the sound.

"Hello?" I asked again but still received no answer.

Now, I was getting creeped out, and I decided that being in a house I didn't know was probably not the best idea. Just as I turned to walk back down the hallway, I noticed a framed family crest hanging beside an enormous grandfather clock.

Intrigued, I moved closer to it and beheld the magnificent medieval emblem—a golden shield embraced by a dark green dragon with its yellow claws fiercely gripping the shield. My eyes went to the surname, and a revelation struck me like a thunderclap. It read Carrier. My jaw dropped in disbelief.

Ready to flee, I turned toward the exit but immediately collided with the chest of an unexpected presence. Looking up into a familiar face, I uttered with astonishment, "Alan?"

"Nina, wasn't it?" he inquired with a Cheshire Cat grin.

"Yes, um... what are you doing here?" I inquired, my confusion growing.

"I could ask you the same thing," he retorted.

"I received a text, and, well, the door was open," I explained quickly as I gestured toward the front door. However, when I looked back, that door was shut. "It was just..." I trailed off in a whisper as my confusion deepened. "What are you doing here?" I asked again to mask my disorientation.

"I live here," he declared with a smirk.

"You're a Carrier?" I questioned in astonishment.

"My whole life," he answered with a smugness that left his breathtaking allure wholly intact.

His entrancing eyes now seemed oddly familiar, kind of like Aaron's. But Aaron hadn't mentioned having a brother. "Are you Aaron's brother?"

"No. Aaron is my nephew," he chuckled, a peculiar dynamic playing into his tone that left me feeling uneasy.

His gaze lingered on me with an unsettling intensity that made me even more nervous. "Sorry, I shouldn't have just walked in," I stammered then attempted to walk away.

As I turned, I caught him smelling the air around me with palpable excitement. He was stunning, yet an undeniable fear gripped me.

"I can see why my nephew is so charmed by you," he remarked.

My steps halted, and I hesitated. I was surprised Aaron had spoken about me. Although my instincts were desperately urging me to run, my heart tugged at me to stay.

"Did he tell you about me?" I asked, but my question was met with Alan's enigmatic silence.

"Hello, Aaron," he said instead even though his eyes were still fixed on me.

I turned around quickly to see Aaron standing at the end of the hall near the front door. He didn't say anything, just stared back at Alan with intensity.

The way they looked at each other made me feel like I was standing in the middle of a duel. I also was starting to feel dizzy and lightheaded, so I wanted to get out of there as fast as I could.

"Hi, Nina. I didn't know you were stopping by," Aaron said in a detached monotone as he continued staring at Alan.

"Um... I didn't really plan it," I said nervously then added quickly, "I should go."

I walked toward the door, but Aaron was still in the way and staring daggers at Alan. I looked back at Alan who had a smirk on his face.

"Um... Aaron?" I said when he didn't move out of the way. "Aaron?" I repeated when I still didn't receive a response.

He looked down at me then moved out of the way. I half ran down the remaining hallway, got outside, and hopped into my car.

*What was that?* my mind reeled, but I didn't give myself time to think about it. I just put my car in Drive and left. I was shaking the entire drive home. The whole experience had been so odd and more than a bit frightening.

Now that I had some distance though, I assessed what I'd learned, including the astonishing discovery that Alan and Aaron were related. I thought back to the first time I'd met Alan and how he'd looked at me. It had made me feel uncomfortable, but he'd also looked at me as though he were trying to understand something. What that understanding was, I still had no idea.

This time had been different though. There had been no trace of confusion on his face. This time, his look had been very primal, almost predatory.

My phone buzzed and interrupted my thoughts. I checked the caller ID, and it was Ian. Irritated, I tossed the phone into the passenger seat. The buzzing persisted and resumed as soon as it stopped. It was Ian again. I still didn't answer. As soon as it stopped buzzing, it started again. Ian again.

I was still mad at him and didn't want to talk. But he had never called me three times in a row before, so I answered. However, when I said hello, no one replied.

I looked at the phone. It seemed to be working fine, so I said hello a few more times before getting frustrated and hanging up. I called him right back, but he didn't answer.

When I walked into the house, Ian was playing a video game with Zay. I was still mad, so I just yelled at him. "Ian! What's your problem? Why did you call me three times then not say anything when I picked up?"

"What are you talking about?"

"You just called me three times, and when I answered, you didn't say anything," I repeated.

"I haven't called you all day," he insisted.

"You did!!" I screamed as I pulled out my phone from my back pocket.

I went to the call list, which showed the three calls from him. Just as I stepped forward to show him the call log, an electric surge came from the phone, which made me scream and drop it.

Both Ian and Zay jumped up immediately and ran toward me. "What happened?" Ian asked.

"It... it burned me," I explained as tears started pouring from my eyes. I examined the third-degree burn on my hand then quickly turned away.

"I'll get the first-aid kit," Zay said then ran out of the room.

I looked back at my hand to assess the damage.

Ian pulled my hand closer to him to get a better look, but as we were examining the wound, it seemed to heal right in front of our eyes. The burn didn't heal completely, but it had healed enough that I wouldn't have to go to the emergency room.

"Did you see that?" I asked as I pulled my hand away from him.

I looked at him, and he was stunned. He nodded. We both looked at each other, not believing what we had just seen. Before we could say anything else, Zay returned with the first-aid kit.

"Pff, this is nothing," Zay said when he saw the burn. He handed me antibiotic ointment and a bandage then went back to playing his video game.

I continued examining my hand, still not believing what I had just seen. I had been injured before, but nothing like that had ever happened. It still hurt a little now but nowhere near as much as it had when it first was burned.

I looked up at Ian and saw him typing frantically on his phone.

"What are you doing?" I growled at him. Just as I expected, he ignored me. "What are you doing?!" I asked louder.

"Getting answers," he said as he walked away.

"Where are you going?" I shouted at him. But before he could answer, he was out the front door.

"Ugh!" I yelled out as I stomped up to my room.

I closed the door and sat down with my back against it. The day was full of questions yet again, and I didn't know what to think.

As I brushed my hair out of my face, I saw the package I had hidden under my bed. I pulled it out and threw it on my bed.

The burn on my hand still hurt a bit, and I had an enormous headache, so I took nighttime pain reliever before laying down in bed.

I grabbed the book and continued reading through the descriptions of the creatures, but I still couldn't find vampires. Despite my interest in the book, in a little while I couldn't fight the medicine, so I fell asleep.

# CHAPTER 9
## APPLE OF MY EYE

The next few days flew by, and it was Friday before I knew it. The teachers at our school had bombarded us with work, so the only other thing I had time for was soccer practice. Even though I didn't like having so much schoolwork, I was happy that the rest of the week was at least normal.

Things were even getting better with Ian. He still hadn't told me what he knew, but with no new odd occurrences, it was like nothing had ever happened.

The day was coming to an end when I received a note from my chemistry teacher, Mr. Andermann. It said I was excused for the rest of the day to complete a project for history class in the library. I wasn't sure what that was about, but I was happy to get out of chemistry, so I collected my things and headed to the library.

When I got there, I wasn't exactly sure where to go, so I approached the librarian and handed her the note.

She was an older lady with white hair and reminded me of Mrs. Farnsworth, except that she always looked mad. I didn't even know her name because I was afraid to ask.

As she took the note, I noticed she had the same pendant that Mrs. Farnsworth did, and I wondered whether they were related in some way.

After reading the note, she didn't say anything. She just wrote down a room number then pointed in the direction of the room. I went the way she pointed and found a group of small office-like rooms at the back of the library. I looked for the room number the librarian had written down.

Finding it, I walked in and instantly was engulfed by the scent of grapes and vanilla. I felt a little lightheaded but walked forward anyway. As I stepped around the corner, I found Mr. Conrad sitting at a desk facing away from me.

"Hello?" I asked cautiously.

He looked up then turned around. "Hello, Nina," he said in a deep voice as he stood.

He was still wearing the same oversized clothes as always, but his mysterious invitation made me feel nervous. He seemed to be hiding something, which made me wonder a lot of whys. *Why did he cover his tattoos? Why did he hide his physique with oversized clothes?*

"Come sit," he instructed as he sat back down, moving farther away from the chair next to him.

"Am I in trouble?"

"No," he replied with a light chuckle. "I wanted to talk to you about your friends. I told you I would look into it."

"Oh, yes!" I said excitedly.

"I called all the numbers they had listed in their files, and I found things a little odd as well. When I called Jen's emergency contact, a man picked up and said she was on vacation. Then when I called Matt's emergency number, a man said the same thing. The odd part was that the man at Matt's sounded exactly like the man I had spoken to when I called Jen's."

"Did he have a thick Indian accent?"

"No, he didn't," Mr. Conrad responded.

"When I called, the man, or men rather, who answered both had thick Indian accents."

"Hmm. Do you know who they were?"

"No. I'd never heard either of their voices before that."

He wrote something down in his notebook then closed it right away. I wanted to know what he had written, but I didn't want to ask. He was still my teacher and didn't have to tell me anything.

I started to feel dizzy again, so I grabbed my head.

"Are you okay?"

"Um, I don't know. I don't feel so good."

Mr. Conrad regarded me with concern then moved even farther away from me.

*Here comes the sour part of the Sour Patch Kid*, I thought as the dizziness cleared a little.

"I want you to understand that even with this information we've found, it doesn't mean either of them are still alive. For all we know, they both had vacations booked and whoever is answering doesn't know they passed away and still assume they were on the trips."

"So, they had two separate emergency contacts, which ended up having the same person on the other end," I said sarcastically but bit my tongue when I remembered who I was talking to. "Sorry."

"According to the school, they passed away. I know that's difficult to hear, but even if we find something, that fact will not change," he said sympathetically.

I smiled and nodded even though I didn't agree with him at all.

"Now, you are welcome to stay here with me and study or you can go back to class."

I didn't really want to go back to chemistry class, so I stayed in the room with him. He put his headphones on and started grading papers while I read *To Kill a Mockingbird* for my literature class.

When the bell rang, I quickly ran out of the room and headed for my locker. Becca was there.

"Hey, how are you feeling?" I asked, not really wanting to bring up Jen but needing to know if she was okay.

"Um, I'm okay. I miss her," she responded with tears in her eyes.

"Me, too," I said as I pulled her into my arms.

"I can't believe it, you know? What was she doing up there?"

"I don't know," I answered, trying to keep myself calm and composed. "Maybe you should talk to someone," I suggested. "The school has set up counselors for anyone who needs to talk."

"Maybe I will," she responded as she pulled out of my embrace.

"But you can always talk to me, too," I added with a sympathetic smile.

She looked up and fell back into my arms. I rubbed her shoulder until Ian came around the corner. I didn't have to tell him what was wrong. He just walked up and pulled Becca into a hug, and she started crying into his chest.

Becca didn't have her car, so we gave her a ride home. After she got out, the rest of the ride was very awkward. Ian didn't say a word to me. He had just been so empathetic with Becca, yet with me, he was distant and just listened to music through his headphones.

As soon as we got home, he ran straight up to his room and shut his door. I was still very annoyed with him but didn't want to dwell on it, so I just laid on my bed. When I opened my eyes again, I realized I had slept through the night. I jumped out of bed and went to take a shower.

Only when I was done did I realize it was Saturday, then I began to get butterflies in my stomach. I hadn't spoken to Aaron at all after the incident at his house, and I wasn't sure if he still wanted to see me.

I decided I would still go to the restaurant where we had planned to meet and spent extra time on my hair and makeup. I wanted to make a lasting impression on him in case this was the last time I saw him.

I cringed at the possibility I wouldn't see him at all. I curled then straightened my hair three times before landing on the look I wanted. After all, I wanted to look good, but I didn't want it to seem like I was trying too hard to look good. I finally ended up just keeping it completely straight.

I looked at my face in the mirror, wondering what color eyeshadow to use with my now paler complexion. I was so used to wearing colors that went with my tan skin. I searched my eyeshadow palettes to find the perfect one, but, ultimately, I ended up using the same shade of purple I wore every other day. It wasn't a bad color; it just seemed plain for the occasion.

This would be the first time I was going to be completely alone with Aaron with no football game or brothers to distract us. I smiled when I thought of Aaron smiling at me as he sat next to me on the couch last week.

After I stopped daydreaming, I finished my makeup with lip gloss that had a hint of red and then stared at myself in the mirror. I was satisfied with my look but still sighed because I knew I would look so much better with tan skin.

I tossed my lip gloss into the drawer of my vanity table and went to my closet. I would have loved to wear a nice dress, but it would be too cold for that, so I put on a fitted, sage-colored, long-sleeve shirt with a scoop neck and buttons down the top-middle. The shirt felt a little on the flirty side, especially since I had left the top button undone. I added black jeans and black knee-high boots with high heels.

I wasn't short, but I wasn't tall either. Ian had surpassed me in height this year, and Zay was just about my height already. Aaron was pretty tall, so I knew the boots would put me a little bit closer to his eye level. I finished the look with my faux leather jacket, so my family wouldn't say anything about my outfit.

Luckily Zay was the only one home, so I didn't really have to explain much. I knew my parents would ask him where I was when they got home, so I told him I was meeting up with Becca.

I didn't like lying to my brother, but my parents were very protective. Every time I went out, they needed to know who I was with, and they also always needed to have met the "who" in person either the day we went out or previously. I didn't want to lie to Zay about anything else, so I rushed out of the house before he could ask me where I was going.

I wasn't at all familiar with the town where I was meeting Aaron, so I left earlier than necessary. I was happy to walk out into a lovely sunny day. The sun beamed on my skin and made the cold bearable, which spontaneously put a smile on my face.

Other than taking a few wrong turns before finding the restaurant, the drive wasn't too bad. I arrived at the restaurant in about 45 minutes. I looked around for Aaron's car in the parking lot but didn't see it.

I was disappointed but not really all that surprised. I hated that I had gotten my hopes up, but I also remembered that he hadn't exactly looked happy to see me when I showed up at his house the other day.

I felt silly just leaving after driving so far, so I grabbed a book from my backseat and headed into the restaurant, figuring that if I read it while I ate, I would look less pathetic sitting there alone.

As soon as I walked in, I smelled the aroma of delicious food being prepared. It was the first time in a while that something had smelled appetizing, so I was excited.

It was a small Italian restaurant I had never heard of. The name was in Italian, so I didn't even try to pronounce it. Inside, it looked like the restaurants in Italy that I had seen in movies, with pictures of happy couples framed all along the right wall of the entryway and antique vases above a fireplace across from them.

I looked toward the dining room and saw that the seating was exquisite. The mahogany chairs had green suede cushions that almost matched my shirt. The décor was very Old World; even the people in the pictures wore old-fashioned clothes. If I'd had to guess, I would say that the pictures had been taken in the early 1900s.

As I looked around, I realized that all the pictures' captions and all the signage in the restaurant were in Italian. I didn't speak Italian at all, so I hoped the menu was in English.

When I walked up to the counter, the girl started speaking to me in Italian.

"Oh, sorry," I said as my cheeks turned red. It was already embarrassing enough to be here alone, but it was even more embarrassing that I might not even be able to order anything by myself.

I smiled apologetically at the hostess and started to turn to walk away when a voice behind me began speaking in Italian. I turned around quickly to see Aaron standing right behind me.

*God, this guy is handsome.*

The fact that he spoke the language like it was his native tongue made him even more attractive. I watched him as he conversed with the hostess, who was obviously attracted to him since she smiled flirtatiously with blushing cheeks while he spoke.

When she walked around the desk, she accidentally on purpose brushed against him. I automatically rolled my eyes and immediately hoped Aaron hadn't seen me do it. I felt better when he put his hand at my waist to guide me toward where she was leading us.

"Shall we?" he asked coyly.

I didn't say anything to him and just nodded in agreement. I could feel his hand on the small of my back, which gave me butterflies in my stomach. I wasn't a small girl, but I wasn't big either. I had an athletic body type; however, in comparison to me, he looked enormous.

His muscular arms seemed like they could carry me away to another world—a world all our own where our problems would just melt away. Again, his smell was intoxicating, and it made my head spin.

I was happy when we made it to the table because I was starting to get lightheaded again. As we sat down, we looked at each other but didn't say anything. I really didn't know what to say, and, judging by the look on his face, he didn't either.

"I wasn't sure if you would come," I finally confessed.

"Ditto," he said with a warm smile. "I just want you to know... that thing at the house... it had nothing to do with you." He paused. "My uncle is just... it's kind of hard to explain," he added in a low voice then looked at me for my reaction.

"It's okay. But I just want you to know that I didn't know that was your house. I am not some sort of stalker," I said nervously.

"How did you end up there anyway?" he asked then took a sip of his water.

"Long story," I replied shyly.

"I'm intrigued," he said with a playful smile.

I then told him about the weird text message I had received as well as how I had met Alan previously. He seemed a little worried about the text but even more so about Alan. Apparently, Alan hadn't said anything to him about the accident at all even after he'd asked him about the damage to the car.

"Alan has always kept to himself and has never really been around, but lately, he seems to be everywhere," he explained, seeming a bit annoyed.

"He looks so young. How old is he?" I asked without even thinking.

"He's older than he looks," he replied with a chuckle. It was the same laugh Alan had given me, like there was some inside joke I didn't understand. "But I don't really want to talk about my uncle," he added, interrupting my thoughts. "I want to know more about you, and..." he paused then added hesitantly, "I want you to know more about me."

"Well, you pretty much know everything there is to know about me. Is there anything in particular you'd still like to know?" I asked flirtatiously.

"Um, what's your favorite color?" he asked lightheartedly.

"Blue," I giggled.

"Cosa posso regalarvi, bella gente?" the hostess, and now apparently also our waitress, said with a smile as she returned to the table.

The girl was very pretty with tan skin and long, wavy brown hair down to her shoulders. I couldn't understand what she was saying, so I looked to Aaron. He smiled and pointed to the menu.

I hadn't had the chance to look at it yet, but I was so hungry that I blurted out the first thing that came to my mind. "Cheese ravioli with alfredo sauce please."

Aaron translated for me and then ordered for himself.

We handed the waitress the menus, and she walked back toward the kitchen. I felt a little self-conscious now because I thought I'd noticed her staring at me peculiarly. I wasn't sure if it was because I couldn't speak Italian or it was something else.

When she opened the kitchen door, I saw the heads of two cooks peek out as if they were trying to see something. She whispered to them then pushed them back into the kitchen.

"Everything okay?" Aaron asked.

"Oh, yeah, sorry," I said, bringing my attention back to him.

Throughout dinner, we settled in to chatting about our lives and ambitions after high school. The food tasted so good that I asked for another plate to take home. I was having a great time. Being with Aaron felt natural. Everything was perfect until we finished eating.

"I know you are aware that I have a girlfriend," he murmured reluctantly.

I could feel the red in my cheeks form as I nodded.

"I like you... a lot," he confessed as his fingers fiddled nervously, "but things are complicated right now. Amanda has been acting strangely, and that might be dangerous. I care about you too much to risk anything happening to you. I want to be with you, but I need some time to figure things out. I hope you can understand," he finished with a reassuring smile as he reached across the table to gently take my hand.

His nearness jumbled my thoughts. I couldn't think when I was with him, but I wanted to be with him, too. I knew what he was saying didn't make any sense, but I couldn't express that clearly, so I just smiled at him.

"And there's more," he began then paused. "My family is different," he confessed as he caressed my hands.

Pulling one hand away from me, he grabbed the saltshaker. He poured the salt directly onto the table then looked around.

"Wha—"

He cut me off with a look as he put his finger to his lips in a shushing manner. Then he smiled and slowly pulled his other hand away from me. Looking around one last time, he closed his eyes and took a deep breath then began to dance his fingers above the pile of salt on the table while mumbling something in another language.

I was really confused, but before I could think about it too long, the salt started floating between the table and his fingers.

"Whoa," I said unconsciously.

He smiled and put his hands down, and the salt fell back onto the table. He casually brushed the salt into his palm and then into the empty plate in front of him. Then he looked up at me nervously.

"You're a warlock," I whispered.

"I'm surprised you didn't say a wizard," he laughed. "You know, because of the whole *Harry Potter* craze."

I wasn't sure what to say to him. I'd already had a hunch his family might be magical, but actually seeing that magic was amazing as well as a little bit alarming.

He offered his hand to me, and I didn't hesitate taking it. I wasn't scared of him. I was happy he had trusted me enough to tell me such a big secret.

"Is Amanda a witch? Is that why you're worried?" I asked as Aaron's phone started buzzing.

"No, Amanda is not a witch," he said, ignoring his phone.

"So, what is dangerous about her then?" I asked.

"I want to be open with you. There's something about you, and... I feel like I can trust you."

"You can," I reassured him as I caressed his hand.

"I want you to trust—" he broke off as his phone vibrated itself off the table and he caught it before it hit the ground.

"Nice catch," I said as he read the text message he'd just received.

His expression changed from contentment to worry in an instant. He looked back at me with a forced smile. "We should get out of here," he said hurriedly as he pulled out enough cash to pay for the dinner two times over and threw it on the table.

We had already started walking out of the restaurant when the waitress came back to our table. She spoke to Aaron in Italian then looked at me with a shy smile.

I smiled back at her, and she immediately looked down guardedly. *That's strange.* I made a mental note to ask Aaron about it after we left the restaurant.

Outside, before I could ask him anything, he stopped and turned to me. "I had a nice time. Thanks for showing up," he laughed.

"Ditto," I giggled.

He took both my hands in his and hesitated. "Screw it," he said suddenly as he pulled me into his body then gazed deeply into my eyes as his fingers delicately caressed my cheek.

Tilting my head into the warmth of his touch, I closed my eyes and felt the rapid beating of my heart as a gentle tremor coursed through my body.

As he brushed my hair behind my ear, I opened my eyes and saw his tender smile. His hand moved down my face until he held my chin between his thumb and fingers. Another smile graced his lips before he drew me into a kiss.

His lips, full and soft, brought a warmth that seemed to envelop us. As they parted slightly, his tongue ventured inside my mouth to create an intimate connection.

His hands traced a path from my arms down to my waist and around to the small of my back while I softly caressed his chest and learned that his body didn't just look amazing but felt amazing, too.

I couldn't stop myself from venturing further and traced every line of his abdominal muscles with my hands, counting each with my touch.

He drew me in closer, sliding his hand under my shirt onto my back, before the warmth of his hands moved down to my outer thighs and sent tingles through my body.

The sensations were overwhelming, and I yearned for more, but I knew we had to stop. There were other people in the restaurant. At any moment, someone could walk outside.

Reluctantly, I pulled my lips away from his and smiled as I gazed into his ocean-blue eyes. His own brilliant smile, radiant against the night sky above, made me linger in the aftermath of our kiss. It had been an extraordinary moment, and, without a doubt, the most passionate kiss I had ever experienced.

"I should go," I whispered on a heavy breath. As I walked away, I could feel him watching me, so I did my best not to trip over anything.

I sat in my car with a gigantic smile on my face and touched my lips, vividly remembering everything about the kiss. I thought back over the incredible night I'd had. Yes, he had family issues. Yes, he had a girlfriend. Yes, he was a warlock. But I didn't care. Nothing could ruin the moment.

I was still sitting there when I thought I saw someone standing in the wooded area across the parking lot. I squinted to see if I could recognize them, but I couldn't see much in the dark beyond it being the shape of a man. I thought it was kind of creepy, so I locked my doors and started to back out of the space. As I did, there was a knock at my window that made me scream.

"Alan? What are you doing here?" I asked after my heart settled back into my chest and I rolled down the window.

"Just taking an evening stroll. What are *you* doing here?" he asked as he bent down to look in the window.

"Umm... I—"

"Ahh, you were here with my nephew. What a playboy."

His words shocked me, and I suddenly felt embarrassed and a little foolish.

"I am *sure* you will be different though. And maybe you are," he said eerily.

I wanted to know what he meant, but I didn't want to ask. This was the second time he had just shown up out of nowhere. As curious as I was, I didn't know him that well, so I didn't want to assume anything. Maybe he had just been in the area. Both times.

Right now, I just wanted to leave, so instead of saying anything, I just smiled.

**BEEEEP**

A car honked at me because I was still in the middle of backing out, which meant no one else could get out of the parking lot. I turned back to Alan to tell him I had to go, but he was gone.

# CHAPTER 10
## THE TRUTH WILL SET YOU FREE

I finished backing out of the space and started my drive back home. It was weird that Alan kept popping up, but I wasn't sure if I wanted to tell Aaron about it yet.

The night had been great, but then Alan had reminded me that Aaron wasn't single. As much as that hurt to hear, he wasn't lying. Aaron was dating Amanda. Even though he'd said he wanted to be with me, he'd never said he would break it off with her.

I was still entangled in my own thoughts when I realized how late it was getting. It was so late that I was surprised my mom hadn't called to find out where I was.

As soon as I stopped at a red light, I searched for my phone in my purse to see if I had missed a call from her. After confirming that I hadn't, I decided to call Lavinia to see if she could meet up before I went home. I was excited to tell her about my night, and I knew that if she came home with me, my parents wouldn't ask about who I had been with.

I looked up to see whether the light had changed to green, and a white Lexus sitting next to me at the light caught my eye. It looked exactly like Jen's car. It was difficult to see through the windows because they were tinted very dark. I knew Jen didn't have tinted windows, so I figured it was only the same make and model as her car.

I was just about to brush it off as a lookalike until the light changed and it passed me. Even in the low light of night, it was impossible to miss the obnoxiously neon green sticker on the car's back bumper, a very familiar parking sticker from our school.

Now, I was sure it was Jen's car, and I was determined to find out who was driving it. Had the family sold it just like they had the house, or was her family still actually in town?

I decided to follow it but not so close that the driver could see me. I was surprised when the car drove back to Hallowed Hills, and not just anywhere in Hallowed Hills: the original Hallowed Hills settlement. The museum was closed, but the gate opened when the Lexus pulled up in front of it.

I wanted to get closer to see what was happening, but my gut told me I shouldn't. Instead, I parked far enough away from the entrance to stay unseen and called Lavinia.

After a brief conversation about it, we agreed it would be better to meet at my house. It wasn't likely we would be unnoticed at the settlement.

When I got to my house, I waited in my car for Lavinia so we could walk in together. She got there only a few minutes after I did. However, no one was there when we walked in, so we stayed in the living room. I told her about my night with Aaron, and she was very excited for me.

Of course, I left the magic stuff out because I didn't think it was something Aaron wanted people to know about. But I did tell her about seeing Alan. I was interested in her thoughts since she had dated him before.

"Don't let Alan get to you. He's just very competitive. If anyone has something, he wants it, too. He's probably just trying to get you to question your relationship with Aaron," she reassured me.

I still wasn't sure what to think, but Alan did seem like that type of guy, so I decided not to worry about it too much.

"How was your day?" I asked to change the subject.

"I went out with my brother during the day then met with Ian for coffee in the late afternoon."

I couldn't help noticing her blush when she said Ian's name. "I'm glad things are going well with you two," I smiled.

"So, what are we going to do about the settlement?" she asked, now her turn to change the subject.

"Um, maybe we can go tomorrow. But what do we do when we get there?"

"I don't know," she answered with a shrug.

"It's getting late. Maybe we can sleep on it. Hopefully after a good night's rest, one of us will think of something," I suggested.

We'd been home for almost an hour when Ian and Zay came home. Ian winked at her, and Lavinia watched him walk up the stairs.

"Go," I said to her with a playful smile.

"Are you sure?"

"Yes, go be lovey-dovey."

Lavinia smiled and threw a pillow at me then ran up the stairs to Ian's room.

I looked around for my phone then remembered I'd left it in my purse, which was in my car. Smiling at the thought of maybe having a text message from Aaron, I went outside to grab my phone.

But when I got to my car, I suddenly felt like I wasn't alone as a cool breeze blew behind me that caused a chill to run down my spine. I turned around quickly, but nothing was there.

I hurriedly grabbed my phone, but as I locked the door, I saw someone standing next to the passenger side of my car. It was dark, so I could only tell that the figure was wearing dark clothes and had a hood covering their head.

Suddenly, I heard someone breathing hard close behind me. I turned around anxiously and braced myself for what I might find, but, again, when I turned around, no one was there. I turned back to where I had seen the hooded figure, but that person was gone, too. I quickly looked around again but saw no one. Terrified, I started running back toward my house, but then I heard a familiar voice.

"Nina."

I stopped dead. "Jen?" I questioned instantly as I placed the voice. I turned around quickly, but just like the first two times, no one was there.

I cautiously walked back toward my car but didn't see anyone. "Hello? Is anyone there?" I asked, but no one answered.

Even though I thought I was going crazy, I still walked around my front yard. I still didn't find anything or anyone. I even looked under my car.

As I started standing back up, I found two large legs inches in front of my face that caused me to scream and fall backward.

"What are you doing?" Ian asked as he laughed.

"You scared me! Where did you come from?"

"Umm... the house. I heard you say something, so I came to see what was happening," he answered while still laughing.

He offered his hand to help me up. I gave him an evil smirk but still took his hand.

"Where is Lavinia?"

"She's in my room. What are you doing? And why are you yelling?"

"I thought I heard..." I started to explain. "Never mind."

I knew I'd heard Jen's voice, but I didn't think Ian would believe me, or worse, he *would* believe me and run off again like he knew something, which would be even more annoying.

I still wanted to confront him about knowing Aaron before just recently, but I thought it would be better to wait until Lavinia left, so I just walked back into the house without saying anything.

I hurried upstairs to my room. I wasn't tired, so I grabbed the strange book that had been sent to me from under my bed. As I went through it again, I found new creatures. There was so much information.

After learning about Aaron's secret, I was excited to read about what else it said about warlocks. As I flipped through the pages, I started getting more and more frustrated at the disorganization of the book. On top of the lack of order, some entries were not in English. I was still trying to find the entry on warlocks when I heard Lavinia say good night to Ian.

I closed the book quickly, jumped off my bed, and grabbed Ian's math notebook with the flyer I'd found inside it. I stayed in my bedroom until I heard Lavinia leave through the front door. I glanced into Ian's room, but he wasn't there, so I went downstairs.

When I stepped off the staircase, I saw he was on the couch in the living room reading a book. I looked at him but didn't say anything. I just tossed the notebook onto the seat beside him.

"Hey, I've been looking for this!" he said excitedly as he picked up the notebook.

Still, I said nothing. I just looked at him with annoyance then tossed the flyer in his lap.

"What's this?" he asked as he unfolded the paper. He looked at it, then his cheeks immediately turned red. "It's not what you think," he said nervously.

"Ian, I don't know what I think. Do you know Aaron? Wait, of course, you do," I sneered before he could answer. "Here is a better question: How long have you known him?"

He didn't say anything for a while then finally responded, "I met Aaron the first week we moved here."

"Why would you keep that from me?"

"Nina, I know you. If you knew that I knew him, you would have wanted me to introduce you."

"And what is wrong with that?" I asked, fully annoyed.

"I told you. The founding families have secrets, secrets that could get people hurt. I don't want you involved with a family like that."

"What does that even mean?" When he didn't answer, I continued, "Fine. And anyway, that's too bad because I was out with him tonight." With that, I turned to leave the room.

"Wait, what? He has a girlfriend, Nina!" he shouted as he chased after me. He grabbed my shoulder just as I got to my bedroom door. "This is serious, Nina. You could get hurt," he said with real worry.

"Then you need to tell me right now what is going on!" I shouted at him.

"I can't... it's not my secret to tell," he responded quietly.

I wondered if he already knew what Aaron was. Maybe that was why he was trying to keep us apart. I was hesitant to tell Ian that I knew Aaron was a warlock. If I was wrong, I would be telling Ian Aaron's secret. Lavinia could be right; Ian might just think Aaron got too much attention from girls. I studied him, and he looked worried at my silence, but I still wasn't sure. And I couldn't tell him Aaron's secret unless I was sure.

"So you've said. Well, unless you give me a good reason, I will continue to see Aaron," I declared then closed my door.

It didn't take long for Ian to knock at my door. "Nina?" I heard him ask.

"Are you ready to come clean?" I asked through the door.

"Can you just let me in, please?" he pleaded.

I unlocked the door, and he walked into the room. He looked at me with utter defeat.

That made me feel horrible, and I realized that I didn't want to manipulate my brother. He was my best friend. Ian was always the one I told all my secrets, and I was always the one he told all his secrets. If he did know about Aaron's secret, I needed a way to let him know I knew without actually telling him I knew.

And then it hit me: the book.

I smiled warmly at him then sat on my bed. "Come sit down with me. I want to show you something," I said.

I patted the spot beside me and put the book on my lap as he sat down next to me. I opened the tome across both our laps then looked up at Ian. I watched his eyes as he glanced at the enormous book open before us.

Almost instantly, his eyes narrowed, and his expression went from indifferent to fixated. He quickly grabbed the book from my lap and eagerly started reading through it.

"Where did you get this?" he asked enthusiastically.

"I'm not sure. Someone sent it to me. I'm not sure who, and I'm not sure why."

I slid down to the end of my bed and reached underneath to pull out the packaging the book had come in. I looked it over again before handing it to Ian. "Here. The book came in this."

Ian examined the packaging carefully, flipping it around multiple times before giving up. "That's it?" he finally asked.

"Yeah. I wanted to tell you right away, but there has been this weird thing with us, and I..."

"I'm sorry. I shouldn't be keeping things from you. It's true. It's not my secret to tell, but it's not really about that. I want you to be safe. Knowing too much can put you in danger," he said sheepishly.

I studied his expression for any indication of his real understanding, wondering if he knew what I was trying to tell him. When he didn't continue, I went to my desk and grabbed my history paper.

"Here. I know you're a fast reader, so read this," I said as I handed him the paper.

It only took Ian a few minutes to read through the entire essay. "How did you get this information?" he asked curiously.

"You're not the only one who knows how to do research," I replied with a grin.

He smiled at me sheepishly and looked down. I could see he wanted to tell me something, but he was still hesitant.

"Oh, and one more thing. Remember how I said I was with Aaron tonight?"

Ian gave me a disapproving look then nodded.

I laughed at him but continued, "Well, he also showed me something, something that I have been questioning since I wrote my history paper."

A smile started forming at the corner of his mouth. "You know," he said quietly.

"I do."

"And how do you feel about it?" he asked hesitantly.

"I'm not sure. I guess it doesn't really feel real. You know me. I love all that science fiction stuff, but I'm not sure if I ever really believed any of it. Sure, I've fantasized about it being real. I thought meeting some of the creatures we've read about would be cool. But I don't think I ever thought it was actually real. Even seeing it tonight, I'm still not sure if I believe it."

"Yeah, I know how you feel. But... it *is* real," he said warily. "I didn't believe it initially either, but there's too much evidence to support it."

We sat silently for what seemed hours, but it was really only a few seconds.

"And it's not just witches and warlocks," Ian began again at last. "According to Aaron, there are many types of creatures that come to Hallowed Hills. They gather here once a year for a conference of some kind. He explained it to me, but my head was spinning at the time, so all I really remember is that they come once a year."

"Who comes? What do you mean? Are you saying we will be surrounded by mythical creatures once a year? What types? What's real? Do they hurt the people in the town?" I rambled as I started feeling a bit anxious.

"I don't remember much, but I do remember that during the conference, none of them can impede the town's normal daily routines. Aaron said that if that happened, not only would that council member be put to death, but their family would be as well. No one has ever broken the law so far."

"Why does the council meet here?" I asked curiously.

"Apparently, Hallowed Hills was built on ancient, hallowed ground. I guess it goes back really far, and I mean, even before the country was 'discovered,'" Ian smirked with the air quotes he always added when he spoke of the Europeans coming to America. "That's where the town got its name."

I was starting to understand why Ian hadn't wanted me to get too close to Aaron. From what he had told me, Aaron's family seemed to be at the center of this supernatural world. If I did choose to have any type of relationship with him, I would have to accept not just his family but his lifestyle as well. I wasn't really sure what that even meant.

Then another question entered my mind like a lightbulb going off. Alan. He was so pale. Even though I'd only seen him three times, it had never been in the sunlight. Could he be a vampire? Or was he just an extremely white warlock who hated the sun?

"What do you know about Alan?" I asked Ian while my thoughts continued going in multiple directions.

"Honestly, not much," he said then paused to look at me.

I shot him a disapproving look.

With a smirk, he elaborated, "I'm serious. After the accident with Amanda, I asked Aaron if he knew anything about the weirdo that hit her. When I described Alan to him, he just started laughing. When he finally stopped laughing, he told me it sounded like his uncle."

"So, what did he say?"

"Nothing. I got the feeling he didn't know much. He told me that he had just met his uncle a few years ago. I guess his uncle travels all the time and hates returning to Hallowed Hills," he explained curiously.

"Yet he lives here?" I questioned, puzzled by the glaring contradiction.

Ian shrugged his shoulders like he didn't know and didn't care either.

"He always seems to appear out of nowhere, and he is really white," I whispered under my breath.

"What do you mean he appears out of nowhere?"

"I don't know," I said with a shrug. "The other day, I saw him at the store and then tonight in the parking lot. He's not there one minute, and then he is."

"That's kind of creepy. I never really pressed Aaron about him, so I don't know much. If you are asking whether he's a vampire, the answer is I don't know. I haven't seen him suck anyone's blood or anything. On the other hand, I haven't seen him in the sun either," he chuckled. "Truthfully, I really don't know what a vampire would look like anyway. There are so many versions in literature and movies. I mean, we have the older versions with pale skin, haunting red eyes, and a feral cast to their features. Then we have those that sparkle in the sunlight." He rolled his eyes at that one. "Even so, all sources seem to have three things in common." Ian paused then continued as he raised a finger for each, "Vampires have pale skin, they must avoid the sun, and they need to consume blood to survive. But if pale skin is the only physical feature we can go by, 80 percent of people in the northern hemisphere could be vampires. It's just best to avoid the entire family."

"But you can be friends with Aaron?" I asked, incredibly annoyed at his double standard.

Ian looked at me with a frown. "You know perfectly well that that's different," he shot back in irritation.

"Why? Why is it different? You're still part of his world, aren't you?"

He stared at me for a few seconds with a look of frustration then answered. "What if you found out Lavinia was a witch?"

"Is she?"

"Well, no. At least, I don't think so. But would it make you see Lavinia differently?"

"No," I answered quickly.

"Would it make you see our relationship differently?" he asked innocently.

I was about to answer quickly, but then I stopped to think about it. Would it make a difference? I knew I wouldn't see her differently as a person, but if I didn't have concerns about her being with my brother when I knew she could physically hurt him, wouldn't that make me a bad sister? I didn't want to admit it, but maybe he was right.

"That's what I thought," Ian responded to my unspoken words.

"Shut up," I said, not wanting to admit defeat. "You know, Lavinia did pop out of nowhere the first day we met her, and she got my car fixed very quickly, almost like magic. She also has really white skin, too. And, come to think about it, I have never seen her out in the sun either," I finished with a grin.

155

"So, now Lavinia is a vampire witch? I don't think so. You just have supernaturals on the brain now."

Before I could continue teasing Ian, I received an email notification on my phone. Looking at it, I simultaneously felt angry and sad.

"What is it?" Ian asked nervously.

"The school just sent out an email. They're having a memorial for Jen and Matt on Monday," I answered then tossed my phone back on the bed.

"What's wrong with that?" Ian asked hesitantly.

When I'd invited Ian into my room, I had decided not to keep any more secrets from him, so I told him what I had uncovered about Jen. I even told him about when I'd followed the suspicious Lexus back to the history museum.

After my admission, I was surprised when it turned out that he wasn't opposed to the idea that Jen was still alive. He was, however, concerned that I had followed a strange car, which I thought was fair. We continued discussing Jen and Matt for a while longer when he suddenly went silent.

"What's wrong?" I asked in confusion.

He suddenly grabbed my hand and looked where I had burned myself only yesterday. The wound was completely healed with no trace that I had even been hurt.

"Is there something *you* need to tell me?" he asked accusingly.

I hadn't noticed that my hand had healed entirely in the short time since the incident. With the pain gone, I had forgotten it had even happened in the first place. I was still inspecting my hand when Ian pushed at my shoulder to get my attention.

"So, now you think *I'm* a vampire?" I asked sarcastically. Ian frowned but didn't answer. "You always see me go out in the sun," I added pointedly.

He continued staring at me without saying anything.

"I am not a vampire, Ian. I don't sparkle. I promise."

At that comment, he couldn't keep back his laughter, and the tension lifted. We went back to reading through the book together for another hour or so before calling it a night.

After Ian left my room, I laid in bed feeling satisfied. I was happy I no longer had to keep things from my brother, and we were both on the same page now. Even though the night had been filled with more questions than answers, I didn't care. I had my brother back, and that was all that mattered.

The next morning was cold like always, but it was also rainy. I called Lavinia to see if she had any ideas about what we were going to do about the settlement, but she said she had a family emergency and couldn't meet me today. We decided to figure it out later in the week.

By only 10 a.m., it looked like it was 9 p.m. The rain finally had stopped, but it was still dark out. I was reluctant to leave the house, but I knew I needed to get ink for my printer. With all the work our teachers had given us, I had none left, and I still needed to write a short story for my literature class.

I put on two shirts and two sweaters before adding my jacket with a hood.

"You look like a marshmallow," Zay laughed.

I rolled my eyes at him and walked out the door.

Once I was in the car, I started to get really hot, so I took off one sweater then put my jacket back on.

On my way to the store, I saw Alan sitting at one of the tables outside Once Upon a Bean drinking his coffee. I thought it was a bit strange that he only wore a leather jacket and didn't seem bothered by the cold at all.

Although I knew it was a bad idea, I decided to stop. After parking my car, I headed to the coffee shop.

"Hi, Nina," Alan said as I walked up behind him.

"How did you know it was me?" I asked as I walked around him to sit in the seat across from him without a thought.

"Just a hunch," he replied with a cocky smile.

"Why are you sitting out here?" I asked.

"Why not?"

"Because it's freezing."

"If I hadn't been sitting out here, would you have stopped?"

I was taken aback by the question. He couldn't have planned for me to stop by. There was no way he would have known I was even out. Clearly, he was messing with me.

"We can go inside if you like," he said as he stood up and entered the coffee shop.

I stood up to follow him before I even knew what I was doing, almost as if he had me under a spell or something. It wasn't like I was interested in him or anything. It was more like I wanted to know more about him.

Inside, we sat down at one of the tables by the window and talked for about an hour. He seemed really interested in my family. I wasn't sure why, and I really wasn't sure why I was telling him about them either.

He was definitely a playboy; every girl who walked in seemed to know him or want to know him. I was curious why he seemed so interested in me and my family, but I was hesitant to ask. I also felt weird because he wasn't flirting with me, and he really didn't seem interested in me in that way, yet he couldn't take his eyes off me the entire time we were there, even when other women came up to talk to him.

My curiosity finally got the best of me. "Why did you look at me so intensely when we first met?" I asked.

The question seemed to catch him off guard because he finally looked away from me. He took a sip of his coffee even though it was obviously cold by that time.

"Well?" I asked when he didn't say anything for another minute.

He sat back in his chair and looked straight into my eyes. "You intrigue me."

"What does that mean?"

"You are special."

"Like, don't-eat-the-paste special?"

"No," he laughed, then the humor left his expression. "You remind me of someone I used to know. She was very beautiful and strong, just like you. She died a long time ago."

"I'm sorry," I said, not really sure why I was apologizing.

"Don't be," he responded with a sweet smile. "Uh oh, here comes trouble."

"What?" I asked as Aaron walked into the cafe with an annoyed look on his face.

"What are you doing here?" Aaron grumbled as he stared directly at Alan.

"Just having a coffee with my new friend."

"Nina, can I speak to you in private, please?"

"Um, sure."

We walked over to a table as far away from Alan's as possible and sat down.

"Why are you here with him?" he asked accusingly.

His tone threw me off. I had never heard him speak that way before. "I am not here *with* him," I declared. "But what would it matter if I was? Don't you have a girlfriend?"

"I told you I need some time."

"So, you want me to stay single while you figure things out with your girlfriend?" I snapped.

When he didn't say anything, I started to stand up, but he grabbed my hand that was still on the table. However, he just as quickly pulled his hand away when one of the baristas looked straight at him.

"I just need some time," he repeated. "Please."

He looked like he wanted to tell me something but was conflicted.

It was still so hard for me to think clearly when I was around him, so I sat back down and looked at him. "I will give you time, but just remember that when a door opens, it doesn't stay open forever," I quipped then stood up and walked out.

When I had driven halfway home, I realized I had forgotten to get my ink. "Crap."

I drove back to the store and grabbed the ink then went straight back home, anxious because I hadn't finished my story yet.

I wrote my paper quickly, but I was satisfied with my work. Even more, I was glad Ian and I were good again because I definitely would need him to check my work this time. I left it on Ian's desk with a sticky note asking him to read it before getting ready for bed.

# CHAPTER II

## THE FROG PRINCE

The next day, I woke up later than usual but felt refreshed and excited. When I sat down for breakfast, Ian and Zay were already eating and laughing. In fact, everyone was in a great mood that morning. It was like any other normal day.

The only thing different was that Dad had left very early that morning, and Mom made us breakfast instead. She wasn't exactly a bad cook; it was just that our dad had more experience.

Until a few years ago, Mom had been the breadwinner of our household while Dad went to medical school. Over the years, he became a phenomenal cook. As much as Mom tried, she could never get her dishes to come out quite the way she wanted them to. Still, she always tried her best, so none of us had the heart to tell her when she overcooked or undercooked something. We ate it thankfully, even if we had a stomachache later in the day. She'd started getting better at it; there were even times that her food actually tasted good, usually when it was something she cooked regularly for us, like pancakes or scrambled eggs.

However, that particular morning, she was trying something new. It looked like some sort of omelet, but I couldn't be sure. Since I couldn't taste anything anyway, I ate two of them to make her feel good about her cooking.

Ian and I stayed in for the rest of the day catching up on the loads of homework our teachers had given us that week. I was happy Ian and I were back to normal and not just because he helped a lot with all the homework. It was really nice to be able to talk to him again.

Zay didn't have much homework, so he went out with his friends. Ian and I waited for him to come home then we all decided to work out together. Usually, we went to the gym, but we decided it was too cold, so we just trained in our basement. Once we had finished our workout, we were all exhausted and headed up to bed.

On the way to school the next day, the three of us spoke more about what we had seen in the backyard a few nights before, but none of us had a plausible explanation for the glaring red eyes.

I also told them about the three figures I had seen. Zay said he also had noticed three weird guys at the bonfire and thought he'd seen one guy's eyes change, but he wasn't 100 percent sure. He hadn't seen anything after that, so he had assumed he'd been wrong. Unsure what to do with that information, we decided to drop the subject for the time being.

"This town is just weird altogether," Zay added with annoyance, "I was yelled at when I said the town was discovered in 1693."

"Who yelled at you?" I asked.

"The know-it-all student aide in my history class," Zay replied.

"The town *was* founded in 1693," Ian answered assertively.

"Well, Little Miss Know-it-All said it was founded in 1765. I swear this entire town is just bat-shit crazy," Zay finished.

Both Ian and I laughed at his annoyance with the situation. I wondered what had happened in just the last few days that had made Zay change his mind. At the bonfire, he had been loving the attention from all the girls.

It was strange that the student aide had said the town had been founded in 1765. I thought back to the plaque at Luna's and clearly remembered the building and names listed below as well as the date above. It definitely had said 1693.

"Oh, by the way, what happened to your burn, Nina? Who are you? Wolverine?" Zay blurted out.

Both Ian and I busted out laughing.

"What? What's so funny?" he asked, obviously annoyed by our reaction. When we didn't answer, Zay crossed his arms and looked out the window. "I hate this place," he mumbled under his breath.

"Zay, we're not laughing *at* you. We promise," I responded sympathetically. "We laughed because last night Ian accused me of being a vampire," I said, trying not to laugh at the memory.

"Well, are you?" Zay asked seriously.

"No, Zay, I am not a vampire," I answered sternly.

I looked over at Ian, who was staring at me with one eyebrow up like he was Dwayne "The Rock" Johnson or something.

"Guys, I am not a damn vampire!" I repeated.

"If you say so," Zay responded.

"The burn was just not as bad as we thought. It healed. Nothing weird about it," I answered.

"Whatever," Zay said as he put on his headphones.

I could feel Ian still looking at me, but I didn't have anything more to say, so I turned the volume up on the radio and continued to drive.

After we dropped off Zay at his school, Ian and I spent the rest of the drive talking about what we had learned about the town, including the founding year. We both agreed that everything we had read said that the town had been founded in 1693. We had to assume that the student aide had been confused.

"So, I talked to Aaron," Ian said.

"Yeah? About what?"

"You," he answered flatly.

"What about me?"

"He said that he told you about him and I could share anything I wanted about his family with you. I didn't tell him I'd already told you, but I was happy when he told me it was okay. I was feeling a little guilty about it last night, but you're my sister and you're more important," he finished with a smile.

I smiled at him. "I'm glad we can talk about everything again."

"Me, too," he agreed.

"Do you think we should tell Zay?" he asked.

"Maybe eventually, but not yet. I don't think it's necessary right now."

We made it to school with 15 minutes to spare. When I got to my locker, Becca was leaning on the one right next to mine, and she looked really sad. I instantly knew what she was sad about. It was Jen's birthday; she would have been 18 years old.

She and Jen had known each other since they were in first grade and had been really close. The three of us had been planning to go to an underage nightclub this weekend since Becca and I were still 17. Jen didn't care; she had been so excited about it.

I thought about giving Becca hope by telling her about hearing Jen's voice, but I wasn't sure if she would believe me. Even though Becca believed in the supernatural and she might believe me, I had proof, so it might have made things worse.

"Hi, Becca," I said in a whisper when I reached her.

She looked up at me with tear-filled eyes.

I pulled her into my body and hugged her tightly then she began to fully cry. She stayed in my arms for a few minutes before pulling away.

"Sorry, my mascara came off on your shirt," she said apologetically.

"Don't worry about it," I responded right away with a warm smile.

She smiled back and handed me her sweater she'd had in her arms. "Here, take this," she insisted.

I didn't want to argue with her, so I smiled and took the sweater. Then I walked her to her first class and went on to mine.

When I walked into history, the bell hadn't yet rung, so everyone was standing around talking. Mr. Conrad was sitting at his desk, looking overwhelmed as he graded papers. I noticed the ones he'd already graded were mostly Cs and Ds, so I regretted not having Ian proofread mine.

I walked up to his desk and placed my essay in the only empty spot I could find. He looked at the newly arrived pages, annoyed, but when he looked up at me, our eyes met, and he smiled.

He quickly turned away, pushed his glasses back up his nose and cleared his throat. It was almost as if the smile had been an accident, and he was trying to take it back. He looked at me again, nodded as if to say thank you, then continued grading the rest of the essays.

I took my seat, and the bell rang a few minutes later to start the day. The rest of class was pretty normal. He spoke about the town's history a bit more and other types of supernatural creatures. When the hour was almost over, Mr. Conrad launched into a lecture about how disappointed he was with our essays.

"I expected more from seniors. I found multiple factual errors about the town, which is concerning," he said while looking straight at me.

His stare made me uneasy, so I quickly looked down at my notebook and pretended to be taking notes. I wasn't sure what factual errors I could have made. Even though Ian had read through the essay quickly, he would have pointed out any errors, so I tried to convince myself that maybe Mr. Conrad had been looking at someone behind me.

"I wasn't surprised that most of you wrote about witches, but I *was* surprised that 75% of you felt they were not real," he continued.

As Mr. Conrad went on, a bright light outside the window caught my eye. It came in three short flashes followed by three long flashes then three short flashes. The odd light continued to flash in the same pattern over and over again.

Completely immersed in the light, I was startled when I felt a nudge. I turned quickly to see Noah looking at me with concern and gesturing with his head toward the front of the class. Mr. Conrad had stopped talking and was staring at me.

"Welcome back, Miss Hart. You know I don't speak for my health. When I am speaking, I expect everyone to pay attention. Now where was I?"

I was shocked at the way he had spoken to me. He was so different when we were alone.

"I would think living in this town would open your minds to the possibility of the unknown. I didn't hold that against anyone; it was just surprising. Now that everyone has turned in their essays, it's time for our class trip," Mr. Conrad said excitedly as he rubbed his hands together.

The class started whispering, wondering where we would be going.

"All right, everyone, settle down," he said as he motioned with his arms for the students to lower their voices. "I need everyone to bring back these permission slips by tomorrow. The trip is on Friday, and I am not going to chase anyone's slips down. If you do not get them in, you will stay with Mrs. Fritter, who will be having class. Any students not going on the field trip will join her class," he explained as he handed out the slips.

The entire class booed. Mrs. Fritter was the AP history teacher. Mr. Conrad was a cuddly puppy compared to her. She was very strict and expected nothing but perfection from her students.

"We will see if we can change the minds of our nonbelievers with a visit to the Museum of Mythical Creatures in Downtown Chicago," he announced.

The class erupted in excitement. I was incredibly confused by their reaction. I had never heard of that museum before.

"What is the Museum of Mythical Creatures?" I whispered to Noah.

"It's a really popular museum about mythical creatures from all over the world. It's hard to get into. You need to be invited to visit," he answered.

"That's kind of weird. How do they make money if they don't let people in?" I asked.

"I don't think money is a problem for them. It's owned by a really rich collector."

Just then, the bell rang, and everyone hurried out of the classroom.

When I walked out the door, I was shocked to see Amanda standing across the hall. The fact that she was back in school was surprising enough, seeing as she hadn't been in history class. However, it was her appearance that shocked me the most.

She was glaring at me, and she didn't look like herself at all. Her previously golden tan skin was now the color of ivory, and she had bluish-purple circles under her eyes as though she hadn't slept in days. Even so, her hair was still perfectly done, and her clothes—a light blue turtleneck and white jeans—looked like they were straight out of *In Style* magazine.

I assumed she was just stopping by the school since she wasn't in her uniform. But even if that were the case, the cute outfit didn't really seem like her style. I had never seen her wear anything that covered her figure so completely when she was out of uniform.

I needed to pass by her to get to my next class, but the way she looked at me as I walked toward her sent a chill down my spine. I decided to make a pit stop in the girl's restroom, hoping that, by the time I came out, she wouldn't be standing there anymore. In the restroom, I went straight into the first stall and locked the door behind me.

Amanda had looked scary. There was no other word for it. I wasn't the type of girl who was intimidated by anyone, but this was somehow different. I felt anxious and overwhelmed as though something really bad was about to happen.

I wondered if she had learned that I had gone out with Aaron, or worse that I'd kissed him. I was immersed in my tumbling thoughts when I was startled by a knock at the stall door.

"Nina? Are you okay?"

Becca's voice instantly made me sigh in relief. I opened the door to see her standing there with a concerned look on her face.

"What happened? Is everything okay?"

"Yeah, I'm fine. Just needed to use the restroom."

Becca looked at me, knowing it was obviously a lie.

"Seriously, I'm fine," I repeated with a smile.

It didn't really seem like she believed me, but she dropped the subject anyway.

I wasn't ready to tell her yet about my night with Aaron. I was embarrassed about being interested in a guy who was already taken. If someone else had told me they'd gone out with another girl's boyfriend, I would be pretty disappointed in that person.

To make things worse, I hadn't heard from Aaron. That made me wonder about his real intentions. But he was with Amanda.

*Why can't I crush on an available guy?* I bemoaned silently.

For all I knew, it had been just a one-time thing. Maybe he wasn't interested anymore and had just been curious like every other guy in the town seemed to be. I saw how the boys looked at me, but none of them ever tried to talk to me. On the other hand, he had called Ian and told him about our conversation. That was a plus, so maybe he *did* see a future for us.

"Okay, well, is your history class going to the museum on Friday as well?" she asked, breaking me out of my tangled web of thoughts.

"Yes, I just have to get my permission slips signed, which is easier said than done."

"Oh right, the train accident," she said with understanding. "Well, at least we're taking a bus. No trains involved!" she added excitedly.

"I'll make sure to let my parents know that," I laughed.

"Is Ian going?" she asked with a blush.

"Um, I'm not sure. Mrs. Fritter will still have class, and Ian has AP History." Becca looked at me hopefully, so I conceded, "I'll ask him tonight."

She smiled then walked toward the door, checking her makeup before leaving the bathroom. I also glanced at myself in the mirror and was ready to follow Becca out when I noticed something different about my appearance.

It wasn't anything really all that obvious, but I looked more refreshed than I should be. I closely studied my face in the mirror. My skin looked smooth and soft. My hair was extra shiny like I had done a deep conditioning treatment. The color of my skin hadn't changed—I was still annoyingly white—but it looked bright, firm, and perfectly moisturized. I hadn't put on any kind of lotion, so it was very odd.

I looked... impossible... as if I were not a real person or like someone had taken a picture of me and filtered out all my imperfections. I continued staring, now studying my arms and stopping where the third-degree burn should have been. I poked at the spot, almost hoping for pain, but there was nothing. It was just like the rest of my body.

I looked at myself in the mirror again. "What is happening to me?" I asked out loud.

A few seconds later, the warning bell rang, making me jump and cover my ears. *Why is that bell so loud?*

I grabbed my bag and ran toward the door. There were only a few stragglers in the hallway by the time I emerged, so I felt relieved. However, the feeling only lasted a few seconds when I realized that the few students in the hallway were all staring at me.

I ran to my next class, trying to avoid seeing anyone else. When I made it to the door, I noticed oddly that I was not out of breath. Sure, I could feel my heart beating, but it was not accelerated like it normally would be after a jog or a run. I felt my pulse, and it was very slow, like I was lying in bed and trying to fall asleep. For a moment, I thought I was dying.

I turned right around and headed toward the nurse's office. Walking in, I immediately let her know what was going on. She took my temperature and found that it was a bit low and agreed that my heart rate was also a bit slow, so she called my parents.

My parents gave her permission to let me drive myself home as long as I felt okay to do so. I had potentially life-threatening symptoms, but I didn't feel sick at all. I felt a little bit anxious, but that was it.

I sent Becca a text message asking her to take Ian home, and she responded right away with a yes. I sent one to Ian as well, letting him know what was going on. He didn't answer, but he was a nerd like that. I knew he wouldn't look at his phone until class was over.

I was a few feet from the main entrance when I heard my name. I turned around and was surprised to see Mr. Conrad.

"Are you okay?" he asked as he continued to walk toward me.

"Umm, I'm not sure. I... I'm not feeling so well," I responded nervously.

When I focused on him, he looked so different that I almost didn't recognize him. His typical oversized clothing had been replaced with a fitted, dark blue button-down shirt that showed the true muscularity of his physique. He wasn't just fit though; he looked like he could easily grace the cover of *Muscle & Fitness* magazine. Even his black pants displayed evidence of his massive leg muscles.

With my attention so fixated on his body, it was only when he casually waved his hand past his face did I even realize he had let his hair hang loose. The beachy waves cascaded down to his shoulders and framed his face with a captivating allure.

As my gaze shifted again, I noticed he wasn't wearing his glasses. Their absence unveiled a whole new facet of his tantalizing presence.

"Umm," I said as I tried to put words together.

Gazing into his eyes, I found myself hypnotized by their intense emerald-green hue. He stood almost directly in front of me, and I remained speechless as my attention lingered on his features. Then it dawned on me that he towered above me. We had never stood in such close proximity, but now it struck me that he was at least three inches taller than my dad.

Feeling a tinge of embarrassment for having stared at him for so long, I blurted out the first thing that crossed my mind. "I have a nurse's pass," I said quickly, praying he hadn't noticed me staring at him.

"I wasn't accusing you of anything, Nina," he answered as one side of his lips raised just a bit to form a playful smile.

Hearing him say my name, and not the usual "Miss Hart," released butterflies in my stomach, leaving me giddy and embarrassed at the same time. He was my teacher, so I couldn't see him as anything more than that. I wasn't sure what was wrong with me or why I was feeling this way, but I also wondered how I had never noticed how striking he was before now.

"I have to go," I muttered before rushing out the door and sprinting to my car. I was so afraid I would say something I wouldn't be able to take back, so I just needed to get away from him.

When I made it to my car, I noticed that my heart rate hadn't changed, and I wasn't out of breath just like earlier. I still wasn't sure where to go. I thought maybe I should head to the hospital, but I didn't know what I would say to them. *Hello Mr. ER doctor, I feel fine, but could you spare some of your precious time away from actual sick people to check me out anyway?* It seemed pointless.

Then Mr. Conrad's face intruded upon my thoughts again. Shaking my head and rubbing my eyes, I decided to just drive aimlessly for now just to escape the confines of the school.

As I started my car, a knock at my window startled me. I let out a scream and instinctively covered my eyes. As I slowly lowered my hands, I turned toward the window, unsure what I expected—maybe the shadow monster again?

However, when I opened my eyes, relief mingled with my nerves as I found Mr. Conrad standing on the other side of the glass. Rolling down my window, I prepared to speak with him.

"Why don't you let me give you a ride," he asked warmly as he knelt next to my door.

I felt like a deer caught in the headlights. His smell was intoxicating, and I was so nervous I started to feel lightheaded. I didn't know what to say to him.

"I'll be okay. I don't want to be a bother," I finally answered.

"I have the rest of the day off, and I was just leaving anyway. It's no bother at all," he insisted as he opened my door.

Before I knew it, I had already stepped out of the car and begun to follow closely behind him, taking in his intoxicating scent. With every breath, I felt more lightheaded, but I didn't care.

When we made it to his car, my body started feeling heavy, so much so that I stopped walking altogether. Mr. Conrad put his hands out to steady me, and I fell right into his arms.

The next thing I knew, I was waking up in Mr. Conrad's arms and staring right into his eyes. I blinked a few times before I could hear what he was saying.

"Let's go," he said with a sigh of relief.

I experienced a strange sensation then, but the pain in my head started improving slightly, and I had a newfound ease in my breathing even though the sense of being off kilter persisted.

By now, Mr. Conrad already had opened the passenger door and extended his hand for me to take.

Eagerly, I accepted it, but before I settled into the car, I locked eyes with him. Instantly enchanted, I felt as if my body had a mind of its own as my free hand reached up to his cheek and caressed it softly.

To my delight, he didn't resist and instead leaned into my touch and closed his eyes. His skin had the most perfect temperature, neither cold nor hot.

When our eyes met again, I felt a magnetic force urging me to continue. Slowly moving my hand, I traced his sharp jawline all the way down to his neck then onto his chest where I felt the sturdiness of his pectoral muscles beneath his shirt.

Intrigued, I ventured further, discovering then that his shirt was already untucked. Unfazed, I boldly moved my hand under his shirt for direct contact with his chest and traced its definition while stealing glances at his lips.

His mouth became slightly ajar, his eyes narrowed, and he bit his lip as if entranced by my fingers dancing along his chest.

Following the creases of his muscles down to his stomach, I met his bewitching gaze again and felt his heartbeat quicken as my fingers continued tracing his well-defined abs.

His newly accelerated breathing heightened my excitement, and our heartbeats seemed to synchronize. I grasped his shirt at the center of his chest from underneath and slowly pulled him toward me.

I glanced down at our proximity then shyly met his eyes. I could see that he knew this was wrong, just like I did, but neither of us had the power to stop.

His enormous hands encircled my waist and drew me into his god-like physique as the rhythmic beating of our hearts echoed loudly in my ears, reminiscent of bongo drums at a Cuban nightclub.

As I leaned closer, my face nearing his, a sudden pain surged through my temples, but I was too engrossed in the moment to care. Then a wave of dizziness overcame me, and my head began to spin.

"Nina..." I heard Mr. Conrad say in a muffled voice.

But I couldn't hold myself up any longer and felt my body start to get heavy and fall into his arms again.

# CHAPTER 12

## FORBIDDEN FRUIT

I was awoken by the smells of antiseptics and metal. Looking around, I found myself in a bed inside a very brightly lit room. I could hear ambulances and electrical equipment as well as the squeaking of an old wheelchair passing by my room and a woman announcing codes over a loudspeaker.

Finally realizing that I was in a hospital, I sat up in bed. I looked at my chest and noticed I was hooked up to a heart monitor. I examined the numbers on the screen, which said my heart rate was 31.

I was no doctor, but I knew that was low. I immediately hoped I wasn't at Osbourne-Palmer Memorial. I could only imagine my dad's face if he read my name on a patient-admission list or something.

Because he was a doctor, he always tried to solve every medical problem our family had. He asked so many questions to try to diagnose us that sometimes it became overwhelming. I knew I would have to tell my parents about this eventually, but I didn't even know what I was feeling, so I couldn't exactly explain it to someone else.

Looking around again, I didn't see my dad, but I did see Mr. Conrad standing outside the room speaking to a nurse. It only took a few seconds for him to notice I was awake. He walked into the room followed closely by the nurse.

"How are you feeling, honey?" the nurse asked sweetly.

"I'm fine," I answered as she flashed a light past my eyes, which made me blink and turn away.

"You seem okay, but your vitals are very low. The doctor wants to keep you overnight for observation."

"I don't think that will be necessary," I said as I started to try to stand up. Both the nurse and Mr. Conrad lunged toward me.

"Whoa, whoa! Nina, you fainted. That's why we are here," Mr. Conrad said sternly but empathetically.

I squinted at him. I was so confused. It was strange that my teacher was here in the hospital with me. I barely remembered anything, only leaving the school then sitting in my car. Then... waking up here. I struggled to try to remember more and was so confused that I just laid back in bed.

When the nurse left, Mr. Conrad sat down next to me.

"What are you doing here, Mr. Conrad?" I asked him sheepishly.

"You don't have to call me Mr. Conrad outside of school. It's Connor," he said with a sweet smile that made my cheeks feel warm. "You don't remember?" he continued.

I shook my head.

"What is the last thing that you *do* remember?" he asked.

"Being in my car. I remember talking to you, but that was before I went to my car," I answered as I rubbed my temples.

"I followed you to your car to see if you were okay," he reminded me.

I thought about it again, and I started to remember seeing him at my window. "Oh, right, you came to my car. You said you would give me a ride," I remembered. "What hospital are we in?"

"Edward's Hospital. It was the closest one to the school. Is that all you remember?"

I looked at him. It seemed like he wanted to tell me something, but I wasn't sure what that could be.

"Um, yeah, I think so. Why? Is there more?" I asked curiously.

"I called your family, but the only one I could reach was Ian. He's on his way now," he said, ignoring my question.

"Thank you for bringing me here."

That was when I noticed he was wearing his oversized cardigan and enormous glasses again, like he was seeking to conceal his true appearance from everyone.

"You put your glasses back on," I blurted without thinking then bit my lip in surprise at my boldness.

"Yes, I did," he said with a luminous smile.

Smiling shyly in return, I looked at him for a moment. "Don't you want to take them off?"

"Do you want me to take them off?" he teased with a cheeky smile.

For reasons I couldn't understand, I nodded.

He waited, seemingly contemplating the decision, before slowly removing his glasses and slipping them into his pocket.

His eyes were spellbinding. I reached over to his hands that were clasped together on the side of my bed and started stroking his fingers with mine.

He watched my fingers massage his hand then looked back up into my eyes with a concerned expression before letting out a deep breath and slowly turning his hand over so he could hold mine.

He smiled hesitantly, and I reciprocated.

Unsure what was happening between us, I took the time to study his face, analyzing the features he kept hidden from the world. He had a strong, diamond-shape jawline and unblemished skin, and his eyes seemed to radiate with an aura that made him undeniably beautiful. I also noticed that his skin resembled mine—not the color; his skin tone was more of a warm beige—but in the softness and smoothness. His hair was silky and extra healthy, again like mine.

Tossing my legs to the side of the bed, I attempted to stand.

"Whoa, what are you doing?" he asked anxiously as he steadied me.

Drawing myself closer to him, our bodies on the brink of touching, I lifted my gaze to meet his, and a knowing smile playing at my lips. "I remember," I breathed, the words dripping with seductive allure.

Balancing on the tips of my toes, I tenderly caressed his face. Tumultuous emotions swirled in his gaze, yet he didn't pull away. I pulled his face toward me and met his full lips with mine, seeking the connection we both yearned for.

My heart sank when he didn't kiss me back. Although he had let me kiss him, that wasn't enough.

I started to pull away when his hands enveloped my face, and a surge of passion sparked between us. His kiss was fervent, igniting a fire within me that burned with an intensity I had never known. He moved his hands away from my face and placed them on my lower back, pulling me into his statuesque form.

A warmth spread through my chest as he lifted me, cradling me in his arms as if I were as light as a feather but also as delicate and precious as a newborn duckling.

Wrapping my legs around his waist, I melted into him, sliding my arms around his neck. Our lips locked in a dance of longing and devotion. Every brush of his fingertips against my skin sent shivers down my spine, making my entire body feel like it was floating as a sense of euphoria overwhelmed me like nothing I'd ever felt before. I brushed his hair away from his face with my fingertips as our tongues continued to dance.

Although I knew someone could walk in at any moment, I didn't care. All that mattered in that moment was the pleasure I felt.

Mr. Conrad—Connor, my mind corrected—pulled away from me slowly and set me back down on the bed. Smiling at me, he looked down shyly then gently removed my arms from around his neck. He placed them against his chest for a moment before looking into my eyes. Holding my hands together in his, he kissed them seductively even as he maintained eye contact before situating them again on my lap.

Before I could say anything, I noticed Ian walking through the door. I looked over at Connor, but he was already sitting back in his chair as though he had known someone would be walking into the room.

"Nina!" Ian exclaimed in panic.

"I'm okay," I said quickly, trying to reassure him.

"Mr. Conrad?" Ian questioned. "I didn't think you would still... I mean, thank you for bringing my sister here."

"You are welcome. I guess I should be going. Take it easy today, Nina," he said as he stood up and brushed a hand over his lips.

He walked out before I could say anything. Ian looked at me then at the door through which Connor had left then back at me.

"What's going on there? Why was your teacher at your hospital bedside?" he asked accusingly.

"Don't be weird, Ian. He was there when I fainted at school," I answered, trying my best to sound indifferent about his presence.

"Yeah, but why was he *still* here?" he asked suspiciously.

"I don't know. Why don't you ask him?" I answered in frustration.

He looked at me like he knew I was hiding something.

"What's wrong with you?" I asked.

"What's wrong with *me*?" he snorted.

"I just want to go home. They haven't been able to get a hold of Mom or Dad, so I'm stuck here," I said, trying to change the subject.

"I spoke to Mom, and she had to interview a witness in Indiana for a case her law firm is working on. Dad should be here soon. He was in the middle of an autopsy when they called the first time."

"What about Zay? Who is going to pick him up?" I asked.

"I couldn't get a hold of him. HHH has a 'no cell phone' policy, but I did leave a message for him with the office. They will let him know that he needs to take the bus home today."

My dad arrived a few minutes later and rushed to my side. "How are you feeling, baby?" he asked frantically.

Before I could even answer, he felt my head and studied my arms then looked up at me and ran out of the room.

"What was that?" I said out loud.

"No clue. That was weird right?" Ian asked.

"Yes, it was."

Before I could say anything more, Ian walked toward the doorway and started listening to the conversation Dad was having with the doctor.

"He's arguing with the doctor. He's telling them that he wants to take you home. He sounds upset," he relayed before looking back at me.

I didn't bother telling Ian that I could hear everything they were saying from where I was. He turned back to look toward the hallway then spun away fast and walked quickly toward me. "He's coming back," he said as he slid back into the chair by my bed.

Dad's stern voice cut through the air like a knife. "We are going home. Now," he commanded, his determination palpable. "Get your stuff. Let's go," he added as he waved us toward the doorway.

Both Ian and I stood up quickly and followed his direction. I was still hooked up to the heart monitor, so I pulled off the leads. To my surprise, it hurt for only a second. I regarded the doctor standing in the hallway. She looked both scared and confused.

"Henry, I urge you to let us keep her here for at least one night," the doctor said to my dad.

But Dad's authoritative tone welcomed no argument. "I'm a doctor, too, Maryam. I can take care of my daughter," he answered authoritatively as he herded Ian and me toward the nearest exit.

"Henry," another doctor called out.

"I'll be right back," he said to us then went to go talk with the man.

They spoke for a while a short distance away, but then the conversation seemed to get intense. Dad looked at us then pulled the doctor around the corner.

"Dad, is—" I started to say but then realized Ian was gone.

Looking around, I found him getting food from the vending machine. I laughed; he was always hungry. I sat down in the waiting area and picked up a magazine to distract myself, but my attention was swiftly diverted when I caught sight of Alan down the hall.

His demeanor was tense, hands clenched as he fixed his gaze on someone in the distance. I rose, drawn toward the unfolding drama, then realized it was Connor facing off against Alan with equal intensity.

I couldn't see his face, but I could see that his fists were clenched as well. Connor turned his head to the side as if he knew I was watching. Then he looked back at Alan and walked down the hall to his left. When Connor was out of sight, Alan started walking toward me.

"Hey," Alan said to me far too casually for the charged atmosphere.

"What was that?"

"What was what?"

"That," I said pointing in the direction Connor had gone.

"Oh, just some dick," Alan dismissed.

"That's my history teacher."

"He's your what?"

"My history teacher..." I trailed off, not understanding why he was acting so strangely. "Why?"

Alan's gaze hardened as he glanced back toward where Connor had disappeared. He exhaled heavily before refocusing on me.

"How are you? Are you hurt?" he deflected, his concern a stark contrast to his previous demeanor.

"You didn't answer me," I insisted.

"It's nothing. I just don't like the guy."

"How do you know him?"

"Through my family," he said flippantly. "But that doesn't matter. What happened to you?"

I didn't like his answer, but I knew I wasn't going to get much more from him, so I responded to his question instead. "I'm okay. I don't know. I fainted. They don't know what's wrong with me."

"So, why aren't you in bed?"

"My dad. He's acting kind of strange," I answered as I turned to look in the direction my dad had gone.

"Well, you do look a little pale. And..." he trailed off as he started examining my eyes and moving really close to me.

"What are you doing?" I asked, unsettled by his sudden intensity.

"Strange," he said.

"What?"

Suddenly, I heard my dad start yelling at someone about a report that had not been submitted. I turned but couldn't see who he was yelling at. A few moments later, he came around the corner stalking toward me again.

I turned back to look at Alan, but he was gone.

"I hate when he does that," I muttered to myself.

# CHAPTER 13
## WRITING IS ON THE WALL

We drove home in silence, and my dad looked really worried the entire time. He kept looking at his phone as if waiting for a very important phone call.

Just as we pulled into the driveway, his phone started to ring. He answered it. "Hey, I'm just getting home. I will call you back in ten minutes," he said in a rush.

"Was that Mom?" I asked.

"No, it was a colleague from the hospital. Let's get you up to bed," he answered as he stepped out of the car.

Once in the house, I started walking up to my room, but I noticed my dad pull Ian to the side. I stood at the top of the stairs and watched him feel Ian's forehead then look at his arms. He studied Ian's arms longer than he had mine then let out a sigh of relief and let go of them.

"What?" Ian asked my dad.

"Nothing," he answered and hugged Ian.

"Umm... okay. What's going on?" Ian asked while being squished by my dad's bear hug.

"I am just glad you're okay."

"What do you mean? Is Nina contagious? What—"

"Where is Zay? I have to go pick him up. I hope..." he started to say then looked at Ian. "I have to go pick up Zay. I'll be back later. Don't let your sister leave this house," he finished as he rushed out the door.

Ian looked so confused and stood staring at the door with his arms left out for a few seconds as though Dad was still inspecting them before turning around to look up the stairs.

We looked at each other, both not understanding what was going on.

He regarded me pointedly for a long moment then asked suddenly, "Why does your skin look like that?"

"Like what?" I asked innocently.

"I don't know, like bright."

"Bright?" I questioned.

"Nina, I don't know. It just looks different. Dad seemed worried about your arms or your skin or something. You didn't look like that this morning." He continued staring at me as if waiting for an answer.

I really didn't have anything to say to him. I had noticed the difference, too, but I hadn't thought it was that big of a deal. So, my complexion was clearing up. For all I knew, it was just part of going through puberty.

"Did you take something?" Ian asked cautiously.

"Of course not!" I answered quickly.

He looked at me with concern as I walked down the stairs and looked straight into his eyes. "Ian, I didn't take anything."

"Okay, I believe you."

"But dad looked at you, too, like he was expecting something to be wrong with you as well."

"Yes, he did. Dad is acting very strangely. Maybe it's some kind of virus," he wondered aloud. "Maybe you're turning into a zombie!" Ian added dramatically.

"Haha, very funny."

"He didn't seem to be worried about himself, just you, me, and... Zay. How are you feeling now?"

"I feel fine. I always felt fine. My heart rate has just been low. I'm thinking the rate got too low, and that's why I fainted, but I didn't really get to ask any questions with Dad shooing us out of there like that."

"Yeah, that was strange, too. Did you have any other symptoms?" he asked.

"Okay, Dad." I rolled my eyes at him playfully.

"I know, but maybe I can find some information about what might be going on," he said sheepishly.

"What would you be able to figure out that the doctors couldn't?"

"Well, I'm kind of thinking it may not be a typical virus. I was only half kidding about the zombie thing," he replied worriedly.

"Ian, I am not a zombie, and I am not a vampire. I am not any kind of supernatural creature," I said with real frustration.

"Nina, you already know about Aaron, and you know about the council meeting. What if there are creatures here and one infected you somehow? I'm going to call Aaron."

He pulled out his phone and walked into the living room. I was about to follow him when the front door swung open, barely missing my shoulder.

"Whoa!" I exclaimed.

"What's going on here?" Zay demanded. "Dad just picked me up from school and literally pushed me into the house. He said I can't let you leave the house. What did you do?" He paused in his interrogation and stared at me. "Umm... what's wrong with your skin?"

"I'm a zombie, and I'm going to bite you!" I quipped.

I walked away before he could ask any more questions and moved into the living room to find Ian just getting off his call.

"Aaron and his grandmother are on the way," Ian said.

185

"His grandmother? For what?" I asked.

"They think it may be something... not normal, too," he whispered then looked at Zay who was standing right next to me.

"Okay, what's going on?" Zay demanded in frustration.

That was when Ian and I made the decision to tell Zay the truth. We told him everything we had found out about the town, including how Aaron's family factored into it. We didn't leave anything out, including the book that had been sent to me.

Zay didn't really seem to believe anything we were saying. We were still trying to explain it to him when there was a knock at the door.

I looked through the peephole to see Aaron and an older woman standing on our porch. I stood back and fluffed my hair a bit with my fingers.

Ian rolled his eyes and shoved me out of the way to open the door.

Aaron walked in and nodded to Ian as he held the older woman's arm to help her inside. I had to assume she was his grandmother.

Aaron and I looked at each other. He was just as handsome as I remembered him; his piercing blue eyes were magnetic.

I bit my lip and stepped toward him. He smiled then took my hand, massaging my fingers for a moment before releasing them.

"Nina, this is my grandmother," Aaron said with a charming smile.

She was a small woman who appeared to be in her 60s. Almost a foot shorter than Aaron, she had thick, shiny black hair with only a bit of white that she kept up in a bun. She had thin lips, dark eyes, and a strong jawline. The wrinkles on her face illustrated her years, but her features were beautiful. She most certainly had been a knockout when she was younger.

"Hello, I assume you are Nina. My name is Beatrice Carrier," the woman said to me in a heavy British accent.

Without saying anything else, she pulled my arms toward her and examined the outsides then turned them over and did the same to the insides, feeling with two of her fingers from my biceps down to my fingertips.

"I am afraid that we are too late," she concluded after her examination.

"Too late for wh—" I started to say but suddenly got a really bad headache and began to feel dizzy again, so I stepped back and sat down on the stairs. I looked over at my brothers who were both rubbing their temples as well.

"Go outside, Aaron, and take this with you," Beatrice instructed as she handed Aaron her pendant.

I noticed immediately that it looked just like the pendants worn by Mrs. Farnsworth and the librarian and wondered whether they could be all in the same coven.

Aaron didn't ask any questions; he just took the pendant and went outside. As soon as he was gone, I started feeling better. I looked over at my brothers, and they seemed better, too.

"The lot of you," she said with a concerned whisper.

"The lot of us what?" Zay nearly shouted.

Ian frowned at Zay and barked, "You're being rude, Zay."

"This is all crazy. Magic is not real. It's only in movies and books," Zay retorted.

"I am sorry that this has happened to you, but there is not much we can do now. The only thing you can do is stay alive."

"Stay alive? Shouldn't that be something everyone should do?" Zay huffed.

"Was there a potion in your pendant?" I asked abruptly. "Is that why you gave it to Aaron and asked him to leave?"

Beatrice nodded in acknowledgment.

"How did you know that?" Ian asked.

"I remember the book saying something about witches and warlocks using potions and spells to deter dark creatures. It made them feel sick," I answered.

I looked to Beatrice for confirmation. She smiled slightly as she nodded slowly.

"Dark creatures? What does that mean? And why would that affect us?" Zay asked with annoyance.

We all turned back to Beatrice who looked concerned. "You are all in transition. Nina is quite a bit farther along than you two, but you are all affected. I will try to explain what I can, but I need to know how this happened. Where did you get the blood?"

"Blood? What blood?" I asked as I stood up.

Beatrice looked at me for a moment then caressed my face with the palm of her hand. Her hands were softer than I had expected them to be. Her touch made me feel safe.

"Nothing has to change as long as you stay alive. Ian and Zay will look more like you in time, but you will be okay. My concern is that if someone did this to you without you knowing it, they may try to complete the transition without you knowing that, too."

"Did what to us?!? I'm so confused my head is spinning," Zay whined as he sat down on the stairs.

I felt my phone vibrate in my pocket, so I took it out right away. It was a text message from Aaron.

I am sorry I can't be in there with you. Please trust my grandmother. She will help you as best as she can. I miss you.

My heart started to melt. He was really worried about me. Oddly, that made me feel good.

"Is there somewhere we can all sit? I am getting a bit tired. I am not as young as I used to be," Beatrice said with a smile.

Ian quickly moved toward Beatrice and guided her to the couch in the living room. She stayed for another half hour or so explaining to us what transitioning actually meant. "There are supernatural creatures that are born, and there are those that are made. Those that are made must transition into the creature they are meant to be," she explained.

"So, we're transitioning into some sort of creatures?" Ian asked.

"It appears so. It seems to be a humanoid creature, similar to a vampire," she added as she inspected my arms again. "But you cannot be vampires because the symptoms are not presenting that way."

"I don't understand any of this," Zay said anxiously then rubbed his face.

Beatrice stood up and sat down next to him then rubbed his back in a grandmotherly gesture. "I know this is quite a lot to understand, and I will do everything I can to help."

Zay looked at her and smiled.

Beatrice smiled back before she continued, "Whichever creature you are transitioning into must be one that is created like a vampire and not born like a witch or warlock. Somehow you have ingested the blood of the supernatural creature into which you are transitioning," she explained then paused. "And because you were unaware, it is very likely someone wants you to make the change without your knowledge."

"Why would someone do that? What would be the benefit to them?" Ian asked.

"That I am not sure, but the thing that concerns me the most is that there are three of you and that you are so closely related."

"Does that make a difference?" I asked.

"I am not sure, but I have heard stories of a prophecy about three supernatural creatures of the same kind that become very powerful, but all those stories were just that: stories," she said but she appeared worried. "I have never seen any type of real documentation on this, so I don't know much about it, but I will try to find out more. For now, just be very careful. Even though we do not know the creatures you are becoming, we do know they are demonic."

All three of us froze. Was she saying we were turning into some sort of demon? We looked at her with concerned frowns, so she explained, "That just means that part or perhaps all of the creature is a demon. We don't know how much control you will have if you fully transition," Beatrice said as she began to stand.

Ian stood up with her and walked her to the door. Zay and I followed behind them closely.

"Just remember, even if it's an accident, if your heart stops beating, you will have no choice but to complete the transition."

With that, she covered my heart with her palm and smiled warmly. "Make sure you keep it beating," she added before walking out the front door.

My brothers and I stood in the hallway in silence for a few minutes, just trying to take everything in. I tried to think of a reason anyone I knew would want the three of us to become supernatural. Even if I had known why, I still had no clue who would want to do that to us. Like Ian had asked, what would be the benefit to them?

"The bookmark," I said then realized I had said it out loud.

"Bookmark? What bookmark?" Zay asked curiously.

I looked at both my brothers then sprinted up the stairs to my room. I could hear them following close behind me. I grabbed the book from under my bed and started frantically flipping through it. I got all the way to the back and then went to the front again. It wasn't there.

"Ugh, it's not here!" I said as I tossed the book onto the bed.

"What are you looking for?" Ian asked.

"When I first received this, it had a bookmark stuck in it. It marked a page on Nyx something, Nyx-being, Nyxed, I don't know… something. It had to do with the goddess Nyx."

"Nyxed? Sounds like something that gets rid of something else," Zay said with concern as he picked up the packaging the book had come in. He put his hand inside and brought out the bookmark. "Is this what you're looking for?"

"Oh no! It must have fallen out," I said with dismay as I took the bookmark out of Zay's hand. I inspected it closely. It didn't have anything written on it. It was just a dark brown leather strap with the image of a crescent moon etched into it.

"What's the big deal? Why is this so important?" Zay asked.

"Someone wanted me to see that entry, so there has to be a reason," I concluded.

"Well, you said it was Nyx, so let's just look through the book," Ian suggested.

"Unfortunately, that's easier said than done. First off, some of the entries aren't even in English, but that's not even the worst part. The entries have no order to them, and they are all wacky," I explained.

"She's right. I have ges-talt-wandler?" Zay sounded out badly. "Not sure what that is, but then right after that it says ogre," he stated as he looked through the enormous book.

"Don't worry about the name right now," Ian said. "Can't you remember anything about the entry?"

"I remember that it said they were descended from the goddess Nyx and were similar to vampires."

"Okay, what did the vampire entry say?" Ian asked.

"Yeah, I could never find vampires in that damn book," I said, annoyed.

"Why don't we each take an hour with the book to see what we can find," Ian suggested. "Zay, why don't you go first? I'll see if I can find any information online about dark creatures that relate to the goddess Nyx."

"Don't you mean demonic creatures?" Zay commented anxiously.

"Let's not jump to any conclusions. Let's figure things out first, and then we can go from there," Ian said calmly.

I smiled. Ian was great in a crisis, always able to keep a cool head. His plan was good, and it made me feel a little better.

I didn't have much to do while my brothers did their parts. I figured that if I started looking things up, I would worry myself more, so I decided to lay down on my bed for a while. I was exhausted. Now that my headache finally had gone away, I wanted to take advantage of it. I felt for my pulse, and it was still extremely slow. Not wanting to worry about it anymore, I turned over onto my side and closed my eyes.

# CHAPTER 14

## BAPTISM OF FIRE

I woke up the next morning feeling very nauseous but happy at the same time. I rubbed my eyes. Glancing down, I saw I was still fully clothed. I touched my shirt and immediately remembered what had happened the day before.

I smiled and stroked my lips with my fingers, remembering what my dream had been about: my encounter with Connor. Closing my eyes, I saw his face in my memory. I knew it wasn't right to be thinking about him, but I couldn't seem to help it.

With the same smile still on my face, I opened my eyes and began to examine my skin. I was relieved when I saw that it hadn't seemed to have changed any more.

I still had my shoes on, so I tried to slide out of my bed without touching the soles of my shoes to the sheets. Although it was still early, I decided to get ready for the day and took a quick shower, brushed my teeth, and got dressed.

I was almost at the stairs when a feeling of extreme nausea resurged, and I had to run to the bathroom. Heading straight for the toilet, I threw up then sat on the floor rubbing my stomach, wondering what I could have eaten to make me feel that way. I threw up twice more before deciding it was safe to leave the bathroom. I brushed my teeth again then looked at myself in the mirror.

Strangely, my chest appeared to have gotten bigger. I took off my shirt and looked at myself in just my bra. My cleavage was spilling over the top, and I could see the under part of my breast as well. It was strange, but I also thought I kind of looked really hot, so I couldn't help smiling. I loosened my bra straps, so my breasts fit better and put my shirt back on before heading downstairs.

The house was really quiet, so I tried not to make any noise as I walked toward the kitchen. I peeked in the garage to see if my parents' cars were there.

"Ugh," I said out loud when I saw that both cars were there. I knew I had to come up with a plan to convince my parents that I was okay. I didn't want to end up having to grow my hair radically long just to be able to use it to climb down from a tower in which I had been locked away.

As I thought about excuses I could use, I started eating breakfast. I had only taken a few bites of my cereal before I got annoyed by the tastelessness.

I threw the bowl into the sink, then I saw a jar of peanut butter on the counter. For some reason, it looked really good. I went to the refrigerator to get jelly but saw a large jar of pickles first. I knew it sounded weird, but for some reason the idea of peanut butter and pickles was really appetizing to me. In no time, I cut up a large pickle, smeared peanut butter on the slices, and began to eat.

It tasted really good, and I was happy I finally could eat something. Once I had finished my odd breakfast combination, I went to sit in the living room to watch a bit of TV with Chloe. She was purring on my lap within a few minutes and looked so peaceful. I never thought I would envy a cat so much. Stroking her soft orange fur helped tremendously with my anxiety.

It wasn't much later when I heard someone coming down the stairs. To my surprise, it was Ian. He never woke up early. In fact, we had to nearly drag him out of bed every morning, so I knew something was up.

He raised his hand to say hello then yawned on his way to the kitchen. He came back a few minutes later with a bowl of cereal in his hand and sat down next to me.

"Good morning."

"Morning," he replied sleepily as he spooned another bite of cereal into his mouth. "I didn't find much last night. There was nothing about any type of dark creatures associated with the goddess Nyx," he said after swallowing.

"I'm not surprised. It's not something I'd ever heard of before. I'll take a look tonight after school."

Ian looked at me with disapproving eyes.

"I am not going to be a prisoner in my own house. Oh, I almost forgot. Is your history class going on the field trip to the museum?"

"Random question, but yes, we are supposed to go on Friday, but I don't see Dad signing the permission slips for us."

"Well, I'm going. I don't care if I have to forge his signature. I am not a baby," I said, seriously irritated.

"There is a little bit more to it. You know that."

"I do know that, but I... *we* have to live our lives. Do you really want to spend the rest of your life in this house?" I asked sardonically.

"Of course not, but I wouldn't mind spending one more day in the house. I still want to read through that book," he confessed.

"Did you find anything on vampires?" I asked him.

"No. I'm thinking that that entry must be in another language. I want to scan some of the entries and send them to a linguist."

"A linguist? Do you know a linguist?" I giggled incredulously.

"No, but I'm hoping Aaron's family has some connections."

"Is he coming over?" I asked with more enthusiasm than I meant to convey.

"You are such a girl," Ian responded with a cheeky smile.

I rolled my eyes at him then turned back to the TV.

"Aaron's family comes from a long line of witches and warlocks, so I'm hoping they know, or know of, someone who can help."

"Well, good luck," I said sarcastically.

Ian looked at me angrily then hissed, "You are not taking this seriously, Nina."

"You heard Beatrice. There is nothing we can do, so why even bother? What happened has happened," I said to him.

"There is always a way."

"A way to what, Ian? Stop us from changing into demons?"

"We have to try," he said with an air of defeat.

I looked at my brother and instantly felt regret. He was just trying to help. "What do you need me to do?"

Ian smiled and jumped up. "I have a feeling that if we find the vampires entry, we'll get some answers," he said excitedly.

"Okay, but there is only one book. We can't both look through it at the same time."

"That's true," he said as he stroked his jawline. "I'll look through the book for the entries I think might be helpful and scan them in. You call Aaron and see if he knows anyone who can translate any of the pages," he instructed.

I was surprised he wanted me to talk to Aaron, but then I figured he thought that nothing worse could happen to me than what already had. I mean, we were already turning into demons.

I nodded in agreement then he ran up the stairs. I looked at my phone and told myself that it was still too early to call. But if I were being honest with myself, that wasn't the actual reason. I thought back to our date, which seemed a lifetime ago. I remembered how his touch had made me feel as he'd caressed my body. It had been like nothing else I had ever felt until... I'd kissed Connor.

I was torn between two completely unavailable men. One was in a relationship with someone else, and the other was my teacher.

I looked at my phone again and tried to put my feelings aside, but I couldn't. Gritting my teeth, I forced myself to call Aaron, nervously listening as the phone rang. After the fourth ring, his voicemail picked up. I hung up before I even knew what I was doing.

Truthfully, I wasn't sure what to do. I was afraid I would spontaneously confess that I had kissed someone else. Then I realized that he was probably still kissing Amanda. I frowned. I wanted to know how he was feeling before I stressed myself out, but I didn't know how. I couldn't just come out and ask him.

I threw my phone on the couch then ran up to Ian's room.

"Hey, can I ask you something?" I asked as he scanned a page from the book into his computer.

"Shoot," he replied without even looking up.

"Are Aaron and Amanda still together?" I asked shyly.

Ian immediately stopped what he was doing and looked up and out the window directly in front of him. He turned to look at me but didn't say anything.

"Ian?"

"I don't want to be in the middle of this. Maybe you should ask Aaron."

That non-answer was all I needed. "Okay then," I said blandly as I turned to walk away.

"Wait," Ian said as he pulled my shoulder toward him to turn me around. "All I know is that them being together was not his idea. I didn't pay too much attention, but it's something about the bloodlines. That doesn't necessarily mean he doesn't have feelings for her, but it doesn't mean he doesn't have feelings for you either."

I knew Ian was trying to make me feel better, but it wasn't working. I was frustrated by the fact that I had already called Aaron so he would undoubtedly call me back. Now, I really didn't want to speak to him, and I was starting to get angrier than I wanted to be. I unconsciously started to ball my hands into fists as I walked into my bedroom.

All of a sudden, my eyes started to burn, and it felt like they were melting in my eye sockets. I screamed as I covered my eyes and fell to my knees.

My entire family ran into the room in a panic. My dad knelt next to me as I continued to cover my eyes. "Baby, let me see," he said as he struggled to pull my hands away from my face.

My eyes were starting to feel a bit better, so I opened them. I looked at my palms, expecting to see blood in them, but there was nothing. I turned to look at my dad, but he fell backward in shock.

"What?" I asked.

My dad looked at the rest of the family. I followed his gaze, and they all looked petrified. Ian's mouth was open in disbelief, my mom had her hands covering her mouth, and Zay stood frozen in shock.

"Your eyes are..." Ian started to say.

"My eyes are what?" I shouted when he didn't continue.

He looked over to my vanity table as if to say I should go look into the mirror. I stood up slowly and walked over to it then bent down to see my face in the mirror. I jumped back and covered my mouth when I saw them.

My dad came to my side and started rubbing my shoulders. I looked at him, and he nodded to reassure me.

When I looked into the mirror again, my irises were magenta, and the scalars were almost the same shade but a bit lighter with almost a glow to them. The area just under my eyes had dark circles with dark blue and gray lines over them that looked like veins.

I closed my eyes until the burning stopped. When I opened them again, they were my natural brown color. Never in my life had I been so thankful to see my brown eyes. I sighed in relief then turned back to my family.

My dad hugged me tightly then pulled away. "I'm going to figure this out."

"Maybe you should just lay down," Zay suggested. "We don't want you eating anyone."

"Zay!" my mom yelled.

"What? We don't know what's happening here. I'm just saying," Zay said as he threw his hands up in the air.

My family all started arguing with each other, and it was really getting heated, so I felt I had to say something. "Zay's right. He wasn't very tactful about it, but we don't know what can happen," I stated levelly.

"But you are fine now," Ian insisted.

We debated for a while longer about what to do, but we couldn't agree on anything. My dad finally put his foot down and said that everyone had to stay in the house while he went to speak to someone he thought could help.

Ian and Zay left the room, but Mom stayed. I wanted to find out how much she knew, but I didn't know how to ask. "Does Dad know what I have?" I asked her.

She looked at me, and her kind eyes made me feel more at ease. "He said it's some sort of blood-borne pathogen, but he doesn't know much about it. That's why he's going to speak to this specialist. He will figure it out.

He always does. Your dad is a wonderful doctor. Whatever is wrong with you, he will fix," she said reassuringly.

I wanted to be reassured by that, but I wasn't. Although I wasn't tired, I started to close my eyes so my mom would think I was falling asleep. She brushed my hair from my face and kissed my forehead and left.

Once she was gone, I slid out of bed. I knew one other person who might have some information. I frantically looked everywhere in my room for my phone then remembered I'd thrown it on the couch before coming up to talk to Ian.

*Crap.* I wasn't sure how I was going to do it, but I knew I had to talk to Lavinia.

I waited a few minutes for my mom to leave the hallway, then I opened my door slightly to see if anyone was out there. When I saw that the hallway was empty, I quietly crept out of my bedroom. I could hear people in the living room, so going downstairs was out of the question.

I went next door to Ian's bedroom and looked around. I was excited when I saw his phone lying on his bed. I quickly grabbed it and ran back into my room. I searched for Lavinia's phone number then called her. She answered right away.

After her surprise at me not being Ian, I explained to her what was going on. She said she would come over as soon as she was back in town and would text my phone an exact time.

I felt better after speaking to Lavinia, but I still had to get to my phone. The good thing was that it was still on silent from the night before so at least it wouldn't ring while it was downstairs.

I was deep in thought when I heard a knock at my bedroom window. It startled me so badly that I fumbled Ian's phone and dropped it to the floor.

I looked toward the sound and saw Aaron crouched down on the other side of the glass. I quickly went to the window to open it.

"What are you doing?" I asked him.

"I have been trying to call you all day. I needed to see you," he said as he hopped into my bedroom. I sniffed the air around him and noticed that it smelled differently.

"I can breathe," I said with a smile. Aaron only smelled refreshed and clean like body wash.

He smiled widely. "I must have taken 18 showers before coming over," he said with a chuckle.

He came closer to me until his body slightly touched mine. Reaching out, he caressed my face with one hand and moved my hair out of my face with the other. He took my chin between his fingers and pointed it up toward his face then bent down and kissed me deeply.

My knees started to get weak, and I put my hands on his chest then tugged on the sides of his open button-down shirt to steady myself. I pulled myself away from his lips and stared into his eyes.

He gently touched his forehead to mine, took my hands in his, and smiled. I smiled back self-consciously and looked down.

"What's wrong?" he asked as he pulled my face back up.

"What about Amanda?" I asked sheepishly.

"I'm sorry," he said nervously.

"What are you sorry about?" I asked, not entirely sure I wanted to know the answer.

"It's complicated," he said then looked at me before continuing. "It's my family's tradition. My mom was the first one to marry outside the coven. And if—"

"Wait, marry? Are you telling me you are engaged to Amanda?" I asked in shock.

"No, we are not engaged, just sort of promised to each other," he said quietly.

I pulled myself away from him and dropped his hands, staring at him in disbelief. I didn't know why he'd even come to me then. I turned around and started to walk toward the door.

"Look, things are complicated," he said as he grabbed my hand and pulled me back.

"Do you love her?" I asked suddenly before he could say anything else.

He stared at me nervously but said nothing.

"Why are you here?" I asked a bit too loudly.

I could feel my eyes start to burn. I tried to calm down because that had seemed to work the last time and closed my eyes until the fire subsided.

"I want you, Nina," Aaron said seductively.

I wanted to just say "screw you" and walk away, but I couldn't. I had feelings for him.

"But you want her, too," I said as I tried to fight the tears developing in my eyes.

"I want you, Nina," he repeated. "Amanda is a great girl, but she was what my family wanted." He paused to look at me. "But I don't want to lie to you. It's been over a year, and I have developed feelings for her. I just need some time to figure things out."

By that point, I couldn't hold back the tears. He moved to wipe them away as he took my chin between his fingers again, but this time I pulled away.

I wiped away my own tears and stepped back from him. "You said that Amanda wasn't a witch," I stated firmly.

"She's not."

"But you said she is part of your coven."

"Her *family* is part of our coven, but she is not a witch. Her powers never emerged. That happens sometimes, but the blood of the coven is still there," he explained.

There was a knock at my door. I moved toward it and cleared my throat. "Who is it?"

"It's me," Ian said.

I opened the door, and he immediately noticed my tear-filled eyes.

"What's wrong?" he asked me with concern then looked around my room, and his eyes met Aaron's. "You. What did you do to my sister?" he yelled as he made his way toward him. Ian grabbed Aaron's shirt and rammed him against the wall.

"Ian, stop, please," I pleaded as I pulled him off Aaron. Ian begrudgingly let go of Aaron and stepped back.

"Leave," Ian growled.

I had never seen Ian so mad, so when Aaron looked at me for guidance, I just gestured my head toward the window. Aaron paused then slowly walked to the window and climbed back out.

"Ian, what's wrong with you?"

"Me?" he asked angrily as he began pacing the room.

"Calm down. You're going to give yourself a heart attack," I urged as he continued his laps around my bedroom.

"I told you it wasn't a good idea to be with him."

"You don't even know what happened," I said to him.

He finally sat on the bed then huffed, "I can imagine."

As much as I didn't need Ian protecting me, I was glad I always had him on my side. I sat down next to him and hugged him around his neck. He patted the arm around his neck then fished my phone out of his pocket.

"Here," he said with a smile as he handed it to me. "No more boys climbing through your window, okay? Because I just might eat the next one," he finished with a laugh.

"Stop it," I said as I laughed and punched his shoulder playfully.

He smiled at me then stood up and left the room.

As soon as he was gone, I opened my phone and went directly to my messages. I found a text from Lavinia saying she would come by that day at about 5 p.m. It was still a few hours away, so I contemplated what to do until then.

I could sit here and cry about Aaron, or I could do something useful. As I was thinking, I received another text message. I looked at my phone screen and saw it was from Aaron. I debated for a few moments whether I should open it, but curiosity got the best of me, so I did.

*I want you, Nina.*

Annoyed, I immediately closed my phone and threw it on the bed then stood up. I went into Ian's bedroom and grabbed the book, which was still in the scanner. I brought it back to my bedroom and started looking through the entries.

I decided to focus on the ones not in English that had drawings of creatures. I wrote down in a notebook the first few I saw, which were: Quỷ đen, Νεφελίμ, and Seeungeheuer.

Quỷ đen had a drawing next to the writing that looked like some sort of devil creature. It was shaded darkly and had the face of a ram, the torso of a man, and the lower half of a bull.

The next one was Νεφελίμ. This one had the body of a muscular man with what appeared to be large angel wings. His hair was electric white, but he still looked young. Even through the drawing, his eyes looked like they were glowing blue. He wore a gold chest piece that belonged in some type of battle. Apart from his glowing eyes and the enormous wings on his back, he looked pretty much like a normal human man in his mid-20s to early 30s.

The last one, Seeungeheuer, looked like some kind of sea serpent. It had the head of an Asian dragon, the body of a very large snake, and four massive fins.

I wanted to look through a few more, but I started getting very sleepy. I hadn't eaten much in the last few days, so I felt completely drained. Ultimately, I decided it would be best to lay down for a bit before Lavinia came over. As soon as my head hit my pillow, I drifted off into a coma-like sleep.

# CHAPTER 15
## INTERVIEW WITH THE VAMPIRE

I was startled awake by a loud knocking that caused me to fall out of bed. I picked myself off the ground and went to open the door, but no one was there. I heard the knock again and jumped, not knowing where it was coming from until I realized it had come from my window.

"Doesn't anyone use doors anymore?" I grumbled as I went to see who it was this time.

"I do have a door, you know," I said sarcastically as Lavinia peered in.

"You said you were on lockdown, so I wasn't sure," she said sheepishly.

"Just come in," I responded, somewhat annoyed, but I quickly realized I wasn't being fair to her and felt bad. "Sorry, thanks for coming over. I haven't eaten anything all day, so I'm cranky," I added quickly as she climbed into the room.

"Don't worry about it," she responded. "I talked to someone about your symptoms."

"You told someone?" I interrupted her.

"Don't worry. I didn't say who you were. I just described your symptoms. They said you're in transition."

I already knew that, so I wasn't surprised. "Yes."

"You already knew?"

I nodded at her then she continued, "Okay, well, I told them everything you told me, and they don't know what you could be transitioning to. They said it sounded like a vampire, but some things were different. To transition into a vampire, you have to die with vampire blood in your system then feed on human blood. Once you feed... bam, you are a vampire. Simple. But you are different. You haven't died, and you seem to be slowly transitioning."

Lavinia peered closely at me for a moment. "I can see that your skin has changed, and you said your eyes changed. That's another thing. Vampires' eyes change red when they get emotional, but magenta is something I've never heard of. Also, the blue and gray veins you described are not the same for vampires either," she explained.

I looked at her for a moment in wonder. "Lavinia, how do you know all of this?"

She looked at me with embarrassment. "Well, like I said, I know some-one. Okay, I may know of a vampire. And maybe I dated him for a while, but that was a long time ago."

I was shocked by what I was hearing. How could she have known a vampire but not told me about it? I thought we had been getting close. I'd considered her one of my best friends and told her everything about myself, never leaving anything out. I felt suddenly betrayed.

"I am sorry," she said as if she could read my thoughts.

"Who is it?" I asked, half expecting her to tell me that it wasn't her secret to tell.

She hesitated for a moment before responding, "Please, don't be mad. I didn't say anything because I didn't want to scare you," she offered. "It was a long time ago, and I was young and dumb. It's..."

"Who?" I asked when she didn't continue.

"Alan," she finally admitted.

As soon as she said his name, I was shocked but not shocked at the same time. Knowing what I knew, I wasn't surprised to hear that a vampire was living in our town. I was, however, shocked to hear that someone I had met was a vampire. But oddly I found I wasn't surprised it was Alan. His appearance was how I would have pictured a vampire, and his appearing and disappearing out of nowhere made more sense now, too. His animal magnetism and sinister demeanor was what I expected from a predator as well. In my mind, I compared it to a Siberian tiger; their beauty can hypnotize you, but you know they are still dangerous, and something inside tells you to stay away.

"Does he hurt people?" I asked cautiously.

"Alan is a bounty hunter."

"A what?"

"A bounty hunter," she repeated. "If someone pays him to hurt someone, he will, as long as he thinks the reason makes sense."

"Is he the one behind all the disappearances? But how would it make sense to kill teenagers?" I asked in retraction.

"I really don't know."

Lavinia smiled at me, but it wasn't her regular smile. It was hesitant, like she had something she wanted to say.

"Is there more?" I asked her timidly.

She didn't answer me, and fear colored her eyes.

"Lavinia?" I urged.

Lavinia looked at me for a few moments then stepped back. I thought she might be frightened by the way I looked now, but my eyes didn't have the burning sensation that indicated they had changed, so I wasn't sure why she would be scared.

I ran to the mirror to check them and held my breath as I looked into the glass. I sighed in relief when I saw my normal brown color. I touched my face, and it felt soft, then touched my arms. I didn't look scary. If anything, I looked prettier than before, so I was confused by Lavinia's reaction.

Then I saw Lavinia walk up behind me in the mirror and stare into the reflection of my eyes.

"There is something I want to tell you," she finally said. "Well, I don't want to tell you, but I need to tell you," she added reluctantly.

She looked at me again then looked down. When she looked back up, I nodded to try to reassure her. She turned around and started walking away.

"The timing is really bad," she said as she turned back toward me. "I don't know how you are going to react."

She started fiddling with her hands then balling them into fists then reopening them. Letting out a large sigh, she turned back around. I waited for more than a minute for her to say what she wanted to say, but she just stood with her back to me.

"Lavinia?" I prompted with concern.

I placed my hand on her shoulder and slowly turned her toward me. When she turned, I was horrified by what I saw and stepped back, tripping over my computer chair and falling to the ground. Lavinia darted toward me with inhuman speed to try to help me up.

"Don't touch me!" I yelled as I sat on the ground looking up at her.

Her eyes were similar to mine when I felt the burn, but her irises were crimson red, her sclera's were black, the areas under her eyes were black, and the veins there were all black instead. Her mouth was slightly open and revealed her sharp fangs.

I picked myself up from the ground with my arms in front of me, letting Lavinia know to stay away.

While I fixed my shirt, I thought of something else. As I looked at her, I started to get angry, leaving no room for fear. I felt the flames in my eyes develop as I pounced on top of her, knocking her to the ground with my hands clamped tightly around her neck.

"You know a vampire?!?" I screeched. "You *are* a vampire! You did this to me! To my brothers!" I screamed as I straddled her on the ground.

She pushed me off her with almost no effort then stood up and shoved me against the wall. "No! I didn't!" she yelled.

She looked at me with angry, demonic eyes. After a moment, she started letting go of me and calmed down. Her eyes began to change back to their natural blue. Then she let go of me completely and stepped back. I stood there in shock for a moment while making sure I didn't take my eyes off her.

"Nina, I didn't do this to you," she said calmly.

I was still mad at her, but I couldn't ignore the fact that we did look slightly different. I was so mad that I didn't even want to ask her anything. Even if she hadn't done anything to me, she had kept a huge secret from me. And, not only that, when she had told me about vampires, she had made it seem like Alan was the only vampire in town. I wasn't sure I could trust her any longer.

"Please, Nina, you are my best friend," she pleaded. She sat down on my bed and covered her eyes as she began to cry.

My first instinct was to sit down next to her and comfort her, but I was afraid. I didn't know if she had complete control of herself. For all I knew, she would attack me without realizing what she was doing. What I knew about vampires came from books and television, and all those different types of vampires ran through my memory and mixed together. I wasn't sure what to believe.

"Does Ian know?" I asked her from where I stood.

"No," she responded nervously. "Please don't tell him."

"He needs to know," I said authoritatively.

"I know," she answered shyly, "but I need to be the one to tell him."

I looked into her tear-filled eyes, but I wasn't sure what to do. On the one hand, she had never done anything to harm me. We had been alone together plenty of times, so if she had wanted to hurt me, she probably could and would have. But, on the other hand, Ian was my brother. My family was the most important thing to me, and I didn't want to take any chances.

"I will give you until the end of the day to tell him. If you don't, I will."

"The end of the day?" she asked nervously.

"Yes," I answered resolutely. "Frankly, you should have told us a long time ago, Lavinia."

"I know. It's just that some people don't react well to it. Case in point," she said, waving her hand in my direction. I looked down with shame at that but looked back at her as she continued. "When most people don't understand something, they get scared, and that can be dangerous for us."

"I am not most people."

"I know, but technically you are not supposed to know about me. Only—"

"Family members," I cut her off as I remembered Connor's lecture.

"How do you know that?" she asked, shocked.

"My teacher told us," I answered.

She looked at me in confusion, but I suddenly couldn't focus on her. Just thinking of his name made me immediately picture his face and our kiss. Butterflies started to form in my stomach. As the memory of his lips on mine flooded my thoughts, just for a second, I almost forgot about all my troubles. Almost.

"We're studying about the town's history," I finally began as I came out of my daze. "During one of his lectures, he mentioned the persecution of the girls in Salem. He said that even though the ones accused were not witches, there *were* witches living in the town. And he said that no one should know of their existence, no one but their family and other supernatural beings."

The next few hours were filled with questions and answers. I started to understand better when Lavinia explained about her supernatural world. She admitted that it had been her choice to turn into a vampire, but that the consequences of that choice had never really been explained to her.

"I was turned by a man who I thought loved me, but it turned out I was just an experiment to him."

"What do you mean by experiment?" I asked with concern.

"He was a doctor named William Rowsley. He wanted to know how things worked," she said hollowly. "I found out later that he had chosen five girls, and he tested how long we could go without feeding on human blood before we died instead of transitioning."

"That's horrible."

"Yeah, well, it's the reason we know that to become a vampire, one needs to feed on human blood within 48 hours of the human death or die."

"That doesn't mean he should have tested it on you or anyone else."

"It was just how things were done back then. Not only by vampires, but by everyone. I was 21 years old, so I was young and naive. From the moment I met him, I was infatuated. He was like a vision of perfection, every aspect of him meticulously crafted to captivate the senses. With his chiseled features and striking brown hair framing his face, he had an aura of timeless elegance. His piercing brown eyes held depths of wisdom and mystery that drew me into their hypnotic gaze with an irresistible pull."

She paused to look at me with a worried glance. I could tell she was reluctant to tell me about someone she had been so in love with in the past. I smiled to encourage her to continue.

"His lean yet muscular frame spoke of strength and grace, and each movement was deliberate and commanding. Standing about 6'1", he towered above others with an air of confidence that commanded attention. But it wasn't just his physical allure. It was his intellect and charisma that truly set him apart from the rest. He possessed a sharp mind, which was matched only by his unwavering confidence. With every word he spoke, he exuded a quiet authority, leaving no doubt in my mind that he was a force to be reckoned with. In his presence, I felt a sense of awe and admiration. I was drawn to him like a moth to a flame. He wasn't just a man but a magnetic force of nature, leaving an indelible mark on my heart and soul," she finished.

"Wow, that's quite a description," I breathed.

She looked down and smiled shyly then continued, "For months, he treated me like a queen. When I told him I wanted to turn, he was so happy. He told me he was so excited that he had found the person he wanted to be with for the rest of his existence."

"Do you think you really loved him?" I asked.

"Honestly, I'm not sure. I want to say yes, but I found out later that vampires produce a type of pheromone to entice their victims. After he'd changed me, he didn't seem interested in me and left me to fend for myself."

"So, he just threw you into a world you didn't understand without any help from anyone?"

"Yes, and I was completely lost. But the worst part was that I didn't understand the urges I was having, so for a while, I gave in to them," she said cautiously and looked up at me.

I smiled warmly at her in understanding, so she continued. "It's still hard to this day, but nowhere near as hard as it was before. I had, and still have, an animal-like instinct to feed. Sometimes it's really hard to control."

"Why are things easier now?"

"Over the years, I figured out most things on my own, and I have done everything possible not to have an episode."

"An episode?"

"It's like having a red curtain covering our eyes. We don't know what we've done until it lifts—vampires, I mean," she clarified.

Hearing what Lavinia had gone through, I felt bad for her.

"I found out some information about the deaths of Jen and Matt that I was afraid to tell you," she started abruptly.

"What is it?"

"Well, Alan attacked Jen and Matt the night of the bonfire."

"What? Why?"

"Alan holds a grudge against all vampires because he was forced to turn into one. He was a warlock before he died and was very proud to be one. When he transitioned, he lost all his magical abilities. He couldn't do magic anymore or even mix potions that worked."

"Who turned Alan?" I asked with fascination.

"Alan fell in love with a woman, but he didn't know she was a vampire. He was so completely in love with her that, when she told him what she was, he still wanted to be with her even though vampires and warlocks are mortal enemies. He promised his entire mortal life to her."

"Okay, so then did he change his mind?"

"No, he didn't change his mind. But, for her, being with him for only one human lifespan wasn't enough; she wanted to be with Alan forever. So, she changed him, not only without his permission but also without him knowing."

"Oh," I said, shocked.

"Yeah. After he turned, he became so angry with her that he ended up killing her before he knew what he was doing. He immediately regretted it, but that left him with even more anger because he hadn't been able to control himself."

"He killed her? When did that happen?"

"Alan was turned into a vampire in 1880, and that was the same year he became a bounty hunter. His focus has always been on killing vampires, sometimes even when there is no bounty."

Still confused about the why of all of it, I asked, "I don't understand why Alan would turn Jen and Matt if he hated vampires."

"Alan doesn't usually kill humans, but he does sometimes lose control. After he feeds, so the person does not die, he heals them by feeding them his blood, but vampire blood doesn't heal instantaneously. If the body is too broken, or too close to death, they can die anyway, even after consuming the blood. If they die with the blood in their system, they become a vampire."

"So, he accidentally turns people into vampires?"

"Well, sort of. Because he wasn't given the choice to transition, he lets the human choose what they want to do. Although they have that choice, he refuses to facilitate the feeding and leaves them on their own."

"Isn't that worse? That would put a lot of people in danger, wouldn't it?"

"I guess he doesn't see it that way, or maybe he just doesn't care. I've never really asked him about it."

It was getting late, and I knew I still had to ask Lavinia an important question. I was hesitant to ask, but I knew I had to. "Are Jen and Matt dead?"

"Technically... yes, but they have fully transitioned into vampires," she answered. "I have been trying to track them down since the bonfire. I've been able to locate Jen a few times, but she always runs away before I can speak with her."

"What about Matt?"

"I haven't seen him at all. The only reason I know he made the transition is because his body was missing from the ambulance. That would only be the case if he transitioned. Otherwise, he would have made it to the hospital or the morgue."

"I hate to say it, but what if Jen drained him of his blood and he died?" I suggested.

"Well, we know he was in mid-transition, so technically he was already dead. If Jen fed on him, she would become very sick. A dead person's blood severely weakens a vampire. If they drink it, they become very ill, and it can take days or even weeks for them to regain their strength. Since Jen is still running around, I know she didn't feed on Matt."

"Where have you seen Jen?" I asked.

"Actually, I saw her go into the settlement a few days ago, but others were there, so I couldn't follow her. I went back to investigate the next day and looked everywhere, but I didn't find anything strange. If Jen stayed there, it probably wasn't for long."

My head was spinning with all this new information, but I was still aggravated I hadn't really learned anything about what was happening to me and my brothers. "Everyone keeps saying we are transitioning into something like vampires, but no one seems to know more than that."

"The person I spoke to about you transitioning is a scientist," Lavinia began, "but he's not just some ordinary scientist. He's an alchemist, which means he's a warlock with no supernatural abilities."

"Okay, so how does that help us?" I wondered aloud.

"Even though he doesn't have the power to create magic, he has the blood and knowledge of a warlock. He can still create potions by adding a drop of that blood. The potions are much weaker than a regular warlock's, but they still work better than traditional mixtures. And the next part is the reason I felt I needed to tell you about me."

"Okay…" I said as my mind processed everything.

"I need a sample of your blood to give to my contact to test. Your blood is the key to finding out what creature you're transitioning into. I was hoping that if I told you everything, you would trust that what I was doing was for the best. After all, I'm putting all my trust into you."

I was still upset that it had taken her so long to tell me the truth, but I didn't think giving her my blood would hurt anything, so I let her take a small vial of it before she left my room.

Now alone again, I felt really tired, but I felt more hungry than anything else. I went downstairs and forced myself to eat a bowl of cereal. Even though the food had no taste, I was glad it at least made me feel full.

When I went back upstairs, I heard Lavinia and Ian talking. I hoped Lavinia would keep her word and tell him she was a vampire. She was one of my best friends, and I would hate to lose her, but I would always put my family first.

When I walked back into my room, I turned on the TV and jumped into bed. It didn't take long for me to drift into a deep sleep.

# CHAPTER 16

## SINNERS AND SAINTS

I opened my eyes only to find that I was sitting in a large field of grass. The ground felt moist, but not damp, more like it had been kissed by the early morning dew. The air smelled crisp and clean as if it had just rained.

Sitting up, I looked to my left and saw a beautiful pond with a large waterfall. I watched as a white, frothy cascade of water plunged into the pond from a rocky ledge about 20 feet above the pond's surface. A majestic white mare with a silver mane and tail stood with her colt, drinking peacefully from the shining water.

Then a large crack came from the forest just to the right of the pond. The thunderous sound echoed across the field. I covered my ears as I watched the two horses gallop past me.

I started to stand, but my head suddenly began to spin. I closed my eyes and held my head in my hands as if trying to prevent it from flying off my shoulders. The pain was unlike anything I had ever felt before, like a knife of ice stabbing into my brain. I felt like I was going to pass out, but then the pain started to fade.

When I opened my eyes, I noticed someone lying face down next to me. The male body wore black jeans and a blue shirt, and his brown hair was damp. Even though I couldn't see his face, I instantly knew who it was.

"Connor!" I yelled in horror as I shook him to see whether he was alive.

Relief washed over me when I heard him moan, but I soon began to tremble with fear when he still didn't move. I turned him over and saw that his button-down shirt was open, revealing an enormous gash across the lower left side of his abdomen. An oddly shiny, golden substance seeped from the wound. The thickness of the substance made it seem like blood, but the color was completely wrong.

I immediately removed my jacket and placed it against the wound with pressure.

"You know that will not work," Connor said with evident struggle then added with a defeated and hopeless smile, "my enchanting goddess." He reached up and stroked my cheek with his fingers.

As his fingers caressed my face, I began to cry.

"You need to protect them," he said as his hand slowly sank back to his side.

Knowing he was gone, I threw myself onto his lifeless body and cried into his chest.

"You could have saved him," an ominous voice said from the dark forest in the direction of the loud sound from only a few minutes ago.

Horror-stricken, I spun around quickly toward the bodiless voice.

**BANG! BANG! BANG!**

"Hey, Nina! It's 12 p.m. Are you going to wake up today?" Zay shouted.

The sound of my brother's voice made my eyes snap open. I was covered in sweat but instantly felt relief when I realized it had just been a dream. I sat up in my bed wondering why I would have a dream like that. It had felt so real.

"Nina," Zay repeated, now fully annoyed.

"Yeah, yeah, I'm up," I hissed at him.

I thought about telling Ian about the dream, but it was really nothing more than that, a dream. Besides, my having a dream about Connor lying next to me would open an entirely different can of worms I'd rather keep shut.

As such, I decided it would be best to not mention the dream at all, and I just got ready for the day as normal and tried my best not to think about it.

Everything else was fairly normal, other than my brothers and I staying home from school. I made sure they both knew about Lavinia because I didn't want to keep any secrets from either of them. I was happy to hear that Lavinia had already told Ian, and Ian had told Zay.

By the end of the day, both Ian and Zay were getting as stir crazy as I was, so the three of us worked on convincing our parents to let us leave the house.

I was being extra nice and doing as many chores as I could around the house, not only to show my parents that I was okay but also to try to suck up. Everything they asked me to do, I did.

I was surprised when one of those things was letting my dad take blood samples from each of us. I thought he knew more than he was letting on, but I didn't want to argue with him and just wanted to get out of the house. I knew that if I fought him on it, he would use that as an excuse to keep us home, so I kept quiet.

However, Mom seemed to think it was just some illness. When she saw that my symptoms weren't getting any worse and that Ian and Zay had none, she joined our side regarding our at-home prison sentence. Thank goodness it was hard for Dad to say no to Mom. Eventually, they both agreed that all three of us could go back to school that Friday.

Ian, Zay, and I spent the next few days researching different types of creatures, and we used various avenues to figure out what the book said about them.

I discovered the languages of the entries for Quỷ đen, Νεφελίμ, and Seeungeheuer. Quỷ đen was Vietnamese for Black Demon, Νεφελίμ was Greek for Nephilim, and Seeungeheuer was German for Sea Monster.

Black Demon and Sea Monster were pretty self-explanatory, but I didn't readily know what a Nephilim was. From the drawing in the book, I thought it might be an archangel or fallen angel, but it turned out to be an angel hybrid. From what I'd read, the Nephilim could be male or female, but the mothers were always human, and the fathers were always angels.

It was all very fascinating but not entirely useful for what we needed right now. The only demon we found was the Black Demon, and when we got that entry translated, we learned it had nothing to do with our issues. The Black Demon was a supernatural creature that was born and not created, so again we had hit a dead end.

We were able to translate a few other entries ourselves because they were written in Spanish, but we still couldn't find what we needed.

We wrote down a few other names of creatures in different languages, including one with a bat next to a name written as βρυκόλακας. The style of the letters looked the same as the Nephilim entry, so I suggested it might be Greek.

Agreeing, Ian messaged the translator at the library we had used before and called it a night. I could only imagine what she thought we were doing.

When Friday morning finally arrived, I was nervous that Dad might back out of letting us leave the house, but he had already called our school to let them know we would be back that day and had even sent in our field trip permission slips. However, his one condition was that he had to drop us off and pick us up from the museum. While not the usual school policy,

Dad had explained to the school about my getting into a train accident on a previous field trip, so they allowed him to do it.

"So, you're just going to chaperone us?" I groaned.

"What? Are you embarrassed by your old man?" my dad chuckled.

I frowned at him, which prompted him to continue. "No, I have to catch up on some paperwork, and I can do that from anywhere. I will be at a coffee shop 10 minutes away," he said with a grin.

Zay was snickering at me, so I shot him an evil look. He didn't seem to care, and, for a second, I wished my eyes would turn that crazy magenta color. But I took that back right away. I knew if that happened, my parents would have never let me leave the house again.

I ran back up to my room to fix my hair and try to perfect my makeup. I was nervous to see Connor again. I touched my lips and smiled as I remembered our encounter at the hospital. Since we were going on a field trip, we didn't have to wear our uniforms, and I wanted to put on something special. But, as always, it was too cold to wear anything except pants.

I finally decided to wear the boots I had worn on my date with Aaron over black pants and a red long-sleeved shirt that showed off my figure. I quickly glanced at myself in the mirror and was more than satisfied with what I saw. My skin was very fair, but the powder-like complexion seemed to fit my features perfectly. I turned around to look at myself completely and smiled with satisfaction before running back down the stairs.

"Why are you wearing those boots?" Ian asked me with suspicion.

"Because I like them," I retorted.

"Your feet are going to hurt."

"I'll be fine," I countered as I grabbed my coat and snuck out the door before he could say anything else.

I was worried he would figure out there was something between me and Connor, so I needed to come up with a reason for the boots. I realized quickly I had a simple one. Anytime I go out, I try to look a little bit nicer, so I could just say I was wearing them because of the field trip.

Satisfied with my holstered explanation, I took my seat next to my dad and waited to be questioned again. However, Ian didn't bring it up. In fact, no one said anything during the entire car ride. Zay passed out, Ian was listening to music, my dad was on a conference call, and I was daydreaming about Connor.

We arrived at the museum almost an hour later after taking Zay to school. Dad dropped us off by the main entrance. We said our goodbyes and promised him we would be in the same spot at the end of the day.

We had already let Becca and Alex know we were being dropped off, so they were waiting for us by the ticket booth. They gave us our admission bracelets, and we flashed them to the security guard as we walked past the entrance of the museum.

When we found our group, I looked around for Connor, but I was disappointed when I saw Ms. Adams, one of the other history teachers at our school. She hurried us toward the first exhibit where a museum employee had already begun speaking.

I peered into the enormous glass case standing behind him at what looked like a unicorn. It wasn't just a drawing either; it was a large stuffed white horse with a horn protruding from the middle of its forehead. I was astonished to see that the creature had a silver mane and tail.

I tried to think back to my dream, but I only remembered seeing horses. As far as I remembered, they hadn't had horns. I looked back at it, amazed by the detail. This unicorn was most definitely fake, but it had been meticulously crafted, right down to dirt on its hooves and a damp look to the mane. Poised with all its weight on its hind legs, the creature looked enormous, much bigger than a normal horse.

As the day continued, we learned more about different fantastical creatures from around the world, but none of them were demons. Knowing that Ian and I couldn't explore together, because two of us gone would be noticed by Ms. Adams, we took turns going off on our own. Both Becca and Alex were happy to cover for us.

When it was my turn to venture out on my own, I snuck away quietly and turned the corner into a different exhibit that instantly filled me with awe. The room was full of enormous stone statues of the Greek gods.

The first one I came to was Zeus; he was seated in a large, rigid armchair and was holding a staff in the shape of a lightning bolt. He had long hair that flowed past his shoulders, and he wore a toga and sandals.

I read the description, which had all the information I already knew, but one thing piqued my interest that I hadn't known before. It read:

*The only god Zeus feared was Nyx, the goddess of night.*

I quickly looked around the room to try to find a statue of the goddess Nyx. I didn't really know what she looked like, so I went up to every goddess I saw and couldn't help reading a little bit about them.

*Achelois: A minor moon goddess whose name means "she who washes away pain."*

*Alcyone: One of the seven Pleiades and daughter of Atlas and Pleione. She bore several children with the god Poseidon.*

*Alectrona: An early goddess of the Sun, daughter of Helios and Rhode, and possibly goddess of the morning.*

*Amphitrite: Goddess of the sea, wife of Poseidon and a Nereid.*

*Antheia: Goddess of gardens, flowers, swamps, and marshes.*

With so many statues, I was starting to get overwhelmed, but then finally I found her.

*One of the oldest deities in the universe, Nyx was born in the first moments of creation from the yawning abyss of Chaos. Nyx was the personification of night and was so ancient and powerful that even the mighty Zeus was afraid to cross her. As an Olympian deity, Nyx possessed supernatural attributes, such as immense strength, durability, speed, flight, and enhanced reflexes. Being a night goddess, she could wield the darkness and shadows in physical ways, including blinding someone or turning herself into a shadow. Her physical form was both beautiful and frightening, with dark blue skin and five large, magenta eyes.*

"Magenta eyes!" I said out loud then covered my mouth quickly.

I looked around to see if anyone had heard me. When I saw that no one else was around, I looked back at the statue of Nyx.

*Was this why the bookmark had been placed on the page in the book?* I wondered.

I continued reading, anxious to maybe find out what was happening to me. I skimmed through most of the description until I found something I thought was more relevant.

Legend has it that, through the children of Nyx, powerful beings were created to fight against a great evil. These creatures were said to be very powerful and only weakened by the Sun.

As I read, I began to feel lightheaded, and a familiar scent wafted through the air. I whipped around to see Connor standing behind me. A silence settled between us, pregnant with unspoken emotions. His expression carried a mix of worry and inner conflict.

Drawing closer, he sighed and lifted his hand up to my face. I responded by tenderly caressing his hand as it lay against my cheek then he moved his hand to my belly. Nervous excitement played on his lips as he continued to rub me there, revealing a peculiar blend of apprehension and anticipation.

His actions left me a bit puzzled, but as I gazed into his bewitching eyes, all confusion faded away.

"There is something I need to tell you," he confessed with some reluctance.

I could sense the turmoil inside him, but it was becoming challenging to concentrate on anything with him touching me. I ached for him, but I realized that it wasn't just a physical pain. It was also fear about what he might reveal. Despite my desire to kiss him again, he seemed poised to share something that might involve him leaving. I simply nodded and braced myself for the impending revelation.

"I was the one who sent you the book, *Invisible Truth*," he admitted nervously.

"What?" As if a spell had been broken, I looked up at him and stepped back. I couldn't believe what I was hearing.

"I'm sorry. It wasn't supposed to be this way," he said shyly. "I was supposed to help you, but instead I just complicated things," he apologized even as his eyes wandered back down toward my stomach. "I was sent to guide you. I wasn't supposed to interfere in your life."

"What are you talking about? And why do you keep staring at my stomach?" I asked anxiously.

Connor didn't answer me. He just looked down at me and pulled my lips to his. The kiss only lasted for a few seconds, but it left me speechless.

He pulled away from me then grabbed my hand as he said, "Let's sit down over here. There's a story I need to tell you."

Connor led me toward a bench in the middle of the room. As we sat down, he put his elbows on his knees and rested his face in his palms then rubbed his eyes before looking at me again. I wasn't sure what he was going to say, but he looked very nervous.

"Just tell me," I urged him sweetly.

He cleared his throat and started. "Okay, I understand that this might sound unbelievable, but bear with me. A long time ago, in the early days of the world before any recorded human history, there was a war. The conflict wasn't between humans but something much more powerful, the Olympian gods. This war spanned centuries and devastated many species, including fairies, minotaurs, and ogres. By 429 BC, it seemed endless, prompting an unknown being to intervene."

Connor paused to let that sink in then continued, "This being cast a very powerful curse that granted three human men god-like powers to end the war. However, these men became ruthless and soulless creatures without remorse, and they began taking down soldiers from both sides with ease."

The sadness of his words was evident as he went on. "At the time, these men had no names, but centuries later they would come to be known as vampires. No one actually knows who created them; some say it was Hades, others say it was Ares. What *is* known is that only a being of evil could have created something of their nature. But no matter which god was responsible for their creation, they still would have needed the help of a dark sorceress. Even so, no one ever claimed credit, probably because they could not control the creatures."

He shifted in his seat as if fatigued by it all, but he pressed on. "The vampires, armed with the power of creation, turned soldiers from both sides into creatures of the night to form a formidable vampire army. The gods, fearing the vampires' dominance, realized they needed help to fight this new threat, but they didn't know what to do. When it seemed as though all hope was lost and the world would belong to these ravenous, unconscionable demons, Muminah, the most powerful sorceress of the time, stepped in and went to the goddess Nyx for help."

My attention homed in on his mention of the goddess.

"Nyx wanted no part of the war, so she had stayed far away from the battles. But Muminah believed that, as the goddess of the night, Nyx was the only one who could create something that could stand against the vampires. After much persuasion, Nyx agreed that the bloodshed was too much, and it was time to help. With a complex enchantment, the blood of Molech, and the blood of the goddess, together they were able to forge something to battle the demons ravishing the world."

I was about to sit back in relief, but Connor was going on. "In a desperate bid to stem the tide of vampiric tyranny, Nyx and Muminah faced a harrowing choice: Unleash a new breed of darkness or succumb to the relentless onslaught of the undead. With heavy hearts, they forged the nyxlings from the very essence of Nyx herself, sacrificing her strongest progeny to imbue the creatures with unmatched power. Despite Nyx's agonizing reluctance, Muminah pressed on, knowing that only by harnessing the bloodline of her kin could they hope to tip the scales in humanity's favor. Thus, from the crucible of divine sacrifice, the nyxlings arose, bearing the mantle of saviors burdened by the weight of eternity. These creatures were bestowed with all the superior abilities of the vampires: heightened senses, increased speed and strength, rapid healing, and, of course, immortality."

Connor took a deep breath then continued, "However, as with any spell, where there are strengths, there are weaknesses. Both nyxlings and vampires have vulnerability to sunlight, bloodlust, and death from a pierced heart. To become a nyxling, one must have the blood of the goddess in the body at death. But not only that; the person also must be part of the goddess's bloodline. While vampires have the power to turn anyone, they lack control. The smell of blood can change them into rabid beasts, unpredictable and uncontrollable. Although nyxlings have the same bloodlust and need blood to survive, they are able to retain most of their emotions and control over themselves."

Connor sat up straight and placed his hand over his heart. "As to the piercing of the heart, a wooden stake will kill a vampire, but only a dagger made of Celestial Gold will kill a nyxling. Once the gods learned that wooden stakes to the heart could defeat vampires, the tables turned quickly, and it didn't take very long to stop their devastation. Vampires were killed almost to extinction," he explained.

He paused to look at me then lightly took my hand before continuing. "As the gods and nyxlings united against the vampires, a truce was struck. Nyx agreed to provide one descendant from every century to be transformed into a nyxling. In return, the gods promised not to victimize Nyx's line."

I couldn't even speak with all this information, but luckily Connor was going on.

"Nyx trusted some of the gods, but not all of them. Each god had a special purpose that would benefit the world of the humans. It was their job to protect them, but some of the gods only cared about themselves. To ensure security for her descendants, Nyx went to Muminah for help. The sorceress took pity on her, understanding the loss of family from the war, so she created a spell that would help the nyxlings by giving extraordinary and unique powers to three creatures of the same species. She called this spell Talaatah. The chosen trio would be able to take on any foe as long as they stayed together."

"Talaatah," I tried out the name on my tongue.

Connor nodded and went on, "The first would be given enhanced hearing that could even penetrate others' thoughts, no matter the species. The second would be bestowed with incredible strength and near invulnerability with strong, nearly impenetrable skin, making weaknesses no more than an annoyance. The third would have the power of consciousness and dream manipulation to control any type of creature or create dreams for them. The only thing these powers could not affect were the other two who were part of Talaatah."

Connor rushed on to explain, "Nyx was reluctant to give such great power to three individuals, but Muminah explained that this spell would only be triggered in light of a great threat. The goddess and sorceress collected the blood of every creature, including nyxlings and vampires, then cast the spell in secret on a night when the moon was at its brightest to siphon the rays of the moonlight, which was key to producing enough power for the spell. Of course, legends spread and books were written foretelling the Talaatah prophecy, but no one could ever prove it. Over time, humans gained power over the world, and supernatural beings were all but forgotten. Most of the creatures still lived among the humans, so, naturally, stories were told and movies were made, but everyone believed it all to be fiction," Connor finished with a sigh.

"Wow, that's quite a story," I finally said timidly, completely over-whelmed with my head spinning. "It's all very interesting, but I'm not really sure what it all has to do with me."

Connor pulled his hand away from mine then placed it on my leg but then quickly pulled it away and clasped his hands together between his own legs.

"It has been more than 2,000 years since all this happened. For the last 500 years, Nyx's descendants have been targeted because of the prophecy. Someone has been trying to transform humans believed to be descendants of Nyx, thinking that the prophecy can only be about nyxlings. It was figured out that if a descendent of Nyx dies with the blood of a nyxling in them, they are transformed. However, they did not take into account that, with every new birth, the blood of the goddess is diluted. So, even if a human is descended from Nyx, there is only a 50/50 chance they will become a nyxling. Whoever is doing this doesn't care about those odds."

Connor paused and looked me in the eye. "And that's where I come in. For so long, all Nyx could do was watch from the heavens with no access to the human world and pray someone would help her family. I..." he hesitated, "I am able to speak to gods and humans," he said nervously. "My mother was human, but my father was an—"

"An angel! You are a Nephilim," I interrupted.

He nodded and took my hand.

"So, I am a nyxling?"

"No, you are still human, but you are transitioning into a nyxling," he corrected. "But you don't have to be a nyxling. I wanted you to know everything before you made the choice. I don't care if that isn't what I was sent here to do. I needed you to know. If you do go through the change, it will not be easy. You are a 'grandchild' of Nyx, but there are thousands of greats before that title. We don't know how the change will affect you or even if the change will happen. It would be safer if you stayed human."

He looked at me, and I knew what his choice would be, but I wasn't sure what I wanted. Having the abilities of nyxlings sounded amazing, but the probability was not good. Even if it did work, my bloodlust could be different than that of original nyxlings.

"Are there any other nyxlings? Someone who survived the change?" I asked.

"Nyxlings are very rare. If there are any in the world, I don't know about them. I'm not sure if anyone knows about them."

"Okay, but why did you say before that you were sorry?" I implored quietly.

"Because I'm supposed to be your teacher, and I don't just mean at the high school. I wasn't even supposed to tell you all this until you turned, but

I needed you to know. I want you to have a choice; and to have that choice, you needed to know all the facts. I was told of a possible nyxling birth in Hallowed Hills, so I came to the town as a high school teacher. I was tasked to be the nyxling's guide, to make sure that after the transformation, they had all the knowledge they needed to stop whomever was responsible for murdering Nyx's descendants. I never imagined I would..." he paused for a few seconds, "feel the way I do about you," he finished.

I placed my hand over his and moved closer to him. "You don't have to be sorry."

He looked at me and smiled. "I am way too old for you, Nina."

"You're not that much older than me."

"I am older than I look," he said with a chuckle. "You should be with someone with whom you can have a future, maybe a smart and attractive quarterback," he said warily.

*Did he know about Aaron?* I blushed and looked down.

He lifted my chin toward him again. "It's okay. You should live your life," he said.

"Why?"

"Because he is better for you."

"He's a warlock," I blurted out then bit my lip. I hadn't meant to say that. I wasn't sure whether Nephilim and warlocks got along, so I could have just put Aaron and his family in danger. If so, I would never forgive myself.

"It's still better than a Nephilim. You can have a long, normal—well semi-normal—human life with him. I am only supposed to stay here to help with your transition or until the blood passes through your system," he said as he looked away.

"What do you mean 'passes through my system'?"

"Right now, there is nyxling blood in your system, but that blood gets diluted more and more with each passing day. When you were given the blood, you would have gotten very sick, but the minute the blood entered your system, it activated the nyxling gene to create the chance for the transformation. However, with no nyxling blood in your system, the chances are minuscule. When there is no more blood in your system, it means that it has passed through your body. In addition to lessening the chance of transformation, with no nyxling blood, your extraordinary abilities will start to fade until they completely disappear."

"So, you are just going to leave?" I asked, fixating on what he had said before.

"Not right away, but there are rules that need to be followed. Us being together breaks all those rules."

I knew at that moment I wouldn't be able to say anything to change his mind, so I dropped the subject while still planning to bring it up again in the future.

"Why were you so mean to me during history? Everyone else who was in your class said you were so nice."

Connor laughed. "I was mad at you," he confessed with a grin.

"Why? What did I do?" I asked in confusion.

"I was mad because I was so attracted to you. I've been around beautiful women before, but you were different, and I couldn't get you out of my mind. I tried my best to stay away, and part of that was pushing you away. But since I had to treat everyone else the same, I decided to be... well, stricter with the class you were in."

I thought about that for a moment. It seemed kind of childish, but I couldn't say I wouldn't have done the same thing if I were in his shoes.

"But then you changed," I said in realization.

"Yes," he laughed. "Your presence overtook my senses, so I needed you to see me," he said sheepishly.

"See you? Do you mean physically? Is that why you took off your glasses and baggy clothes?"

"Yes," he smiled shyly.

I looked at him now in his white fitted shirt and gray pants, which made his physique look powerful. Then I took in his entire appearance, thinking back to when he'd said he was too old for me. I was curious whether Nephilim aged, but then I realized they were born, so he must have meant he was only a few years older than me.

"What are you, like six years older than me?"

Connor looked at me then turned away. "I was born in 1926," he said hesitantly.

"You are 81, no wait, 83 years old?" I gasped.

He nodded his head shyly.

"Well, I don't care," I said sternly as I stood up.

As though a floodgate of relief had been opened, Connor rose from his seat as well and drew me into his intoxicating embrace. As his lips met mine, the warmth and perfection of them enveloped me as his hands encircled my waist and he drew me closer. With deliberate slowness, he traced his lips along the contours of my jawline and down my neck, igniting a flutter in my heart and a warmth that permeated my entire being.

"My enchanting goddess," he said as he pulled his lips off my neck.

"What did you just call me?" I gasped, vividly remembering the dream I'd had a few nights before.

"I'm sorry," he said shyly and pulled away from me.

"No, it's not that," I said quickly, realizing how my question must have sounded. Quickly, I told him what I had dreamed and that he had called me the same thing right before he'd died. "But you are an angel, so you can't die," I concluded.

"I can die, but there's only one blade that can kill me," he explained. "That blade hasn't been seen for centuries."

"Why do you look so young?"

Connor laughed then continued, "Nephilim age up to a certain point, but we don't all stop aging the same. Some, like me, stop aging in their 20s, but others continue to age until their 40s. We don't know why exactly. Some think it has to do with the age of our mothers when we were conceived, but it's never been proven."

I had so many other questions to ask him, but he started to back away from me. "What are you doing?"

"People are coming in," he whispered as our entire class stepped into the room.

I knew I couldn't ask him anything else with everyone watching, so I went to join my classmates, sneaking into the crowd without anyone seeing. It was then that I noticed Ian wasn't with the group.

"Where's Ian?" I asked Becca.

"He's right..." she said as she turned around and saw he wasn't there. "Huh, I have no idea," she said, baffled as she continued to look around. "Wait, where's Alex? And who was that you were talking to?"

"It was Con... Mr. Conrad," I corrected myself.

"Mr. Conrad!?!" she exclaimed. "I knew he was cute, but since when has he looked like that?"

"What do you mean?" I asked nonchalantly. "He just took off his glasses."

"What is he, some kind of wizard?" she asked with a huge grin on her face.

I laughed with her, knowing she wasn't much off the mark. I looked around to find him, but he was nowhere to be seen. As I searched the room, I saw Ian and Alex standing in the doorway. Becca and I walked toward them.

"Hey! Where have you guys been?" I asked but soon figured it out when I saw that Ian had two hotdogs in one hand and a huge fountain drink in the other.

"Hungry," Ian said with a mouth full of hotdog.

I scrunched my nose at his full mouth then turned to Alex. "You weren't hungry?"

"Yes, I was. I just don't eat like a grizzly bear who just came out of hibernation," he laughed. "I don't know how you are not 500 pounds, man," he added to Ian.

Alex joined the rest of the group with Becca while I waited for Ian to finish eating since food wasn't allowed in the gallery.

"Are you done yet?" I asked impatiently.

"What's the big deal?" he asked.

I stepped aside to show him what was in the room. His eyes lit up, and he pushed his remaining food and drink into my arms.

"Hey!" I shouted as he walked into the room without me. I stood there, fully annoyed, when I suddenly started feeling lightheaded again. But it was a pain I was happy to have.

I turned around with a smile on my face. "Aaron?" I said with surprise.

He looked utterly amazing, and his mesmerizing blue eyes rendered me momentarily speechless. Despite my intention to be angry with him, I found myself unable to resist him when he delicately caressed my hand with his fingertips.

"Hey, Nina," he murmured shyly as he withdrew his fingers from my hand.

"What are you doing here?" I asked.

"Class trip," he replied with a half grin. "I need to get back to my class, but I wanted to talk to you. I want you to know that Amanda transferred to CWA, but not for the reasons you may think."

"Okay. Why then?"

He sighed. "She was attacked by something in Hallowed Hills, something our kind has been feuding with for centuries."

"Please, just tell me," I pleaded with him when he didn't continue.

"I can't," he said.

He might as well have told me that it was not his secret to tell. I turned around and started walking away, but he jumped in front of me before I could go anywhere.

"Please, don't," he pleaded.

"Listen, Aaron, I'm starting to get a headache, so if you're done, I'm going to go back with my class. I get it. She moved closer to you to be with you. Just please leave me alone," I said past the lump in my throat.

As much as I'd tried not to care for him, I couldn't help it. The way he smelled drove me wild, both in good and bad ways. I thought back to the first time I'd seen him at Luna's. No one had ever caught my attention the way he had... at least until I'd really seen Connor. Frustration consumed me; I detested feeling so strongly for two different guys.

"No! I'm transferring back to VP this month," Aaron said, immediately snapping me back to reality.

"You are?" I asked quietly. "Why?"

"I think you know why," he said with a smile. "When I left your house, I realized I wasn't willing to lose you. So, I told my mom I would be transferring back to VP and ending things with Amanda. I'm 18 now, so I don't need my parents' permission to switch schools." He shrugged. "She was mad at first, of course, but she really couldn't say much about it since she married my dad. She just said that if I was going to live in Hallowed Hills, I had to wear the protective cologne our family makes."

He paused briefly then continued, "Anyway, yesterday was the first time I'd seen Amanda since the bonfire, and I told her I couldn't be with her. We'd talked over the phone since then, and I could tell she wasn't herself, but I didn't know what had happened to her. I spoke with my parents about her, and they told me what was wrong."

"Did Alan attack her, too?"

"You know about Alan?" he asked in surprise. I nodded, and he continued. "Alan says it wasn't him, but I don't believe that." He paused. "What do you know about him?"

"I know he's a vampire," I said quickly, so tired of all the secrets.

Aaron looked at me in shock.

"And I found out what I am, too. Well, at least what I am transitioning into."

"You did?"

"Yes. It's called a nyxling, but if the blood passes through my system, then I stay human."

"How long does that take?"

"It..." I stopped to think about that for a second and realized Connor had never told me that part. "I'm not sure," I confessed after a brief silence.

At that moment, Ian came back and took his food from me. I was surprised when he didn't say anything to Aaron and just went to sit down on a bench to finish eating.

Aaron's teacher then started to wave him back toward his group, so he had to go, but he promised he would come to my house the next day.

After Aaron left, I sat down with Ian and told him everything Connor had told me and about what he was. Of course, I left out the romantic part because I didn't want Ian knowing, and it wasn't relevant anyway.

Ian found the statue of Nyx and read about the magenta eyes to confirm for himself that the change had something to do with her. He then also told me he had already talked to Aaron and knew he had broken it off with Amanda. That explained why, when he saw us talking, he had been okay with it.

Ian then showed me a notebook with all his notes from the day. I scanned through the pages and saw a bunch of different handwriting styles. Suddenly I realized why there were a few blank pages after the nyxling entry in the book, *Invisible Truth*. It was an ongoing story meant for more information to be constantly added. I told myself I would add to the nyxling entry when I made it home.

Dad picked us up from the museum then we went to go pick up Zay, who read through Ian's notebook while we drove home. Ian was texting on his phone with a huge grin on his face, so I figured it was with Lavinia. Feeling pretty tired, I fell asleep.

It took even longer to get home with all the traffic, but when we finally did, I ran straight upstairs to write in the book. With so much information, I didn't know where to start, so I just began to write.

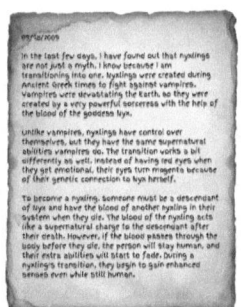

I still had so many things to ask Connor, including the time it took for the blood to pass through. I didn't want to add much more right now because the rest didn't necessarily have to do just with nyxlings, so I closed the book and crawled into bed.

I had so many thoughts running through my mind that it was very difficult to fall asleep. I couldn't stop thinking about Connor, but I also couldn't stop thinking of Aaron either. I was deeply immersed in all those thoughts when a knock at my window made me jump.

Peering over at the window, I saw that it was Alan. Getting up from the bed, I opened the window and took a few steps back then stared at him with arms crossed. "I am not inviting you in," I said sternly.

"Fair enough."

"Why are you here? Did you kill my friends?"

"That highly depends on who your friends are," he said noncommittally.

"Good night, Alan," I said as I moved to close the window.

"I'm joking. No, I haven't killed anyone, at least not for a long time."

"What do you want then?"

"I heard that you spoke with Lavinia."

"Yes, she told me what you are and that you're a bounty hunter."

"Gotta make a living somehow," he said with a smirk. "I just wanted to tell you to be careful. Not everyone is who they seem."

"What does that mean?"

He looked at me for a moment, seeming almost conflicted. I had never seen him like that before.

"Alan?"

"You don't have to let me in, but maybe you can come out here for a minute?" he said seriously. Then he immediately followed that up with a teasing, "I promise I won't bite."

I wasn't sure why, but I agreed and climbed out into the tree with him.

"A few months ago, I received a call from one of my colleagues who said a threat was coming to Hallowed Hills. I told my family, so they moved out of town so I could investigate. However, I couldn't find anything that might be a threat, and the only thing new to the town was your family."

"My family?"

"Yes. My family might be a bunch of jerks, but they are still my family. My colleague claimed that your family was part of a community that hunted witches, and if you and your brothers weren't dealt with, the magic community would be at risk. I had no reason not to believe him, so I started following you and your brothers." He paused for a moment, looking at me anew. "But when I saw you, I couldn't believe how much you reminded me of Maria."

"Who's Maria?"

"She's the one who turned me."

"The one that you..."

I stopped talking as he turned away at the obviously painful memory. He turned back to me and seemed to be trying hard to contain his emotions. I placed my hand over his.

He cleared his throat and continued, "The more I followed you, the more things didn't add up, so I called my colleague again. That's when I found out he was killed the night after he told me about your family."

"So, what does that mean?"

"I think someone wants you and your brothers dead, but for different reasons than I was led to believe."

"So now what?"

"Now, I find out why I was lied to," he said with a look back toward my room. "You better get back in. Someone is walking toward your door."

"Thank you," I said then gave him an unexpected hug.

"Go on. We wouldn't want you to get in trouble," he said with a half-smile.

I jumped back into my room and quickly turned on my TV then snuck into my bed. The door opened slowly, and my mom peeked her head in. When she saw I was in bed, she closed the door again and left.

I lay there thinking about what Alan had said and wondered who could have told him those things. I had no answers.

Not wanting to think about it anymore, I flipped through the channels until I found something to take my mind off all the new questions from the day. I eventually came across an episode of *The X-Files*, so I started to watch it, and the crazy storylines helped me start to get sleepy. Finally, I was able to fall asleep.

# CHAPTER 17
## THE HOUR OF DEATH

The next day, I happily awoke to a text from Aaron. I hadn't wanted to admit it, but I was starting to think Connor might be right. Aaron was my age, and he was human, so maybe he *was* better for me. As long as the nyxling blood passed through me, the chances of my becoming one were almost zero.

I was anxious to find out how long it took for the blood to pass through my system, but I had no way to contact Connor. The only thing I could do was wait until Monday when I saw him in school.

Aaron's text had said he would be at my house in a few hours, so I jumped out of bed and started getting ready. I was excited to see that the sun was shining brightly outside, so I opened the window and delighted in the feel the warm air as it came into the room.

I grabbed my phone and raced to my closet to try to find the perfect thing to wear. While I searched, I decided to call Lavinia and tell her everything I had learned about nyxlings.

"Hello?" she answered.

"Hey, Lavinia, it's Nina. Well, you know it's Nina, duh. Anyway, I have news!" I rambled.

"Hey, Nina," Lavinia laughed.

"So, my school went on a field trip to the Museum of Mythical Creatures, and I learned so much, but the best part is that I finally figured out what I am transitioning into."

"You did? What?" she asked excitedly.

"It's called a nyxling. They're descendants of the goddess Nyx and are sort of like—"

"Oh, my god," she cut me off.

"What?"

"Nothing. I just feel kind of dumb. Duh. Nyx has magenta eyes. I know a bit about the Greek gods, so, ugh, I should have known that. I thought nyxlings were just a myth, so I didn't even think about it."

"You've heard of nyxlings?"

"Yes, but only in stories. The last I heard, they disappeared along with the Olympian gods."

"Oh, well that's weird. So then how could I have gotten their blood in my system?"

"No clue. I've always put nyxlings in the same basket as unicorns. They may have existed at one time, but they are no longer around," she answered then paused. "Wait, you found all this information at the museum?" she questioned.

"Well, sort of," I answered sheepishly.

"What do you mean by 'sort of'?"

"Well, there might be this guy..."

"Aaron?"

"No, not Aaron."

"Oh, sounds juicy. Who?"

"His name is Connor."

"Who is that?"

"Well..."

"Nina? What? Is he some kind of serial killer or something?" she asked when I didn't continue.

"No, definitely not a serial killer."

"Then what?" she pressed.

"He's my history teacher," I said finally after another long pause.

"Okay. What is so scandalous about that? Sure, it's odd he knows so much about nyxlings, but isn't that what teachers do? Teach?" she asked. "Nina?" she asked again when I didn't answer.

"Well, there may have been a kiss... or two," I revealed.

"Wait, what?" she asked excitedly. "Well, *that* certainly is scandalous," she giggled.

"He is... I don't know. He just... I can't explain how I feel around him, but he's my teacher."

"How old is he?" she asked curiously.

"Um... I never asked, but he looks like he's in his early or maybe mid-20s."

"Oh, so he's fairly young," she said with a bit of relief in her voice.

"What? Did you think that he was like 42?" I giggled.

"Well, I don't know. You said he was your teacher, so I just pictured my teachers from my school years," she chuckled. "So, are you guys together?"

"No," I answered disappointedly.

"Is it the age thing?"

"I don't know. I guess. He did say I would be better off with someone my own age, but the way he looks at me..." I trailed off then snapped back to the conversation. "I have never had a guy look at me like that before."

"He told you that you would be better off with someone else?"

"Yeah," I answered. When a long silence followed, I pressed her for more. "What Lavinia? What does that mean?"

"I don't know, Nina. Maybe it is the age thing, or maybe he feels that it's wrong because you are his student, but in my experience if a guy is telling you to be with someone else, it's most likely he is trying to let you down gently."

I thought about that for a moment. Maybe that was true, or maybe it really was because he was a Nephilim. I didn't know, but I wasn't going to tell Lavinia about that, at least not yet.

"What about Aaron?" Lavinia asked.

"He said he broke up with his girlfriend and he's switching schools, but I don't know."

"Switching schools? What do you mean?"

"He's returning to VP."

"To be with you?"

"That's what he implied."

"You don't sound so sure," Lavinia observed.

"Aaron is a great guy, but he scares me," I admitted.

"It sounds like you really like him and are afraid he's going to hurt you. That's normal," she reassured me. "Honestly, without knowing Connor, and even knowing how Aaron's family feels about outsiders, I think Aaron would be the better choice for you."

"How much do you know about his family?"

"A lot," she laughed. "The Carriers are a very powerful coven," she finished.

"Oh, so you know."

"Yes. Alan was a warlock before he changed. Warlocks are born, so his family must be full of warlocks, too," she explained.

"Oh, right. Duh."

"Hey, I want to get a bit of sleep, but I'll come over as soon as the sun goes down," she said with a yawn.

"Oh, yeah, right. Go get some sleep."

"Okay, see you in a bit."

As I hung up the phone, I started to think. I was so happy to have Lavinia in my life. Even though I hadn't known her for very long, I trusted her, and I knew she trusted me. Plus, I could talk to her without feeling embarrassed. I had always wanted a sister, and with Lavinia I felt like I had one.

I decided to take a quick shower before getting dressed, but while I was in there, I started feeling a bit nauseous, so I stayed in the bathroom until the feeling passed.

When I walked out of the bathroom, I almost ran straight into Zay as he sped past my door.

"Hey, where are you off to so fast?" I asked.

"Going to the park with some buddies to play football."

"Where is everyone else?"

"Umm, Ian is downstairs, Mom had to meet with a client, and Dad went to meet one of his friends from the hospital for coffee," he answered as he rushed off.

We didn't get many nice days after the end of July, so I didn't blame him for wanting to take advantage of the nice weather.

With Zay departed, I focused again on my wardrobe. I knew that the weather probably wouldn't last, so I still had to wear jeans, but I wanted to wear a nice shirt with that. I searched through my closet until I saw a little bit of royal blue fabric hanging in the back.

I pushed the rest of the clothes to the side and brought out a fitted razorback tank top with spaghetti straps. It had a low neckline, and it scrunched up in the middle of the chest. It was the shirt I'd worn the first time we went to Luna's. Of course, I'd had to wear a sweater over it because it had ended up being too cold, but I'd still worn it.

This time, I wouldn't have to wear anything over it with how beautiful the day was, so I put on the shirt with black pants and black pumps.

When I looked in the mirror, it seemed like something was missing, so I went to search through my jewelry. It didn't take long for me to find the perfect necklace: a long silver chain with little circles all around it that I could wrap to make it look like I wore two necklaces.

I put it on then started on my hair. As I added some curls to it, I started thinking about Aaron and how I felt about him. The butterflies surged in my stomach as I daydreamed about him.

But then, of course, I thought about Connor. I knew I had feelings for him, too, but I wondered why being with him made me feel lightheaded. I knew I was lightheaded around Aaron because of the cologne he wore that was mixed with a potion.

Curiosity got the better of me, so as soon as I finished my hair and makeup, I pulled the book out from under my bed and looked for the translation of the Nephilim entry. I found the page I had stuck into it with the translation. I hadn't read the entire entry before because I hadn't needed to, but now I read through the paper until something caught my eye.

The sweat of a Nephilim is very potent and can cause dark creatures to become weak and even experience diminished abilities. This is why witches and warlocks use the substance to create potions. In addition to serving as a defense mechanism, Nephilim sweat is a very powerful pheromone, similar to that produced by vampires, only much stronger. These pheromones make Nephilim irresistible to many creatures and can promote feelings of love or infatuation.

After reading that, I didn't know what to think. Were my feelings for Connor just caused by those pheromones? And since Aaron wore the cologne, were my feelings for him because of that as well? I didn't want to believe it, convinced that my feelings for them both were real.

I continued reading through the page when I heard the doorbell ring. Realizing I had lost track of time, I sprinted down the stairs and pushed Ian out of the way to open the door.

"Geez!" Ian exclaimed as he stepped back.

I opened the door with a smile on my face, and Aaron was standing in the doorway smiling right back at me. I noticed immediately that he didn't have his cologne on, and I was very grateful for that.

"That color blue looks beautiful on you," he commented as he stared at me.

I was happy he had noticed, so I smiled coyly at him as he walked into the house.

Ian was standing behind me regarding us.

"Hey, man," Aaron said to Ian.

Ian nodded at Aaron before walking toward him. They were about the same height, so they stood at eye level while they stared at each other. That's when I realized Ian had grown several inches in the last few weeks. I wondered if that was because of the nyxling blood or just a regular human growth spurt.

"Treat my sister right," he snarled.

"Sorry," I mouthed.

Aaron shook his head as if saying not to worry about it.

"At least he didn't assault you this time," I added after Ian walked into the kitchen.

We both laughed, then I grabbed his hand and pulled him into the living room. Even though my parents weren't home, I didn't want to be alone with him in my bedroom in case they came home while he was here.

We sat down, and I turned on the TV, stopping at the first movie I saw. I didn't know what it was, but the scene showed warriors wearing what looked like ancient Roman armor in the middle of a battle.

"I don't understand this movie," I laughed.

"Well, that's probably because we started watching it in the middle," he chuckled.

"Probably. Do you know what movie it is?"

He leaned in closer, his touch sending shivers down my spine as one hand rested gently on my thigh while the other tenderly caressed my cheek. "Honestly, I'm more interested in you than any movie," he confessed as his gaze locked with mine.

His thumb brushed softly against my lips before our mouths met in a tender yet passionate kiss. Heat surged between us as the embrace grew more intense and his hands roamed from my face to the curve of my neck. I found myself tangling my fingers in his hair, drawing him closer until he was pressed against me.

Breathless and dizzy with desire, I reluctantly pulled away, our lips lingering just inches apart. "My brother is in the kitchen," I gasped, my heart still racing from our heated exchange.

"I know," he whispered then sighed. "I just needed to kiss you."

"What happened to your cologne?" I asked when I could form words again.

"My grandmother made me a pendant with the potion, but I left it in the car to come into the house."

I smiled at him then thought about that. I wasn't fully transformed, so I had no bloodlust. Initially, I hadn't understood why he'd worn it around me, but then I remembered there were other dark creatures living in Hallowed Hills. Maybe it wasn't about me at all.

"Do you have any other plans this weekend?" I asked coyly.

"I'm hoping to spend the weekend with you. I actually wanted to ask you a question," he said shyly.

"Okay."

"I was wondering if you wanted to come to my house tomorrow to meet my parents."

"Your parents?"

"Yes."

I felt excited and nervous at the same time, so I just stared at him dumbly.

"You don't want to meet my parents?" he asked with a chuckle.

"It's not that. It's just... well, maybe we can wait a few days? Or weeks? I just want this blood thing out of me before I meet them."

Aaron smiled and pulled my hand into his lap. "My parents know what you are."

"You told them?" I gasped.

"Well, my uncle is a vampire, so they are 100% okay with a nyxling," he laughed.

I frowned at him, not thinking it was as funny as he did. Technically a nyxling was still a demon, and witches and warlocks were not too fond of demons.

"I didn't think your family cared for demons," I voiced.

"No, but you are a very cute demon," he laughed.

"Not funny."

"A little bit funny," he smiled.

I smiled back at him and playfully punched his shoulder, then he put his arm around me and kissed my forehead. I pulled myself into his chest, letting myself indulge in the scent of his skin without the potion.

"So, what time should I pick you up tomorrow?" he asked playfully.

I looked at him with wide eyes then couldn't resist answering. "Whatever time you want," I said, before burying my head back into his chest.

"Hey, I know you guys are all lovey-dovey again," Ian said brashly as he walked into the living room, "but we still don't know who was trying to turn us into nyxlings."

I scowled at that harsh reminder of our reality. "I just want this stuff out of me. I don't want to worry about it anymore."

"Yeah, but even if the blood passes through us," Ian countered, "we still don't know how it got there in the first place. Who's to say that whoever did it the first time won't do it again?"

I sighed because I knew Ian was right. We needed to figure out who had done this to us and couldn't just ignore the fact that someone wanted us to change into nyxlings.

Still, I protested, "I just want to be a normal teenager. I only want to stress about the normal things, like school and soccer."

"Too bad," Ian retorted.

"Don't you have anything better to do?" I asked Ian as he made himself comfortable in the armchair next to us.

"Nope," he responded around a mouthful of food.

"Why don't you go call Lavinia or something?"

"I talked to her already. She will be here after—" Ian stopped abruptly and looked at Aaron. "She will be here a bit later," he finished then continued eating.

"Let's go for a walk," I suggested, intertwining my fingers with Aaron's and guiding him toward the front door.

In addition to the walk being a way for us to be alone, the day was so beautiful that I didn't want to waste it indoors. Hand in hand, we ventured out into the sunlit neighborhood, our conversation flowing effortlessly as we enjoyed each other's company. I was starting to feel safe with Aaron, so I smiled at him.

"What?" he asked with a smile.

"Nothing. I'm just happy."

"Me, too," he whispered. Drawing me to a stop and cupping both my hands in his, his gaze locked with mine.

I was thrilled when I heard my heart beating faster and faster as his face inched closer to mine. It was beating so fast that I wondered if the blood was almost out of my system.

As his breath mingled with mine, I caught the faint scent of the mint he'd had on his breath when he'd first arrived at my house. His gentle touch brushed my hair aside, drawing me irresistibly closer, and then his tongue was in my mouth, plunging in like a boat on the roiling sea.

As we lost ourselves in each other's embrace, it was as if time stood still and the world faded away. This feeling, plus knowing he had stood up to his parents and switched schools for me, made me believe that he really did care for me.

After a moment, he forcefully pulled my body into his as his hands slowly traced the curves of my body. He lifted my shirt up slightly near my stomach and caressed me there softly.

Just like the last time, I didn't want to stop, but I knew we had to. We were standing out in the open, and this time we were right by my house, so either of my parents could drive by at any second. Reluctantly, I pulled myself away from him, but not before stealing one more kiss as I backed away.

He smiled at me and sighed. "I promised Zay I would meet him at the park to play football."

If I wasn't sure before that he cared about me, I was after hearing that. He was even going to help my brother. He didn't have to do that.

In that moment, any doubt about his feelings for me vanished. His willingness to help my brother showed his genuine care and consideration. Although I wished he could stay, I was grateful for his kindness toward my family. "Thank you," I whispered as my heart swelled with love and appreciation.

We walked back to my house, and I kissed him again before he got in his car. I waved goodbye then walked inside.

"You know you should still be careful," Ian said.

"What? Were you just standing behind the door?"

"Even if the blood passes through us, he's still a warlock, and his family is still dangerous," he lectured then added, "*He* is still dangerous."

"Did you ever hear anything about that last translation?" I said to change the topic because I didn't want to argue with him about Aaron.

Ian frowned at me, knowing my intent, but still answered, "I haven't checked yet."

"Well, let's go check," I said and ran up the stairs toward his room.

He followed me and opened his email. The first message was from the librarian, and it had an attachment with it. Ian promptly opened the email and then the attachment.

11/02/1692
Vampire

Never before had I encountered a fouler beast than the one I met, a soulless fiend that slays without remorse. Erstwhile 'twas told to take fifteen soldiers to fell a single vampire. Even armed with stakes of wood, 'twas nigh impossible. Fortune smiled upon us when an unknown man came to our aid. Having dealt with such creatures afore, he imparted wisdom that the blood of the deceased could enfeeble a vampire.

Thus, we devised a charade to beguile the vampire. Placing one of our freshly departed brethren abed within a dwelling frequented by the fiend, we waited through the watches of the wee hours of night for his arrival. Upon his entrance to the chamber, we beheld the hideousness of this creature in truth. Gaunt of frame yet sinewy, slender with a nose long and nostrils arched above a broad yet bony chin. The pallor of his countenance accentuated the dried blood that lined his lips, and he emitted a sweet scent that mingled with the foul stench of human wastes. I nearly retched as he passed by my place of concealment.

Observing the creature bend to feed upon the corpse, we swiftly emerged from hiding. Three brethren and I, driving our stakes into his breast in turn until one pierced his heart. In an instant, the fiend turned to dust. At last, the beast lay vanquished.

I longed to express gratitude to the stranger who had bestowed upon us this invaluable knowledge of vampires, but he vanished ere I could make good on that longing. Methinks he may have been supernatural himself. Ere his departure, he divulged that vampires had been blighted by an unseen hand, cursed during the time of the

Greek gods in a bid to sway the tides of war. Yet these
demons soon turned on both factions and this rent the
battlegrounds. United, both sides fought to quell the
horde of vampires that arose, a feat that must have
proved Herculean.
The strangers shared further insights, which I transcribe
herein:

Strengths: Acute senses, swiftness beyond mortal ken,
strength surpassing all, regenerative powers, eluding
pheromones, and eternal life.
Weaknesses: The rays of the Sun, demise from a pierced
heart (by wooden object), and blood as the decreased (when
imbibed)

Creation: The blood of a vampire must be ingested and
remain within one's veins at the hour of mortal demise.
Upon awakening, the nascent vampire must consume human
blood to seal the transformation. Should that fail to
pass, death shall claim them.

"So... I guess they really didn't like vampires," Ian said sarcastically.

"I guess not."

"The way they described the vampire is completely different from what I have experienced," Ian commented.

"Yeah, it's weird. It sounds more like how they portrayed vampires in old movies, but..." I paused.

"What?"

"Well, maybe it's both. Maybe they evolved? It pretty much sounds like the vampire in this story was nasty and unclean. So, if vampires figured out that being that way got them noticed... maybe they figured out how to stay under the radar a bit more. And, maybe once they did that, they realized the pheromones they produce attract humans..." I trailed off again.

"What's wrong?" Ian asked.

"Vampires produce pheromones."

"Yeah, so?"

"Well, have you ever thought that those have been used on you? Maybe by Lavinia?" I asked cautiously.

Ian looked at me for a moment before answering, "Maybe. But I don't think she would do it on purpose. I don't think it's really something they can control. And, anyhow, nyxlings have it, too. I know we haven't turned, but we do have some 'abilities,'" he said with his typical air quotes. "Pheromones could explain why so many kids in our school seem to be drawn to us."

"Yeah, I guess so. Since you've brought up abilities, have you experienced any changes?"

"Do you mean, am I Wolverine now?" he chuckled.

"Well, yeah," I laughed with him.

"Honestly, I haven't really noticed much other than being able to hear people from farther away, and I heal a little bit quicker, but nowhere near as quickly as you."

"Should we test it?" I asked as I grabbed a pen and gestured toward him with a stabbing motion.

"No!" he laughed.

"Look, I have a scab where I cut myself on a piece of glass this morning. See, it's still healing. It's definitely healing faster than usual, but no testing is needed."

"Okay. Well, do you think we should add to the book?"

"That's not a bad idea."

Just then my phone started ringing. When I saw it was Aaron, I smiled involuntarily. Ian rolled his eyes and started writing in the book.

"Hi, Aaron. Wait, what? Slow down. I can't understand you. What? Who?" I said frantically into the phone, unable to process the new information.

"What's going on?" Ian asked.

"Where?" I asked into the phone.

"Nina, what's going on?" Ian demanded again.

I didn't answer him. I just stood frozen, then my arms went limp, which caused me to drop the phone.

Ian scrambled to pick it up. "Hello? Yeah, it's me. What the hell is going on? What?! What happened? Okay, okay. We are on our way," he said then ended the call. "Nina, let's go. They're at Osbourne-Palmer," Ian said to me as he dragged me out of the room.

When we arrived at the hospital, we found Aaron in the ER waiting room with a blood-soaked shirt.

"I am so sorry," he whispered with tears in his eyes.

Still in shock, I couldn't respond.

"Where is Zay?" Ian jumped in.

"He's in surgery."

"What the hell happened?" Ian asked.

"I don't know. One minute, we were playing a scrimmage game, then all of a sudden there was a black car on the field."

"On the field?" Ian asked.

"Yeah, the car drove right up onto the field. And that's not all..."

"What?" I finally asked.

"Well, there were three other guys standing way closer to the curb than Zay was, and the car went around them. It was like..." he trailed off to look at me. "It was like it was aiming for him."

I transitioned from shocked to scared to angry in about 2.5 seconds. I clenched my hands into fists and could feel the fire start to form in my eyes, but I didn't care.

"Calm down, Nina!" Ian shouted. "Stop, stop, stop!" he urged frantically.

"Nina!" Aaron exclaimed and jumped into my line of sight. He grabbed my face between his hands. "Breathe, beautiful," he said calmly. The gentle timbre of his voice swept away the storm of anger in an instant.

I closed my eyes and covered my face with my hands then began to cry. I felt my eyes change back as tears rolled down my cheeks. I couldn't believe what was happening. Zay had gotten sick after Ian, so if Ian couldn't heal, there was no way he could.

"What are you doing here?" Aaron yelled.

I looked up quickly to see Alan walking toward us. Aaron quickly closed the distance and punched Alan right in the face. Alan's face turned with the impact of the punch, but then he turned it right back around and snorted.

Ian ran toward the confrontation. "Hey! Whoa, whoa. What is going on?"

"He is not supposed to be here!" Aaron yelled as he started toward Alan again.

This time, Ian jumped in front of him. "Bro, you are going to get kicked out of here," Ian pleaded.

"You don't understand," Aaron said to Ian while his eyes were locked on Alan.

I calmly walked toward them despite not fully understanding what was going on, but I had an overwhelming feeling that my entire family was in danger.

Although at a distance, I stood facing Alan, and he grinned. But this wasn't a flirty smile. It was 100% evil.

I let my eyes become consumed by the supernatural magenta and watched as the blue drained out of Alan's to reveal the crimson red that I had seen the first time we'd met.

"Get him out of here!" Ian screamed as he started pushing me to the other side of the room. "Do you want to end up in an insane asylum or worse—a science lab?" he pleaded with me.

I was still staring across the room at Alan who was refusing to leave. Even in my rage-induced state, I heard what Ian was saying. I blinked my eyes until they returned to normal.

"Is everything okay in here?" a security guard asked as he walked up behind us.

"Yes, we're fine," Ian answered then pulled me back to the seating area.

Just then, our parents came rushing into the emergency room. Mom was crying hysterically, and Dad was trying to hold it together, but his eyes were filled with tears. They walked up to us and hugged us.

"Have you heard anything?" Mom asked.

"Just that he's in surgery," Ian answered.

We explained to them what had happened, apart from the car aiming for Zay.

It was so hard sitting in that waiting room and not knowing what was going on. We must have gone up to the nurse's station 15 times to ask for updates, but there was never anything new.

Finally, after hours of torment, the surgeon came out to speak to us. "Dr. and Mrs. Hart?"

"Yes," they answered one after the other.

"Are you Xavier's parents?"

"Yes," they both answered at the same time.

"I'm sorry we had to meet this way, Henry," the doctor said sympathetically then continued, "We just finished your son's surgery. He has multiple contusions, two broken legs, a broken jaw, a dislocated shoulder, a hairline spinal fracture, and an intracerebral hemorrhage."

"Oh, my god," Mom said and covered her mouth.

"Is he…" Dad asked without finishing.

"Your son is alive, but the next 48 hours are critical. He is in intensive care now, so you can go see him. Please prepare yourselves because his injuries are very severe. Maybe just the two of you for now," he said with a glance in our direction.

Ian and I stood back as our parents vanished through the double doors to the ICU. I felt so hopeless and useless. Not knowing what to do, we just sat and waited again.

Aaron sat down next to me. "Hey. sorry, I didn't introduce you to my parents," I said lamely.

"Don't worry about it," he replied as he put his arm around me.

"Why was Alan here?" I asked when I realized he wasn't in the room anymore.

"I don't know. I don't even know how he could have gotten here, but he's gone now."

"Do you think he had something to do with this?" I asked.

"No. I don't think so, but I really can't be sure."

"Where is Lavinia?" I suddenly asked.

"Oh, crap! She's probably at the house by now," Ian answered as he patted his chest then his pants pocket. "Crap! I don't have my phone, and I left yours in my room."

"We have to find her," I insisted as I stood up and threw my jacket over my arm. "Let's go!" I demanded when they didn't move.

I sprinted to the car, not realizing Ian and Aaron couldn't keep up with me.

"Geez, Nina, what's going on? I really don't think we should leave the hospital," Ian pleaded.

"We have to find Lavinia," I countered as I put the car into Drive.

I had learned so many things about the supernatural world in the past few weeks, including that vampire blood heals. I couldn't say anything about it to Ian with Aaron in the car, so I wrote down the word *blood* on a piece of paper and handed it to him.

He read it and his eyes widened then looked back at me and nodded as he placed the paper in his pocket.

I looked in the rearview mirror to see if Aaron had seen us, but he was on his phone.

We made it home quickly, but I was disappointed not to find Lavinia's car in the driveway. Ian ran upstairs to find his phone while I ran to his room to grab mine. It was almost 7 p.m., so Lavinia should have been here.

I called her, but she didn't answer, so I tried again right away. Nothing.

"She's not answering," Ian said to me as he walked into the room.

"I know."

"What do we do? Do you think we should try your blood?" he asked me.

"I'm not fully transitioned, so we don't know if that would even work."

As we were talking, Aaron walked into the room. Both Ian and I went silent.

"I didn't mean to eavesdrop, but I couldn't help it, and it sounds like Lavinia is a vampire." He paused. "And it also sounds like you're trying to find her so she can give Zay her blood."

Ian and I looked at each other but didn't say anything.

"I get it. I've been living in the supernatural world all my life, so I know how important keeping secrets is. I have known vampires are real since I was nine years old, but I only found out that my uncle—" He stopped himself then corrected, "More accurately, my grandfather, was one only a few weeks ago."

"Alan is your grandfather?" Ian asked.

"Technically, he's my great-great-grandfather, but that's beside the point. Anyway, I called him, and he says he will heal Zay."

"He will?" Ian and I both asked in surprise.

"Yes."

"What does he want?" Ian asked skeptically.

"According to him, he doesn't want anything."

Ian continued, "There's something off here—"

"Do it," I said, cutting him off.

Aaron nodded and stepped out of the room to call Alan back.

"Nina, we don't know what he wants," Ian cautioned.

"It doesn't matter. It's Zay," I said sternly.

Seeing how serious I was, Ian nodded, and we both walked downstairs to Aaron.

"He will go later on tonight during the shift change," he explained.

I sighed in relief but then remembered something else. *If the body is too broken, or too close to death, the person will die anyway, even after consuming the blood. And if they die with vampire blood in their system, they will become a vampire.* Ian didn't seem to have thought of that, so I didn't say anything. Zay being a vampire would be better than him being dead.

Aaron left about an hour later, and Dad called to let us know that Mom would be staying at the hospital, but he was coming home. Ian and I both fell asleep on the couch waiting for him.

When I woke up the next day, I found a note from Dad saying that he wanted to be back at the hospital by 8 a.m. I quickly changed my clothes then headed out to the car. I wanted to be with Zay and to know whether Alan had fed him his blood.

"I'll wait for you in the car," I shouted up the stairs as I opened the front door.

I could smell freshly mown grass as soon as I stepped outside the door. The sun was strong, and the air was warm. It felt like summer again. Distracted by how beautiful the day was, I belatedly realized that Chloe had snuck out behind me.

"Stupid cat."

I chased her until she managed to squeeze under a nearby car parked by the curb. I bent down to see underneath the car, and her demonic amber eyes looked straight into mine.

"Chloe, you are going to get run over!" I shouted at her. I never understood why cats always tried to escape from their loving homes where everything was just given to them. They didn't have to work for anything at all. It was the perfect life.

"Ian, can you please help me get Chloe?" I shouted to him through the opened door.

"Oh, crap!" we both exclaimed as we watched Miley, our third cat, make her escape and run in the opposite direction.

Miley was a bit smaller than Chloe, so she always managed to get stuck in weird places, and that made her a little bit harder to wrangle up.

"Okay, Ian, you get Chloe, and I'll get Miley," I laughed.

"Deal," he agreed.

I turned to look for Miley as Ian bent down to try to grab Chloe.

I quickly caught up to Miley and grabbed her by the tail as she was about to run into the street. I had her in my arms and was stroking her soft brown fur when I heard rap music in the distance getting closer and closer. I turned toward the sound of the thunderous music and saw that Chloe had run out from under the car.

Ian was just about to pick her up out of the middle of the road, but a white Cadillac Escalade was only a few feet away from them.

I ran toward my brother and the rapidly approaching vehicle, reaching them in under three seconds. I grabbed Ian by the collar of his shirt and pulled with all my strength, sending him and both cats soaring through the air away from the Escalade. Unfortunately, that left me twirling right into the oncoming vehicle.

"Nina! No!" I heard Ian's horrific cries from the pavement.

I looked into the driver's eyes as he hopelessly attempted to stop the enormous vehicle.

The sound of the SUV impacting my fragile body was horrendous, and I felt my left arm and both legs crack as the fender plowed into me. My head hit the front windshield and bounced off like a rubber ball. I continued to roll over the top of the Cadillac, leaving a long streak of blood behind me until I finally hit the rigid pavement behind it. I heard one more crack, but I didn't know where the sound had come from because I couldn't feel anything after that.

*My spine must have snapped.*

I opened my eyes as the vehicle sped away and left me in a pool of my own blood. I looked up to see Chloe, unharmed, sitting right beside me and just watching me.

I smiled, glad she was okay, then saw Ian limping toward me with tear-filled eyes. He dropped to my side and took my hand.

My dad, who was already joined by half the neighborhood, ran immediately to where I lay. He was crying uncontrollably and being comforted by Mrs. Radloff, the elderly woman who lived across the street.

I couldn't be sure because things were starting to blur, but it must have been Ian who called for an ambulance. I closed my eyes and listened to all the familiar voices around me. I didn't want to reopen my eyes, not so much for myself, but more for the people around me. I thought if they assumed I was unconscious, it would be easier than knowing they could do nothing as I lay there dying.

Only a few minutes had passed when I heard the sirens quickly approaching in the distance, but I wasn't very hopeful. I didn't think they could help me; my injuries were too severe.

"You're going to be okay. The ambulance is here," Ian said to me.

I could hear him trying to control his emotions as he hovered over me. I wished I could do something to make him feel better, but I wasn't able to move. I couldn't feel anything, but I could hear the shifting of sounds around me, so I knew the paramedics were there and I was being moved.

I opened my eyes slightly and saw my brother arguing with a paramedic. "What do you mean I can't go with her? She's my sister!"

"Sir, if you want us to do everything in our power to save her, it is best for no family members to be around. You can meet us at the hospital. We will be there in less than ten minutes."

The man smiled sympathetically at Ian and my dad then nodded before joining the other paramedic already loading me into the ambulance. They climbed in. As I heard the doors shut behind me, I felt a single tear roll down my right cheek.

*This is it.* I wondered how long it would take for the change to happen, but then I had a terrible thought. *What if the blood has already passed through me?* It's what I had been hoping for, but now, faced with death, I prayed that the blood was still there.

"I can't feel a pulse! Hand me the paddles!"

I felt the pressure of a metal instrument being stuck down my throat, and then heard the paramedics continue inflating and deflating the manual breathing aid as I lay there.

"We're losing her! Go again! 1, 2, 3, clear!"

But it was no use. I heard two more beeps from the heart monitor, then it was followed by a continuous blaring sound.

# CHAPTER 18
## GROWING PAINS

I felt like I couldn't breathe, like I was drowning and hopelessly trying to reach a surface that would never come. But I only started to panic when I realized I couldn't open my eyes.

I felt vulnerable and weak, which made me angry. Between my bursts of anger-filled rage, I thought about my parents and how they must have been completely devastated. It was bad enough having one child hit by a car, but having the same thing happen to another child, within days, must have been world-shattering.

I tried opening my eyes again, but I couldn't control my body. Although I couldn't move, I could hear everything. I heard people shuffling around and someone writing on a metal clipboard.

I thought maybe I had died, and what I was experiencing was death. Would I spend eternity laying in a box, hearing the outside world and not being able to move?

I was becoming more and more anxious, but then thankfully my sense of smell started working again. Little by little, I began feeling a bit better, but I still couldn't move, so I didn't know whether I was dead or not.

I could now smell the strong chemicals and metal that engulfed the room. I heard a muffled voice, but I didn't hear another one, so I had to assume the person was on the phone. Then the voice started to get clearer. It was a man.

"Yes. No, don't do that! Stop what you are doing. I'm coming up."

The man stomped away, and I soon heard the door slam shut. Then there was just silence.

As I lay there, I had started believing I actually had died when I heard someone enter the room. The way their feet shuffled made me believe it was someone different this time.

Suddenly, I felt my body lifted from the metal platform. Not knowing what was happening, I became nervous and tried with all my strength to move, but it was impossible. A few minutes later, I felt myself being placed into a vehicle, and then we started to drive. We drove for so long that I fell asleep.

I woke up sometime later gasping for air and not knowing where I was, but I could finally move again. That was a relief. I sat up and looked around. I was in a room I had never seen before. It was very small and had no windows. The only furniture was a small desk and the bed I occupied.

I got up from the bed and examined my body. It didn't look much different, but my skin felt more firm and tougher, as though a rock-like substance sat underneath the thin layer. It was definitely not feminine.

My skin was firmer. Did that mean what I thought it meant? Had I completed the transition without knowing it?

I walked over to the desk where I saw an empty glass, a notebook, and a pen. I opened the notebook and accidentally hit the glass, sending it flying to the ground. It shattered.

As I looked down at the broken pieces, I realized that my human life was like that glass. My time as a human had been shattered, and now I was something different. As I studied the shiny pieces of glass on the floor, they reminded me of the clock at VP. I wondered again what had happened to it and how a school with so much money had let that go unfixed. Had it been a sign?

Suddenly I heard the door begin opening behind me. I spun around quickly, not knowing what to expect. As the door continued to open, fire began to rage in my eyes, but now there was also something new. I felt a throbbing pain in my gums, like they were being torn open. Then I felt a stabbing pain on the inside of my cheek.

"Ow. Ugh. What the..." I said out loud and covered my mouth.

As I held my mouth, I heard a light giggle. I turned toward the sound and was relieved to see Lavinia was walking in. She had with her a large bag and a cooler.

"Lavinia!" I exclaimed as I ran to hug her, forgetting the stabbing pain in my mouth.

She was still laughing.

"What's so funny?"

"You bit yourself."

I looked at her blankly for a moment before realizing what she was talking about. Curious, I put my finger in my mouth and touched one of my canines. They were elongated and very sharp, and the teeth to the right of each were slightly elongated as well.

"Ouch!" I shouted after my finger started to bleed.

"Now, why would you do that?" she asked me while laughing even harder. "You need to relax. Otherwise, they will never change back."

"How am I supposed to relax, Lavinia?"

"Well, you can relish in the fact that you saved your brother's life." She winked at me and shot me a warm smile.

She was right. I had been able to save Ian.

"What's going on? Where am I? How long has it been?"

As my focus shifted, I began to feel the wound seal in my mouth. It was an odd sensation, like my skin was being pulled back together. I looked down at my finger and watched as the gash disappeared before my eyes as well.

"Okay, that's cool."

"Well, let's see, Lavinia began. "You are at my uncle's house, it's been about a month, and... what was the other question?"

"What is going on? Where's my family?"

"Okay, okay. Well, the night you died, your ambulance disappeared along with the paramedics, just like it did when Jen and Matt died. I found you yesterday in a morgue 500 miles from Hallowed Hills."

"What?"

"I contacted morgues throughout the region with your description. Finally last night someone reached back out to me. You had just arrived yesterday as a Jane Doe."

"What about my family?"

"They think you died more than a month ago," she said sympathetically.

I wasn't sure how I felt about that news. On the one hand, if they thought I had died, maybe Ian and Zay would think the blood had passed through my system. Then they could live normal lives.

"Zay!" I said suddenly.

"Zay is fine."

"How?"

"Alan healed him."

"He actually did it?" I said with a mixture of surprise and gratitude.

"Yes."

I was so thankful Alan had healed Zay, but I didn't know why he would have done it despite my asking him. Healing Zay had no benefit to him.

"Here," Lavinia said as she tossed me the small cooler.

"What's this?" I asked as I examined the bag.

"Blood. The whole nyxling thing is different than a vampire, but I am assuming you still need blood."

I unzipped the container to reveal bags of blood inside. I pushed them around and read the labels, which showed all different blood types. I wondered whether each type would taste different.

"What's in the big bag?"

"Just some essentials... clothes, a toothbrush, things like that."

"Thank you." I smiled at her warmly.

I felt so grateful she was in my life. She was an amazing person. She had even taken care of the little things.

"How do you feel?" she asked directly.

I didn't say anything for a moment because I hadn't had the chance to think about that. I felt stronger, but I also felt drained. "Confused," I finally answered.

"Why?"

"Well... who fed me human blood? I mean, wouldn't I have needed that to complete the transition?"

"Um, I think so," she answered.

"What do you mean you think so?"

"Well, like I said, your transition is different than a vampire's, but I assume it works pretty much the same," she answered. "You look really tired."

"Thanks," I chuckled.

"No, I mean, when I turned, I felt exhilarated," she giggled. "So, it's just different."

"Well, what now?" I asked idly.

"You need to adjust to your new life."

"What about my family?"

"They have mourned you already. It's up to you, but it might be safer if you just stayed away," she suggested sheepishly.

"Safer?"

"While you were missing, Ian and I found some stuff out. Whoever fed you the nyxling blood thought you and your brothers were part of some kind of prophecy about three beings of the same type becoming a great power. It says that the three would be closely related. So, with you gone, there can be no three, so maybe they will leave Ian and Zay alone."

I remembered Beatrice mentioning that the three in the prophecy would be of close relation, so Lavinia had a point.

As much as I wanted to see my family again, their safety was more important. We still didn't know who had given us the nyxling blood, so if I returned, that person would know the transformation worked. That would make them assume it would work on Ian and Zay, too. With that in mind, I made the decision to stay away for their own protection.

"By the way, happy birthday," Lavinia said to me as she gave me a box.

"For becoming a nyxling?"

"No," she laughed. "It's October 23, your actual birthday," she answered with a sweet smile.

"Oh, really?"

"Yes, quite a coincidence."

I opened the box and found a locket inside. It was pretty and made of white gold with three small diamonds on the front. When I opened it, inside was a picture of me and my brothers.

"Wow, it's beautiful. I love it. Thank you so much," I said as I hugged her.

"Okay. Well, you should get some rest. We have so much to learn."

As she said those words, I realized just how exhausted I was, so I took her advice and crawled back into the bed. I fell asleep quickly and had the best sleep of my life.

For the next few weeks, Lavinia taught me all the ins and outs of being a creature of the night. It was hard adjusting to eternal night, but at least the cold didn't bother me anymore. Unfortunately, I did start to feel bloodlust, so I had to feed. I hated to admit it, but it actually tasted really good, and I discovered that B negative was my favorite.

Don't get me wrong. There were many perks to being a nyxling. I was faster than I ever thought was possible. I was unimaginably strong, and my senses were incredible. And we discovered something else. Lavinia's skin could break, but the only thing that could penetrate mine were my own fangs. I just wasn't sure if it was a nyxling thing or if it was just me.

Lavinia told me that I seemed to have more control than a new vampire. When a vampire turned, the only thing on their mind is feeding, and that usually lasted for a few years. I didn't feel uncontrollable bloodlust. I knew I needed blood, but it wasn't the most important thing.

Lavinia suggested that we move far away from Hallowed Hills, so I could live a semi-normal life without the fear of someone recognizing me. I could even finish high school from home, so at least I would be doing something. Maybe after a few more months, we would try it out. Lavinia volunteered to be my teacher because she had multiple degrees in many fields.

We even went so far as to look up the best places to go and settled on Alaska. It had two months of nearly complete night. A full 23 hours of darkness would make it easier to live without worrying about people finding out about us.

We also were able to connect with two other nyxlings. Lavinia had known of some ancient vampires—or so she thought—but it turned out they were nyxlings. They were thousands of years old, and they had believed they were the only ones until learning about me.

We spoke to them, a woman named Adaline and a man named Arthur, a few times over the phone until we decided we should meet in person. They lived in Greece, so it would be a long trip. We hoped things would settle down in a few months so we could confirm our plans to visit.

I was doing well controlling myself, so we eventually left the old, abandoned house that used to belong to Lavinia's uncle and moved into an old inn located in a nearby town. The town was small and had no major streets running through it, so there weren't many visitors. It was safe enough, but I wondered whether people would begin to ask questions when they only saw us come out at night.

But Lavinia had been living in darkness for a long time, and she said that people rarely ask. Either they think it's just a coincidence, or they just don't care. I was skeptical about that at first, but it proved to be true, and no one seemed to be the wiser.

I loved being with Lavinia. She was great and provided everything for me and more because she was very comfortable with money. She had invested in different companies that had made her a millionaire.

Even with all her attention and care, I began to feel depressed as I only ever interacted with her. When she noticed, she told me I should go explore the area, so that's what I did.

She lent me her car, a black 2010 Audi. (She told me the model, which had a few letters, but I could never remember what it was, only that it wasn't available in the U.S., and she'd had to get it shipped from Europe.) She kept it in a storage unit about 20 minutes away from the inn, so she dropped me off in the car she had rented. The Audi stood out a bit, and we didn't want people asking too many questions, so she had opted for a rental car to use on a daily basis.

When I opened the door of the car, I got in and instantly sank down into the black and red racing seat. It held my body like it was made just for me. I wondered why she would need a racing seat, so I made a mental note to ask her about it later.

The smell of the leather was breathtaking. I wasn't a car aficionado or anything, but the car was amazing. I ran my fingers around the red-leather steering wheel and down to the performance shifter. I stared at the futuristic-looking gauges. I had no idea what most of them did, but they looked pretty.

I sat in the car for a few minutes before starting up the engine. As it roared to life with a sound resembling a powerful locomotive, the smell of exhaust and gasoline overtook all the other smells of the night.

A dog started barking in the distance, and a light turned on in one of the homes just across the street. Even so, I continued to be mesmerized by the sights and sounds of the beautiful machine and pressed the gas pedal gently to rev the engine. I knew many people would find the blustering sound a nuisance, but to me it was exciting.

I let the car warm up before putting it into reverse. I could feel all the power transferring from the engine into my hands as I backed out of the storage unit. I slowly drove out of the lot, but as soon as I made it to the road, I floored it. The seat acted like a giant baseball mitt, catching my body as I was pressed back into it. That's when I understood the purpose of the racing seats.

I rolled down the window and felt the cool breeze blowing through my hair. I pressed down the gas pedal even more, and my face broke into a giant smile. It was thrilling to know that my reflexes were so quick that I could drive as fast as I wanted without the fear of crashing. And even if I did crash, nothing would happen to me. I put my hand out of the window and watched as the pressure of the wind pushed it backward.

Suddenly, I heard a whooshing sound ahead of the car. I grabbed the wheel with both hands and turned back to look at the road just in time to see something very large land in front of me. I stopped the car only inches from what had landed.

"What the hell!" I exclaimed as I tried to identify what was in front of me.

I looked out over the dashboard in shock. A man was kneeling in front of the car, but it was immediately apparent that this was not an ordinary man. He had giant white wings that flared out in front of his body as if protecting him.

I watched as he started to stand and revealed a bare chest as his wings spread out. The tops of the wings by his shoulders were the purest white I had ever seen while the tips of the wings were gold. The impressive span was nearly as tall as his body as the wings arched off his back like a concave reflection. Each long, narrow feather tensed and shook in his heavenly aura, and his torso bore tribal tattoos that wound sensually around his waist and chest up to the base of his neck.

I knew him. I quickly got out of the car and ran toward him. "Connor," I said with a smile.

He stood before me, a silent enigma. When he opened his eyes, they emanated a glowing neon green that cast an intense otherworldly gaze. It seemed like he didn't recognize me, and panic surged within me as I began to fear he had been sent to kill me.

As I started backing away, his eyes returned to normal and his face relaxed, immediately dispelling the ominous air that had surrounded him.

"Nina," he whispered with a smile.

I let out a sigh of relief when he said my name then ran toward him and jumped into his arms.

"Ouch," he grunted.

"Oh, sorry." I looked into his eyes and smiled broadly. I couldn't believe he was here, holding me close and kissing the top of my head. "Are you real?"

He smiled and laughed. "Yes."

"They are beautiful," I said about his wings.

"Thank you. Are you okay?" he asked as those very wings disappeared behind him.

"I'm okay," I answered as he lowered me back to my feet. I noticed a necklace around his neck. It was a silver Byzantine cross on top of a circular platform adorned with a single green gem in the center. Only the top portion of the cross was on the platform while the lower end hung over the bottom of the circle. Despite its apparent age, the silver symbol showed no signs of wear.

I focused back on him as his scent enveloped me. Like an intoxicating and addictive drug, I knew it wasn't good for me, but I couldn't resist breathing it in. Struggling to focus, I fought to remain on my feet, not wanting our time together to end simply because his fragrance weakened me.

"I have been looking for you everywhere," he said.

"You have?"

"Of course."

"Lavinia has been helping me."

He looked shocked. "Lavinia? Who's she?"

"Ian's girlfriend. Well, I'm not sure if she still is, but..."

"Ian's girlfriend?"

"Yeah."

"And why is she helping you?" he asked with narrowed eyes.

"Umm, well, she is helping me with the transition."

"How?" he asked sternly.

I was a little taken back by his reaction. I wasn't sure if I wanted to tell him, so I asked a question of my own. "Did you come here to kill me?"

"What? No, of course not. Why would you ask something like that?"

"Well, you looked kind of scary a minute ago."

"I was sent here to help you, not kill you," he offered with reassurance.

"I know, but nyxlings aren't really angelic creatures," I said shyly.

"No, but they are godly," he responded with a smile.

I had thought of that before, but I hadn't believed it could be true since nyxlings were ever only compared to vampires. Technically, nyxlings had the blood of a goddess in them, so perhaps that made us demigods. But, then again, gods didn't have to drink people's blood to survive. Plus, I was pretty sure a demigod was the child of a god not the "greatest" grandchild of one.

Then I wondered how Connor knew I would be able to stop the car in time. "Did you know?"

"Did I know what?"

"That I had made the transition."

"Not until a few hours ago," he admitted.

Without warning, I began to smell the most delectable scent I had ever encountered and instinctively took a big whiff of the air. I slowly stepped away from Connor when I realized what the delicious aroma was.

"What's wrong?"

I didn't want to tell him that his scent now not only made me feel lightheaded, but it made me hungry as well. I wondered for a second what his blood would taste like, but then quickly pushed the thought out of my mind.

"Um, I'm just not feeling well," I deflected, not willing to tell him the real reason.

"I'm sorry," he said apologetically. "I don't have my sweater with me.

"Is that why you wore that ugly thing?" I blurted out.

"Yes, it has a sort of shield in the lining," he answered with a chuckle. "My scent is very strong, even to humans. It doesn't hurt them, but it does attract them. Most clothes help diminish my scent a bit, but I had that sweater made specifically for working at the school. I didn't think having students attracted to me would be a good idea in a high school."

"Yeah, probably not. What about the glasses?"

Despite asking the question, I didn't hear his response because I couldn't help staring at his chest—his pec and ab muscles were amazing. I wanted to dive into the warmth of his skin, but I knew I couldn't.

"Don't you have a jacket or something?" I asked suddenly.

"No," he chuckled.

"It's not funny. How about I take off *my* shirt then?" I said brazenly as I started to pull it up.

"Nooo," he protested, grabbing my shirt just as I was about to pull it up past my upper stomach. "Don't do that. Please."

"Well, now you know how I feel."

"I get it," he laughed, "but I still don't have a jacket."

"Fine," I said, pouting as I crossed my arms. "What did you say about the glasses?"

"They are just normal, ugly glasses. None of that is important now. Things are happening that you may not be aware of."

"What do you mean? Like what?"

"When I said *I* have been looking for you, I should have said *we* have been looking for you."

"What do you mean? Who's we?"

"The Carriers and I have been looking for you."

"The Carriers? All of them? Do they know about you?"

"The Carrier family and I go back a long time. I knew Beatrice when she was a young woman. She has known about me since then, but I told the rest of the family just recently."

"All of them?"

"Yes, Aaron knows, too. He has been helping to find you. He is a very powerful warlock, so when even he couldn't locate you, we knew you must have turned."

"He knows? Who else knows?"

"The Carrier family and I know, but no one else." After a pause, he said quietly, "He misses you, you know."

I felt frustrated at that. I didn't know why he kept trying to push me toward Aaron. Even though I did have feelings for Aaron, I hated that Connor wanted me to be with him.

"Right, because you are just my guide," I said with snarky annoyance as I started to turn back toward the car.

I was about to open the door, but Connor held it closed.

"You know that's not true."

"Isn't it? You come down here acting like my savior, but then you tell me you want me to be with another guy."

"That's not exactly what I said. I just want you to be happy. You do care about him, don't you?"

I looked away from Connor shyly, not wanting to admit that he was right.

"It's okay. He is your first love, but *I* intend to be your last," he said with an irresistible smile.

I didn't know what to say to that. I didn't want to let him know how much his words meant to me, but I wanted to grab him and kiss him. I wasn't sure if I could control myself, so I just smiled shyly at him as another question resurfaced. "How did you find me?"

"When Aaron couldn't locate you, I knew only one other way to find you. I had to ask the gods themselves. I started my journey a few weeks ago. As soon as I was able to locate you, I came back."

"The gods?"

"Yes. The goddess Nyx to be exact. She told me where you were."

"So... is that where you came from? I mean, just now."

"Yes."

"And the glowing eyes?"

He laughed. "When we transport to and from the heavens, we go into a sort of trance. It's sort of like being in an airplane; we sit back and watch as we make the journey. We must be in that state to pass through the boundary between Heaven and Earth," he said lightly then his face grew more serious. "Your location is not all Nyx told me. She said you may be in danger."

"In danger? In danger of what?"

"She didn't say. The gods are very careful with what they reveal, and they are hesitant when it comes to altering the lives of those on Earth."

"Unless someone is going to throw me into the Sun, there's not much they can do to me."

"What do you mean?"

I explained to him about my skin and how it didn't break, careful to not reveal that Lavinia's skin was able to break. I still wasn't sure if I wanted to tell him everything about her.

He looked a little confused and dug into his pocket then brought out a large hunting knife.

"Whoa! What are you doing?"

"May I?" he asked as he put out his hand.

I was a little hesitant, but I still gave him my hand. I turned my face away as I felt the knife touch my skin. He sliced into my arm, but thankfully nothing happened.

I let out a sigh of relief, glad I hadn't been wrong.

"Hmm," he said cryptically.

"What?"

"I guess it's true."

"You guess what's true?" I asked with wild curiosity.

"That you are part of the prophecy."

"What do you mean? Aren't all nyxlings like this?"

"Definitely not. It appears you are the strength part of the prophecy, and that means…"

"What?" I asked when he didn't go on.

"I think you may be able to walk in the sunlight."

"Are you serious?" I asked, both shocked and excited.

"Have you tried to go out in the day?"

"Of course not."

Just then, my phone started to ring. I looked at the device with no buttons on it. Lavinia had said it was the newest thing. I clicked the green phone icon on the screen to answer it.

"Hi, Lavinia, I was just…"

"Hey," she interrupted. "I checked Ian's voicemails, and I think we need to get back. I'll text you the details and an address of where to meet me."

"What?" I asked in confusion.

"I'll see you soon," she said urgently then hung up. I got her explanation and the texted address a few seconds later. As soon as I read why we needed to go, I was already pulling open the car door.

"What's going on?" Connor asked at my abrupt change.

"Get in," I commanded as I checked the text message again for the address.

Although I wanted my old flip phone back, I was grateful to Lavinia for talking me into this new phone. It had a guided map on it, so I could get anywhere from wherever I was. I put the address into the guide, and it told me exactly where to go.

I explained everything to Connor as we drove back toward Hallowed Hills. I had been reluctant to tell him about Lavinia, but I had to before he met her. He was a bit upset and lectured me about the dangers of vampires, telling me more than I had ever known about them.

"In the past, vampires were uncontrollable creatures that lacked remorse. *Some* have evolved in the last hundred years or so, but they are still driven by the need to feed. Even with the control they can develop, it still takes years for any new vampire to focus enough to do so. It's something they have to work on, and they have to *want* to work on it," he explained then paused. "Even so, the first years of a vampire's life are filled with bloodlust, and no vampire has ever been able to stop themselves from hurting humans during that time," he finished.

"Well, Lavinia isn't like that," I protested.

"As far as you know," he countered. "Vampires are also really good at keeping secrets. The only time they put anyone's feelings or needs before their own is if they truly have feelings for them. But still, that can only happen later in their existence."

"Okay, Mr. Half Angel. I'm pretty sure you have no room to talk about keeping secrets," I teased.

"That is not the kind of secret I'm talking about. They are predators. They hurt people. Angels do not hurt people," he said sternly.

"Ian trusts her and cares for her," I argued.

He huffed and crossed his arms.

I went on. "If it wasn't for her, I don't know what would have happened to me. She was the one who found me, the one who took care of me after my transition."

He still didn't say anything, but he seemed to relax a bit.

Only then did I tell him why we were headed back to Hallowed Hills. "Lavinia's text explained that she listened to Ian's messages. He said some strange men were looking for me and that even when he told them I'd died, they didn't believe him and stayed around to watch our entire family. Ian also told her that both his and Zay's skin had returned to normal, but they were afraid the men might try to test them with harm because they thought they were lying."

Connor thought for a moment then said, "I think the men might be part of the Supernatural Council. They track every supernatural being ever born or created. They don't usually hurt anyone, but they hate to be lied to." After a pause, he went on, "I wonder if they might want to make an example out of your family."

As soon as he told me that, I started driving even faster.

We were making excellent time and only stopped for gas and food for Connor. I didn't want to admit it to him, but I was getting hungry, too.

"That smells gross," I said as he took a bite of his burger.

"It's delicious. Do you want some?" he asked teasingly.

"Yuck."

"Are you hungry?" he asked seriously.

I didn't say anything. I didn't want to lie to him, but I didn't want to tell him how hungry I was either.

"Do you want—"

"No!" I answered quickly before he could even say it. "Sorry, I'll be fine."

"When was the last time you fed?"

"A few days ago."

"A few days ago? Nina!"

"Well, I didn't know I would be leaving."

"You have to feed," he said as he pulled out his knife.

"Stop!" I yelled. I had never fed from anyone before, and I wasn't going to start with him. Even through his skin, I could tell his blood smelled different than what I was used to, and I wasn't sure I would be able to control myself with a regular human let alone him.

I was afraid of what would have happened if he used his knife and was relieved when he put it away.

While we drove for the next few hours, I told him all about my change and how I'd felt before Lavinia had found me. He told me that it sounded like my body had been trying to fight the infection off to let me die.

Connor shared more about himself as well, saying that he had never met his father but had loved his mother very much. Angels that came down to Earth never stayed for the birth of their offspring, so all he knew about his father was that he was very powerful and respected in the kingdom. He also said that the angels had not come to Earth in a long time, so now for their species to continue, Nephilim had to mate with each other.

As soon as he admitted that, I wondered whether it was why he was pushing me toward Aaron. My mind spun, realizing it meant that he had to keep his species alive by being with Nephilim women. So, when he'd said he wanted to be with me in the end, what he'd really meant was that he wanted to be with me after he slept with hundreds of others.

Watching my reaction to what he'd said, he immediately changed the subject, apparently realizing his mistake. Luckily, we were only about ten minutes from Hallowed Hills, so we wouldn't have to sit with that between us in the car for long.

When we arrived at the address Lavinia had given us, we exited the car and stared up at the building. It was a large, half-constructed warehouse. I noticed a light on in one of the windows, so I started walking toward the door closest to it. The door opened, and Lavinia walked out, but she fell backward in fear when she saw Connor.

"Why?" she asked.

I had never seen Lavinia so terrified, and I looked over at Connor. His eyes were neon green again.

"What—"

Before I could ask him anything, his wings emerged with such force that it almost knocked me to the ground. Thinking Connor was about to kill my friend, I wracked my brain to think of something that would help the situation. Suddenly, I remembered Aaron's face when he had calmed me down in the hospital. His voice and his touch had instantly comforted me, so I held my breath and jumped in front of Connor.

"Breathe, Connor," I said to him as I caressed his face.

Although I couldn't see his pupils anymore, his gaze turned from Lavinia to me. He then closed them and shook his head. When he finally looked back at me, I could see his exquisite emerald-green eyes and a small smile as his wings disappeared behind him. I smiled back at him and then ran toward Lavinia.

"Are you okay?" I asked as I helped her up.

"I think so," she said, keeping her eyes on Connor. "Do you know what he is?"

"Well, yeah. The wings are a dead giveaway," I laughed.

"Yeah, but you know he's a hunter, right?"

I immediately turned toward Connor who hadn't taken his eyes off Lavinia since I'd calmed him.

"Connor? Are you going to be okay?"

He didn't say anything, but he nodded.

I had never thought about what being a Nephilim meant for Connor. We had talked about many things, but he had never said anything about being a hunter. I wondered if all Nephilim were hunters or if it was just him. I couldn't really ask him right then with Lavinia there, but I knew I had to bring it up once we were alone.

We walked down a long corridor that led to a set of double doors. I looked back at Connor who was nervously glancing up at the ceiling. I wanted to ask him about it, but I thought it might make things worse. If he said he didn't trust Lavinia, then Lavinia would say she didn't trust him, and we would get nowhere.

We walked up three flights of stairs before reaching a door at the top. I was surprised when we walked into an exquisite loft with beautiful hardwood flooring and vaulted ceilings with a skylight. I thought it strange to have a window in the ceiling that could let in sunlight, but I didn't ask about it at that time.

As we continued through the loft, I realized just how big it was. To the right was a large kitchen with all black appliances and granite countertops. To the left was a dining area with a sturdy black table surrounded by chairs.

Farther in, we came to a living room fully equipped with a large television, a surround sound system, and white leather couches sitting on light gray rugs with baby blue designs.

"What is this place?" I asked.

"This is my home," Lavinia answered then glanced warily at Connor. "But I might be looking to move here shortly."

"Maybe you two should sit on opposite sides of the couch," I suggested half-jokingly, but they were staring each other down like it was some kind of contest. "Okay! Enough," I commanded, at last fed up with the entire situation. "I don't know what is going on, but that's enough from you both. We are here to help my family."

At my words, Connor took his eyes off Lavinia and looked straight at me. Lavinia went to grab three file folders from the coffee table and handed them to me.

I opened the first one and saw my picture with the word MISSING stamped across it. It had information about my entire life. The file was what I imagined an FBI profile would look like. I opened the other two and saw similar profiles on Ian and Zay.

"What are these?"

"I stole them from the car of one of the men who was at your house," Lavinia confessed.

"What does this mean?"

"Did you read the first part?" she asked me.

I turned back to the first page of my profile and read:

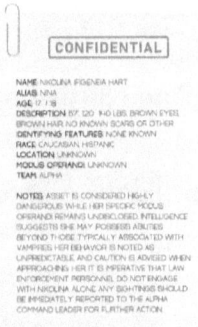

"They think I'm a vampire? And what team?" I asked.

"That's what I don't know. What I do know is that they are aware that Jen and Matt are vampires, so I figured they assume you must be one as well since you went missing in the same way."

"But what even made them investigate us? And why do they have profiles on Ian and Zay, too?"

"That I don't know."

"Let's find out," Connor jumped in.

"How are we going to do that?" I asked.

He gestured for the files, so I gave them to him. He scanned through the pages but focused more on the image adorning the front of the folders. He snapped a picture of it with his phone then handed the files back to me.

"I will be back in an hour," he said as he walked away.

Curious, I looked at the logo on the front of the top folder. It was a circle with a sword going through it and the letter G over it. It reminded me a little bit of the logo on the book that Connor had sent me.

I looked at Lavinia and showed her the logo, but she just shrugged her shoulders.

"We can't wait for him," I said as I started walking toward the door.

"Wait, Nina," Lavinia pleaded as she jumped in front of me. "As much as I don't trust Connor, maybe we should see if he finds something out before we go rushing in there. I mean, I'm not really ready to take on the entire Supernatural Council. Are you?"

"I honestly don't even know what that means. All I know is that my family is in danger, and I have to help."

"I get that, but we have to be smart about it. The council doesn't know for sure you're alive, and maybe we should keep it that way."

"Why? What does that matter?"

"I don't know," she admitted, "but it sounds like they want you for something, and until we know what that is, I think it's best we stay away, at least for now."

My thoughts were running all over the place. The profile said I could be an asset, so maybe that meant they wanted to turn me into a weapon. The more I thought about it, the more I agreed with Lavinia, so we stayed and waited for Connor to return.

The hour he was gone seemed to take days, but finally I heard a whoosh from outside, and a few minutes later, Connor came through the door followed closely by Aaron.

"Nina!" Aaron said as he ran toward me then picked me up and hugged me.

I was so confused. I didn't know why Connor would bring him here, but I was glad he had. I hadn't realized how much I'd missed Aaron until I saw him. His smile made my heart melt.

"What are you doing here?" I asked, unable to control my own smile.

"Connor told me what was going on, and I asked him to bring me to you."

I turned to Connor who was standing away from us and being very quiet.

"He insisted," Connor finally said.

Aaron stroked my face. The warmth of his hand felt amazing against my cold skin, and I let my face fall into his hand as he continued to caress my cheek. Then he pulled me toward him and kissed me softly on the lips.

I pulled away slowly and instinctively looked over at Connor, but he had a stone look on his face like he didn't even care.

"Is everything okay?" Aaron asked me.

"Yes, I just have to be careful," I said, not wanting to tell him the whole truth. It wasn't really a lie, but it wasn't really the reason I had pulled away from him.

Second guessing my hesitation, I grabbed Aaron's hand and pulled him toward the couch with me. I sat him down then sat on his lap gently so I didn't hurt him. Then I took his face in my palms and kissed him. "Hi," I said with a smile.

Aaron smiled and kissed me again. I looked up at Lavinia who looked really confused, so I slid off Aaron's lap and sat next to him but still kept my legs over his.

"Did you guys find anything out?" Lavinia asked.

"The folder has the mark of a secret organization named the Guardians," Aaron answered.

"Who are they?" I asked.

"No one really knows much about them, but we do know that they are some sort of team created by the government."

"The government? Like the U.S. government?"

"Yes."

"They know about us? What do they want with me and my brothers?" I asked.

"No clue, but my grandmother knows someone in the government, so she's reaching out to them," Aaron explained.

"And what happens when they find me?"

"We don't know," Connor jumped in, "but until then, we don't want any surprises, so we need to stay here."

"Can you put on a shirt or something?" Lavinia snapped at Connor before I could respond.

"I don't have one," he barked back at her.

Lavinia pulled the blanket off the couch and threw it at him. He narrowed his eyes at her as she walked away.

"Do I want to know what's going on there?" Aaron laughed.

"Probably not."

"I am not wearing a blanket," Connor bit out.

Aaron stood up from the couch and started to take off his jacket. "Here, man, take this," he said as he threw his jacket to Connor.

Connor nodded at Aaron and dropped the blanket on the ground then put on the jacket, which was far too small for him, but at least it covered him for the most part.

"So, what are we going to do now?" I asked.

"We wait," Connor said. "I'm not leaving your side. I'm supposed to be—"

"My guide, yeah, yeah," I cut him off.

"Yes, but I am supposed to be your protector as well."

"I don't need protection," I hissed with certainty.

"That may be so, but your brothers might."

"So go protect them," I hissed.

"They *are* being protected," he insisted.

"By whom?"

"My family has their eyes on them," Aaron said. "They will be okay."

"So, now *you're* staying here, too?" Lavinia asked Connor with annoyance.

His answer was smug. "I will stay wherever Nina stays."

Lavinia rolled her eyes and went to the kitchen. She came back quickly with two large cups and handed one to me. Right away, I could smell what it was. I saw Lavinia's eyes change to red, and I felt mine change as well as we both took sips of the dark red liquid.

"Sorry, I don't have any people food," Lavinia said to Connor with snark once she'd had her fill.

Connor rolled his eyes and walked away to sit at the dining room table and read through the files again.

We all joined him shortly after and discussed our sleeping arrangements, which placed Lavinia and me in the bedroom and Aaron and Connor in the living room.

As soon as Lavinia and I were alone, she asked me all kinds of questions about Connor. I didn't really want to talk about him, so I told her there was nothing between us and we were just friends.

After what he had told me in the car, I had promised myself that was all he would ever be. And seeing how much Aaron cared for me had made the decision that much easier.

With Connor in her home, Lavinia was scared to fall asleep, so we put the dresser in front of the door to make her feel better. I fell asleep fast, exhausted from the day.

# CHAPTER 19
## LIKE A LAMB TO THE SLAUGHTER

I was in a deep sleep when I felt myself shaken awake. My eyes flashed open, and I rubbed them sleepily then saw Lavinia standing over me.

"What's the deal?" I asked.

"We have to go."

"Where?"

"I got a call from a friend. He said that your brothers and dad have been kidnapped."

"They were what?" I shouted.

"Shhhhh," Lavinia said as she put her finger to her lips. "They said no angels, or they will all be killed."

"What? Who said that? Your friend?"

"Yes, the ones who took your family told my friend to give us that message."

I jumped out of bed, not caring that none of it made much sense. "Let's go."

I looked around for my shoes and remembered I had left them by the front door. Lavinia threw me a pair of high-heeled boots and started toward the window.

"Umm, how am I supposed to run in these?"

"Run on the balls of your feet. You'll be fine," she said as she opened the window. "Go! I will be right behind you."

After I landed on the grass three stories below, I rubbed the mud off my shoes and moaned, "Yuck. Come on, Lavinia, let's go," I whispered up to her, and she landed next to me much more gracefully than I had. "So, what's the plan here?" I asked.

"We need to help them without the kidnappers or your family knowing we did."

"What? How are we going to do that?"

"Very carefully."

"Thanks. That explains so much," I said sarcastically.

"Let's just head to your house, and we will figure it out then."

"My house?"

"Yes, that's where my friend is. He has a letter there that only you can open. Apparently, it's sealed with a magic spell."

More questions, but I didn't care, so I just started to run in the direction of my house with Lavinia close behind me. While we ran, I thought about my family being in danger and how that was partially my fault. I knew I had to do whatever it took to keep them safe.

We followed the long, narrow hiking path while the trees blurred continuously by us. We were so fast. I can't compare it to anything in the human experience. The wind blowing through my hair felt so nice that the running made me feel calmer. I was sure all that could be seen of us were thin, colored blurs.

Then the wind shifted suddenly, and I breathed in air that smelled like fire. I came to a complete stop.

"Hey, what's the deal?" Lavinia asked, stopping about 25 yards in front of me.

I wasn't paying any attention to her. I had heard the whisper of a familiar voice. When at last I looked over at Lavinia, she turned her head to the north and took in the smell in the air as well.

"I hear... Zay... and fire," I observed.

"You hear fire?"

"Yes."

I didn't wait to explain it to her. I just turned to follow the scent. I didn't think I could run any faster than I had before, but I did. The stench of the fire got stronger and stronger until we arrived in front of an old, abandoned building in the middle of the woods that was, indeed, burning.

I listened as hard as I could for the sound of Zay's voice again, but it was my dad's voice that I heard scream frantically, "Oh, my god. Ian! Zay!"

Without a second thought, I ran into the burning building. To me, it looked like the ceiling was caving in on my two brothers in slow motion, but I knew that in a matter of seconds, it would crush them.

I leaped toward the biggest piece of falling debris. As the piece of concrete landed on my shoulders, it sounded like a car hitting a brick wall at 100 miles per hour. I shrugged it off my shoulders and into my hands so they could escape.

"Nina!" my dad screamed when he saw me.

I could smell the blood spilling from his leg.

*Control yourself, Nina.*

Ian and Zay were still on their knees covering their heads when they heard his voice, and they both quickly looked up, saying almost simultaneously, "Nina?"

"You guys have to get out of here," I grunted. I knew I could hold the enormous piece of fallen building forever, but I needed my brothers to get out. I needed them to be safe. My dad was still just staring at me.

"Dad, please get them out of here. Ian, please go help Dad up," I implored as I watched my dad struggle to his feet.

When he stood up, not only could I smell the blood, but I also could see it pouring from an injury on his left leg.

Luckily, not even a second later, Lavinia scooped him up in her arms then ran toward the door with Ian and Zay following close behind them.

After Zay was out, I looked for a place to drop the large piece of concrete, but before I could do so, I heard Ian cry out in pain. I turned quickly to look toward his cry.

"No! Leave him alone!" I yelled.

A man in a black cloak and black mask that looked like a Japanese lion had grabbed Ian by the shoulders and was now choking him. I heard Ian's bones crack as the man squeezed. I glimpsed the man's yellow eyes through the mask as he slowly took Ian's left arm and twisted it until his bone cracked. Then he threw him into the concrete wall behind him, leaving a bright red streak of blood where his head hit the wall.

"Finally, I can get my revenge on your kind," the man said in an almost mechanical voice.

I lunged at him, grabbing his throat with one hand and his shoulder with the other. The impact of our bodies smashing against the wall caused the doorway to cave in.

"You can't save him," he said to me with a chuckle.

I bit down on his right shoulder as he tried to struggle free, and he screamed out in pain. I knew using my teeth was kind of cliché, but they were also my strongest weapon.

Unbidden, Aaron's face flashed into my mind. What would he think if I killed this man? What would I think? I didn't want to kill anyone, but I was filled with rage.

Those thoughts fled as the man attempted to fight back by stabbing me with a weapon he'd had under his cloak. When the blade broke against my skin, his yellow eyes widened, and I noticed they had some red in them.

I smiled cheekily at him.

"What are you?"

I flashed him a wicked smile and prepared to attack again, but I stopped myself. Even though I easily could take this man's life and he might deserve it, I couldn't.

I still had a tight grip around his neck, and he was kicking frantically to try to free himself, but I stared into his eyes and let go of his neck, which sent him crashing to his knees. I made sure to keep my foot on his cloak to keep him in place. He still needed to answer for attacking my family.

He looked at me, stunned. I took my eyes off him only for a second, but then he was gone, leaving his cloak behind. I didn't care to chase him.

Then reality sank in. I couldn't believe I had let my brother die. Even with how strong I was, I had failed. I leaned my head against the cool wall. I wasn't ready to see my brother's lifeless body yet. Defeated, my eyes were reverting to their natural brown when I heard it: a faint heartbeat. He was still alive!

I blurred over to where he lay drowning in a pool of his own blood. The sight of the blood made my eyes flare back to magenta. I closed them and held my breath until they went back to normal.

"Ian? You're going to be okay," I said as I tried not to cry in front of him. But I could feel my eyes filling up with tears as his eyes started to roll back into his head.

I screamed out for Lavinia to come back then spoke to him. "I need you to listen to me, Ian. Stay with me. Do not let your heart stop beating," I urged.

Lavinia came back quickly and kneeled next to us.

"What do I do? I don't know what to do," I stated.

"You have to feed him your blood," she instructed.

"What? No, you do it," I insisted.

Lavinia looked at me with concern. "If I do it, he might change into a vampire."

"Don't change him. Just heal him," I pleaded desperately.

"You know that's not how it works," she reminded.

"So, do it then. Change him," I said as my tears dripped into Ian's blood.

"Trust me, Nina. You don't want that."

I looked up at her and remembered what Connor had said. *Vampires can't control themselves for the first few years.* Alan had killed his girlfriend without even meaning to, and she had been a very strong vampire.

"This way, either he will heal, or he will become a nyxling," Lavinia said.

But I knew those weren't the only two options. His body could reject the change, and he could still die. It was one of the differences between vampires and nyxlings. The moment I sensed his heartbeat slowing even more, I stopped thinking and desperation took over. I bit down on my wrist then fed Ian my blood.

I held my breath, waiting and watching anxiously until he finally drew in a deep, life-giving breath. Relief washed over me momentarily then was replaced by a surge of intense love as I clasped him tightly while he gasped for breath.

When I released him, he smiled weakly up at me and said, "I've been looking for you."

I scooped him up and jumped up to the second floor of the house. Running toward the first window I saw, I effortlessly kicked out the pane of glass then dropped outside, not even shifting Ian in the process.

Zay ran over to me with my dad close by his side.

"Oh, my god. He was right behind me. What happened?" Zay's voice trembled with fear.

My dad remained silent with his gaze locked on his son's fragile form.

"He's going to be okay," I reassured him as I gently set Ian on the ground.

It only took a few moments for Ian to sit up on his own.

"Ian!" A mixture of joy and disbelief echoed in my dad's voice as he cried out and hugged him tightly.

"What's going on? You died months ago," Zay said, his voice wavering barely above a whisper. "Are you a..."

"Yes, I died. I am dead," I confirmed even as a playful laugh escaped my lips.

For a long moment, Zay studied me as his realization hung in the air like a heavy shroud. "You are undead, aren't you?" he finally said under his breath.

I laughed at him and nodded. Suddenly my head started to spin with a weighty scent of blood filling my senses and making it very difficult to concentrate. Stepping away from my family, I sought solace in the distance. I shook my head, attempting to clear my animalistic impulses from my thoughts.

Once I felt a little better, I walked back toward my family again, only to freeze as my dad gasped and recoiled. Guilt gnawed at me as I approached. His stunned expression cut me to the core.

"Dad, it's me. I'm sorry," I pleaded.

Uncertainty clouded his features as he continued to study me from a distance, still looking unsure.

Then Zay stood up from where he sat with Ian to come and hug me. I heard his elbow crash into my body as he put his arms around me. He pulled away and let out a loud shiver. "Ouch. I think that's going to leave a mark," he commented as he rubbed his elbow.

"Nina, is it really you?" my dad asked as he hobbled up next to Zay.

"Oh, Dad, please sit down," I pleaded with him, my heart aching at the sight of his struggle.

"My only daughter is alive. Why would I want to sit down?" He smiled cautiously, and his embrace became a bittersweet reminder of the life I had left behind.

"Is Ian... umm... going to be like you now?" Zay asked.

"No, I fed him my blood to heal him. For him to turn, he has to die with my blood in his system and then..."

Like an ominously tolling bell within my mind, my focus shattered as the rumbling of voices dimmed to a whisper then vanished altogether. In the silence, I inhaled deeply, feeling a primal shift within me as my eyes transformed and my fangs elongated.

My gaze fixated on the source of that intoxicating scent: the crimson river cascading down my dad's leg. A ravenous hunger consumed me, demanding satisfaction.

My rationality faltered as I teetered on the edge of primal instinct. Thoughts of what Alan had gone through filled my head. He had killed the woman he'd loved because he couldn't control his instincts.

I tried to fight it, but I couldn't help staring at my dad's leg. I stepped closer to him and his open wound and felt a low growl rise in my throat as I prepared to leap at the easy prey.

Zay quickly threw his jacket over my dad's leg to cover the blood, and Ian jumped up and ran in between them and me, shielding them from the savage beast I had become.

"Nina, it's okay," Ian said to me in a soothing voice.

With a blink, my eyes reverted, and shame flooded through me. I averted my gaze, retreating inward, only to be jolted back to reality by the deafening crack of a gunshot.

I instinctively ducked and covered my head, forgetting that it was completely unnecessary. I quickly turned toward the origin of the sound, but it was too late. In horror, I watched Ian's descent to his knees as a crimson stain blossomed over the front of his shirt near his heart.

"No!" My anguished cry echoed through the night, but even as fast as I was, it was too late. Ian was gone before I could reach him. I held his lifeless body in my arms as Zay and my dad cried next to us.

I looked around for the gunman, but when I couldn't find him, I knew I needed to get Zay and my dad out of there. I grabbed Zay and rushed him far into the forest away from where I'd heard the gunshot, then I went back for my dad. Both of them were on the ground throwing up when I returned with Ian's body.

"Sorry," I said, but they shook their heads as if to relieve me of guilt from making them nauseous.

"But he had your blood in him," Zay said as he continued holding his stomach.

I didn't have the heart to tell him that the change wasn't guaranteed, so I lied, "I have to take him, so he can complete the transition." I turned to Zay as I picked Ian up. "Call an ambulance for Dad," I instructed as I picked Ian up then blurred away.

As I ran off, I realized Lavinia wasn't with me. I hoped she was okay, but I couldn't worry about her. I ran back toward the warehouse loft, trying not to get lost. Thankfully I got there quickly. I kicked the door down as I entered, causing both Connor and Aaron to jump up off the couch.

"What happened?" Aaron asked.

"They killed him," I explained as tears rolled down my cheeks.

"Who killed him?" Connor asked as he went right to Ian and placed his hand over his heart. A golden light glowed from beneath it. I watched, hoping there was something he could do. "I'm sorry," he said after the light disappeared from his palm.

"He had my blood in his system," I confessed.

"That's good, right?" Aaron asked.

Connor and I looked at each other.

"What?" Aaron asked.

"There's only a 50/50 chance the transition will work."

"What?" Aaron said, shocked.

"All we can do now is wait," Connor explained.

"I lost Lavinia," I whispered.

"What do you mean? She's dead, too?" Aaron asked.

"I don't know. She's just... gone. I'm not sure if they took her or she ran off," I explained as I stood up. "I have to go find her."

"You can't leave," Aaron said to me.

"There's nothing I can do here right now. We just have to wait, and Lavinia might be in trouble."

That's when the smell started to get to me, and I started to fall but caught myself on the couch.

Aaron came running over to help me stand up straight. I shook my head and smiled at him, but then I saw he was wearing a necklace with a brown pendant and the same blue liquid and symbols I had seen on Ms. Farnsworth.

He saw me staring at it and pulled it off over his head. From his pocket, he took out a small box made of what looked like crude iron and placed the pendant inside then put it back in his pocket.

"Thanks."

"What were you thinking?" Connor shouted at me.

"I'm leaving," I said as I ignored his comment.

"Where are you going?" Connor asked, but I was gone before he could say anything else.

I ran back to my house, thinking about what had happened. The Carriers were supposed to have been protecting my family. What had happened to them? Why was there a letter sealed with some spell? Had the Carriers had something to do with what had happened?

I was deep in thought when I saw something inhumanly fast pass by me. I stopped and looked around.

"Lavinia?" I asked in a loud whisper.

I heard rustling in a tree across the way, so I started walking toward it.

"Hello, Nina," Alan answered as he walked out of the darkness.

His appearance startled me so badly that I lost my balance as my heel got stuck in mud. Alan blurred to me and caught me as I was falling.

"I'm fine," I said to him, trying to shrug off his touch.

He threw his hands up in the air.

"Sorry," I whispered then turned on him with a question. "What are you doing here?"

"Going for a midnight jog. What are *you* doing here?"

I wasn't sure whether he was being serious. Was it really a coincidence that he was here?

In the last few months of my life, I felt like we had been getting closer. That was until I thought he'd had something to do with hitting my brother with a car. No time like the present. "Did you hit Zay with a car?

He rolled his eyes. "If I were going to hurt someone, it wouldn't be with a car," he said with a flash of his fangs.

"Why did you act that way in the hospital then?"

"Aaron had just punched me in the face. I didn't know what was going on. It was instinct."

"Why were you there?"

"I had a little thing with one of the nurses the night before, and I was kind of stuck inside," he said arrogantly. "I was just walking around when I saw you."

"Why was Aaron so mad at you?"

"That you will have to ask him."

I don't know why I did, but I believed him. He was an ally, not an enemy.

Settling into that thought, I told him what had happened tonight and in the past few months. In turn, he told me that his entire family and Connor had been trying to find me, doing everything they could, including bringing in a medium just in case I had crossed over into the afterlife.

When I told him I hadn't woken up until a month after the accident, he grew suspicious and told me it only took someone a few hours to wake up after dying with vampire blood in their system. After thinking a few moments, he hypothesized that I likely had been put under a sleeping curse after I was turned.

I wasn't sure what to think about that. I had no idea what had happened during the month I was missing.

Switching gears, I informed him that the change wasn't guaranteed for nyxlings, so I wasn't sure whether Ian would survive. Thinking about that again made me start to cry. He reached out and hugged me gently. For a moment, I let him, but then I pulled back and wiped my tears away.

He stepped back and smiled at me. "What can I do?"

That was when I really started to see him. I don't know if I had been afraid of him before, but I don't think I had ever really seen him for what he was: a strong, smart, handsome, and loyal man.

He wore the same maroon jacket and black shirt he always did, and I wondered idly how something so plain could look so good. As I stared at him, the moonlight seemed to glisten off his pale skin, making it almost shimmer.

He just stared back at me with his baby blue eyes.

I took a deep breath and smelled how fresh the air was. It was nice to be able to stand next to a guy and do that. Since Alan was a vampire, I would never feel sick or weak around him, and he was immortal just like I was. I started thinking that things would be so much easier if I were with someone like him.

Of course, he was a big flirt, so I really didn't know how he felt. Daringly, I stepped toward him and slowly put my hand on his chest. He held it there gently and smiled charmingly at me as I ran the fingers of my other hand over the stubble on his cheek to see what his reaction would be.

He just stared at me intently, patiently waiting for my next move.

"I have to see that letter," I said suddenly, pulling my hands off him as I realized just what I was doing.

"Let's go," he directed as if nothing had passed between us and started running toward my house.

"Hey!" I exclaimed when he left me behind.

When we reached the house, it looked normal. No lights were on, and I figured Zay and my dad were still at the hospital.

"Stop," Alan said as he put his arm up.

"What are you doing? I'm going."

"We have to be smart about this. We already know someone has been watching your family, so I'm going to take a lap around the place and make sure it's clear. You stay here," he said then blurred away.

He was right. If I had just walked in there and someone was watching the house, they probably would try taking me away. We still didn't know why they wanted me, so it was too dangerous for me to just walk in there.

"Clear," Alan announced as he stopped in front of me only a few seconds later.

"Are you sure?"

He rolled his eyes. "This is what I do."

We walked up the driveway and looked around but didn't see anything out of place. Alan walked onto the porch while I looked around the front yard.

"Is this it?" Alan asked as he grabbed for the letter on top of the mailbox attached to the house. "Ow!" he yelled when the letter zapped him.

"Are you okay?" I asked, pulling his hand toward me and glancing at the wound, but it was already healing. "You're fine."

"It still hurt. Well, at least for a second. Thanks for caring," he responded with an egotistical smile.

I quickly dropped his hand and went to grab the letter. I didn't get zapped, so I opened it.

"What does it say?"

"It's blank," I answered while holding it up to him.

He poked at the piece of paper. When it didn't shock him, he grabbed it from me.

"What are you doing? It doesn't say anything."

"Maybe not to the untrained eye."

He flipped it over a few times then handed it back to me. "It doesn't say anything on it."

I rolled my eyes at him as he went to sit on the porch swing.

"You know what this means, don't you?" he asked leadingly.

"What?"

"Come on, Nina, think."

When I didn't say anything to him, he got up and walked back over to me. "A letter only you can open, yellow eyes, fire, gone in the blink of an eye…"

"I don't know."

"You were set up. As sure as death and taxes, it was by some kind of fire-breathing demon."

"Death and taxes?"

"Give me a break. It's what we said in my day."

Despite the old phrasing, what he was saying made sense.

Alan continued, "And then your brother gets shot minutes after you fed him your blood? Yeah, I'm not buying it. It was all a set up. Where's that little handy-dandy book of demons you have?"

"It's not a book of demons."

"Whatever. Where is it?"

"It's under my bed," I answered as I looked for the spare key in the plant next to the door.

"What are you doing?"

"What do you mean? I'm getting the book," I said as I slid the key into the door lock.

"Umm… I wouldn't do that if I were you."

"What are you talking about?" I asked behind me as I opened the door and began to walk over the threshold. Before I could, I felt an electrical shock that sent me crashing to the ground beyond the porch.

"Told you," Alan said as he helped me off the ground.

"What was that?"

"Didn't anyone teach you anything? We have to be invited into a home."

"But I walked into Lavinia's house without being invited," I argued.

"Let me rephrase that. We have to be invited into any living person's home."

"What about the inn. I walked right in there."

"Meh, hotels and inns are kind of gray areas. Vampire 101 will have to wait for later. Come on," he said as he started walking down the front path.

"Where are we going?"

"To ahhhh—" he screamed as he was taken straight up into the air.

"Alan!" I yelled as I looked up into the sky to see what had grabbed him. Then I heard a crash behind me and turned around with my fangs bared.

Upon seeing what it was, I scolded, "Connor! What did you do? Where is Alan?"

"Away from you."

"He was helping me," I growled.

"He's a vampire."

"And?"

"And they are unpredictable and dangerous," he reasoned.

"Connor, you just swooped in and grabbed a man and sent him to God knows where. You can't get any more unpredictable and dangerous than that."

Annoyed, I started to walk away from him, but he grabbed my arm. I turned back and looked at him.

"I am supposed to be really strong," I warned as I glared at him with my magenta eyes ablaze. "Shall we test it?"

He promptly let go of my arm, and I continued walking away. Then I felt something run past me. I turned back toward Connor and watched Alan punch him in the face and send him tumbling to the ground.

"Dick," Alan said as he shook his hand off. "Ow."

Alan was dripping wet as though he had gone swimming in a lake with all his clothes on. My gaze involuntarily lingered on his figure. The shirt he wore clung to his chest, accentuating every contour of his physique. He took his jacket off in one fluid motion and let it fall carelessly to the ground. Even through the long-sleeved shirt, I could see the muscles in his arms ripple as he ran a hand through his soaked hair. The intensity in his gaze was arresting. *Holy shit.*

"I have to get away from this douchebag, so I can heal. Meet me at the hospital. We need Zay," Alan directed, snapping me out of my trance.

Before I could say anything, Alan was gone. I glanced over to Connor who was just now getting back up. "You kind of deserved that."

"I am just trying to protect you," he said.

"I don't need your protection!" I yelled as the fire started in my eyes again.

"Why are you being so difficult?" he asked pointedly.

"Oh, why don't you go find a Nephilim to mate with," I threw at him then bit my lip. I hadn't meant to say that. I didn't want him knowing that he had hurt me badly when he'd told me about keeping his species alive.

Not waiting around for a response, I ran as far as I could before I started to cry. The tears made it difficult to see, so I stopped and sat against a tree.

Why did I care so much about that? He wanted to be with other women, and he wanted me to be with Aaron. I felt bad for thinking of Aaron as a consolation prize because he wasn't. He was amazing. I was the terrible one.

I heard the beat of Connor's wings nearing, so I wiped away my tears the best I could and stood up. "Just go away, please," I said to him as he approached. "I get it. You have a job. But there are three of us, and I'm the one who needs you the least. Go protect the only one of us actually still alive."

He stared at me with regret and longing. "I care about you so much, Nina," he said quietly as he started toward me.

"Just stop! Please."

He stopped walking and nodded. "Okay, but I need you to be honest with me. You can't just go running off. I could have helped save your family."

"They said no angels."

"Who did?"

"The people who took my fam..."

I realized then that there was one family member who was not with them. "My mom."

"Your mom?"

"Yeah, she wasn't there. I have to go."

"Nina!"

"Connor, my family is in danger. If you care about me like you say you do, stay away from me. I'm going to the hospital. And before you think of joining, Alan will be there, too."

I ran away from him as fast as I could.

Just when I thought I was getting over him, seeing him for only a few moments made all my feelings come rushing back. I felt a little more sound of mind now that I was away from him and decided I wouldn't cry anymore over a guy who didn't want to be with me.

When I walked into the ER, I found Alan flirting with the nurse at the front desk to try to get her to let him in, and it sounded like it was working.

"Alan," I said behind him, and the nurse quickly shied away.

"Hey, Nina."

"What was that about?" I asked, referring to the nurse's quick departure.

"Nina, have you seen yourself? No one could compete with you."

"I'm not competing with anyone for anything," I said flatly.

"Alright," he said as he rolled his eyes.

He put his arm around me and pulled me toward the double doors leading into the ER. We were walking down the brightly lit hallway when Alan suddenly put his arm out to stop me.

"What?" I asked with a frown.

"What's the deal with you and my nephew?"

"You mean your great-great-grandson?" I laughed.

"'Nephew' is less confusing. What's the deal?" he restated.

"What do you mean?"

"Well, are you together or not?"

"We've never defined what we are," I answered vaguely.

"Aaron seems pretty sure, so you better figure it out fast. I see how that damn angel looks at you. Aaron may be blind, but I'm not," he said then started walking down the hall again.

I was shocked at how mad he was and embarrassed that Alan thought I had feelings for Connor. He wasn't wrong, but I didn't know what to say to him. I hadn't been considering Aaron's feelings at all. On the other hand, he had never told me he wanted us to be exclusive, and there was still that whole Amanda thing, too. If he wanted to be with me, he would have brought it up. When things calmed down, I'd talk to him about it.

Alan walked into a room ahead, and I followed him. My dad was lying in the bed laughing with Zay, who was sitting in the chair next to him.

"Nina!" my dad exclaimed when he saw me.

"Dad, are you okay?"

"I'm fine. My leg is broken, but I've had worse," he replied with a smile.

"How much does your dad know?" Alan whispered to me.

"I'm not sure. I've kind of been away for a while now."

"I told him everything," Zay chimed into our exchange.

"Well, in that case, do *you* want to feed him, or do you want me to do it?" Alan asked me then added flippantly, "Nyxling or vampire?"

"My dad is not Greek," I snarled at Alan. The fact that people were after my family wasn't funny at all. "You do it."

"Hold on. What are we going to tell people when Dad suddenly doesn't have a broken leg anymore?" Zay asked. "Let's just wait until we get home to start with all the supernatural crap."

Zay was right. If a doctor came to check on him and found him completely healed with no injuries, there would be a whole lot of questions that would be very difficult to answer.

"I'm fine. They gave me something for the pain."

"Oh, and, by the way, Becca knows," Zay reported.

"Becca knows what?" I asked.

"Everything. So maybe you should call her."

I wasn't sure how I felt about that. On the one hand, I was glad she knew because that meant I could get in contact with her. She was always good at making up believable stories, so maybe she could figure out a way to explain my absence to everyone else. On the other hand, her knowing could put her in danger.

"Zay, we need you to come with us," Alan instructed while I was still thinking.

"Why?" he asked defiantly.

"We need to get the book from Nina's room, and neither of us can get in the house."

"Why?" he asked again.

"Because we haven't been invited in," I informed him.

"That stuff's true?"

"Yes. Now let's go," Alan said as he grabbed the back of Zay's collar.

"Geez, I'm coming," Zay complained, hitting away Alan's hand.

We said goodbye to my dad and headed back to the house. Meanwhile, Alan went to Lavinia's because he wanted to talk to Aaron.

Zay didn't like that I had to carry him again while running to the house, but we had no other way to get him home. After the nausea passed, Zay invited me into the house. I grabbed the book, and we left.

I dropped Zay back off at the hospital in my car so he could be with our dad then left the car there so they could get home later.

Just as I got to the parking lot at Lavinia's house, I started to get a striking headache. It was something I had never felt before and was a hundred times worse than being next to Connor. The pain radiated into my eyes.

"Ahhh!" I screamed as I covered my eyes and dropped to my knees.

I felt warm liquid dripping into my hands then Alan's voice sounded next to me as I felt him wrap his body around mine.

"Nina, open your eyes. Let me see," he said as he touched the area next to my eyes.

The pain was so unbearable that I couldn't focus on what he was saying, but I heard the sounds of the night start slipping away until I heard nothing at all.

# CHAPTER 20
## TROJAN HORSE

When I woke up, I still felt the throbbing pain in my eyes, so I sat up slowly and touched my eyelids. They felt okay, and there wasn't any more warm liquid, so I opened my eyes slowly. Everything was extremely bright like I was looking directly into a car's headlights. The pain was worse with my eyes open, so I closed them again.

I didn't know where I was, so I felt around the area where I lay. I was on a couch.

"Nina?" Ian's voice asked.

"Ian? Is that you?" I asked excitedly.

"Yeah, I can't see anything," he replied.

"I can't see anything either, but I think we're at Lavinia's house."

"Nina, we are at Lavinia's," Aaron's voice confirmed. "Ian woke up grabbing his eyes, likely experiencing the same pain as you. He passed out, too, but woke up a few minutes ago. Alan gave him some blood, and he's okay."

"But neither of us can see. That's not really okay."

"Focus," Connor said.

I rubbed my eyes then tried to focus as Connor instructed. Still nothing. I started to cry, afraid I would never be able to see again. As I began to think of all the wonderful things I would miss seeing, the pain suddenly started to fade.

I wiped my tears away and tried opening my eyes again. The light was still there, but it wasn't as bright as the first few times I'd tried opening them. I rubbed my eyes, blinked a few more times, and then thankfully I was able to see again.

"I can see," I voiced with relief.

"Whoa," Alan said as he came to stand behind Aaron who was immediately in front of me.

"What?" I asked.

"Your eyes changed colors," Aaron answered.

"What do you mean? Like magenta?"

"No... definitely not magenta," Alan answered, still stunned. "Umm... they're like a moonlight gray."

"What?"

I turned to see Ian rubbing his eyes and looking around. I jumped off the couch and ran to him.

"Ian!" I yelled as I hugged him.

He rubbed his eyes again and turned to me. I saw that his eyes were not brown anymore either. They were gray, just like Alan said mine were.

"Your eyes are gray," Ian commented.

"Yours, too," I said quietly then grabbed him and hugged him again. "I'm so glad you're okay."

"Ouch, Nina. What's with your skin? Why is it so hard?"

I touched Ian's skin, and it was nothing like mine. It was soft and smooth just like before he had changed. As I was looking at his skin, Alan came up and sliced Ian's arm with a hunting knife.

"Owww! What's wrong with you?" Ian yelled at Alan as he put pressure on the open wound.

315

"Alan!" both Aaron and I screamed.

"It's not healing," Aaron stated.

"Do you mind?" Alan said to Connor, who rolled his eyes and walked out the door.

"Is this far enough?" Connor called from behind the door.

"Oh, look, it's healing," Alan said sarcastically.

"Connor, you can come back now," Aaron yelled.

"Who?" Ian asked suddenly as he turned to Alan. "Who!?" he demanded again but this time turning to Connor.

"What are you, some kind of owl?" Alan chuckled.

But Ian wasn't paying any attention to Alan anymore. He was fixated on Connor. Then he turned and looked at me then back to Connor. He shook his head then leaned it back against the couch with his eyes closed.

"What's wrong?" I asked.

"There are just some things you don't want to know," he said as he rubbed his eyes.

I wasn't sure what Ian was talking about until I turned to look at Connor. I didn't think a Nephilim could blush so hard, but his cheeks were bright red. When I thought about what Ian had said and Connor's embarrassment, I instantly knew what was happening.

Ian had received an ability, too, and that ability was mind reading. Although I didn't want Aaron or Alan knowing what Ian probably had seen in Connor's thoughts, I needed to know if I was right.

"Can you hear what people are thinking? Can you hear what I am thinking?"

"Yes, I can hear, and *see*, what they are thinking," he answered then indicated everyone around us, "but no, I can't hear what you are thinking, thank god." He then turned to Alan. "You know, Alan, the more you try not to think about something, the more you do," he scowled at the vampire.

Alan's smirk vanished, and he walked into the kitchen. Ian shook his head as if trying to forget something.

"What happened? Are Dad and Zay okay?"

Before I could answer, Alan yelled to us from the kitchen, "Someone set you up!"

"That's Alan's theory at least," I said.

"As much as I don't like the guy, that makes sense," Connor agreed reluctantly.

"Told you!" Alan yelled again from the kitchen.

After catching Ian up on what had happened the day before, we started working on a plan to keep Zay and the rest of our family safe.

I learned that Mom had taken my death really hard and had committed herself to a psychiatric facility. As terrible as that was, we decided that the best thing for her would be to stay where she was. Once everything got back to normal, I would tell her about me and hopefully she would be okay.

Since those men might still be watching our house, we decided to let my dad and Zay know they could stay at Lavinia's for a while. We planned for Aaron to pick them up in the morning and bring them back here.

However, Lavinia was still missing, so we needed to find her before we did anything else. That produced a 20-minute argument about who should go with whom, but we ultimately decided that Alan and Ian should go with me, and Aaron and Connor should go together.

Connor didn't like the arrangement, but it made the most sense because Aaron would need protection. Since he had to wear his pendant, it was best he went with Connor. And since Connor made Alan and Ian weaker, it was best they went with me. Furthermore, at night all five of us could search, but Alan and Ian would have to be inside before sunrise. Tomorrow I would test whether I could walk in the sunlight.

That night, Alan, Ian, and I searched every square inch of the town, but we found no sign of Lavinia. Aaron even had cast a locator spell, but he couldn't find her either. He said that the only other time it hadn't worked was when he had been trying to locate me when I'd gone missing. It was odd.

Not knowing where else to search for her, we returned to the abandoned building where the mysterious man had taken my family.

Alan didn't like that Ian could see his every thought, so he searched on the opposite side of the building's ruins from Ian. It wasn't as though Ian was happy to know every little thing Alan was thinking either, so he was glad when Alan was far enough away that he didn't have to hear.

While Ian searched the back of the building, Alan and I went to where Ian had been thrown against the wall. It still had dried blood smeared on it, and that made Alan's eyes change.

"What's the matter with you?" I asked.

"It's blood," Alan said with mild annoyance.

"So? It's dried."

"It's not something I can control," he explained.

"So, the sight of any type of blood makes you transform?" I observed thoughtfully.

"Human blood," he corrected, "but yes."

I flashed back to when I had seen Lavinia pick up my dad and run him out of the house. He had had blood dripping down his leg, and Lavinia's eyes had never changed.

"So, you're saying that when a vampire sees even a little bit of blood, they involuntarily transform?" I asked.

"That's what I said. Wait, why?" he asked when he noticed me deep in thought.

"Well, Lavinia picked my dad up while he was bleeding, but she never transformed."

Ian must have heard our conversation because he blurred right next to us. Still getting used to his speed, he tripped on a piece of debris and hit the wall.

"You okay there?" I asked with a giggle as he brushed himself off.

He stood up straight but didn't say anything for a moment. "No," he finally answered.

"You are not okay?" I asked.

"No, I mean yes. I wasn't talking to you," he explained as he stared intently at Alan.

I looked at Alan then back at Ian. "Okay, what is going on?" I asked in frustration.

"He thinks that Lavinia is somehow involved with the kidnapping," Ian explained as his eyes started changing to magenta.

"Whoa, whoa, listen," Alan said, holding up his hands toward Ian. "I'm just saying maybe she hasn't been 100% truthful. That's all."

"What do you mean?" I asked with a scowl. "I have no idea what you guys are talking about."

"There's just no way that any vampire can be near blood and not transform. It's not in our DNA. So, the only way she wouldn't have reacted to the sight of blood would be if she'd had a spell cast on her."

"A spell?"

"Yes, it's possible, but not many witches can cast it, and not many vampires would let that type of spell be cast on them."

"Why not?"

319

"Because it weakens us. Yes, it takes away our bloodlust, but it also se-verely diminishes our supernatural abilities." Alan thought for a moment. "But how would Lavinia know she would be near blood?"

"Maybe she was just being careful," I suggested. "I mean, she knew Ian would have been there, and she wouldn't have wanted to attack him if he was bleeding."

"Maybe, but I doubt it. You also said that she told you she wouldn't feed Ian her blood," Alan reminded.

"Yeah, so?"

"Why? Vampire blood heals. Ian was conscious, so he wasn't close to death. All the vampire blood would have done was heal him," Alan rea-soned.

We all thought about that for a moment then Alan began again, "The only ones who knew we were protecting your family were my family, Con-nor, and Lavinia. As much as I don't like Connor, I don't see him betraying you. My coven is strong, and they would have seen an attack coming... unless there was an inside man, well, in this case an inside woman."

I couldn't believe what Alan was saying. I looked at Ian. He had been quiet the entire time and was now leaning against the wall deep in thought.

Suddenly, Ian pushed himself off the wall and walked over to us. "No. I know Lavinia. She would never betray us," he said finally.

"I am—"

"I said no," Ian cut off Alan.

"Listen, I'm more than a hundred years older than you, so don't get on my bad side," Alan growled at him as he poked his chest.

Ian's eyes started blazing magenta as Alan's eyes became red.

"We all need to just calm down for a minute," I said as I jumped in between them. "There's nothing here to help us, so let's just go meet up with Connor and Aaron at the house."

As we started walking out of the dilapidated building, I grabbed Alan by the arm as he walked past me and turned him to face me. "If you ever threaten my brother again, you *will* be sorry," I whispered to him while my eyes blazed.

We both knew it didn't matter that he was older than me. I was stronger and would always be stronger than any vampire. He regarded me for a moment but didn't say anything then just walked away.

When we got back to the warehouse, Connor and Aaron were already there. We told them about Alan's new theory, and, to our surprise, they had come to the same conclusion.

Ian and I still didn't want to believe it, so he said he would look through Lavinia's things to prove she'd had nothing to do with hurting our family.

With the sun coming up in the next hour, Alan and Ian had to stay in the house. I was still concerned about the huge skylight, but Alan told us he had been here before and knew the window was made from UV-blocking glass. He was right, and we were able to watch through the glass above us as the sun came up. It felt warm but did no harm to any of us.

"Are you ready, Nina?" Connor asked me.

"Maybe this isn't such a good idea," Aaron argued.

"I'll be there to protect her if something happens," Connor reassured him then turned to me and noticed the frown on my face. "If something happens, I can cover you with my wings."

"Maybe Aaron's right," Ian agreed. "I mean, nowhere in the history of time has a vampire or nyxling been able to walk in the sun."

"Let's look at the facts," Alan chimed in. "She is the only one of us that this dickhead's abilities don't work on," he said with a flippant gesture at Connor.

Connor's eyes started glowing green.

"Calm down, cowboy. I'm on your side here."

"His scent does make me lightheaded," I supplied, "and I get dizzy around him."

"Yes, but your other abilities still work," Alan reasoned.

"Still..." Ian hedged.

"Ian, I have to try," I interrupted, starting to see Alan's point.

Aaron nodded in support and grabbed my hand, starting toward the loft door. The walk down the stairs and corridor seemed longer than it ever had before.

"Are you ready?" Connor asked as he stopped in front of the door.

I nodded, and he opened the door. Connor walked out first and spread his wings then gestured for me to come forward.

I walked toward him into the sunlight. The sun was so bright that I had to block it from my eyes, but my skin didn't burn. I studied my arms for a moment then looked back at Connor who had a huge grin on his face.

Suddenly Aaron was hugging me and twirling me around.

"See," Connor announced proudly.

I nodded to him, and all three of us walked back inside to tell Ian and Alan. Ian was anxiously waiting by the door to the loft. When we walked in, he was so relieved that he hugged me tightly.

That question now answered, Ian began to snoop around Lavinia's place with Alan while Aaron and I went to go to pick up Zay and my dad. Connor was tasked with trying to find out more about why the government was looking into our family.

We took Lavinia's car to go pick up Zay and my dad. As much fun as it was running really fast, doing that to go everywhere was getting tiring. And even though the sunlight didn't seem to hurt me, I noticed I felt a bit more sluggish than usual, so I wanted to conserve my energy. I wasn't sure what we were going to do with my car, which was still at the hospital, but I wasn't too worried.

When we picked up Zay and my dad, they were both a bit shocked by the new color of my eyes.

"They are moonlight gray," he said.

"Why does everyone keep saying 'moonlight gray'? Why not just call it gray?" I asked.

"Because they *are* moonlight gray. The color comes from the rays of the moonlight in the spell for Talaatah. The spell has started. It just needs the third to be complete," my dad said distantly, somehow knowing that Ian had transformed.

"What do you mean the spell has started? I thought the spell was cast a long time ago."

"The spell was cast, yes, but now it's been activated. It's kind of like a radio. You know it can be turned on, but since you have no batteries, you don't bother trying to make it work. But now batteries are being added, and the parts are starting to gain power."

"What happens when it gains full power?"

"I don't know," he said hollowly.

Already shocked by what our dad was saying, that shock deepened when he started telling us things we'd never known about him. When he'd first met our mom in Greece, he had been researching the supernatural, specifically the Olympian gods. He hadn't known much at the time, but during his trip he learned many things, including details about Talaatah.

He confessed then that the real reason we had moved to Hallowed Hills was because the Carriers had offered protection for our family. After the train accident, my dad immediately had thought someone was trying to transform me into a nyxling.

Since he already had known about the only 50/50 chance of the transformation working, he had looked into who could help us. He had known about Hallowed Hills and its ties to the supernatural world. The town

323

itself having a spell around it that could identify supernatural creatures in a subtle way.

"In fact," he related to us, "the town's actual settlement year can only be read by supernatural creatures. The founders hung a plaque in Luna's Grill with a spell on it. Whoever could read the town's settlement year as 1693 was supernatural. Most of Illinois wasn't settled until the 1700s, but Peoria was settled in the late 1600s." My dad paused and looked at Aaron. "The next part you probably know more about," he said with a gesture at him.

"It's been a long time since I heard the story," Aaron began, "but I do remember that my family knew the French settlers in Peoria. When my ancestors needed a place to hide, they fled to this area. The French leaders were not too keen on letting outsiders into their settlement, so my family settled about four hours away. Wanting to remain hidden, they didn't officially settle Hallowed Hills until 1765, but the town was actually founded in 1693."

"But that's more than a hundred years after the Salem witch trials. I'm no cartographer, but I don't think it would take that long to get from Massachusetts to Illinois," I laughed.

"Very observant," my dad jumped in. "It's not just the town's founding year that appears differently to humans. It's also the reason. We, I mean humans, see that the town was settled by the ancestors of the people accused in the Salem witch trials. Supernaturals see the truth."

It finally made sense why everyone else had thought we were crazy when we'd told them the founding year. I scowled to myself. The next time I saw Connor, I would yell at him for marking down my history paper for putting the founding year as 1693.

The most surprising information was yet to come. "When I met your mom, she had nyxling blood in her system, but she had no idea. I was already falling in love with her, so I explained to her everything I knew. She had already heard all the stories, but she hadn't believed them. It took both your grandfather and I explaining what was happening to her for her to finally believe."

My dad smirked then continued, "She had been sent to Greece by her parents to learn about her culture, but they had never imagined what would happen to her there. I was the first to notice and brought her back safely to the United States. I met with her parents and told them I would always take care of her, and ever since then, I have."

My dad then confessed that they had only planned to have one child. They would have loved a huge family, but they wanted us to be safe. After I was born, that put two possible nyxlings in the family, so they didn't want a third, but then my mom got pregnant with Ian.

A few years passed, and our family seemed just like any other, so they figured they could live their lives how they wanted. My mom really wanted another baby, so they decided to have another child. They got that normal life for almost 20 years before our family was targeted again.

At first, I was upset with my dad for having kept all this from us, but he said that knowing so much was a burden. He was always looking over his shoulder for the supernatural, even if there was no way it could be there. "Your mom and I both thought it would be best if you didn't know about it at all, so you could live normally," he explained. "But now that you do, I have a few journals from my time in Greece at my office that I'll bring home so you can read them."

Aaron and I dropped Zay and my dad off at the warehouse then left again to continue searching for clues about Lavinia's disappearance. As Aaron drove, I just stared at him. First, I noticed how muscles in his arms bulged ever so slightly when he changed gears. Then I thought back to what Emily had said about him being the best-looking guy. That felt like a lifetime ago. He was certainly handsome, but I had never imagined how good of a person he would be. The way he was helping protect my family even though it put him in danger was amazing.

"What?" Aaron asked when he caught me staring at him.

I didn't say anything and just smiled at him. He smiled back and grabbed my hand then kissed it while he watched the road.

I thought about what Alan had said about our relationship. I wanted to ask Aaron what we were to each other, but I was scared. I wasn't sure what he had done while I'd been gone. If he'd thought I was dead, I couldn't blame him for finding someone else. But I didn't want to ask him because I didn't want him to feel like I was smothering him. Alan had hinted that he considered Aaron and me a couple, but that could have just been his assumption.

My silence must have been louder than I thought because Aaron started to pull over to the side of the road.

"What are you doing?" I asked.

"What's on your mind, beautiful?" he asked seductively.

*Is he a mind reader too, or is it just that obvious?*

When I didn't volunteer anything, he started driving again and thankfully dropped the subject for another, saying, "I'm a bit hungry. Is it okay if we stop at my house to get some food?"

I nodded at him, and we made a U-turn to head toward his house. When we arrived, no one else was there.

"Hmm, I wonder where everyone is?" he said.

For my part, I was relieved. I still hadn't met his parents, and I was nervous to meet them. Glad for their absence, we stepped out of the car, and he invited me into the house.

"I'm going to make a sandwich. You can come with me, of course, but Alan never really likes the smell of our food, so if you want, I can meet you in the living room. You know where it is."

Grateful, I opted to go to the living room and wait for him. While there, I looked at all the items—more artifacts really—on display in cases throughout the enormous room. There was no information listed for any of them, so I didn't know what they were, but everything looked very old. I was immersed in surveying all the treasures when I heard Aaron walking toward me.

"Do you want to sit for a bit?" he asked as he put his hand out to me.

I took his hand, and we walked to the couch and sat down. I didn't know why I was so nervous, but I felt like I had the first time I'd met him with the butterflies in my stomach going crazy. I nestled in next to him, and he put his arm around me then pulled my chin toward him before kissing me deeply.

"We're supposed to be looking for clues," I replied shyly after the kiss.

"Do you want to go look for clues?" he asked quietly.

"No," I responded then kissed him again, grabbing his face with my hands.

Although I was trying not to be too rough, a whirlwind of emotion drove my actions, and I leaped onto his lap, straddling him as our fervent kisses persisted. Urgently, I unzipped his jacket and let my hands explore beneath his shirt as I locked eyes with him, our foreheads almost touching.

The rhythm of his heavy breathing matched my intensity. Grabbing my face, he initiated another passionate kiss. He pulled back but kept my face between his palms. He gazed into my eyes as my fingers traced the contours of his chest. I tossed his jacket aside, and his shirt soon followed suit.

In a surge of desire, he pulled me into him then lifted me effortlessly onto the couch before his body covered mine. A cascade of sensations assaulted me as he trailed kisses from my neck to my chest then pulled my shirt upward to access my stomach with his lips.

Responding to his intense energy, I took control and shifted so my body was on top of his.

"Sorry," I murmured, a hint of apology in my tone as I felt the need to temper my eagerness.

"I don't mind," he replied, his smile laced with flirtation.

My fingers delicately traced the contours of his abdominal muscles as he lay beneath me. Our eyes locked, and he again took charge, gripping the back of my neck and capturing my lips once more. With a tender touch, his hands slipped underneath the back of my shirt, and he skillfully unclasped my bra.

Suddenly nervous, I pulled away from him a little.

"Is this okay?" he asked at my abrupt stop.

I nodded, a mess of nerves and desire, before sealing my consent with another lingering kiss. I had never wanted anyone more than I wanted him.

"Ahem."

The sound made us both jump off the couch, and we found an attractive woman standing with Connor only a few feet away. The woman was tall, thin, very pretty and looked like she was in her early 20s. Her long blonde hair was tied back in a ponytail, and she was wearing a black skirt suit.

"Jess!" Aaron yelled. "Where's my shirt?"

I would have told him, but I was too busy trying to get my bra to snap back together. Aaron turned me around and quickly did it for me then found his shirt behind the couch.

"You are supposed to be able to hear people coming," he whispered to me ironically as he put his shirt back on.

"I was kind of in the moment," I murmured.

"Um, Nina," Aaron began slowly with an extended hand. "This is my sister, Jess." To her, he asked, "What are you doing home?"

"Nice to see you, too," Jess said. "And nice to meet you, Nina," she added as she held out her hand to me.

"It's nice to meet you, too," I replied shyly. I was mortified that this was the way his sister was first meeting me.

I looked over at Connor. He didn't seem bothered by it at all. By this point, his reaction didn't surprise me, but it still irritated me. I wished I didn't still have feelings for him, but I couldn't help it, so I did my best to not look affected.

"Well, now that we have that out of the way," Jess said with a smile. "I'm here because I was called in to help."

"Help? Help with what?" Aaron asked.

"Just because I don't practice magic doesn't mean I don't know how to do it," she explained pointedly. "Besides, I bring more than magic to the table. You might not know because you're clearly in your own little world," she said with a flick of her hand to indicate our indiscretion, "but I recently started interning for the U.S. government, specifically, the Defense Department. The division where I work tracks any unusual threats to our country."

"Unusual threats?"

"Yes, and that brings us to you," she said then looked straight at me.

"I'm a threat to the U.S. government?"

"Umm... that remains unclear. It's above my pay grade."

"Do interns even get paid?" Aaron asked with some snark.

"Not the point," she dismissed. "All I know is that they are keeping a close eye on you. I'm here for the same reason as everyone else: to help protect your family."

That admission made me relax just a little.

"I brought important herbs that will help brew a protection spell for your living brother," she continued. "It was supposed to be for both brothers, but Connor just filled me in on the ride from the airport."

Jess then stepped close to me. Taller than me, she had to bend down a little to look into my eyes. "Are you wearing contacts?"

"No," I said flatly.

"Your eyes are so pretty."

"They're new," I admitted.

"Huh?"

"Long story," Connor jumped in.

When he said that, I realized he had never commented on the new color of Ian's and my eyes, and I wondered if he had expected it. I squinted at him in question, but he turned away quickly. He was definitely keeping something from me.

"Anyway, I'm going to get started on that, so you two kids have fun," she said with a wink as she walked out of the room.

That left just the three of us standing in the room together. I felt so uncomfortable being alone with both Aaron and Connor. Although it clearly didn't bother Connor, I still felt guilty.

Luckily, Connor launched right into business. "I spoke to Ian, and he hasn't found anything to implicate Lavinia in any way. However, I think he might just be seeing what he wants to, so I asked Alan to help, but he hasn't found anything out of the ordinary either."

I was happy to hear that Lavinia still had nothing to do with it, but the question remained about why she hadn't reacted to the blood.

I suddenly felt very tired and said as much. I hadn't slept or fed in a while, and both Aaron and Connor noticed. Connor suggested that Aaron and I go back to Lavinia's house for the blood bags so I could get my energy back. He didn't tell us where he was going, and I didn't want to ask.

On the drive back to the warehouse, Aaron again pulled over to the side of the road.

"Is this our new thing?" I asked with amusement.

He smiled then looked at me shyly as if he wanted to say something but didn't know how.

"What?" I asked.

"I want you to know how much I care about you. I know things were a little rocky when we met, and I'm sorry about that. I will never let someone else dictate my love life again." He looked away then met my eyes directly. "I have never felt this way about anyone. I know things might get complicated because we're different, but I think it's worth it."

I smiled and kissed him, whispering into his ear, "Me, too."

He smiled then grabbed my hand. "I want to do something for you, but I'm not sure how you will react. I promise I've thought it through," he explained. He kissed me softly then whispered, "I want to be your first."

I immediately pulled away from him because I knew exactly what he was talking about, and it wasn't sex. "I can't."

"I trust you, and you need to feed," he stated. He kissed my neck then looked into my eyes again. "I trust you with my life."

I peered into his ocean blue eyes and saw his complete trust in me as he placed his forehead against mine and caressed the side of my face. Grateful, I let out a shaky breath.

"Yes," I said at last, realizing what he actually meant to me. He was an amazing guy, and the most unselfish person I had ever met, but most of all, he had always been open with me and had never kept anything from me.

That was when I knew there was no reason for me to look elsewhere. I had found the man I wanted to be with, and I was sure I was falling in love with him. That's also when I knew I could stop because I would never do anything to hurt him.

Giving into the desire, I kissed his lips then started kissing his neck. His skin felt so warm against my lips as if his blood was heating up just for me. I sucked slightly on his skin, and it felt like the blood was pooling between his skin and my lips as if there were a magnetic attraction. I pulled away then kissed his neck again, letting my eyes become consumed by fire and my body fill with lust.

I felt my fangs grow, then I bit down on his neck. The feeling was like nothing I had ever experienced. It was stimulating and animalistic. Blood had never tasted so good before.

I didn't want to stop, but I knew I had to. I pulled away slowly, and he stared into my eyes with a smile. I licked my lips, welcoming every last drop into my system.

"Are you okay?" I asked.

He grabbed my face and kissed me deeply then pulled back slowly. "Yeah. It hurt, but it also felt good, and I mean *really* good," he said with a sated smile.

I bit my wrist and presented it to him. "Here. We can't have you walking around with holes in your neck," I giggled.

He laughed then put his lips to my wrist. I didn't think it would feel like anything, but as he drank my blood, I gasped, feeling like I was going to explode with pleasure. I threw my neck back, and he let go of my wrist.

"Did that feel as good to you as it did to me?" he asked with a sexy smile.

But I didn't answer him. I just pulled him toward me and started to kiss him. I wanted him, and I knew he wanted me. He pulled off my jacket as I clawed at his to try to get it off.

Around us, the windows were all fogged up. If anyone passed by, they would know what was happening, but I didn't care. The front seat was uncomfortable and made it difficult to maneuver, but again, I didn't care. I pulled him toward me, and he climbed over the gear shift into the passenger side then flipped me over to be on top of him.

"Someone's coming," I said suddenly with a start.

Aaron quickly scrambled back to the driver's seat and rolled down the window to see who was there, but he couldn't see anyone.

We put our jackets back on and stepped out of the car to locate what I'd heard. As we stepped out of the car, we found Connor standing in front of it with his neon green eyes.

"Connor?" Aaron asked then turned to me. "What's wrong with him?"

"I don't know. Connor, what's going on?"

I wasn't sure what was happening, but the only time I'd seen him look this way was when he had met Lavinia for the first time. I stepped between him and Aaron and said his name again, at the ready in case he brought out his wings. Instead, the color of his eyes returned to normal.

"Beatrice found something," Connor said simply.

"What?" Aaron asked.

"She just said it was important. We need to go meet with her," he said as he walked around us and got into the back seat of our car.

"I guess he's coming with us," Aaron announced with thick sarcasm.

The drive back to the Carrier house was very awkward. I hated that being so close to Connor confused me so much. I tried to focus on the feeling I had just experienced with Aaron, but it now felt impossible to grasp. I closed my eyes and tried not to think about it, but I couldn't get Connor out of my mind.

I felt ashamed that after being so intimate with one guy, I still had intense feelings for another. Then something occurred to me. My feelings were only this strong for Connor when I was near him. I knew the feelings were real, but I also knew I was smarter than that. Whenever I wasn't near him,

I just wanted to be with Aaron. That made me wonder whether it was Connor's pheromones that created the intensity of my feelings for him.

I opened my eyes, getting madder the more I thought about it.

"What's wrong?" Aaron asked.

"I have a headache," I answered, not wanting to talk about it.

I wanted and needed to talk to Connor about so many things—my eyes, my feelings, and whatever else he was keeping from me—but I knew that being alone with him would only make things confused. It would probably be best for me to forget about getting any answers and just stay away from him. In fact, the longer we sat together in the car, the more my head actually started to hurt. But thankfully, the ride didn't take too long.

When we arrived at the Carrier house, about 15 cars were parked in front of it.

"What is going on?" I asked.

"No clue," Aaron answered as we stepped out of the car.

I stood there with Connor on one side and Aaron on the other. "Maybe we should call first?" I suggested.

"No, why?" Aaron asked.

"Well, I don't know. We were here only about an hour ago, and no one was here. It's just weird. And my eyes aren't exactly unnoticeable."

"Just say you have contacts in. We will be fine," Aaron reassured me.

"But I don't have contacts in," I mumbled under my breath.

"Let's go," he said as he pulled me toward the house while offering Connor his jacket, "but maybe you should put something on."

I laughed as Connor rolled his eyes.

When we walked in, no one was in the front hall, but we could hear multiple voices farther in. Aaron took my hand and led me toward the sound.

I held my breath as we turned the corner. All conversations came to a screeching halt, and everyone was staring directly at me. I involuntarily stepped behind Aaron and gripped his hand tighter. He shifted to put his arm around me and held me close.

"It's true," one of the women scowled in a heavy Italian accent.

"Where did she come from? Did she come from outside?" another woman asked.

"But the sun is still out," a man said.

"What is she?" posed another man.

"She must be dangerous, a vampire the sun doesn't affect," said a different woman.

"It's unnatural," hissed the woman farthest away.

They continued to talk about me, but I couldn't make out the rest of it as everyone began talking at the same time.

"Silence!" Beatrice shouted as she banged her fist down on the long, rectangular table.

Everyone stopped talking and sat up straighter. She sat at the head of the table and clearly had authority over everyone present. She stood and walked toward me with open arms, pulling me into her body with a hug.

"No one is going to hurt you here, my dear," she whispered into my ear.

"Beatrice, your grandson cannot be with her. She is a vampire; he is a warlock. It cannot happen," implored an elderly woman with black hair, dark skin, and a thick German accent.

I looked at Aaron. Mad, he removed his arm from around me and stood in front of me. "You have no—"

"Aaron," Beatrice said as she put her hand up. "What my grandson does is frankly none of your business, Lucille," she announced authoritatively. "Now, we are here to discuss how to help this young lady's family. She did not ask for any of this. And, for the record, she is not a vampire. She is a nyxling."

"Nyxlings are extinct," a man protested.

"Obviously not," Beatrice said in a tone that welcomed no objections. "There is only one sibling left alive, but there is a mother, too."

"My mom?" I asked then looked up at Aaron. He returned my gaze but was just as confused as I was.

"The family is obviously being targeted because of the Talaatah prophecy," Beatrice explained.

"That spell was created so nyxlings would not have to be the great power," said an older man with white hair, dark skin, and an accent straight out of New Orleans.

"The spell used all creatures' blood, did it not?" Beatrice asked the man. That seemed to quiet him down quickly. "Now, as I was saying, her family is being targeted because of the spell, so we need to protect the last two still alive. To do that, we need to know who is targeting them," she explained as a large book was passed to her. She put on glasses that hung from a chain around her neck.

"Germany, Spain, England, Italy, and Greece," Beatrice listed. "These are all the places that people with Greek blood have been attacked in the last 50 years. Unfortunately, none of them survived. Since the killings were so far apart, no one really put it together until now. Every instance involved accounts of a man in his late 20s and a young lady in her early 20s with the victims. The man has been described as handsome with light brown hair and dark eyes, only seen at night. The woman is described as beautiful with blonde hair and blue eyes, also only seen at night."

"Vampires," one of the men stated.

"Or nyxling," a woman scoffed.

"All nyxlings are related. I highly doubt they would target their own family," Beatrice denounced that theory as she looked at the woman over the tops of her glasses. "Now, Bruce. You said you had a few pictures."

A man with fiery red hair and pale skin stood and walked over to her with a large envelope.

She opened it and spread the pictures out on the table. I pulled myself away from Aaron and approached the table. As I saw the pictures, I instantly felt my eyes become engulfed with fire.

The three people seated closest to me jumped out of their chairs and moved away from me.

"Lavinia," I said angrily.

# CHAPTER 21
## OVER MY DEAD BODY

I closely studied the pictures on the table. The first was of a man kissing a blonde woman, but I could only see the sides of their faces, so I moved on to the next picture. The next was of the man. He was tall and thin and very handsome with pale skin, dark hair, and brown eyes. He was dressed sleekly in a brown suit and smoked a cigarette. I didn't recognize him, but I wasn't all that interested in him at the moment.

My focus remained on the blonde-haired, blue-eyed girl I'd glimpsed when Beatrice had first placed the pictures on the table. The first few were not very clear, but the one with her in profile was. It was indisputable. She wore the same black, double-breasted peacoat Lavinia had worn the first day I'd met her. And there were more pictures of her. Some showed her kissing the mystery man, and some were of her and, I assumed, the victims. My relatives.

I looked up from the pictures and saw that some of the people around the table had changed form. One now had the head of a bull. Another had the head of a snake. Surprised and feeling threatened, I bared my fangs, which made two other women transform and four of the men's eyes start to glow yellow.

I glanced behind me and saw that Connor's eyes were glowing as well and he had spread his wings. Aaron's hands now held floating balls of blue and white flames.

With both men standing there, I knew they would do anything to protect me, and I knew how much they both meant to me. I wouldn't let them fight for me, especially with nothing to fight about, but I understood the reaction from the others in the room. Everyone fears the unknown, even if they were supernatural creatures.

"I'm sorry," I said to try to calm everyone down. I let the fire die down in my eyes and retracted my fangs then turned to both Aaron and Connor with a smile.

Aaron looked at me right away, but Connor's eyes continued to glow. "Connor, it's okay," I whispered to him and walked in front of him. Eyes still aglow, at least they came off the crowd and focused on me. I smiled at him sweetly, and his eyes finally returned to normal.

"We are fine," I said to the anxious crowd then gestured at the photographs. "I don't know who the man is, but the woman's name is Lavinia."

The rest of the room calmed down as well, and everyone sat back in their chairs.

Beatrice nodded at one of the men at the table with a pile of files in front of him. He looked like a typical bookworm with brown hair, light skin, and black-rimmed glasses. He grabbed a large binder and flipped through it with inhuman speed, stopping abruptly to read something on a page. Then he scanned through more of the piles of folders until he found what he was looking for.

He pushed the glasses up his nose then began to read out loud. "Lavinia Sava, born 1608, in Borsa, Romania. She was turned into a vampire in 1629 by Dr. William Rowsley."

"Any information on the doctor?" Beatrice asked.

"Let me see," he said as he rummaged through the pile of files again. "Ahh, yes. Dr. William Rowsley, born 1499, in Limerick, Ireland. Turned into a vampire in 1529. He... he was born into the O'Brien coven," he said with surprise.

"So, he is or rather *was* a warlock," Beatrice assessed.

The man nodded and looked back at the file. "There is no information on who he is personally, but this says that he worked for the Romanian government, specializing in innovative weaponry," he explained before reading on silently to himself.

"What is it, Francis?" Beatrice prompted.

"Well, it looks like he has been working on a project called Triadic. But that's all it says about that."

"Is he still alive?"

"I have no date of death listed, but... here, there is a photo of him. It's not too clear, but..."

"What?" Beatrice asked when he didn't continue.

"I'm not certain, but it could be the same man in those photos." With that, he stood up and brought the file to Beatrice.

She put her glasses back on as he handed her the file. "Hmm, it's possible. Is this the only picture of him?"

"Yes ma'am."

"That's hardly right," Beatrice said with pursed lips then turned to the man sitting next to Francis. "Thomas, make a note to update all the profiles with clear photos ASAP."

The man nodded and started writing on the notepad on the table in front of him.

I couldn't help wondering how they had so many files and whether they had profiles on every supernatural creature. As just file folders, the records didn't seem very secure. I couldn't even imagine what would happen if some human got a hold of them. In the wrong hands, all this information would be extremely dangerous.

Even as I considered that, everyone at the table continued looking through profiles and talking among themselves. I didn't want to be rude, but I knew I had to go warn Ian and the others about Lavinia. While thinking of an excuse to take my leave, my phone started to vibrate. I glanced at the caller ID and saw it was Alan.

"Nina," Beatrice said, startling me and instinctively making me put my phone away. "I am sure you have many questions for us as we do for you."

I nodded.

"But for now," she continued as she turned to her grandson, "Aaron, please take your friends into the living room while we finish our meeting in here."

Connor and I followed Aaron back to the living room. I sat on the couch, and Connor sat down on the other side as far away from me as he could.

"I can't just stay here. I have to go talk to Ian," I said just as Aaron's phone started to ring.

He pulled it halfway out of his pocket then silenced it without looking at it before returning it to its place and saying, "We should wait to see what my grandmother says first. For all we know, your family may not be at Lavinia's house anymore."

"What do you mean? Where would they be?" I asked anxiously.

"Maybe Jacob thought they weren't safe and had them moved," he explained.

"Who is Jacob?" Connor chimed in.

"He's someone on the council."

"Oh, you mean those crazy creatures in that room?" Connor asked bitingly.

"You have no room to talk," Aaron countered.

"I'm an angel, not a bull or snake creature. Come on, a snake? What does that tell you? All we need is to let a vampire in on the decision making, and we will all have gone crazy," he huffed.

"I'm a nyxling," I said with a bristle. "It's like a vampire."

"No. As a nyxling, you are a demigod," he replied.

Aaron looked at me in confusion.

Most of what we found about nyxlings had referred to them as similar to vampires, but Connor was prompt with the reminder. "If you'll recall, nyxlings have the blood of the goddess in them... always, not only when they turn. They are descended from her line. You can't be a nyxling unless you are related to Nyx. Hence, all nyxlings are, in a sense, demigods."

"Who told you that?" Aaron asked.

"Who told me?" Connor asked incredulously as he stood up. He took off Aaron's jacket and tossed it onto the couch. "I am an angel. I speak to the gods. Oh, and it's also just common sense," he said dismissively as he started toward the door.

"Where are you going?" Aaron asked.

"To the warehouse," he responded and walked out of the room.

"Why is he so angry?" Aaron asked.

I shrugged and stood up to follow Connor. "I'm sorry, Aaron, but it's my family at stake."

"Fine," he said as he grabbed his jacket off the couch.

As we walked out the door, we saw Connor fly off into the distance.

"People in this town are going to think they're going crazy with all his flying about," Aaron surmised as he watched Connor go.

I laughed. I couldn't imagine my reaction at looking up and seeing a man with giant wings flying over my head if I didn't already know about supernaturals. I wasn't even sure I would tell anyone about it.

While we stood in the driveway, a man came out of the house. He looked normal and in his late 20s, with brown hair and eyes, but he wore a bulletproof vest, which made me think he was a police officer.

"Hi, Jacob. Nice to see you, man," Aaron said to him as he shook his hand. "Oh, Nina, this is Jacob."

"Hi, Jacob," I replied anxiously.

Although I didn't want to be rude, I was eager to get back to the warehouse, so I started walking toward the car. Aaron noticed right away and ran to catch up with me.

"He's going to think I'm a bitch," I muttered to Aaron as he got in the car with me.

"No. He knows you're worried about your family, but he could help us with..." he trailed off as his phone started ringing again. "It's Alan. This is the second time he's called," he explained then answered. "Hello... You did? What did you find? Yeah, we found out some things about her, too. Wait, he did what? We're on our way," Aaron said in a rush before hanging up.

"What?" I asked with wide eyes, realizing that I hadn't been paying enough attention to the phone call.

"They found something."

"And?"

"He didn't say what it was, but..."

"But? But what?" I asked anxiously.

"He said Ian went to look for Lavinia."

"What? How? The sun is still out!"

"I didn't get all the details. Alan just told me that there was something we had to see at the warehouse."

I gave Aaron a look and pressed the gas pedal to the floor, making him grab onto the handle above the top of the window.

We made it back to the warehouse in less than five minutes, and I blurred inside and up the stairs into the loft.

"Where is he?" I asked when I saw Alan.

"He left."

"How?"

"I'll show you," he said as he ran out through the loft door where we ran into Aaron who was just getting there.

"Where are you guys going?" he asked.

When we didn't answer him, he followed us back down the stairs.

We got almost to the door that led outside, but Alan turned to the left and went down another hallway. It led to a set of double doors through which he hurried. We entered an enormous garage with six vehicles in it and two other empty parking spaces. Alan went directly to a car covered with a dusty gray sheet. He grabbed the bottom of the sheet and pulled it off.

"My car!" I said in surprise. Indeed, it was my blue Celica, but it was still banged up. I looked inside, and it still had all my papers and garbage on the floor, too. "I don't understand."

"Like I said," Alan quipped, "you were set up."

I narrowed my eyes at him then looked back at my car. Lavinia had never had my car fixed. She'd had a new, identical one waiting. And that meant she likely had caused the accident.

Until that moment, I had always thought that somehow it had been Alan. "So, it wasn't you?" I asked him.

"Me?" he asked with blatant offense. "What possible reason would I have to total your car?"

"I... This is... I," I stammered.

"What happened to your car? And how did it get here?" Aaron asked as he walked up to us.

I'd never told Aaron and Alan what had happened to my car, so I filled them in. After my story, Alan said he remembered Lavinia talking to someone about a car when they'd hooked up a few nights before the accident, but he hadn't cared then to listen to any of the details.

They had been together on and off for years, so they always had their own things going on. Apparently, Lavinia had never stayed for more than a few nights with him before, so when she'd decided to find a place in town, he had thought it was a bit odd.

"Ian. How did he leave?" I asked to bring them back to the immediate point.

"He took the one car with blacked out windows."

"Why didn't you stop him?"

Alan scowled. "The asshat opened the damn garage door. What was I supposed to do?"

"I can do a locator spell on him. I just need something that belongs to him," Aaron announced as he started back toward the loft.

Alan and I followed Aaron upstairs and looked around the loft for anything we could use for the spell. Finally, we found a toothbrush; however, we weren't completely sure whether it was Ian's or Zay's. If it was Zay's, we figured it would just lead us to the high school and we would know it was the wrong one. We had to try anyway.

Aaron started the spell as we waited anxiously. While we waited, Alan drank a blood bag, but when he offered me one, I declined. I was secretly hoping I could feed off Aaron again. I didn't want to hurt him, but the taste of his blood and the feeling it gave me was extraordinary and addictive.

Alan looked at me askance when I'd said no to the blood bag, but he let it go.

As Aaron finished the spell, it didn't point to the high school, so we were hopeful it had found Ian. We all ran downstairs and looked through the cars in the garage. There were two trucks, an SUV, and three sedans left.

I let Aaron choose the car and, unsurprisingly, he picked one of the trucks. It was a pitch-black Ford F-150. I wasn't much for trucks, but it was very pretty. The cab was so tall that Aaron had to help me get in on the passenger's side.

"I guess I'll just stay here then," Alan yelled sarcastically after us as we pulled out of the garage.

Aaron had a satisfied smile on his face the entire time we drove. And since he knew Hallowed Hills so well, we had no trouble getting to our destination: the original Hallowed Hills town settlement.

"Why would he be here?" I asked.

"No clue, but this is where the spell said he is," Aaron explained.

We walked through the front door, and everything appeared pretty normal. A cashier was at the front register, and a few customers were in the store.

Looking around, I was surprised to see Becca sitting there on a bench. I checked my watch. It was only 1 p.m., so she should have still been in school.

"Becca?" I asked, which made her stand up quickly.

"Nina!" she exclaimed and hugged me. "Oh, my god! I missed you so much!"

I felt tears of joy build up in my eyes. As I hugged her, I made sure not to hold her too tightly. "I missed you, too," I said as we both wiped our tears away.

"What are you doing here?" she asked.

"Umm... I was about to ask you the same thing."

Becca looked shyly at Aaron, which made me realize that I had never introduced them. She knew of him but had never actually met him before.

"Oh, this is my... this..." I stammered, not knowing exactly what to say. After everything that had happened, we still had never discussed our relationship status.

"Hi, I'm Aaron, Nina's boyfriend," Aaron chimed in with the save.

I smiled and blushed at his words, but Aaron just grabbed my hand and held onto it.

"Nice to meet you," Becca answered shyly.

"So, what are you doing here?" I asked again.

"I asked her to come," Ian explained as he walked up to us.

"Ian. What are you doing here? How did you even get here?"

"Have you been to the warehouse?" he asked.

"Yes."

"So, you know."

I nodded and proceeded to tell him everything else we'd learned that day. He began to get so mad that his eyes started to change. Since Becca had never seen the change, she moved a little behind Aaron.

"Relax," Aaron said to him.

Ian's eyes quickly changed back to normal when he realized he was scaring Becca.

"Sorry, Becca. I'm fine," he assured her then turned back to us. "Lavinia told me about a secret room in the settlement that vampires couldn't enter.

Originally, I figured that meant that nyxlings wouldn't be able to either. Becca was the only human I knew who was aware of me, so I called her."

"Why didn't you just ask Aaron?" I suggested. "It's more dangerous for Becca than it is for him. He can..."

"Can what?" Becca asked as her eyes widened with curiosity.

I looked at Aaron then back at Ian who was shaking his head.

"She knows about you, too?" Aaron asked me, going back to what Ian had said.

I looked over at Becca because, honestly, I wasn't sure how much she knew. However, her shy smile confirmed that she knew everything. "Yes," I answered simply.

"And you trust her?" he asked.

I turned to Becca again and smiled. "With my life."

"Then I trust her, too," Aaron said then proceeded to tell Becca about him and his entire family.

All in all, Becca didn't really seem too surprised. Ian had told me that in the past few months, she had learned so much about the supernatural that most things didn't bother her. The only thing that really had shocked her was the existence of nyxlings since she had never heard of them before.

With everyone on the same page, the four of us started to look around the store and the settlement. Of course, Ian was stuck inside the store, but the rest of us looked through all the original homes now set up as museums. I was excited because I had always wanted to see the museums but had never had the chance to do so.

After a while, we decided to split up. I went to the original Osbourne home while Aaron and Becca looked in some of the others. When I walked into the house, it smelled of damp wood and disinfectant. Although the home had been kept up pretty well, I could still see chipped walls and cracked floor panels. I walked around the home, touching the walls as I went through the hallways.

Barriers blocked the entrances to most of the rooms, but I had to look through them. Moving my hair away from my ear, I listened carefully. Certain no one else was around, I stepped over the velvet rope to look in the living room first.

I knocked on all the inside walls but didn't find anything, then I continued into the other rooms. As I walked around and felt the floor crack under my weight a few times, I started to understand why there were barriers in front of some of the rooms. After painstakingly looking through the entire house, I still hadn't found any secret rooms, so I left.

As I was walking down the porch stairs, Aaron and Becca were coming toward me.

"Anything?" I asked.

"Nothing," Aaron answered.

"I didn't find anything either, just smelly old houses," Becca reported as she scrunched up her nose.

"Well, maybe Lavinia lied. It wouldn't surprise me. She's lied about everything else," I said bleakly as I looked back at the Osborne house.

It was then that I noticed outside doors leading to a cellar. It wasn't really a hidden room, but no one would have a reason to go down there. Without a word, I walked over to the double doors leading into the ground, and Aaron and Becca followed me. There was a padlock on it, so I glanced around to check for onlookers. Seeing none, I crushed it with my palm.

"Whoa," Becca said. "Remind me never to piss you off," she added in awe.

I turned to her and laughed then opened the doors. As the doors dropped open, they made a loud bang. We all stopped moving and looked around to see if anyone was coming toward us. The settlement was pretty quiet because it was the middle of the day during the week, so we got lucky. No one seemed to have noticed.

Turning back toward the opening, we walked down the creepy stairs and found a lightbulb hanging from the ceiling. I pulled on the chain and surprisingly it worked.

"Now, why would that work unless there was something to hide down here?" Becca voiced.

Aaron closed the doors to the outside, and we all walked into an even creepier hallway. The odor of damp, moldy mildew was so strong that I could tell even Aaron and Becca smelled it.

The first lightbulb illuminated the narrow stone hallway all the way down to another light. I pulled that one, too, and we continued walking down the hallway, avoiding the water that was dripping from the ceiling and creating various puddles on the floor.

We finally made it to the end of the hallway to find a lonely door barely visible in the light from the last lightbulb. I pushed on the door and found that it was unexpectedly heavy. I pushed harder and finally opened it all the way.

Entering, I looked behind the door and saw there was a giant concrete slab attached to it. Whoever had put it there had to have known only certain people would be able to open it.

We walked farther into the room. It was mostly empty but had a large couch in the middle and a brown antique desk in the corner. On the farthest wall was another door.

I walked toward it and opened it, but when I tried to walk in, I immediately felt an electric shock and fell to the ground.

"Nina!" Aaron and Becca shouted simultaneously as they ran to me.

"I'm fine," I said as I brushed myself off. "I just can't get in."

After Aaron and Becca laughed a little at my expense, they went inside the room while I sat down on the couch.

They were taking a long time, so I sent a text to Ian letting him know what we had found. I didn't want him doing anything crazy like trying to run to the house while the sun was still out because he hadn't heard anything from us. Ian promised he would wait until sunset before coming to explore the cellar.

When I finished texting him, I got up to peek inside the room where Aaron and Becca had gone, but I couldn't see anything except a bare wall and another hallway leading to the left, which went beyond my line of sight.

Anxious, I walked around the room I was in, and the desk caught my eye. I tried to open the top drawer, but it was locked. I pulled harder, and the drawer front broke off in my hands, which made a bunch of papers spill out all over the floor.

Annoyed at the mess, I sat on the floor and started picking up all the papers. I tried to read some of the pages, but they weren't in English. I was excited when I found a small sticky note in Spanish that I could read.

El plan de la niña funcionó. Los tres están ahora en Hallowed Hills. William ha sido informado.

I could understand Spanish and speak it pretty well, but my reading wasn't the best. Even so, I understood exactly what the note said. I assumed the girl mentioned in the note was Lavinia, and the "three" mentioned were me and my brothers, but I didn't understand how her plan had worked to get us to town. It had no date or anything else on it, so I wasn't sure if whomever had written it had informed this William.

"Did you find something?" Aaron asked suddenly.

"Geez," I cried out, grabbing my chest as if my heart still beat.

"You know, for a nyxling, you sure let a whole lot of people sneak up on you," he said playfully.

I smiled at him then stood up and grabbed the back of his neck, pulling his face to mine and kissing him deeply.

"What was that for?" he asked with a grin.

"Nothing. Just remembering the last time someone snuck up on me."

Aaron caressed my cheek, pulled me into his body, and kissed me again. I pulled away from him when I actually heard someone approach this time.

"Did you guys find anything?" I asked as Becca walked through the door.

"Umm, yes," Becca said sheepishly as she handed me a file folder.

"What?" I asked as I looked at her and then back at Aaron.

They both looked very worried, so I quickly opened the file. The first page had my picture and under it a date with a checkmark next to it. I read the date: *09/19/2009*. It was the day I'd been hit by the car; the day I'd died.

I flipped to the next page. It had a picture of Ian and underneath a date with a checkmark as well: *11/24/2009*. That was the day *Ian* had been shot; the day he'd died.

Anxiously, I flipped to the next page and put my hand to my mouth in shock when I saw it. A picture of Zay had a date under it, too: *11/26/2009*.

"What's today?" I asked nervously.

"It's November 25, the day before Thanksgiving," Aaron answered hollowly.

"Where is Zay?" I asked as I handed Aaron the file.

"I don't know. School?"

I started to run toward the door.

"Nina! What are you going to do?" Becca called after me. "You can't go to the school. Everyone thinks you and Ian are too sick to leave the house," Becca said to me.

I stopped in my tracks. "What do you mean people think I am too sick to leave the house? I thought everyone thought I died."

"My family didn't want to make the announcement until they knew for sure. They convinced your dad to tell the school you had been sent to a specialist out of the country after your accident," Aaron explained.

"Wait. My parents? They agreed to that?"

"My family had documents made to confirm the transfer."

"But my mom thought I was dead. That's why she..." I paused, not wanting to say the words out loud.

"As far as I know, my family worked only with your dad. I'm not sure how much your mom knows," he explained then paused. "As the story goes, when you recovered, you were able to go back home, but then you got sick."

"Lavinia told me my family thought I was dead," I argued, still trying to reconcile the stories.

"Lavinia lied," Aaron stated.

"Your dad told the school Ian got sick days before you came back into the country. Because your immune system was weakened, you were the only one in the family to catch what he had," Becca explained. "It worked because a few days before... um, you know... he was killed, he wasn't in school because he and Alan had gone out of town to try to find you."

"What illness do I have?"

"Not sure. Your dad took care of that part, but that was before we knew you could walk in the sun."

"Wait. Hold on. Connor said that only he and the Carriers knew I wasn't dead. Connor wouldn't lie to me," I stated with certainty.

"He didn't know Ian and I knew," Becca answered shyly. "I kind of gathered that he and Alan didn't really get along," she laughed.

As I tried to wrap my head around all this new information, I thought of something else. "But Ian only changed yesterday. How could the school know all of this?"

"My family helped," Aaron said with a smile. "No one questions the Carriers."

I was annoyed with my dad, but I had to trust there was a reason he hadn't told my mom about me. Still, he couldn't have known until recently. The way he had looked at me in the abandoned building in the woods had been complete shock.

Aaron took my hand, pulling me out of my thoughts. "We'll go," he said then kissed me softly on the lips before he and Becca headed toward the door.

Becca stopped too and hugged me. "We will find him," she reassured me.

"Becca, it might be really dangerous."

"I'll be okay. Besides, I have a warlock protecting me," she quipped.

I smiled at her and slowly pulled her into my arms. "Thank you."

I followed Aaron and Becca back to the settlement store where we found Ian asleep on the bench. We woke him up and told him what was going on.

He wanted to go help, but he knew he couldn't. As Aaron and Becca left, I told him I'd stay at the settlement with him until the sun went down.

"This is so dumb. We can just use the blacked-out car parked downstairs. It's in an underground garage, so there is no risk at all," Ian argued.

"There is a risk. First off, I know that Lavinia loves unique cars. What type is this one?"

"A 2010 Rolls-Royce Phantom," he said under his breath.

"I knew it. Come on, Ian. Even if we make it to the car and out of the garage, you know there is going to be some police officer who gets curious. They will find a reason to pull us over, even if it's just to see who is driving it. When they find out that the car isn't ours, they will probably make both of us get out."

"That sounds ridiculous and made up," he huffed.

"Let's just drop it for now. Aaron will call us when he has some information," I insisted.

He didn't respond, but he didn't disagree either. "How have you been these last few weeks? I missed you," I smiled.

"I missed you, too," he smiled back. "Other than not having my sister, things have been good. I've learned so much from the Carriers about the supernatural world, but I spent most of my time with Connor," he said, looking at me as if he wanted to tell me something.

"That's good," I said nervously, not knowing what kind of information he knew about Connor. Right now, I didn't want to know.

"You know, the thing with you and Connor... it really shouldn't have happened. You were in a parking lot. Not only could someone have seen you, but now there will always be the question of what could have been."

I wasn't entirely sure what Ian was talking about. He hadn't mentioned the kiss in the hospital room. The parking lot? Nothing had happened in the parking lot. Either way, I didn't want to continue talking about Connor and me, so I quickly changed the subject.

"You know, Becca could get hurt. You shouldn't have brought her into this."

"I know, but I would never have let anything happen to her. If I thought being here would be dangerous, I wouldn't have asked her. But I guess anywhere in this town could be dangerous," he realized.

We were getting bored just sitting around, so we started wandering around the store a bit, but the employees were starting to get suspicious. Ian had been there for hours and hadn't even gone to see the museums.

To allay some of their concern, we bought a book about the town's history and sat down to flip through it.

While we were reading, my phone started to ring, so I answered it. "Hi, Aaron."

"Zay is not here," he said right away.

"What?" I asked too loudly as I jumped up from the bench.

"Meet us at my house," he said abruptly.

"I'll be right there," I finished then hung up.

"I have to go," I said to Ian.

"I'm coming, too," he said definitively. "I heard."

Of course, he'd heard. He was a nyxling.

I nodded, knowing there was no use arguing with him. Zay was in danger, and he wouldn't just sit back and wait. Ian turned to walk down the hallway to the parking garage elevator, and I followed. Once we were in the garage, he blurred over to the giant black car.

Getting inside, I admired the beautiful, glossy black interior and black leather seats. Every window was completely blacked out. For a normal person, it would be very difficult to see out.

"We are definitely going to get pulled over," I said.

"That's okay. We just won't stop."

Ian pulled the car up to the massive garage door, and I grabbed his hand. I was still scared for him to go into the sun, but when we drove into the daylight, I was relieved that he was fine. "Jesus. I swear that if I had a heartbeat, I would have had a heart attack right there," I breathed.

Ian laughed and continued to drive, picking up Alan from the warehouse on our way to the Carrier house.

Alan told us he had found hidden cameras all over the loft, which meant that Lavinia knew everything we'd done the entire time we'd been there. As such, she was not going to let us find her unless she wanted to be found.

When we arrived at the Carrier house, we drove into the garage where Alan kept his car; it was blacked out as well, but he only used it in emergencies. It was a simple, brand-new BMW sedan but nowhere near as noticeable as the boat we were driving. As I examined it, I realized it was the same car he had been driving the first day I'd met him.

Beatrice was waiting for us when we walked into the house, but Aaron and Becca were not there yet. I knew it from her face before she said anything.

"They took Zay," I said but not as a question.

She nodded in sympathetic confirmation. "I have men searching for him. Aaron and Becca already picked up your mother and father. We thought it best for them not to be around, so we put them on a plane as soon as we heard about Zay."

"They left?" I asked, not sure if I was hurt or glad.

"We didn't give them much of a choice. We knew that if we were able to save Zay, your mother would be the next target."

I looked at her askance for a moment then realized I had never flipped to the last page in the file at the Osbourne house. I had forgotten that my mom could be a target, too. Although I didn't want to be away from my parents, I understood why it was best for them to be far from here.

Aaron made it to the house only a few minutes later, saying he had dropped Becca off at her house. I was thankful for that. As much as she wanted to help, it was very dangerous for her.

We set to working with the council to try to find out where Zay could have been taken. It became frustrating very quickly. Even though there were supernatural creatures on the council, none of them were as fast as nyxlings and vampires.

I knew Alan and Ian couldn't search in the daylight, but I could. Even so, Beatrice forbade it, saying that I was still just a child and the council had it covered.

I didn't want to go against her wishes, but I had to. As soon as Beatrice went back into the office, I told the boys I needed to go help with the search. Ian was semi-okay with it because Zay was his brother, too.

"If you're going, I'm going," Aaron insisted.

I was hesitant to let him. Even though Aaron was very strong as a warlock, vampires were still stronger. Not only that, but vampires didn't care who they hurt to get what they wanted. I felt bad thinking that way about vampires, especially knowing Alan, but he was an exception, not the majority.

"Aaron, I'm not going to take the car," I said, hoping he wouldn't feel comfortable with me carrying him around. When he didn't say anything more, I figured I was right.

"Call me as soon as you find something, and I will be right there," Aaron said as he stroked my hand.

Ian hugged me goodbye then I walked toward the large archway leading to the hall. However, right then two very large men stepped out in front of me. I rolled my eyes and easily picked up and moved the bigger of the two with his arms still crossed in front of him. With a smirk, I glanced back at the second one who was still big but not quite as big. He looked at me with wide eyes then stepped out of the way.

"I'll call you," I turned to say to Aaron before blurring away.

As I ran, I could feel myself getting weaker. I had been in the sun for more than seven hours at this point, I hadn't fed much, and I hadn't rested at all. As much as I didn't want anyone else to get hurt, I would need help once I found where Zay had been taken.

I ran around town for a little over an hour before stopping abruptly, bending down and putting my weight over my knees. There were no cars, for which I was thankful, because I hadn't noticed where I'd been running. I was on the side of a fairly large road. If someone had seen me just pop up out of nowhere, I could have caused an accident.

As it was, I saw a woman jogging about 200 yards in front of me. She had her earbuds in, so she probably wouldn't even hear me coming. I shook my head to try to get that predatory thought out of my head, but I was so hungry. I ran closer to her but stayed more to the forest on our left.

The girl stopped when I blurred by her. "Hello?" she asked, removing one earbud.

I could feel my eyes being engulfed in magenta as she peered into the trees. As she got closer to me, her sweet smell began to drive me wild. I pressed the back of my head against the tree where I hid, feeling utterly ashamed of myself. She was only a few inches from me when I blurred away.

When I stopped next, I found myself in the middle of the woods. That made me think of the abandoned building where Ian had been shot. Looking around, I realized I had no idea where I was, so I just picked a direction and started running.

At last, I made it to a familiar street and was able to get to the building from there. It was immediately apparent that it wasn't empty. Smoke was coming from the roof, which still looked half demolished from where I stood.

Listening carefully, I heard someone struggling and like something was covering their mouth. I quickly climbed up a nearby tree. When I got to the top branches, I peered through the mostly caved in roof and saw Zay sitting inside the building. From there, I watched a strange-looking man walk out of a door and bend down over Zay.

"I don't know why he thinks a little shit like you would be part of this, but here we are," he said as he pulled the covering away from Zay's mouth.

The bulky, heavyset man perhaps in his 50s wore all black. His hands and arms were covered in thick brown hair, but he had none on top of his head, which instead bore a scar going straight down his forehead and over his right eye. Pretty large, he reminded me of the bouncer-type guys at the Carrier house.

"Here, eat," he said as he dropped a metal plate and cup in front of Zay.

The man removed the ropes from around Zay's hands and walked back out through the same door. I watched Zay devour the offered sandwich.

I wondered for a moment why the kidnappers had left him out in the open like this, but I quickly realized why. They didn't know I could walk in the sun, so a pool of sunlight would be the best place to prevent a nyxling or vampire from trying to rescue him.

I thought of just going in and grabbing him, but I was so drained that I was afraid I would make things worse and get myself captured. Instead, I pulled out my phone and sent a text to Aaron to let him know where I was. I also suggested it would be better if fewer of us went to the building because I wasn't sure what they might do to Zay. We agreed to limit the rescue party to him, Ian, Connor, and Alan and have them meet me at an intersection close by.

Before heading off to meet them, I listened for any sounds or voices. I could make out two distinctly different men and a bunch of rustling. With all that interference, I wasn't sure how many people were inside.

I wanted to let Zay know I was here without anyone else knowing, but I wasn't sure how. I searched through my pockets and found a folded-up piece of paper. It was a note card I'd used for math class. I ripped off pieces and tried to make it look like a crescent moon, which I had learned during my time with Lavinia was part of the symbol for Nyx.

Using what felt like my last bit of energy to jump from the tree onto the roof, I dropped the crudely shaped paper down to Zay and jumped back off the roof before he saw me. I scrambled back up the tree to see if he had gotten my message and was happy to see him holding the paper and smiling.

As I stumbled to our designated meeting spot, exhaustion crashed over me like a relentless tide. Alan blurred to my side in an instant, his concern evident in the gentle support of his arms as he helped me to my feet.

"Thanks," I murmured, leaning into him for a moment of respite.

With a gentle yet determined stride, Aaron joined us and wrapped his arms around me. Finding solace in the warmth of his embrace, my worries momentarily melted away. I nestled in closer, seeking refuge in the safety of his chest as I felt the steady rhythm of his heartbeat beneath my cheek. In that moment, enveloped by his presence, I felt a sense of peace wash over me along with a silent reassurance that everything would be all right as long as he was by my side. With a contented sigh, I surrendered to the comfort of his embrace and allowed myself to momentarily forget the challenges that lay ahead.

"Nina, you look drained," Connor's voice cut through my haze of weariness. His tone was laced with worry. "When was the last time you rested or fed?"

Ignoring his pointed inquiry, I turned to him with a furrowed brow. "Where have you been?" I demanded, my frustration bubbling to the surface.

But Connor wasn't one to be deterred. "When was the last time you fed?" he persisted, his gaze unwavering.

My frown deepened, but I straightened, attempting to muster some semblance of composure. "I'm fine," I insisted, although the weariness in my voice betrayed my bravado.

Aaron intervened, taking charge with a firm hand as he guided me toward the sheltering canopy of the forest. "Come on," he urged gently, his touch both comforting and reassuring as we ventured into the darkness of the woods.

When we were far enough away, he held out his wrist to me. I didn't hesitate taking it and bit down, drinking a bit more than I had the first time.

"Thanks," I said with a smile.

Aaron kissed me and pushed me lightly against a tree, his touch sending electric waves of pleasure coursing through my veins. "I will do everything that is in my power to save Zay," he promised intimately.

"I know," I responded then bit my wrist and presented it to him.

He grinned and drank from my wrist. His blood tasted really good to me, but the feeling of him taking mine was exquisite, almost erotic. He drank for longer from me than I had from him, but I didn't care.

When he finally released me, his gaze burned with intensity, then his lips claimed mine in a fervent kiss that left me breathless and yearning for more. It was as if he was exploring every inch of my soul with each touch and setting my very being ablaze with desire.

"Um... guys," my brother's voice came from afar, pulling us back to reality with a jolt.

Reluctantly and more than a bit embarrassed that my brother heard us, I pulled myself off Aaron but held his sharp blue gaze and looked deeply into his eyes.

He put his forehead against mine and closed his eyes. "We are never going to get a break," he whispered, his voice filled with playful irritation as he caressed my cheek.

I smiled at him and pulled him toward the others.

"Welcome back," Alan quipped with a knowing grin. "How was it?" he added as he waggled his eyebrows suggestively.

Aaron pushed him playfully, then we started to talk about our plan. It was dark now, so they would be expecting all of us to be looking for Zay. Our only hope was that they would underestimate the time it took us to find where he was.

I described the man I'd seen, and Aaron said it sounded like one of the men on the council who was a Nandi bear, a creature who was able to shift his form into a very large bear but was still extremely hairy in his human form.

Aaron and Alan were enraged that the council could have been infiltrated. "I have to let the council know," Alan said as he started to type a text message.

"Just don't tell them where we are," I begged him.

"Nina, they can help us. They can send multiple teams of agents," he argued.

"But if the kidnappers see an entire army approaching, they might hurt Zay," I explained.

"One hour," Alan said sternly. "If it takes longer than that, I will be calling them."

"Deal." I smiled.

Regrouping, Alan suggested, "Nina and I should run to the house while you three go together in the jeep we brought. Nina and I will walk up to the front and let ourselves be seen."

"You want to use her as bait?" Connor scowled.

"Nina can take care of herself," Alan said to him.

I smiled at Alan when he said that, happy to know that at least someone didn't see me as the "damsel in distress."

"You three should go around the back. The hope is that they won't expect Ian. As a nyxling, he has more control, way sooner than a vampire. If they think vampires and nyxlings have the same bloodlust, him being here might throw them off."

"This is not a good idea," Connor warned.

"Lavinia also knows you and Alan don't get along, so they might think it's just the two of us here. That adds more to the element of surprise," I added with a smile toward Connor.

He didn't say anything, but he seemed to relax a little bit. It was the best plan we could come up with in so little time.

I didn't tell them, but I also hoped that because I had told Lavinia there was nothing between Connor and me, she would think I wanted to be as far away from him as possible.

When Alan and I got to the building, I could tell something had changed. Instead of only smoke, fire engulfed the building.

"Again?" I said in full irritation as I jumped up to the roof where I'd last seen Zay, thus throwing our entire plan out the window.

When Alan and I reached the top, we found a vaguely familiar man with two bear-like creatures standing behind him. It clicked. This was the man I had seen in the pictures at Aaron's house. We knew he was a vampire. All three of them immediately turned to look at us, and that's when I saw Lavinia standing next to Zay.

"Let him go!" I yelled as I felt magenta flood my eyes and my fangs grow. Glancing at Alan, I could see his eyes were red, and his fangs were out as well.

The two Nandi bears stepped in front of the man as if guarding him.

"Ah, you must be Nina," the man said as he moved lazily in front of the bears. "But where is our Ian? Still looking for Lavinia?" he asked with a chuckle.

I had forgotten about Lavinia's cameras in the loft, so they probably knew Ian had already made the change. But luckily, we hadn't gone back to the loft after the settlement, so they didn't know we had caught up with him there.

"I'm sorry," the man offered almost politely, "I haven't introduced myself."

"We know who you are," I declared angrily.

"Oh, you do now? Interesting. And how do you know who I am? I know Lavinia didn't tell you," William drawled with a gesture toward her.

"No. I have friends, *real* friends," I asserted with a pointed glare at Lavinia.

She turned away quickly and held Zay tightly as he made an attempt to get away.

William moved toward them and grabbed Zay by the back of his jacket collar. He walked him toward the roof's edge and held his arm out over nothing, dangling Zay three stories above the ground.

"No!" I yelled.

"Let me go!" Zay yelled as he kicked the air around him.

"Stop, Zay!" I yelled. The more he kicked, the more anxious I became. William might be able to hold him, but I didn't want to risk it.

"You don't agree with us because you don't understand. People have been looking into this prophecy for hundreds of thousands of years, but they have never really understood what they were looking for," William explained. "Muminah was smart to collect the blood of all creatures to throw everyone off the scent, but ultimately Talaatah could only be about nyxlings. I knew that the second I heard vampire blood was collected. She would only do that if she knew the prophecy wasn't going to be about them," he explained.

"You don't know what you're talking about," I hissed at him.

"Don't I? Love the new eyes, by the way," he said evilly.

I dropped my gaze to the ground then glanced at Alan.

"Yep. Pretty noticeable," Alan whispered.

I thought about just running toward William and grabbing Zay. Even if he fell, I could still blur to catch him, but only if no one got in my way.

I closed my eyes and tried to hear the others, but I couldn't. That was almost a relief. If I could hear them, William could, too.

"Please," I pleaded with him. "You don't even know if his body will accept the change."

"Why wouldn't it? There are two already. We just need the third."

"Even if you are right, what do you get out of it?" Alan shouted.

I was surprised to hear his question, but also surprised I had never thought about that. What *would* the benefit be to William if we were part of Talaatah?

I turned back to William and waited for his answer.

"Why would I tell you?"

I rolled my eyes, mostly at myself for thinking he would reveal why. Then William brought Zay close to him and put a knife to his throat.

"Wait!" I shouted. "He doesn't even have nyxling blood in him!"

"Ah... finally... the point. So, you'll feed it to him then?"

"Yes," I answered reluctantly.

"And you'll let my friends put these beautiful bracelets on you?" he asked as he gestured toward the two bears.

The bears then turned back into humans, revealing their completely naked bodies, which instinctively made me look away. When I turned back, they wore basketball shorts and were rummaging through a bag sitting next to William. Then they pulled out a large iron box that opened to reveal several blue bracelets like the ones you'd get at a carnival, only made of leather.

"What kind of bracelets are those?" I whispered to Alan.

Alan clenched his jaw. "They're saturated with a poison infused with Nephilim sweat and spelled so the sweat will enter the bloodstream. The council uses them to weaken us and severely diminish our powers. They were made for vampires. I assume they work the same for nyxlings, and apparently, they assume that, too."

"Well?" William prompted.

"Yes," I regretfully answered.

The two men approached us with the iron box. Alan glared at the man with the scar through his right eye. The man only grinned at him as he approached until they stood right in front of us and waited.

Alan rolled his eyes then put out his wrist. I followed his lead and did the same. As soon as the bracelet was on Alan, he sank down to the ground, and the man kicked him in the stomach, which made him tumble over.

I blurred over to him and bared my fangs at the man.

"Ah, ah, ah," William said as he repositioned the blade near Zay's throat.

I let my fangs return to normal, but I still stood between the man and Alan as I presented my wrist to him.

As he slapped one bracelet on, it felt like a knife stabbing me in the wrist. I winced at the pain, but I didn't fall to the ground like Alan had. I realized my mistake when I saw the look of surprise on the man's face.

"Let's do two for her," William instructed as the man held up a second one.

As soon as it was on, I slowly fell to the ground. It was definitely painful, like little needles piercing my skin over and over again, but I was still okay. Then I felt something very cold flowing into my system like I was hooked up to an IV bag.

The two men picked me up by my shoulders and dragged me toward the other three. I acted like I felt really dizzy and laid on the floor while one of the men brought out a huge hunting knife. The other man picked me back up and placed me on my knees while William brought Zay over to us. The man took my arm, put the knife to my wrist, and sliced at it.

"It won't cut," the man said when he realized my skin wouldn't break.

I looked up at him and grinned, and his expression quickly went from confused to worried.

I forcefully shoved away the man holding me, and his body careened through the air before crashing to the ground below. Upon witnessing my display of strength, his accomplice faltered, but his resolve remained. With a glint of menace in his eyes, he brandished the knife and lunged toward me.

Reacting swiftly, I dropped to my side, deftly evading his attack, and hooked his arm in a swift motion. As if a practiced maneuver, I leveraged his momentum, pulling my sternum into his tricep, sending him spiraling over me with perfect execution. A smirk of satisfaction crossed my lips as I realized the hours I'd spent watching wrestling had paid off.

As my assailant regained his footing, I pounced, fangs bared and eyes ablaze with primal fury. The taste of blood filled my mouth as I tore into his neck, my instincts taking over in a savage frenzy.

With crimson stains still fresh on my lips, I turned my gaze toward William with a predatory glint in my eyes. Slowly, deliberately, I stalked toward him, the anticipation of the hunt coursing through my veins just as Connor, Ian, and Aaron appeared on the other side of him and Zay.

"Took you guys long enough," I quipped, sarcasm lacing my words.

"We were waiting for our moment," Ian said jokingly. "Where's Alan?"

"They put bracelets on us," I answered as I showed him my wrists, but I never took my eyes off William. "I guess they don't work on me," I grinned.

"Go help Alan," Connor instructed Aaron who quickly went running toward him.

But William was just smiling. I thought that was kind of odd now that he was so outnumbered, but then I saw two blurs run past me. I took my gaze off William to see something hit Aaron from behind just as he made it to Alan. Something else grabbed Connor's and Ian's feet through the roof and pulled them both through.

Aaron got back to his feet, and I could see what hit him. "Matt?" I whispered.

Not even a second later, Connor came crashing up through the roof with his wings spread wide and Jen dangling from one of his hands. He dropped her in front of William and Lavinia.

With a look at Connor, Lavinia grabbed Jen by the hand and ran off into the night.

By the look of surprise on William's face, I wondered whether Lavinia had told him about Connor, but that confused me based on how scared she was of him when she'd first met him. I would have guessed she would have warned William.

Seconds later, Ian jumped up through the hole in the roof that had just been created. I nodded at him, but, out of the corner of my eye, I saw William move to throw Zay off the roof.

"No!" I yelled as my brother's body flew out into the dark sky.

Connor was still too high up to get to him, so Ian and I started running toward him as William blurred away in the opposite direction.

I glanced up into the sky where Connor had changed direction as well, but I knew he would never make it, so I ran as fast as I could even though I could feel that I was slower. Ian was still a few inches behind me.

Zay's eyes met mine, and then I only saw his hand, so I leapt from where I was.

"Got you," I said as I barely caught his hand. I pulled him back up onto the roof as Connor landed next to us.

At sounds of fighting, I turned and saw Aaron throwing fireballs at Matt to protect Alan even while blood dripped from his neck.

I blurred over to Matt and grabbed him by the back of his jacket the same way William had grabbed Zay. "What are you doing?" I asked as I held him.

A fireball hit me in the back, so I turned around. "Ow," I said to Aaron, more annoyed than hurt.

"You just ran out right in front of me," he laughed uneasily.

In my distraction, Matt wriggled his way out of his jacket and blurred away. I rolled my eyes before throwing the jacket to the ground and running to Alan's side.

"How can we get it off?" I asked as Aaron tried to break the bracelet off Alan's wrist. It looked almost on the verge of snapping when Connor walked up and pulled on the bracelet until it finally broke apart.

"Ahh, thanks," Alan muttered through a cough.

Connor said nothing as he walked over to me and snapped my bracelets off as well then went back to Zay and Ian. He was acting so cold and distant, but I did my best not to let it bother me and ran over to hug Zay.

While I hugged my brother, I noticed that Connor was staring at me. I let go of Zay, then Ian pulled Zay into him as well. I could see that Ian was watching Connor as he continued staring at me.

"We should call Beatrice," Connor said abruptly when he noticed Ian's gaze then quickly turned away.

"I already did," Alan informed him as he and Aaron walked up to us, "but there's not much for them to do now."

I noticed right away that Aaron's wounds had healed, and I knew Alan had healed him. I smiled at Alan, but he didn't seem to notice.

"Maybe they could do something about the raging fire underneath us?" Ian asked sarcastically.

"Right. I'll let them know, and then I'm going to go and rest up a bit," Alan said then looked at Connor.

"Not a bad plan," Aaron agreed as he put an arm around my shoulder.

"Are you coming back with us?" I asked Connor.

"I have a few things I have to take care of," he grumbled then flew off into the night sky.

"He's moody," Aaron noted.

"Well, you would..." Ian started to say then stopped himself and shrugged. "I'm tired. Maybe we should get going," he suggested as he blurred away with Zay.

I heard Zay scream all the way to the ground then start throwing up when they stopped.

"Don't even think about it," Aaron said with a laugh at me.

I kissed him then we climbed down a ladder on the side of the building before walking to the jeep where Ian was still laughing at Zay.

"Are you done?" Ian asked.

"I think so. Don't do that again," Zay grumbled then quickly jumped into the front passenger side of the jeep.

My brothers and I went home, but Aaron went to his house to speak with his grandmother. When we arrived at the house, I was so exhausted I went straight to my bedroom and began to undress. Then I heard a whooshing sound.

"Alan!" I shouted as I tried to cover myself.

He grinned then turned around. "My bad."

"What are you doing here? How did you even get in?" I asked as I put my shirt back on.

"Zay invited me in. I didn't get a chance to talk to you before we left. I wanted to see... ugh. Can I turn around now?"

"Fine," I said as I crossed my arms.

He turned around and continued, "I wanted to see how you were feeling. With what happened tonight, I mean."

"What are you talking about? About William getting away?"

"No..."

"Then what? Alan, I'm tired. I don't have time for games."

"I know it was in the heat of the moment, but I also know you," he said as he scratched off a bit of dried blood from under my lip.

I finally understood what he was talking about. I had killed two people. I sat down on my bed and gazed into the distance as he came to sit next to me.

"I... I don't know," I answered as the truth settled in and tears started filling my eyes. I covered my face as I began to cry.

He pulled me into his chest and started to caress my head. "Shhh, it's okay."

"But it's not okay. Who am I to take someone's life?"

"A very good sister, that's who," he declared as he lifted my chin up toward him.

In that moment, I knew how good Alan actually was and wondered why he didn't let the world see that good in him. Everyone else saw him as this sarcastic vampire who didn't care for much, but that's not really who he was. He was a genuinely good person who understood how people felt.

"Will you stay with me for a little while?"

"Sure," he answered, then we both laid back on the bed.

"Thank you," I said as I snuggled into his chest.

He nodded and closed his eyes as he continued running his fingers through my hair.

We had only been like that for a few minutes when I heard a faint knock at my bedroom window. Alan blurred away, and my head hit the pillow in his absence.

I stood up and opened the window. "Aaron?"

"Hi," he said as he stepped through the window into the room.

"You know my parents aren't even here, right?"

"Yeah, but this is more exciting," he laughed then sobered as he assessed me. "You look exhausted."

"Thanks," I laughed.

"You know what I mean."

"Well, I *was* lying down until *someone* decided to play Tarzan at my window."

"Okay then, let's go lie down," he said with a sweet smile as he led me to bed.

I laid down, and he took his place next to me. He still had a bit of the scent of his pendant on him, so I held my breath for a little while. Even so, I wasn't able to fight my exhaustion for long and fell asleep in Aaron's arms minutes later.

# CHAPTER 22
## LOVE AND THUNDER

When I opened my eyes, I was in my bed. I stretched my arms and smiled. For a moment, I almost thought the past few months had just been a dream. That was until I inspected my skin. Then there was no denying I was a nyxling.

Sounds of laughter came from downstairs, and I smiled when I heard Aaron's voice alongside my brothers'. I jumped out of bed and ran to my vanity table to make sure I didn't look too crazy. After I brushed my hair and my teeth, I ran downstairs to join the boys.

When I entered the kitchen, Aaron stood up and hugged me. "Hey there, sleeping beauty."

"What do you mean?"

"You have been asleep for three days," Zay laughed.

"I have?" I asked, fully confused.

"Yeah, I guess you were tired," Zay teased.

Looking around, I was happy to see that everything seemed normal. My brothers were home, and everyone was safe, even our parents. I was about to ask about them when I felt a sharp pain in my stomach. I rubbed it and bit my bottom lip.

"Here," Ian said as he put a large cup in front of me. "Drink. There are children in the house for God's sake," he chuckled. In response, Aaron removed his arm from around me and sat back down in embarrassment.

"What?" Zay asked in confusion.

"Vampire 101," Ian said as he sat down next to Aaron whose face was now beet red.

"I don't get it," Zay muttered but didn't care enough to follow up, so he left the room.

Of course, Ian knew exactly what was going on. Not only could he read Aaron's mind, but he had also dated a vampire.

I was just recently experiencing that myself. The few times Aaron and I had shared blood, it had been nothing short of intoxicating. Each drop tasted exquisite and sent shivers down my spine as the blood mingled with his essence. It was an experience beyond the physical; it was deeply sensual, as if his very life force surged into me and intertwined with my own, amplifying every sensation.

With each gentle stroke of my tongue against his skin, I could feel his essence pulsating through me, heightening the intimacy of our connection. It felt like I was offering a piece of myself in a sacred exchange of life force that bound us together with undeniable intimacy. The urge to surrender to him, to lose myself in his embrace, was overwhelming. In those moments, nothing else mattered, and the pull toward him was irresistible, a primal longing that transcended all rational thought.

Shaking myself out of that memory, I drank the cup of blood Ian had offered me instead, and we spent the rest of the day watching TV and laughing, just being ordinary teenagers. It felt like things were finally getting back to normal, but I was skeptical of that lasting.

Ian caught me up on what had happened the last few days. He said they had talked to the school principal, and Ian would be able to continue school from home, but I would return in January after the holiday break.

I thought that wasn't fair, but they had debated and decided it was best to keep up appearances if we wanted to stay in Hallowed Hills.

Aaron said his parents had spoken to mine, and they had bought them a vacation package in California. My parents were using the time to catch up with some close friends and wouldn't be back until after the long weekend. He also told me they had spoken with his grandmother and had decided my brothers and I would stay at his house until our parents returned.

I was nervous about staying at Aaron's house. I still hadn't met his parents, and meeting them like this could be awkward. Of course, it would still be better than meeting them the way I had met his sister.

I told the boys I needed to go start packing since both Ian and Zay were already done. When I got upstairs, I got a suitcase from my closet and threw it on my bed, grabbed a bunch of shirts and a few pairs of jeans, and started packing.

I smiled when I heard someone opening my door. I knew instantly who it was. As the door closed behind him, his hand began sensually caressing my hips. Pushing my hair aside, he began to kiss my neck with a gentle touch and slowly turned me around.

Aaron's gripping blue eyes locked on mine and delved into the depths of my soul. Pulling me close, he kissed me softly. His hands gripped my legs, and I leapt into his arms. Moving us to the bed, he laid me down with him on top.

Kissing my neck, Aaron skillfully opened my shirt, undoing each button one by one until the fabric laid to the side. His lips explored the delicate skin between my breasts, sensually tracing a path down my ribs.

The touch of his lips on my body sent shivers through me. Looking down, I watched him with fascination as he used his tongue to massage my skin. The tingling sensation overwhelmed me, but the realization that we were finally alone made it even more intense.

When he unbuttoned and unzipped my jeans then kissed even lower, I felt my eyes set ablaze. I pulled him back up and turned him over then straddled him, glaring at him with my magenta eyes.

He smiled at me, sat up, then continued to kiss me.

Removing his shirt, I tossed it aside and pushed him back down with a mischievous grin. My hands roamed his hard, muscular chest. Not realizing my fangs were already out, I bit my lip, and a droplet of blood escaped, which caught his attention.

He wiped it away with his thumb then put it in his mouth. His eyes rolled back as the blood touched his tongue, then he looked at me again. He grabbed my face and started to kiss me aggressively as he fully removed my shirt and pulled me close to his body then rolled back on top of me.

His phone vibrated in his pocket, but neither of us could be bothered.

My palms traced the indents of his abs, journeying down to unbutton his pants as we continued our passionate exchange.

The phone buzzed again, a mere distraction.

But as I unzipped his pants, a gentle knock echoed on my bedroom door.

"Ugh, we are never going to get a break," Aaron exclaimed in frustration as he flopped down beside me.

I rolled back on top of him and started to kiss him again as I toyed with the lining of his pants. He smiled and sat up then caressed my back as we continued our kiss.

"Um, Nina?" Ian asked shyly through the door.

"Go away, Ian!" I shouted.

"Believe me, I wouldn't be doing this now if it weren't important."

The fire died down in my eyes, and I stood up and grabbed a shirt from my suitcase, pulling it on while I stalked toward the door. I looked back at Aaron still lying on the bed.

"I need a minute," he said as he wiped his face up and down with his palms.

I giggled at him as I cracked open the door.

"Alan called. He knows where William and Lavinia are," Ian explained. That made my eyes immediately change to magenta.

"Aaron, we have to go," I announced without looking back then ran down the stairs.

"I still need a minute," I heard Aaron say under his breath when I was already halfway down the stairs.

I nearly stumbled over my own feet when I found Connor waiting at the bottom of the stairs.

*Why does it seem like he's always around when Aaron and I don't want to be interrupted. And why can't he ever wear a shirt? Doesn't he get cold?*

With that thought, my gaze lingered on his sculpted chest and abs. I was frustrated that every encounter with him set off a riot of butterflies in my stomach. Maybe it was only because I couldn't have him, but sometimes it felt like I had stronger feelings for him than I did for Aaron.

As we went into the living room, I tried not to think about that as Ian filled me in on what was going on. However, that proved impossible as I looked at Connor's perfect face and alluring emerald eyes.

Although I heard Aaron's movements upstairs, Connor's presence was impossible to ignore. Even while Ian shared the information, I remained captivated by those enchanting emerald eyes. He was the epitome of masculinity. His chiseled jawline and broad shoulders would make any girl weak. A masterpiece of perfection, his chest and stomach were accentuated even more by the unearthly tribal tattoos.

Lost in the study of those tattoos that looked more like an integral part of him than mere ink, I forgot to conceal my admiration, and Connor caught me staring. I quickly looked away and back toward Ian who was visibly in pain from sitting so close to Connor, but not saying anything about it.

I also could feel a burning in my throat, like I was drinking fire. I swallowed and realized I hadn't been paying any attention to Ian, so I had no idea what he was talking about.

I hoped I hadn't missed anything important, but by that time, he was explaining how Lavinia had found Alan in the woods. I was curious how that had happened but didn't want to ask and admit my inattention.

She had told Alan that William would let Matt and Jen go if we met him in downtown Chicago on the roof of the Waldorf at 9 p.m. tonight. I didn't recognize the name of the building, but Ian said it was still under construction.

Lavinia also had told Alan that if we involved the council, William would continue turning townspeople into vampires.

"So, what's the plan?" I asked.

"Alan said he should be able to get a few of those bracelets, two or three at the most," Connor relayed. "Since we already know there will be four vampires, that makes us short by one or two. From what Alan told me, the bracelets he can get aren't as powerful as William's. They will be able to keep a vampire down, but they might take longer to work. Our best bet is to weaken them before we put the bracelets on," he surmised then looked at Ian.

Connor continued, "We know they're not just going to hand over Matt and Jen, so we need to be prepared for anything. The bracelets William had were very powerful, so it's a good bet he will have them again," Connor predicted then looked in Ian's direction.

"What are you getting at?" Ian asked, annoyed.

"I know everyone wants to help, but their bracelets didn't just diminish Alan's abilities, they crippled him. He couldn't even move. I think it would be best if Alan and Ian stay away from the fight tonight," Connor assessed.

"Absolutely not," Ian said firmly.

"Ian, he makes a good point," I said in support. "Aaron was attacked from behind when he went to help Alan, and they bit him. If the bracelets had worked right on me, it would have been an entirely different story."

"But they didn't," Ian declared.

I nodded then countered, "But I could feel myself become slower and weaker the longer they were on me. They may not work on me the way they do on others, but they *do* diminish my abilities, too," I emphasized. "Even if Connor isn't by you and Alan, and if William has those bracelets, we don't know what may happen. I'm sorry Ian, but we can't risk it."

Ian looked at both of us then stood up and huffed out of the room. Aaron had just made it down the stairs and was still buttoning his shirt as Ian brushed past him on his way to the kitchen.

"What's going on? Is he okay?" Aaron asked, completely confused.

Connor stood up and approached Aaron. Although he was only about four inches taller than him, Connor seemed to tower over him. He just glared at him, not saying anything, and Aaron looked at him like he didn't understand what was going on.

"It's just going to be the three of us tonight," Connor finally said then promptly walked out the front door.

"Ooo... kay."

Aaron came farther into the living room where I was sitting and plopped down onto the couch next to me then put his arm around me and kissed my cheek. "So, what's going on? What's the plan?"

"I'm not really sure," I answered with my eyes fixed on the front door.

Aaron's phone started to ring, so he picked it up and walked into the dining room to answer it. I heard Alan's voice on the other end, so I thought he might be a while.

I needed to get Connor out of my head, so I went to talk to Ian in the kitchen. "Hey," I said as I walked in. He was sitting at the table, and I knew that he had heard me, but he didn't say anything. "I know it's frustrating, but—"

"No, you don't know. You don't have all this power that you can't do anything with," he explained in frustration. "I feel useless."

"You are not useless, Ian. We need you and Alan to protect Zay. You are so smart. The council could use a guy like you," I said with an encouraging smile. "So, turn that frown upside down, and let's get in the car and see what you can do to help," I said with annoyingly optimistic pep.

"Thanks," he mumbled with a chuckle. "Maybe I can go through some of the files and see if William has any associates in the city."

"See! Now you're thinking like Youlian Phineas Hart."

He rolled his eyes and laughed at my use of his full name then stood up to walk toward the front door.

"Zay!" I screamed up the stairs. "Let's go!"

I glanced in the dining room and saw that Aaron was still on the phone, so I pointed to the front door and gestured like I was turning a steering wheel.

He nodded and winked at me. Zay ran past me and out the door, almost knocking me over in the process. I laughed then followed him outside.

I turned to pull the door closed then turned back around and ran straight into Connor. "Sorry," I said lamely.

"Can we talk?" he asked abruptly.

"I don't think we have anything to talk about," I replied and started to walk past him.

Before I could get away, he grabbed my hand. I stopped, and he stroked the top of my hand with his thumb then looked deeply into my eyes.

I hated that his touch made me feel amazing. He was the one who'd said we couldn't be together, and now I felt like he was playing games, like he wanted me to want him but didn't really want me. We stood there gazing at each other, hand in hand for what felt like forever.

"Why are you doing this?" I finally asked.

"I... I don't know," he admitted.

"You don't know? Yeah, well, that's nice," I bit back at him sarcastically.

"Nina," he said as I pulled my hand away from him.

"Connor, I can't."

He lowered his head then looked back up at me nervously.

I wasn't sure what he was going to say or do, but I couldn't hold back my tears any longer, so I blurred away into the night. I ran so far that, by the time I stopped, I didn't even know where I was anymore.

Looking around, I found myself within a wide expanse of grass surrounded by large hickory trees that almost created a perfect circle.

I was so upset. I had promised myself that I wouldn't cry over Connor anymore, and here I was with tears running down my face... again. The worst part was that he hadn't really said anything. For all I knew, he had just wanted to talk about the plan for the night. I felt so childish.

I looked at my phone and saw that I had missed a call from Aaron. I was about to call him back when I heard the beat of Connor's wings. I turned away from the sound and tried to compose myself as I felt the cool breeze from his wings as he came in for a landing. Then I felt his breath on my neck and knew he was standing behind me.

"Nina."

When I turned around, he was so close that we were almost touching. He put his hand on my cheek and caressed it.

Once again, I was instantly enchanted by his touch and smell. I already felt dizzy, but I still couldn't help breathing in his scent. I looked up at him with tear-filled eyes even as one salty drop escaped.

He stepped even closer and wiped the tear away.

"No," I said as I pulled away again. "You told me that you wanted me to be with Aaron."

"That's the last thing I want," he countered.

"But you said you did."

"I said he would be better for you," he corrected sweetly. "But every time I see his hands on you, it infuriates me," he admitted then turned and walked a few steps away.

"But you don't want to be with me," I said to his back.

"I never said that either," he responded as he turned back to me.

"Do you *want* to be with me?" I asked nervously.

He walked closer again and gently cupped my face. "I want nothing more," he replied, "but things are very complicated, and I don't want to hurt you or stand in your way."

"Things are *complicated*?" I spit the word back at him. "You mean the fact you have to impregnate other Nephilim to propagate your species?" I reminded him incredulously as I pulled away.

He looked down and dropped his arm to his side. "We are very different. I might not look much older than you, but I am. You are only 18 years old, Nina. I am 83. People romanticize immortality, but they don't consider the fact that the mind of a teenager is very different from the mind of a...

let's say an octogenarian. You still have so much yet to experience in life, so many choices you haven't had a chance to make," he said sympathetically. "But I need you to know that I have never felt this way about anyone in my entire life. I know I must be confusing you. I'm confusing myself, too," he admitted then stroked my arm with the back of his finger. "You are the most important thing in my life."

My mind urged me to retreat, but my heart... my heart insisted on staying. Even so, I took a step back to distance myself only to collide with a tree. He advanced, and I pressed my body into the tree, seeking its solid support.

Although I could have turned away, some inexplicable desire compelled me to stay. Still struggling to stay strong, I placed my hands at my sides, gripped the tree trunk, and lowered my gaze, allowing my hair to cascade over my face.

Connor gently moved my hair aside and tilted my chin up toward him. Tracing my jaw with the backs of his fingers, he produced a shiver throughout my body with just his touch. Confused and overwhelmed, I turned my face to the side and closed my eyes.

His hand began to trail down my neck, which caused another quiver to run through me. Turning back to him, I met his eyes as his fingers continued their sensual journey down to my chest. His seductive gaze mesmerized me, leaving me frozen in place. Closing the gap between us, he pressed his chest against mine then began a trail of kisses along my neck.

A soft moan escaped my lips. Although I knew I should resist, I was powerless. Fully inhaling his intoxicating scent made my dizziness resurge, and I placed one hand on his bare chest to steady myself. But his lips on my neck felt heavenly; I was under his spell.

His kisses stopped as his hand moved to the back of my neck, and he pulled me closer. Our foreheads touched as his hand sensually traced my face. As our eyes locked again, the world faded away.

Then his lips touched mine and ignited a fire within me. The moment consumed us, and nothing else mattered—no worries, no fears, nothing. There was only the heat of the moment, an electrifying passion that surged through our kiss. I could almost feel tiny shocks of energy on my skin as the intensity grew and grew. His heartbeat echoed in his chest as our lips molded together with a gentle urgency.

His arms wrapped around me, drawing me ever closer as we lost ourselves in the moment. My eyes transformed, and my fangs extended, responding to the primal energy between us.

"I'm sorry," I said quietly as I covered my mouth and fangs.

"Don't be. I want all of you, just the way you are," he said then pressed his neck to my lips.

The excitement I felt in that moment had no rival. "Are you sure?"

He looked up at me and nodded then presented his neck to me again.

I smelled his skin and touched his neck with the tip of my tongue, which made him shiver. I put my lips on his neck and pressed my fangs into his skin.

He winced at the pain but then used his hand at the back of my neck to push my fangs deeper.

I drank vigorously from the warm stream that flowed from the puncture wounds. His blood was like nothing I had ever tasted, and a feeling of pure pleasure flowed through me. It began as a mild trickle that rapidly surged into a river that threatened to sweep me away as it circulated through my body.

It was like I had been running on empty for a long time and was instantly being recharged. It wasn't just the energy I felt; light tremors were building into rumbles of exquisite pleasure.

Sated at last, I pulled away from him slowly and watched his wounds close on their own.

He turned to me with a smile then kissed me again. We explored each other's mouths with sweet passion, our tongues intertwining in a dance of desire. He picked me up and pressed my back against the tree, so I wrapped my legs around his waist, and my arms circled his neck. I wanted him to feel the same pleasure I had, but I wasn't sure whether he wanted to taste my blood.

I pulled away from him and bit my lip then waited for his reaction. He stared at the small droplet of blood then met my eyes. Fearing he didn't want to, or, because he was a Nephilim, he couldn't, I wiped it away with my finger.

He grabbed my hand, looked at it for a moment then licked the blood off my finger.

"More," he whispered.

I bit my lip again, and he immediately sucked the blood that surfaced. He pulled away suddenly and threw his head back. When he looked back at me, his eyes were glowing green, which excited me even more.

I bit my wrist and presented it to him. He took it right away and drank forcefully. I hadn't felt real pain in a long time, but he sucked so hard that I could feel it, and I was fully surprised when the pain started to feel very good.

As he continued to drink, my body wanted to explode with pleasure. The pain and ecstasy were immeasurable.

He threw his head back again, and his wings burst forth as his eyes continued to glow. He then forcibly lifted me from the tree, guided me to the ground, and, with an intensity that mirrored possession, he fervently removed my shirt. A man consumed by desire, he began to kiss my neck then descended to my breasts, his hands cupping them as he kissed each one.

Pleasure coursed through me. My back arched in response to his sensual touches as his lips continued their exploration toward my stomach.

Looking up from my body, he locked eyes with mine as his glowed brightly. With a tantalizing flick of his tongue, he traced the line of my jeans right below my belly button and skillfully released the top button with a snap.

After one last kiss on my stomach, his eyes returned to their usual state, and his wings gracefully retracted. Taking my face in his palms, he kissed me deeply before pulling back.

"Ughhh," he growled before looking back up at me.

He seemed to be fighting a battle within himself and brushed his face with his palms then met my eyes. We gazed into each other's eyes in a shared understanding that something profound had unfolded between us.

It became clear that this was an experience that would be etched into the fabric of my being—a moment of unbridled love and passion destined to linger in the recesses of my memory forever.

"I'm sorry. I kind of lost myself for a second there," he said as he knelt in front of me.

I wanted to tell him that I hadn't minded, but my voice didn't seem to work. I just wanted to kiss him again. I smiled and picked myself up off the ground, moving to sit on top of him as I again wrapped my arms around his neck. I kissed him, and he excitedly caressed my back and hair.

"You are so beautiful," he said before pulling away again, "but we can't."

Hearing those words instantly made my anger surge. He was doing the same thing yet again. I jumped off him, but he grabbed my wrist before I could get away.

"Wait," he said then pulled me into him for another kiss. "I need you to understand. You could say I'm sort of old fashioned, but there are other people's feelings we need to consider, too," he said sheepishly.

My eyes widened in shame. How could I have forgotten? Aaron had just called me his girlfriend days ago, and I had been in bed with him only a few hours before being here with Connor. Again, I pulled away, and this time he let me.

"I'm sorry," he repeated. "I just can't control myself when I'm around you. You enchant me."

I turned back to him and cupped his face in my hand. I couldn't be mad; it wasn't just him. I couldn't control myself around him either.

"You're not saying anything. What are you thinking?" Connor prompted.

I wanted to tell him I loved him, and had loved him for a long time, but I was scared.

"I'm thinking... that you probably should stay away from Ian for a while," I responded with a soft laugh.

He looked confused then understanding dawned. "That's probably a good idea," he laughed, "but how are you feeling?"

I waited for a moment, not really wanting him to know yet how I actually felt. "I think you're right. There are other people's feelings to consider, so things are indeed complicated. But I've never felt anything like that before."

That's all I could tell him. I hoped he knew how I felt, but I knew I couldn't say the words to him. I loved him so much, but I was afraid that if I told him, he would pull away.

"Maybe you should put a shirt on?" he said with a laugh.

"You first."

"I don't have one, but you do," he quipped as he grabbed my shirt from the ground.

I smiled and pulled my shirt over my head then noticed my phone on the ground. Connor picked it up, looked at it, and then handed it to me.

"What?" I asked when he didn't say anything and just looked guilty.

I looked at the phone and saw I had three missed calls and one voicemail from Aaron. I listened to the voicemail, my face fell. "I'm supposed to meet everyone at the train station," I conveyed to Connor. "Aaron said Ian told him I was going to Becca's house."

"I asked Ian to cover for us. I told him I just needed to talk to you and didn't think Aaron would be okay with us being alone."

"Why would you think that?"

"Well, I may have fought with Alan about you a few times while you were gone."

"Fought with Alan? What does he have to do with any of this?"

"He's a pain in my ass, but he is very observant, so he told Aaron I had feelings for you. I'm not sure if Aaron believed it, but he's a good guy. The truth is that I didn't plan any of this. I just wanted to talk to you, but it's like you put a spell on me. I can't control myself."

I looked at him and smiled because I felt the same way about him with his bewitching touch.

"When did you tell Ian?"

"I didn't tell him exactly," he said, pointing to his temple.

"Oh, okay," I said then looked at my watch. "So, I have to be in Chicago in about 30 minutes, and I can't exactly run there without being noticed."

"Then we fly," he said with a smile as he lifted me into his arms. "Ready?"

I nodded, and then we were in the sky. The world below unfolded in a mesmerizing tapestry—the bustling cityscape morphing into a mere speck and its activity reducing to a faint hum while the fragrance of the clouds enveloped us in an intoxicating embrace that was pure and invigorating. With a sigh of wonder, I let my head rest on Connor's chest as we continued our journey.

We landed on a rooftop a few miles away from the train station where Aaron told us to meet, deciding that I could run from there to meet up with everyone else while he flew to join us later.

I placed my hands on Connor's chest as he looked down at me, more the picture of a Greek god than an angel. I wanted to kiss him, but my thoughts went to Aaron.

Sensing my internal conflict, Connor smiled warmly, and a silent understanding passed between us. With a tender gesture, he leaned forward and pressed a gentle kiss to my forehead.

When I arrived at the train station, the mood was heavy and the tension palpable in every exchange. Aaron's expression was a mask of barely contained turmoil as I approached. His smile was strained and fragile.

"Have you guys figured out what we're going to do?" I ventured, trying to break through the thick fog of apprehension that enveloped us.

"Where's Connor?" Alan's accusatory tone cut through the air like a blade as his eyes narrowed with suspicion.

"I'm not sure," I replied carefully as I struggled to maintain my composure. "He's not here?"

"He's not with you?" Aaron's surprise was evident, his voice tinged with concern.

"No. Why would he be with me?" I retorted, attempting to deflect further scrutiny away from myself.

Aaron started to smile and put his hand out for me. I took it right away, but, out of the corner of my eye, I could see the skepticism in Alan's gaze.

For what felt like an eternity, we engaged in heated debate, our voices rising and falling in a cacophony of conflicting opinions. Our plan, if one could call it that, was flimsy at best. Our only semblance of strategy revolved around Aaron calling the council as a last resort. Other than that, the only plan was for Alan and Ian to stay close while Aaron, Connor, and I assembled on the roof. Ian had discovered multiple supernaturals in the city, but none of them had a connection to William or Lavinia.

"So, we're pretty much winging it," I remarked bitterly.

"Pretty much," Ian agreed.

As the moment to meet the vampires approached, anxiety filled the air as the guys expressed concerns about Connor's absence. Ian called him, and Connor told him he was on his way and would meet me and Aaron on the roof of the Waldorf.

Aaron and I said goodbye to Ian and Alan then started our drive to the building. Thankfully it only took a few minutes because it was almost 9 p.m.

As we parked, I reached for the door handle to exit the car, but Aaron caught my hand before I could step out. "I need to talk to you about something," Aaron confessed warily, his words heavy with the weight of an impending revelation.

A wave of apprehension washed over me as I became afraid of what he might say.

Now, looking deep into his ocean-blue eyes, I couldn't fathom a future without him, but his expression was one of heartbreak, as if he somehow knew about my encounter with Connor in the woods.

With trembling lips, Aaron spoke, his voice strained with the agony of confession. "I know you have feelings for him," Aaron said as he focused on our clasped hands, "but I know that it's partially my fault, too. If I had just broken up with Amanda the first time we went out, I don't think he would even have been a factor," he said nervously. "It wasn't fair for me to ask you to wait," he added then lifted his eyes to mine.

His words hung in the air like a guillotine poised to sever our fragile bond. "I am sorry," I blurted out unintentionally.

His gaze fluttered down again, but he quickly met my eyes once more. "You know I will never hurt you, Nina. I will do everything in my power to keep you safe and happy," he vowed, his voice laced with raw sincerity. "I love you."

In that moment, time seemed to stand still as his declaration echoed in the caverns of my soul. A swell of conflicting emotions threatened to consume me, yet amid the chaos, one truth remained undeniable—I loved him, too. He was an amazing guy who had captured my heart the first time I'd seen him. I remembered the swarm of butterflies in my stomach and how I only wanted him.

"I love you, too," I said with a genuine smile as happiness surged through me at his words.

Aaron pulled my face to his and kissed me softly. Although brief, the kiss felt incredible as his perfect lips barely grazed mine, igniting a warmth throughout my body. I pulled him into me and started kissing him with more passion and enthusiasm.

Pulling back a little, I caressed his lips with my thumb before stealing one more kiss. I didn't want to hurt him. Even though I loved Connor, I loved him, too. I had to decide what I wanted to do, and now was when I had to do it. Aaron loved me back, and he'd not only told me he did, he'd shown me. He had never told me to go be with another guy. Plus, he was absolutely gorgeous, inside and out. Ultimately, there was no other choice.

"I love you, Aaron," I repeated. "I want you."

He smiled crookedly and kissed my hand then stroked my face before pulling away slowly.

When we stepped out of the jeep, desperation clawed at my chest as I watched him walk away, his words ringing hollow in the silence that followed. I couldn't help wondering why he hadn't said he loved me back the second time. Was he second guessing his feelings? Maybe I was just feeling self-conscious, but I didn't like the feeling, so I stayed back, leaning against the jeep as Aaron made his way toward the building.

"Is everything okay?" he asked when he noticed and walked back to me.

I looked up at him then reached out to caress his face before pressing my lips to his. As he pulled away, a moment of hesitation and reflection passed between us.

Things were undeniably different. It felt like it was more than my having feelings for Connor. He was right. When we'd met, he'd also had feelings for another girl, and I'd given him time to figure things out. Maybe I'd unconsciously pulled away from him when he'd taken that time to make his choice, but I had let myself fall for him despite loving Connor as well. Still, I knew Aaron was the better choice.

Scared of losing him, I stopped thinking and turned him around, pushing him back against the jeep and kissing him passionately. I aggressively pushed against him and thrust my tongue into his mouth.

He willingly reciprocated, and his hands grabbed my face as I began to remove his belt. The sound of his heartbeat echoed like the rhythmic pounding of a jackhammer as I unzipped his pants and slipped my fingers under the waistband of his boxer briefs.

"Whoa, we can't do this here," he said suddenly, restraining my hands and pulling them away.

I didn't know what to say, so I just watched as he buckled his belt.

In that moment, I felt my heart breaking. I knew it was just an excuse. There were several times we shouldn't have been getting intimate and had been interrupted. The only thing he'd ever said before was that we never got a break. However, no one was here to interrupt us this time. He was the one to stop it. He didn't want to be with me.

As much as it hurt, I had to try to put it out of my mind, at least for a while, so I turned away from him and started walking toward the building without another word.

"Nina, wait!" he pleaded as he ran to catch up with me.

I stopped when he stepped in front of me, but I couldn't look at him because my eyes were welling up with tears.

"Let's just go," I urged, hearing the strain in my voice.

"I... I just don't think it's the right time," he stammered.

"It's fine. Let's go," I said again.

Focused again on the task, we started looking around the building to find a way to get in. I could just break the door down, but an alarm could go off, so we look for another way.

"We can get in this way," Aaron explained as he turned the corner. It was the door to the sprinkler room, but it was locked. He put his palm against the door and started to chant, then the lock clicked. He looked back at me and smiled as he opened the door with ease.

We made our way through the sprinkler room and found a door indicating that it led to the main lobby. As we stepped into the colossal entry space, grandeur beyond imagination greeted us. Marble floors gleamed with an exquisite luminescence while a magnificent golden W loomed behind a lavish reception desk. Scaffolding hugged the walls like sentinels, hinting at the ongoing transformation of this palace of luxury. Every piece of furniture, even shrouded in protective plastic, whispered tales of extravagance—each item a testament to the wealth permeating the building.

Emerging from my daze, I noticed Aaron standing by the elevator doors plated in the same gold that had painted the W on the wall.

I tried hard not to think about what had just happened between us, but I couldn't help it. "I'm just going to run up the stairs," I told him as he pressed the elevator button, "but you take the elevator. I'll meet you up there."

"Are we okay?" he asked sweetly as he grabbed my wrist.

I wished I could dismiss the turmoil inside me, but it gnawed at me. Unable to contain my thoughts any longer, I blurted out what lingered in my mind. "Do you love me, Aaron?"

My question caught him off guard. But although it seemed to surprise him, I felt he should have responded immediately if he truly loved me.

Instead, Aaron stared at his hand on my wrist then looked back up at me. The silence between us was deafening, planting more seeds of doubt and making me think that maybe he only wanted me to think he loved me to keep me away from Connor. I didn't know why he would have cared if I was with Connor, but my mind was running wild.

"Yes, I do," he finally said. "I love you, Nina."

But it was too late. I was too scared. "I'll meet you up there," I said to him as I blurred away.

I couldn't believe what was happening. Yes, I loved both Aaron and Connor, but now it seemed like neither truly wanted to be with me. I ran halfway up to the roof then stopped and sat down for a moment. I thought about the things Connor had said to me and then what Aaron had said.

I put my head in my hands and made myself cry. I knew tonight was important, so I needed to get everything out before I made it up to the roof. I let myself cry for a few minutes before I stopped feeling sorry for myself. If they didn't want me, I would be fine. I could be alone.

When at last I made it to the roof, both Aaron and Connor were already there. I turned my gaze away from them both and cleared my throat, announcing I was going to look around before anyone else arrived to see if there was anything we could use. Really, I just wanted to stay away from them.

It was only a few minutes later when William blurred onto the other side of the roof, and seconds after that, Lavinia, Matt, and Jen were there, too.

As I locked eyes with Lavinia, an uncontrollable surge of emotion swept over me. The mere sight of her ignited an inferno within me, and an unparalleled rage consumed my senses. I hesitated, struggling to restrain myself, but wary of the potential consequences of succumbing to any impulsive reactions. My gaze burned at her with intensity as I positioned myself defiantly in front of my once-close friend.

# CHAPTER 23

## RAGNAROK

I had faced my fair share of pain and disappointment, but the turmoil in that moment eclipsed it all. Lavinia hadn't just been a friend; she'd been like a sister. Discovering that the very bond we'd shared was tainted by betrayal felt nearly unbearable and left me feeling utterly alone.

"How could you do this to us?" I finally expressed aloud as my emotions broke free. Despite the anger simmering within me, I stood my ground and attempted to temper the fury in my voice as I pressed, "You were like my sister."

Lavinia turned, and her silence cut through the air as her gaze shifted to William. Something was different about her. At the abandoned building just a few nights before, she had seemed conflicted as though she had still cared. Now an icy detachment replaced any semblance of warmth.

"Lavinia has told me so much about you," William remarked, his eyes shifting between Connor and Aaron. "You're a very popular girl, aren't you?"

My eyes blazed with anger. Every confidence I had shared with Lavinia had become fodder for her betrayal.

"I have been researching Talaatah for hundreds of years," he continued smoothly. "Failure after failure, disappointment after disappointment...

until now. For your family to be given something so important, and for you not to even care, is maddening."

I turned my gaze back to Lavinia and found her avoiding my gaze. Although both Matt and Jen looked like they were in pain, they still stood with William as well.

"I will not stop until Xavier is a nyxling," William went on, "but don't think of that as the end. Think of it as the beginning. That is what I'm giving him: the start of eternal life. Once he turns and completes the three, you and your brothers will have absolute power."

"I don't need absolute power. I just need my family to be safe," I retorted. "And you don't even know if his body will accept the change."

"Oh, it will... and, if it doesn't, well, there's always your mother," he added confidently.

Those words propelled me forward, but Connor's firm grip on my shoulder stopped me. "He's baiting you," he warned.

"We're not going to let you near him or our mom," Ian shouted as he and Alan ran up behind us.

"What are you doing here?" I hissed at him. "We told you we could handle this. You could—"

"We're in this together," Ian interjected firmly, his stance unwavering as he took his place between Connor and me.

"What the kid said," Alan chimed in with a smirk, his confidence evident as he moved to stand next to Aaron as a united front against the threat looming before us.

The five of us faced William confidently, knowing we now outnumbered them with Alan and Ian. Connor's abilities could weaken them all and make it easier for us to use the bracelets. Having more of us would make that even easier. Plus, having Ian here would be a tremendous help since he could listen to their thoughts and instantly know their next moves. I couldn't stop myself from smiling.

"Jen and Matt are confused," Ian explained. "They see us and know us, but don't understand how they know us. Their memories are flashing fast. I can't understand any of it," he added as he rubbed his temples.

William regarded Ian curiously. I was sure he'd heard what he had said, but he seemed to be trying to figure out what Ian's words had meant.

"What are you going to do? Kill all your friends?" William snarled.

"You know they're no match for us," I said defiantly.

"I do. Why do you think I chose them?" he laughed. "But enough of this," he said then balled his hand into a fist. "Now!" he commanded as he signaled toward us.

Suddenly, several dark figures began to jump over from the building behind him. As they came into the light and stood by his side, I now counted ten supernatural creatures—three more vampires, two Lycans, and three other creatures I had never seen before alongside Jen and Matt.

The unknown creatures had leathery, dark gray skin, yellow eyes, and noses with the tips cut off, which made their faces resemble skulls. I realized quickly that their eyes were the same as the three men we'd seen at the bonfire, but I was confused because then they had had faces and normal-looking skin. But I also recalled that creatures on the council had changed forms, so I concluded that these must have a human form as well.

Taking a moment to study the vampires, I was shocked to realize I recognized them. They were Kenny, Crystal, and John—the kids who had gone missing months before.

"I need the nyxlings alive and brought back to me, but apart from that, kill them all," William commanded then walked away with Lavinia close behind him.

The creatures dutifully began walking toward the five of us. We stood our ground, waiting for their attack. Connor flew up into the air and swooped back down at the crowd but was suddenly grabbed by something with giant bat-like wings.

"Connor!" I yelled.

The bat-winged man came crashing back down to the roof on top of Connor and punched him in the face. Connor retaliated by turning him over and punching him back as their battle continued.

"What the hell is that?" Alan asked as we began fighting off the rest of the creatures.

"I don't know," Aaron answered, "but Connor is our ace in the hole against these vampires, so that's an issue."

I pushed away the three gray creatures bent on attacking me and blurred over to Connor, ramming the creature off him. I took in the creature. Like Connor, he was bare chested and in very good shape, but the rest was like his complete opposite. He had black hair past his shoulders, scarlet skin, two horns coming out of the sides of his head, and gigantic, dark red, almost black, bat wings.

The creature stood up slowly and stared at me as Connor regained his footing and came to stand next to me.

"You're bleeding," I said to Connor as I noticed the golden liquid seeping from a cut on his head.

When I said the words out loud and realized his blood was golden, I blanched. I hadn't noticed its color earlier today, but now that I saw it, I winced at the thought of my dream coming true. I'd had that dream before I knew he was a Nephilim, and that fact scared me even more.

Connor wiped the blood away from his forehead, and I snapped back to the present. I stared at him in horror when I saw that the gash wasn't healing. I looked back at the demon-like creature. He was grinning back at us, his own black blood dripping from a cut under his eye.

"What is it?" I asked Connor.

The creature didn't give him time to answer as it grabbed me and tossed me to the side. I hit the side of the building so hard that a piece of concrete broke off and went tumbling down to the street below.

Quickly peering over the ledge, I sighed in relief when I saw no one was there. My attention swung back over to Connor, and I saw that the creature was attacking him again.

I was about to help him when I realized Ian was being outmatched by the three gray creatures and the vampire John. Ian had blood on him, but no visible wounds. For a moment, I was glad Connor was far enough away from him to limit his weakening effects, but that also meant the other vampires were far enough away as well.

I stood torn, my mind racing as I assessed the dire situation. Connor grappled fiercely with the demon, his strength faltering against the overwhelming force. Meanwhile, outnumbered and overpowered, Ian faced a relentless onslaught from John and the gray creatures.

In a desperate split-second decision, I sprinted toward the demonic creature, determination blazing in my eyes. With swift precision, I seized the demon's shoulders with both hands, using my momentum to propel my legs upward and around his neck. I crossed my legs together before spinning around his chin, launching him into a powerful flip, and sending him hurtling across the rooftop and crashing into the creatures that were attacking Ian.

"Thanks," Ian gasped, gratitude evident in his voice as I joined him at his side.

I nodded then watched the demonic creature stand back up. Before I could react, Connor flew past me, plowing into the demon in a fierce collision of strength and fury, their battle raging on.

Ian's eyes suddenly went wide, and he quickly turned around. He gasped as I heard a stabbing sound and looked down to see a knife going through his stomach.

"Ian!" I yelled before catching him as he was about to hit the ground. I looked up to see John, his face twisted in a sadistic grin as he held the bloodied knife, reveling in his cruel deed. "It's not healing," I said in horror when I noticed that blood continued to pour out of the fresh wound.

In a heartbeat, Alan came up behind John and effortlessly snapped his neck. John's body flopped down onto the ground as Alan knelt beside us, his action a testament to his unwavering loyalty and resolve.

"It's not healing," I repeated.

"He'll be fine," Alan assured me. "We just have to get him out of here."

"Connor is too close," I said when I realized his weakness. "Alan, please take Ian away to heal," I begged him.

Before Alan could say or do anything else, one of the gray creatures attacked him from the side, and they began to fight.

Not knowing how any of the nyxling injury stuff really worked, I tried shielding my brother's body. What if I left him and they tried to cut him apart or something? He wouldn't be able to heal then.

The thought of that made me really angry, and the fire in my eyes started to sear. I looked down at my hands and saw an aura of magenta light around my whole body.

Standing up, I played with my hands, swaying them around in the air. I heard thunder boom across the sky as lightning pierced the dark night and flowed straight into the tips of my fingers. The magenta light around my body started to become electrified.

Curiously, I touched my fingers together, and small bits of pink lightning came out of them. I grinned and pulled my hands away from my body then clapped them quickly back together. As my hands met, I heard an ear-piercing sound as a giant burst of magenta lightning flew out of them. A pink lightning burst hit the two Lycans and the three gray creatures, sending them all flying away from Aaron and Alan.

Jen and Matt looked at me then at each other then back at me as lightning sparked again from my fingertips. As I prepared to strike again, they blurred away.

I turned toward Connor and the demon. Connor had him pinned, but they had stopped fighting to watch me.

I could feel electricity coursing through my whole body. Instead of being painful, the feel of the electric current passing through me was energizing.

Regaining his focus first, the demon kicked Connor in the chest to push him off and flew away. Connor quickly assessed Alan and Ian's injuries then flew away as well.

Connor was still bleeding, so I was worried about him, but Ian and Alan needed him away from them so they could heal, so him leaving was necessary. As for me, I watched my magenta aura melt away then ran to Ian's side.

"Ow," Ian muttered as he started to sit up.

"Ian!" I exclaimed as I hugged him. "You're okay."

"Of course, I'm okay," he declared with annoyance.

I laughed at him through my tears of joy as Ian stood up and looked around. "Where did everyone go?"

"Your sister was a badass, hot pink Raiden," Alan jumped in.

"What?" Ian asked as his brow furrowed in confusion.

"We'll explain later. Right now, we have to find William and Lavinia," I said.

I located Aaron and saw Crystal and Kenny lying on the ground. I stood up and walked over to him. "Are they dead?"

"Sort of."

"What?"

"When you kill a vampire but don't use a wooden stake, they go into a trance that begins to heal their bodies. So, technically, yes, they are dead but not for long," he explained with a smile as he began to put bracelets on them.

I sighed in relief, knowing they would not wake up for at least a few hours. I wasn't sure what we were going to do with them, but it hadn't been their fault they had been turned into vampires.

"Should we leave them here?" I asked.

"I'll call my grandmother," Aaron offered. "She will send someone to pick them up."

"Isn't she going to be mad?" I asked.

"Without a doubt," he said as he turned away and dialed his phone.

"I think I might have an idea about where they went," Ian claimed as he walked up behind me.

"Where?" Alan asked.

"There's a cabin where a river turns into a waterfall. It sits in a huge field at the bottom of the falls."

I immediately thought of my dream again and remembered the two white horses running away after the sound of thunder. I looked down at my hands and thought of the lightning that had come from them. Thunder and lightning went together. In my dream, Connor had died after I'd heard that thunder.

"Nina?" Ian asked.

I shook my head and came back to the present. "Okay, let's go," I answered, knowing I had no other choice.

We started to run toward the door to the stairs, but before we made it there, a powerful gust of wind threw us all to the ground. We turned back around to see three men floating in the sky. Clad in black cloaks, they all looked exactly the same, with pale skin and long white hair. Behind them on the roof stood William and Lavinia.

"Are you serious? It's like we cut one head off, and three more grow back," Alan said.

"Then we cut all three off and gut the body," I said angrily.

"Whoa, that's dark," Ian commented.

"They are warlocks, and they're wearing pendants," Aaron noticed.

"But that means William and Lavinia will be weaker, too," Alan snarled as he bared his teeth.

I was already feeling weak and had a horrendous headache, so I could only imagine how Ian and Alan felt. I glanced over at Alan who was starting to lean to the side and shake his head. Ian didn't look much better, but at least he was upright.

Aaron glanced my way and seemed to know my thoughts. Alan and Ian wouldn't last long, and soon it would just be me and him.

"Do your little lightning trick," Alan suggested.

"I don't know how it works," I confessed.

"Then we're screwed," he said sarcastically.

At that moment, Connor landed right in front of Alan and Ian.

"Connor," I whispered with a smile, but that smile quickly vanished when I realized his injuries hadn't yet healed. He also had bruises on his chest, face, and a new cut on the side of his stomach that was bleeding.

"Go," he said to Alan and Ian.

"Come on, kid," Alan encouraged Ian. "We won't go too far." At first, Ian was reluctant to leave but finally turned away and blurred off with Alan.

Connor walked over to stand by my side while Aaron stood on my other.

"You really don't know how to do your lightning thing?" Aaron whispered to me.

"No," I cringed.

"Well, at least we know who your greatest-grandfather is now," Connor said as if it were obvious.

I looked at him, waiting for him to continue, but he didn't. Instead, he opened his wings high then brought them back down quickly, producing a powerful gust of wind that blew the three warlocks farther back in the sky. Then he charged toward William and Lavinia.

Aaron and I followed him toward our two enemies. Aaron and Connor took on William while I approached Lavinia. Stopping just in front of her, I didn't say anything and just stared at her.

"I am so sorry, Nina. I didn't—"

I punched her in the face before she could finish, and she was thrown back several yards. I wasn't sure what she was going to say, but I wasn't going to ask. Even though she looked like the girl I remembered, her coldness and lack of care was fresh in my mind.

I started to run at her again, but all three warlocks returned and grabbed me, pulling me up into the air. I frantically kicked the air to try to get them to let me go. The first two had my arms while the other one attempted to restrain my legs.

I bucked and kicked the one off my legs then pulled myself up to the one holding my left arm and bit down on his hand. He immediately let go, and I pulled at the last one with all my strength to send him crashing down to the rooftop. I dropped from about 50 feet up and landed right next to him.

My anger surged again, and the magenta aura reappeared around my body. Thunder roared as the lightning hit my hands again, and I immediately threw the pink streaks toward the warlocks, which sent one crashing against the side of the building.

Out of nowhere, my side was blasted by a fireball. I looked the way it had come but became distracted when I saw Connor lying against the wall and Aaron kneeling beside him. Then I saw the origin of the fire. William stood with another ball of yellow flames in one hand and was preparing to throw it toward me.

William was a vampire, so I was caught off guard by his use of magic. He shouldn't have been able to. I had learned so much in the past few months, including that when someone transitioned into a vampire, the blood took over the body. Any supernatural gifts or qualities they had had before dying were essentially erased by the vampire blood.

He threw the ball of flames, and I jumped out of the way then blurred toward him. I was about to jump on him when I felt an excruciating pain in my head—like hundreds of needles piercing my brain—made me drop to my knees.

I looked up through the pain to see William concentrating hard on me. His eyes were pitch black.

Aaron stood up and started to run toward me.

"Aaron, stop!" I yelled.

If I was in so much pain, William doing the same thing to him would probably kill him.

"Yes, Aaron, stop," William said lazily with a chuckle. He walked toward me slowly as I held my head against the pain.

"Put the bracelets on her," he instructed one of the warlocks still standing.

As the warlock approach, I saw the tip of a knife pierce his chest from behind. When the body dropped, Lavinia was standing there.

"Stupid girl," William sneered then threw a fireball at her. It sent her flying over the edge of the building. "Go get her," he ordered the last warlock after he put four bracelets on me.

With the bracelets on, I felt the needles in my head stop. I still held my head so William would think I was still in pain. I could feel the poison working its way into my body from the bracelets, but that at least was bearable.

William started toward Aaron who was awaiting his attack. Aaron threw balls of fire at him, but William easily dodged them all.

William reached for Aaron quickly and grabbed him by the throat. I tried to blur to him, but I was significantly slower than usual. I managed to jump onto William's back, making him drop Aaron. I bit him on the neck a few times as he scrambled to get me off him. Finally, he pulled me over his head and tossed me into Aaron.

I stood back up to fight, but I stumbled before regaining my balance and grabbed my head to try to focus. "Get these off me!" I screamed to Aaron.

As Aaron desperately worked to remove the bracelets, I watched William pull a dagger from his cloak. It had a black-tipped blade and an emerald-green handle.

William blurred over to me and lifted the dagger, but I stopped his arm with my free hand as it came down at me. He felt so strong, but I was able to hold him at bay—that was until he started pushing with his other hand as well. With his full strength, he pushed me down to my knees.

The blade was almost to my chest when I heard a snap as Aaron managed to get off one of the bracelets. I felt a little bit stronger and was able to slowly push William's arm and the blade away from my body.

William's black eyes glared at me.

"I can't get the rest off!" Aaron shouted furiously.

William grinned at me as he pushed the blade harder back toward my body.

**CRAAAACK**

William's body suddenly fell to the ground, and Ian appeared behind him.

"Ian!" I yelled then stood up to hug him.

"Ow," he winced as the three remaining bracelets touched his skin.

"Oh, sorry," I apologized as I stepped back.

"Well, that was anticlimactic," Alan said as he came to stand next to Ian.

"Connor!" Ian gasped and ran toward him as Aaron stood up and Alan hugged him hard.

"Thank you," Aaron said to him.

"You know I couldn't leave my grandbaby to face a bunch of evil war-locks for too long," Alan smirked.

"Shut up," Aaron said as he playfully pushed him away.

It was done. Everything was good. Well, everything except for Connor. I still couldn't blur quickly, so I ran to him as fast as I could using human speed.

"Is he alive?" I asked, trying not to show how heartbroken I was. I had never seen him look so fragile. I just wanted to grab him and hold him tightly. I was thankful Ian couldn't read my thoughts because I didn't know what he would think of that.

I took Connor's hand and stroked it. Ian watched me then gave me a smile of understanding. I half smiled back at him then turned my full attention on Connor.

"Yes, he's still breathing," Ian answered. "I just don't know what to do. Do angels have the same anatomy as humans? I mean, I know he's half human, but is he more human than angel or more angel than human? It's not like we can just take him to a hospital. Let's at least try to stop the bleeding," he rambled as he ripped the sleeves off his shirt.

Ian laid Connor down and put pressure on the wound on his stomach.

"Aaron!" I yelled so he might come and assist, but when I turned around to find him, I saw that William's body had long white hair. I walked over to the body and turned it over.

"It's one of the triplets," Alan observed as we now stood over the body.

"The who?" Ian questioned.

"They are three warlocks who looked exactly the same," Alan answered. "What would *you* call them?"

"But how?" I asked, struggling to grasp the complexity of the situation.

"Glamor spell," Aaron explained. "He made himself look like William, but when he died, it wore off."

That explained why William had been able to produce magic. It hadn't been him at all. His supposed magic had been nothing more than an illusion, a clever façade to deceive us all.

"But how did we not notice them change? Are we sure there aren't four of them? Was William ever even here?" Ian asked in rapid succession.

"I don't know. Do I look like a crazy warlock to you?" Alan asked sarcastically, then his face darkened. "I knew that was too easy. I don't think this is over yet."

A sense of unease settled over us, the weight of the impending danger hanging heavy in the air. With Connor's safety at stake, I knew we couldn't afford to let our guard down for a moment.

"If that's true, we need to get Connor out of here," I instructed. "If that demon creature comes back, it will kill him."

"So, now it's the four of us against four vampires and two warlocks?" Aaron mused, casting a meaningful glance at Alan and Ian. "I think we might need help."

"Yes, call them again," I agreed, knowing that involving the council was our best chance of facing the looming threat head-on.

Aaron turned away to make the phone call.

"I think it will only be three vampires and one warlock," I said when he returned.

"What do you mean?" Ian asked.

"Lavinia killed one of the warlocks who was attacking me."

An instant smile appeared on Ian's face. "She did?"

"Yes, but don't get your hopes up. We still don't know what her intentions are," I cautioned.

"I know," he said, but he wasn't quite able to hide his smile.

I looked up into the sky and saw the last warlock floating toward us, then William, Jen, and Matt blurred in behind him. I looked at the warlock's chest and noticed that his huge amulet looked like it had two of three parts. I watched as he put out his hand and another amulet flew from the body of the warlock Ian had killed.

As the three pieces came together, a red aura glowed around them and seemed to seep into the warlock's body.

"Great, a super-powered warlock. That's all we need," Alan said sarcastically.

"Get behind me." My voice resonated with commanding authority as my eyes blazed an intense magenta glow.

With a sense of purpose coursing through me, I watched as the skies roared in response to my power, and the thunder echoed my determination. As I raised my hands, the bolts of lightning surrounded my entire body in pink electricity. A surge of energy enveloped me, crackling with the sparking tendrils, as I unleashed the lightning at the warlock then held it in two streams against his body.

"I'll keep him away. You guys take care of the other three," I directed.

With a sense of urgency, the others charged our enemies, their determination matching my own as the clash of power filled the air. I maintained the charge on the warlock, but soon one of the streams started to fade. I concentrated all my efforts on holding the other, unleashing a powerful surge of energy that sent the warlock crashing to the ground. But, to my dismay, he rose again, a sinister grin twisting his features as he retaliated with a fiery onslaught that engulfed my jacket in flames.

"Holy crap!" I exclaimed, scrambling to extinguish the inferno that threatened to consume me.

Before I could regain my composure, the warlock descended upon me, his relentless assault driving me to the ground with a forceful kick to the chest.

Struggling to regain my focus amidst the chaos, I sought solace in the distant rumble of thunder, but it eluded me as it became drowned out by an onslaught of pain and fury as the warlock continued punching and kicking me. With a desperate effort, I attempted to defend myself, but his relentless barrage left me vulnerable and defenseless.

Alan blurred over to me and pulled the warlock off then kicked him so hard that he went through the window of a small tool shed on the roof. As Alan moved to help me to my feet, my heart sank at the sight of William, his malevolent intent clear, as he brandished a wooden stake and got into position to strike from the shadows.

"Alan, look out!" I shouted in desperation.

With every ounce of strength I could muster, I tried to rise to my feet, but the weight of the cursed bracelets still bound to my wrists and being drained from channeling lightning left me powerless, a mere bystander in the face of impending tragedy.

I watched in horror, my limbs heavy with helplessness, as the life of my friend hung in the balance. Time seemed to slow to a crawl, each second stretching into eternity as the cruel weapon inched closer to Alan's heart.

Then, in a flash of bravery and selflessness, Ian lunged forward, pushing Alan out of the way, sacrificing himself to be stabbed in the heart instead.

"Ian!" I cried.

"Stupid kid," Alan said frantically, his voice trembling with emotion as he rushed to Ian's side. His hands shook as he desperately tried to staunch the blood flowing from the wound.

A blue fireball came in suddenly, striking William with a ferocity that sent him hurtling through the air like a ragdoll.

I looked toward its origin and saw Aaron. He was now battered and bloodied, and his neck showed a tapestry of savage wounds that oozed crimson with every labored breath. He had been trying to protect us and fight off Jen and Matt at the same time. They seemed much faster and stronger than the last time we'd seen them.

Alan blurred over to Aaron to help him with the two other vampires while I went to Ian. I noticed the wooden stake was no longer in him but was immediately distracted as the warlock emerged from the shadows of the shed.

I left my brother on the ground and turned my attention back to William and the warlock. I slowly tried to stand, but I couldn't keep myself upright, so I fell back down. I was so dizzy now and could barely hold myself up, but I knew I had a job to do.

Determination burned within me like a flickering flame in the darkness, urging me to press on despite the overwhelming odds stacked against us. Though my body screamed in protest, I knew that I couldn't give up. The safety of my loved ones and the fate of our world was at stake. I attempted to pull myself up, but my strength faltered once again. I looked up to see that the warlock was hovering over me with a cruel grin plastered on his face.

The warlock's harsh grip tightened around my hair as he hoisted me into the air, and I desperately clung to his hands. With a sinister grin, he produced two more bracelets, determined to seal my fate.

My gaze darted to Allen and Aaron, who were locked in combat with Jen and Matt, then to Ian's lifeless form sprawled on the ground. Hope dwindled as my strength waned.

The warlock threw me to the roof, knocking the wind out of me. I closed my eyes and resigned myself to the inevitable. *This is it*, I thought as I opened my eyes to see the warlock only a few feet from me. He knew I had nothing left.

As he pulled my wrists toward him, an enormous bicep appeared around his neck. Gasping for breath, the warlock stumbled to his knees, and his grip on me loosened in his shock. Through bleary eyes, I beheld a towering figure, a form radiant with an otherworldly power.

"Connor," I breathed as he emerged from the shadows.

Connor loomed above me, his eyes ablaze with power. Despite his own injuries, he exuded an aura of unwavering determination, a beacon of hope in our darkest hour. He fixed his gaze on me, concern for me evident on his face. His eyes reverted to their normal state as he realized the difficulty I was having to stand and go to him.

"Nina," he murmured, his voice deep and sensual.

Weakly, I managed a smile in response, but my joy was short-lived. A sudden movement caught my eye, and before I could react, a gleaming dagger sliced through the air and embedded itself in Connor's right shoulder with a sickening thud. Time froze as he crumpled to the ground beside Ian, the agony etched on his face mirroring my own inner torment.

"Nooooo!" My anguished cry echoed through the chaos as tears blurred my vision. Summoning as much strength as I could, I crawled over to Connor and shielded him the best I could.

While William hesitated, I checked for a pulse. It was weak but still present. I desperately scanned the area for anything to secure the blade.

"I'll be right back," I whispered to Connor then pressed a deep kiss to his lips.

Despite the absence of visible wounds, every movement of my body sent searing pain coursing through me as if I bore the curse of a thousand broken bones.

Summoning the last shreds of my strength, I rose unsteadily to my feet with fierce determination. With an emboldening crack of my neck, I braced myself as I prepared to unleash whatever remained of my dwindling energy.

With every ounce of power and fury I could muster, I pounced toward William, driven by primal instinct. But even in my desperation, I was swatted away like an inconsequential pest, and I hit the ground near a wall and sat up against it.

"You are weak," William taunted, his voice dripping with contempt as he loomed over me. His malevolent grin sent shivers down my spine.

He looked me over then took my wrist and bit down. I was astonished when my skin broke, and he began to drink my blood. His eyes opened and turned magenta for a moment before turning back to red. "Yes!" he shouted as he straightened.

I watched as blood continued to drip from my wrist. Standing above me, William was coming back for more when he suddenly stopped, and his body crumbled to ash in front of my very eyes before a wooden stake clattered to the ground atop the remnants of his form.

"Lavinia?" I asked weakly, disbelief coloring my voice as I saw who had dealt him the final blow.

She smiled nervously as she knelt next to me and worked on getting the bracelets off my wrists.

I could see her skin burning as she tried pulling them off with her hands. She blurred away then came right back with a dagger in her hands. I could barely keep my eyes open anymore, so I started to close them.

"Nina! Stay awake! I'm so sorry. I didn't know."

I heard her and tried to open my eyes, but I was so tired.

Then I heard a snap. My eyes instantly opened and became filled with magenta fire. I briefly smiled at her and nodded then ran right toward Alan and Aaron, who were still fending off Jen and Matt. Lavinia came alongside me and began to help as well.

"These vampires are not Jen and Matt. They are two ancient vampires with a glamor spell on them," Lavinia explained as we battled the vampires.

"Wait, what?" I exclaimed, barely able to process Lavinia's revelation amidst the chaos of the battle. The realization sent a chill down my spine, now knowing that we faced not just any vampires, but ancient beings cloaked in deception.

As Alan deftly evaded a vicious blow aimed at his head, his words echoed my own thoughts. "Well, that explains a lot," he quipped, his voice laced with a mix of incredulity and determination.

Lavinia blurred back to William's ashes and put the wooden stake in her pocket. "Three of us need to focus on one first," she instructed upon her return, her eyes ablaze.

I met her gaze with a resolute nod, knowing exactly what I had to do. I concentrated hard, seeking the familiar rumble of thunder that heralded the arrival of my elemental power.

This time, it worked. As soon as the lightning hit my hands, I unleashed a torrent of electricity upon one of the ancient vampires while my friends took on the other. Despite my efforts to overwhelm him, the vampire proved resilient, his ancient strength barely contained by the force of my lightning assault.

Meanwhile, the other vampire blurred all around Lavinia, Aaron, and Alan, their combined efforts the only thing standing between us and certain doom.

"Bite me," Aaron suddenly yelled at Alan, a desperate plea piercing through the chaos of battle. His voice strained with urgency as he sought any means of gaining an advantage.

"What? No!" Alan protested.

"Just do it!"

"No, Aaron, I can't. I'm barely holding it together now. The scent of your blood is driving me crazy. I love you, kid, but I don't know what I would do if I got a taste of your blood right now."

They stared at each other for a moment before Lavinia broke the awkward silence. "I can do it," she said shyly.

"How much longer will the bloodlust spell last?" Alan asked accusingly.

"A few more hours."

"Are you sure?!" Alan screamed.

She nodded, then Alan looked over at Aaron and nodded to him as well. Lavinia bit down on Aaron's wrist, which caused the vampire to focus on him.

I was still holding the pink stream on the other vampire, but he was starting to get up, so I jumped toward him and held him down as the lightning shot off my body.

Lavinia now was on the other vampire's back, and he was swinging her around, but Aaron took out his legs, which caused him to fall back on top of Lavinia. Finally, Alan pounced on him and stabbed him in the heart with the wooden stake.

The three of them walked over to me, Alan with the stake still in hand. "Are you ready?" he asked.

I nodded and stood up but kept two lightning streams on the remaining vampire. I dropped them both to let Alan stake him, but before he could, the vampire blurred away into the night.

"Did we win?" Ian asked as he walked up behind abruptly.

All of us screamed.

"Ian! How?" I asked in awe as I pulled him into a hug.

"Lavinia," Ian remarked in surprise.

"When I came back, I separated Connor and Ian so he could heal," she answered shyly.

"You did?" Ian asked with a huge smile on his face.

"Where's Connor?" I asked.

"I pulled him over to the side so he would be safe from the fighting," Lavinia answered then started to run toward that end of the roof.

We found Connor behind a huge air-conditioning unit. The awful blade was no longer in him, and Lavinia's sweater was wrapped tightly around the wound to put pressure on it.

I looked at her and smiled, and she smiled back.

"I..." she started to say, but I stopped her as I pulled her into a big hug.

# CHAPTER 24
## WELCOME TO MY NIGHTMARE

With Connor's state understood, I frantically looked around for Aaron. When I saw him, our eyes met like magnets.

He ran toward me and kissed me deeply. "I love you, Nina."

I smiled and kissed him again, so glad he was okay. I hated seeing him hurt, but that made me understand how much I cared for him. He didn't have to be here. He had risked his life for me and my family.

"I love you, too," I answered then placed my head on his chest and wrapped my arms around him. I was so happy.

I looked back up at him, and he was smiling. He kissed me again then pulled me into his arms and held me tight. The combination of the scent of his potion and his blood was making me feel sicker, but I didn't care. I didn't want to pull away. As I started to feel dizzy again, I leaned more of my weight on him.

"Whoa. Are you okay?" Aaron asked as he felt my shift.

I nodded at him then massaged my temples as he quickly pulled off his pendant and threw it to Alan.

"Ow! What the hell man!" he grunted as he caught it out of reflex then dropped it quickly.

We both laughed as we held on to each other. I took a deep breath in and exhaled. I was finally able to breathe again. His blood still smelled good, but at least it wasn't painful.

I looked back over at Alan. He was getting out his phone to make a call when I heard footsteps coming up the stairs. I pulled myself off Aaron and blurred over to the rooftop door to open it. I looked down the winding stairwell.

"It's the Safeguard," Aaron said next to me as he looked down the stairs as well.

"The who?" I asked.

"It's like the supernatural police. They're the ones the council called."

"Do you think they can help Connor?"

"Yes. They usually show up with a sort of paramedic team just like the human police except these guys have the medical knowledge of supernatural creatures. I'm sure one of them will know what to do," he explained as we stepped back out onto the roof.

Six officers burst through the rooftop door behind us as the elevator beeped, and three more officers came out with two gurneys.

"These guys would have been helpful about five minutes ago," Alan complained sarcastically.

I noticed Jacob was leading the team, and Aaron went to speak with him to tell him we had an injured angel who was the priority. Jacob signaled to another officer who started to take his shirt off.

"Whoaaa, buddy, this is not Chippendales!" Alan shouted.

As the officer finished removing his shirt, a pair of enormous light gray wings emerged. He flew over to Connor, scooped him up, and took him up into the sky.

"Where is he taking him?" I asked Jacob.

"Heaven," was his response.

"What?" I asked in utter horror.

"No, it's okay. He's not dead. He just needs to be healed, and that's the only place they can recover," he explained then frowned. "There isn't much that can hurt an angel. What did this to him?"

"I don't know what it was, but it had horns, was red, and had giant bat wings, but it still looked kind of human."

"That sounds like it might be a cambion."

"What is that?" I asked.

"It's a half-human, half-demon hybrid. The logistics of the birth are complicated, but that's another story. There are only two ways an angel or a God can be injured: by an equal or by Asmodeus's dagger. The latter will kill them, and a demon or angel can injure or kill them just like humans can with another human."

We watched as the rest of the officers secured the area and took away the bodies of the warlocks and other supernatural creatures. Thankfully, the Safeguard also had a knife with a red ruby blade that was able to quickly cut off the two remaining bracelets. I felt so relieved.

Looking around the roof, I saw it had pretty much been destroyed. Several holes looked like they went down multiple floors, and pieces of the brick exterior were missing. Then I noticed that the officers seemed to be damaging the roof even more.

"What are they doing?" I asked Aaron.

"They're covering our tracks," he said. "Apparently, the city experienced a strange and severe thunderstorm this evening during which lightning destroyed the top stories of this building," he finished with a grin.

"Weird," I laughed.

He put his arm around me as we started to walk, and I noticed him start to limp. "You're hurt," I said as I inspected him closer.

In addition to the bite marks on his neck, he also had them on his arms and shoulders. I looked at his right leg and noticed he couldn't put any weight on it.

"It's no biggie," he said, brushing it off.

"Stop," he whispered as I bit my wrist.

He pushed my arm down. "Maybe not here," he winked.

"Here," Alan said as he gave Aaron his wrist. "Well, I'm sure you're not in love with me. At least I hope you're not because if you are, we're going to have a whole other set of problems," he said jokingly.

Embarrassed, Aaron and I looked at each other. Alan knew exactly what we had been talking about.

"You have so much to learn, young Skywalker," Alan said to me as he pulled his jacket sleeve back down once Aaron was done.

Once we'd all gathered again, Lavinia told us what she knew about William's plan. It wasn't much more than we already knew. She had been told we were a threat and needed to be dealt with. I nodded, remembering Alan had once thought much the same. Lavinia had believed what William had told her because he had turned her, and that built an inherent trust. She hadn't seen him for years, until 1948 when she'd started helping him. She'd pretty much followed him blindly after that until she'd fallen in love with Ian.

Ian was happy to have her back with him. Although I was happy as well, I still didn't fully trust her. I knew the bond between a vampire and their creator was one of the strongest in the world, so it had been hard for her to kill William. I figured that meant she must really love Ian.

After the night's ordeal, my brothers and I went back to the Carrier house to rest. Thankfully, the council was gone when we arrived, so it was just Aaron's family and the three of us.

Ian and Zay were given a room to share, but I got my own. As I walked into my room, I heard Beatrice's muffled yelling at Aaron for not calling them sooner. I felt bad because I was the one who hadn't wanted to call them.

I laid on the bed and tried to drown out the voices, but that proved impossible as Beatrice scolded Aaron for a few more minutes before stalking away. I got up to see if I could talk to him, but then I heard other footsteps.

"When?" I heard Ian ask in the hallway.

When no one answered him, I assumed he was reading someone's thoughts.

"When?" he asked louder.

"When she was gone," Aaron answered in a whisper. "When we didn't know if she was alive."

"But when we knew she wasn't dead?" Ian prompted angrily.

Aaron didn't answer, but I heard another pair of footsteps join them.

"You know he slept with her, too," Ian said before a pair of footsteps stalked off.

Then I heard someone hitting someone else.

"Ow! What was that for?" Alan asked.

"You slept with Amanda," Aaron whispered angrily.

"Oh, that."

Then another pair of footsteps stalked off, and I peeked out of my room, but all I found was Alan holding his jaw. I closed the door before he could see me and went to sit on the bed.

I couldn't believe what I'd heard. Why was Aaron so upset Alan had slept with Amanda? If he didn't have feelings for her, it shouldn't have mattered. I started to think back to earlier that night when he'd pulled away from me. Maybe it hadn't just been the wrong time and place. Maybe it was because he still had feelings for Amanda. My heart broke just thinking about it, and I knew I couldn't be in that house anymore.

Throwing my phone onto the bed, I opened the window. As I was about to swing my second leg out, there was a knock on the door. I stopped and watched as the door opened slowly.

"Nina?" Aaron asked.

I looked him directly in the eyes then jumped out the window. I blurred into the night without looking back.

I didn't know where I was going. I thought about heading to Lavinia's house, but I still wasn't entirely sure about her. Then I thought about going to Becca's, but her parents still thought I was sick. The only other place I could go was home.

When I got to the empty house, I instantly felt horribly alone. Even the cats were gone, which made the house even quieter.

I knew my brothers would be worried about me, so I grabbed the house phone in the kitchen and called Ian to let him know I was safe.

Not wanting to cry anymore, I went upstairs to check my email. There were many from VP, so I started opening them. They contained the lessons from each day that I had missed.

"Ugh," I said then closed the laptop.

Even though it could have been a good distraction, I didn't want to deal with that at this time. I ended up sending an email to my parents to tell them I missed them then went downstairs again.

When I got to the front door, I saw it was open. I looked around but didn't see anyone, then I heard the TV turn on, so I blurred toward the sound and stopped in shock. "Alan? What are you doing here?"

"You know only bad girls sneak out of their rooms," he quipped.

"It wasn't my room," I pouted.

"Semantics. Come over and sit. I want to talk to you about something," he said as he patted the spot on the couch next to him.

I didn't want to argue with him, so I just went to sit down.

"I know you heard some things tonight," he said.

Pulsing with renewed anger, I started to get up.

"Eh," he said as he grabbed my wrist and pulled me back down. "Just hear me out. Aaron is a really proud guy, and he's not used to being with a... well, such a desirable girl. The kid has a big ego, just like his granddad," he smirked cockily.

"I don't know what you're trying to say," I ventured.

Alan sat up straight and cleared his throat. "He has never had any competition for the object of his affection, and now that he does, he's protecting himself."

"He wouldn't have hit you if he didn't still have feelings for Amanda," I argued.

"Umm, debatable," Alan posed.

"I don't think so," I said as I stood up.

"I saw you kiss Connor," he said accusingly.

Those words froze me in place. I thought about continuing to walk away then decided to turn back around instead.

Alan met my gaze. "I know it was that whole death thing, but Aaron was right there, and you kissed Connor. So, let's not pretend you don't have feelings for him."

"Aaron doesn't want to be with me," I said hollowly.

"Now, what makes you think that?"

"I just know," I answered, not wanting to tell him about our moment at the jeep.

In a rush, Alan got up off the couch and stalked toward me then grabbed my arm and pushed me against the wall. I sucked in a breath as the cold surface hit my back. He held my forearm while his other arm rested on the wall beside my head. His face was so close to mine that I could see his pupils dilate.

*What is happening?*

"What are you doing?" I asked breathlessly, taken back by his actions.

He had just been pushing me toward Aaron, but the way he now looked at me painted a completely different story. I sniffed the air around him and breathed in deeply. It felt so good to be able to do that.

"He would be crazy to not want to be with you," Alan admitted as he moved the hair out of my face then caressed my jaw with his thumb.

His touch felt nice, and I felt no urge to recoil because our bodies were the same temperature. Frozen in place, I looked into his eyes. He shifted his gaze from my eyes to my lips.

"Shit," he muttered under his breath as he looked down quickly and removed his hand from my face then stepped back.

I stood there in shock for a moment trying to figure out what had just happened. I just stared at him as he sat back down on the couch, relaxed, and went back to being his cocky self. It was like he was a completely different person as he grinned at me and spread his arms across the top of the couch.

After a few more moments of silence, I tried to remember what we had been talking about before the very odd encounter, but I couldn't. Trying to break the now very awkward silence, I said, "I want to learn more about Talaatah. My dad told me that he had some information."

"I think that's a great idea," he said as he adjusted his position again on the couch but still didn't say anything else.

"Earlier today you said something to Aaron," I began, my voice barely above a whisper and laden with uncertainty and a tinge of fear.

"Okay..." he prompted when I didn't continue. The tension in his voice was palpable as he awaited my next words.

"When I offered Aaron my blood and he declined, you suggested he take yours instead. You said... you said something about him not being in love with you."

"Okay..." His tone urged me to continue as he sensed the weight of my words.

"What did you mean by that?" I implored, my voice trembling with a mix of apprehension and desperation for answers.

"She really didn't teach you anything, did she?" he bit out sarcastically.

"What does that mean?"

"Blood sharing can be a very intimate practice, but it only becomes intimate if one party is in love with the other. Now, when both parties love each other, it's... indescribable. The feeling of intense pleasure and need is all-consuming. You feel every small touch as an explosion of pleasure. I, myself, only ever experienced that when I was human, but I have been told that, as a vampire, the feeling is even more intense," he said then paused, obviously deep in memory. "But even though my experience was long ago, it is still a feeling I will never forget."

"Is that how you knew you were in love?" I asked him cautiously.

"No," he replied, a wistful edge seeping into his tone. "I knew I was in love before I ever tasted her blood, but when I smelled her blood, it was sweet. Humans do not typically want to drink blood," he chuckled. "Before that time, blood had always smelled coppery to me, so when she offered it to me and it smelled so enticing, I couldn't resist."

I felt my cheeks flush as I listened to his explanation. I dared to ask, "So, what happens when neither party loves the other?"

"Nothing," he answered simply, his tone devoid of emotion. "We feed, and that's all. Vampires do not give their blood freely to those who do not hold their hearts. If we have to, it is as little as possible. Vampires need to consume blood to survive, but we do not need to give our blood away to just anyone."

Before I could fully comprehend what Alan was saying, I remembered what I had been about to say before he distracted me. "Ian was mad at Aaron tonight, too." I paused, trying to remember exactly what Ian had said. "He saw something in his thoughts and asked him 'When?' Aaron said it was when he didn't know she was alive, or something like that. I'm assuming I'm the 'she.'"

Alan looked to the side and seemed to be trying to remember. "Ohhhh, that..." he replied, then he became very quiet.

"What?" I asked.

"Well, we might as well get it out now because Ian is just going to tell you anyway. When you were gone, Aaron slept with Amanda. He told me about it, and he said it was a mistake, that he didn't know if he would ever see you again and—"

I blurred up the stairs, the weight of my emotions crashing around me like thunder. With a forceful slam, I shut myself in my room, feeling like I was drowning in an ocean of anger and confusion.

"Nina, come back," his plea echoed through the halls.

I heard him blur up the stairs and knock, but I didn't answer. After a minute, I heard him walk back downstairs and change the program on the TV.

Although I was fuming mad at the news, I honestly was glad he stayed. At least I knew he was there if I needed him.

Lying on my bed, I gazed up at the ceiling, thoughts drifting to the world above. I wondered whether Connor had been able to heal or if he'd even made it there. The uncertainty of his fate clawed at my heart, the fear of losing him forever a relentless nagging haunting my every thought. Tears began to flood my eyes.

Restless, I got out of my bed and walked to my parents' room to grab the phone they kept in there. Sitting on their bed, I dialed Becca's number and told her almost everything, even about what had happened with both Connor and Aaron that night. I only told her what Alan already knew about Connor because I knew he could hear me. I planned to tell her the rest when we had more privacy.

She tried her best to make me feel better, but it didn't work. She even tried to cheer me up by saying she would take me out that weekend to help me forget about both men. Becca's birthday was only a few weeks before mine, so we could finally go to the nightclub she had been talking about since the first week of school. We had been chatting for about half an hour when she suddenly gasped.

"What Becca? What happened?"

"Ahh, it's nothing.... Chloe just jumped on the bed," she answered. "I'm still getting used to having cats in the house," she laughed.

I sighed in relief. "Thanks for taking them, Becca. And thank your mom for me, too."

"You're welcome. I love you, girly."

"I love you, too. Goodnight."

I hung up the phone feeling a little bit better. At least I still had someone. Becca was a really good friend. The more I thought about it, the more I realized that Alan had become one of my best friends, too. I smiled at that comfort.

I knew I still wouldn't be able to fall asleep, so I looked through the emails from school. There were so many because I had missed so much. Although I could probably read through everything pretty quickly, I thought it would be better to ask Ian for help.

I opened the last few emails with the current subjects we were on and started reading through the material. I was doing pretty well, so I decided to look through one more, but that was a mistake. That next one was U.S. History, taught by Ms. Adams.

I closed my laptop and went to lie down in bed. Seeing Ms. Adams's name instantly made me think of Connor again. I looked over at the clock. It said it was already 12:55 a.m. I pulled the covers over my head and curled up, but then there was a knock on my door.

"Nina?" Becca asked.

I jumped out of bed and ran to the door. Throwing it open, I hugged her hard and pulled her into my room. "What are you doing here?"

"Alan came to pick me up. He said you might need a friend," she explained sweetly.

I smiled and hugged her again. "Thank you."

"Thank Alan. It was actually him at my window when I told you that Chloe scared me," she laughed. "He is so hot."

I looked at her with disapproval.

"What? So, he's a little older than me. No big deal."

"A *little* older? Becca, he's more than a hundred years older than you," I laughed.

She shrugged then crawled into my bed. I went to lie down with her, and we talked for a little longer before we both fell asleep.

I was awoken by an unusual sound. Blinking my eyes open, I looked around. Becca was no longer there next to me. The unusual sound reached my ears again. It was moaning—distinctly pleasurable moans. My mouth dropped when I realized what it was and that it was coming from the other side of the wall. I could hear Becca's and Alan's voices as they whispered to each other.

Wholly amused, I buried my face in my pillow and burst into laughter. Their passionate escapades persisted longer than I could handle, so I eventually turned my radio up loud to try to drown the noise out. A few seconds later, I heard Becca shushing Alan and then Alan laughing.

About ten minutes later I heard the shower running. Feeling awkward at the prospect of seeing either of them, I went downstairs. As I entered the kitchen, my eyes widened at the sight of Alan standing in front of the counter, shirtless with only black sweatpants on.

I had never seen him like that before, and I was surprised to learn that he had two full-sleeve tattoos. I wanted to inspect them closer, but before I could, he turned around.

"Hi," he said cheekily.

Captivated by his appearance, I was left momentarily speechless. First off, his sweatpants were baggy, but they perfectly accentuated his masculinity. Feeling red with embarrassment, my eyes darted away and up to his arms. Tattoos adorned both arms and extended onto his perfectly sculpted, rock-hard right pectoral muscle. The intricate tribal designs gracing his chiseled abs reminded me of Connor's. *Jesus, this man is so hot.*

When my eyes finally reached Alan's face, his cocky smile revealed that he was well aware of his sex appeal, and I realized he'd likely heard me walking down the stairs and had done nothing to hide his overtly sexual appearance.

Thankfully not mentioning it, he took a sip from the coffee mug in his hand then handed me a file folder.

"What's this?" I asked, grateful for the distraction.

"It's all the information your dad had."

"You went to get this for me?"

"You said you wanted it," he answered then started digging in his pocket.

I tried my best to keep my eyes on his face, but the traitors started to wander down his body.

"Here's your phone, too. Thought you may need it," he added with a cocky smile as he walked away.

I couldn't help watching him go. Coupled with his trim waist, his broad shoulders were hypnotizing. The tattoos were just the icing on the cake.

I shook my head to clear it. All I needed was to have a crush on him. Not only would that make it three guys, but it would be the worst choice ever. Alan was one of those guys who didn't have relationships. He had conquests.

Now alone, I sat down at the kitchen table and opened the file. There were so many papers inside with different dates, ranging from 1987 to 2006. My dad didn't have the best handwriting, so most of it was really hard to read. I flipped through them to try to find anything about Talaatah, but before I could, Alan walked back into the kitchen.

"I have to get going. You're the only cool kid that can go out in the sun. Have a good night," he winked.

"Bye," I said distantly.

I didn't quite understand him. He knew I'd heard him with Becca, but he was still flirting with me as if I would be interested in a guy who had just slept with my best friend. Annoyed, I closed the file and went back upstairs.

"I know you're not asleep," I said to Becca as I laid down next to her.

She sat up quickly with a huge smile on her face.

"Go ahead, tell me about it," I said as I playfully rolled my eyes.

She started telling me about Alan and their sexual encounter without missing any detail. As I sat there listening to her, oddly I found myself getting a little jealous. I wasn't sure if it was because it was Alan or the fact that she had gotten to feel that kind of pleasure.

After she finished her story, she told me she had spoken with her mom, and I could go stay with her. She'd told her mom I wasn't sick anymore, so her mom said she would be happy to have me. However, since her mom worked at the school, she was also expecting me to return to school the following day.

We slept for a few hours then woke up so I could take her home before her mom found out she was gone. I opened the garage to take my dad's car but noticed my car behind it in the driveway with the keys on the windshield.

I saw a note under the wipers, so I grabbed it. It read:

*Thought you might need this, too.*

*~ Alan*

Alan had gone to get my car from the hospital. I smiled at the note but put it away as soon as Becca walked out. I wasn't even sure why I'd hidden it. It didn't have anything scandalous on it.

Becca opened the passenger door and got in without asking any questions, and she was asleep before I even got in the car. When we made it to her house, I shook her awake, and she climbed back up to her room.

I told her I would just stay around the corner since her mom expected me to arrive in about an hour anyway. I grabbed my bookbag and reviewed the current lessons from my classes with the time I had.

When I went back to her house, I spoke to her mom while Becca got ready for school. She informed me that Becca had a new curfew, and she expected me to follow it as well.

I listened to her and agreed to all her terms. Of course, she would be worried. This town used to be safe, then all of a sudden, teenagers started going missing. I wished I could tell her that it was all over, but I knew I couldn't.

Soon Becca was ready, and we headed to the school. She swooned over Alan the entire drive, but luckily she lived much closer than I did, so we made it in only a few minutes.

As we walked into school, I instantly noticed that all eyes were on me, and everyone was whispering. I could hear them all. Most of them thought I must have been really sick to have been out so long, but others were speculating that I'd left to get plastic surgery. Those people thought Ian was getting plastic surgery as well and he would look different when he returned, too. It was absurd. Sure, my complexion had changed, but my features were still all the same.

"This whole nyxling thing is pretty cool, but right now I hate that I can hear what everyone is saying," I whispered to Becca as I leaned against the lockers.

"Don't let it get to you," she advised. "They're just jealous."

"If you say so," I responded glumly.

"I do say so," she said as she closed her locker.

Then I heard people start whispering about someone else. "There he is," a girl said.

"Oh my god. He is so cute!" another girl whispered.

I turned toward the ripple of voices and saw exactly who they were talking about. He was tall with light skin and a muscular body, not like Connor or even Aaron; he was more on the thinner side. He had green eyes and short brown hair that was buzzed on the sides and spiked up in the front.

"Who is that?" I asked.

Becca turned around to see who I was looking at, then she smiled. "New guy: Calix Dewar. He just transferred here from Scotland. So hot. He hasn't really been interested in any girls here yet," she said, "but it looks like he's staring at you, so I guess that's about to change." She winked at me.

I turned to see what she was talking about but averted my eyes quickly as they met Calix's. "Stop," I replied in embarrassment.

"Umm, we should get to class," Becca said suddenly as she looked behind me.

"What?" I asked as I turned around.

I completely lost my breath. I had forgotten that Aaron had transferred schools, and he was talking to a few guys from the football team when he turned and saw me. He looked surprised to see me, but then he started walking toward me. I turned around quickly to walk the other way.

"Oh, sorry," I said as I crashed into someone.

"Hallow thir," Calix announced in a very thick Scottish accent.

"Oh, hi."

"They ca' me Calix. 'n' yer?"

I could barely understand what he was saying, so I had to think about it for a second. He was asking my name. "I'm Nina," I finally responded.

"Urr ye freish?"

"Umm, excuse me?"

"Freish tae th' skool. Sorry, new," he self-translated.

"Ohhh, no. Well, yes, but not really. I'm returning, but I'm still kind of new," I rambled on.

"Hey, Calix. I see you met my girlfriend," Aaron said as he walked up behind me.

"Marking yer territory, urr ye?" Calix chuckled. "Ah will catch ye efter," he said as he walked away.

Aaron stepped in front of me then leaned against the nearest locker. "What did he just say?" he laughed.

I didn't laugh with him. I just stared at him in silence.

"We have to get to class," Becca coughed and started to pull me away.

"Nina, please. Just talk to me," he pleaded as he grabbed my arm.

Both Becca and I looked down at my arm for a moment. For a second, I wasn't sure if I wanted his touch or wanted to bite off his hand.

"I'll just be a minute," I said to her.

"Are you sure?" she asked quietly.

I nodded then turned back to Aaron. "What's up?" I asked casually, trying to sound like I didn't care about anything, but I couldn't even look him in the eyes. He was so amazingly handsome that every time I looked into those eyes, I would get lost in an ocean of blue. Right now, I wanted to be strong.

*He slept with Amanda. He doesn't want me*, I reminded myself.

"I talked to Alan today. He said you'll be staying with Becca instead of us."

I looked up at him in confusion. *How would Alan have known that?* Realizing I was looking at him, my eyes darted back to the floor.

"Is there anything I can say that will change your mind?" he asked sweetly.

I shook my head and started to pick at the notebook in my arms.

"Nina, please just say something."

"Not here," I whispered without looking up.

He grabbed my arm and pulled me into an empty classroom right next to the lockers.

"Aaron, that's not what I meant. Not here, not now," I said, looking straight at him. "I'm not sure if even ever," I added then looked away.

"Please don't say that," he pleaded and pulled me toward him. He lifted my chin up and brushed my hair to the side. "I love you."

"I can't, Aaron. We—"

Then he kissed me.

My knees nearly gave way to the intoxicating blend of passions that surpassed any kiss we'd shared before. I had to force myself not to pull him into me, but I also didn't do anything to stop the kiss either. Our connection deepened and deepened until the door started to open.

We pulled apart immediately. Seizing the opportunity, I hurriedly exited the room, leaving behind the hushed whispers of incoming students.

Aaron's voice called my name, but I didn't stop. I sprinted to my first class, desperately trying to hold back the tears threatening to surface. I quickly made it to History and apologized to Ms. Adams for being late. She was really nice and nothing like Mr. Conrad.

I tried not to think about Connor, but it was really hard. Everything in here reminded me of him, even the smell of the classroom. I was resting my head in my palms when I felt something hit me in the back.

I turned around to see Calix smiling at me. I reflexively smiled back, then he pointed to the floor. I looked down and saw a crumpled piece of paper, so I picked it up, opened it, and read it.

Is that your boyfriend?

I assumed he was talking about Aaron, so I really didn't want to answer. I just looked back at him, and he lifted one of his eyebrows. I shrugged my shoulders and looked down then turned back to my textbook and continued to read.

I couldn't wait to get out of that room. The girls who weren't talking about my presumed plastic surgery were saying how unfair it was that Calix seemed to be interested in me. I wondered whether the girls had been that mean before I'd changed, but I just couldn't hear it.

As soon as the bell rang, I rushed out of the class. I ran faster than I probably should have, but no one was around yet, so I figured it was okay.

I stopped in between a set of lockers to think. I had to get a book for my next class, but I was afraid Aaron would know where my locker was. I was debating whether I should just leave when I felt a presence behind me.

I turned around quickly to see Calix smiling at me. My first thought was that he was a vampire. There would be no other way he could have gotten here so fast. But then I realized that the sun was out, so he would have had no way of getting to the school since there was no underground parking lot. He would have no way to avoid the sun even if he had a blacked-out car. I smelled around him to see if I could detect the distinct scent of the pheromones that vampires produced.

"I smell nice, dinnae," he said with a chuckle.

"Sorry," I responded, embarrassed that he'd noticed. "How did you get here so quickly?"

"Short cut."

I looked at him in confusion. What short cut was he talking about? He sure didn't smell like a vampire, but was he something else?

"Yer eyes are lovely," he commented.

"Um, thanks," I replied as I looked away quickly.

"They said ye hud contacts, bit ah see that's nae true."

I smiled at him for his observation, but I still felt weird about my eyes, like I was lying about the color of them.

"Kin ah walk ye to class?" he asked.

Not sure what else to do, I nodded, and we started to walk. I held my books tightly to my chest as he talked to me.

It was difficult to understand him at first, but the more we walked, the more I started to get used to his accent. He told me that he and his family had moved to Hallowed Hills two weeks ago because of his dad's job. In turn, I told him about my family—well, at least the non-supernatural stuff—and I found that he was actually a really nice guy and easy to talk to.

The halls were starting to fill up, and yet one of the football players was throwing a ball around. We stopped by one of the locker blocks so people could pass by, and I saw that same football player whisper something to another, but I couldn't hear what he said with all the other noise in the hall.

Calix was still talking to me when I saw the player with the ball throw it straight at the back of his head.

I was about to tell him to look out, but before I could, Calix turned around and caught the ball as it was about to hit him. He waved at the football player, who looked wildly astonished, then threw it back at him so hard that it knocked the wind out of him.

"Umm, great catch," I said to him, staring at him with even more curiosity.

"Wow, that was amazing!" another girl exclaimed as she grabbed his arm.

Calix started to talk to her as well as another two girls who walked right in front of me to talk to him, so I took that opportunity to sneak away.

I wondered how he could have done that. If he wasn't a vampire, maybe he *was* another type of supernatural creature. I supposed a human could be that quick, but how could he have known that the ball was coming? He looked normal and smelled normal, but he had to be something more than human.

I started to think about what my dad had said, that knowing about supernatural creatures makes you see them everywhere. I told myself I had to brush it off for the time being, but if I saw anything else strange, I would ask Ian to help me look into him.

I moved to put my folder in my bag as I turned the corner, but I missed the opening, so all my papers spilled out everywhere.

Ugh," I said as I slumped to the ground to gather them.

Suddenly, the papers started to float. I looked around and saw Aaron standing there, concentrating on the papers with a grin on his face.

"Aaron, stop! Someone might see," I hissed under my breath.

The pages fell back to the ground, then he walked over and started helping me pick them up normally.

"Thank you," I said blandly.

"You're welcome."

We stood up at the same time, and he tried to hold my hand, but I pulled it away, acting like I wanted to move my hair out of my face.

"I don't know why that boyfriend stealer even wants Calix if she has Aaron. God, why can't she just leave at least one for the rest of us. Mr. Conrad probably left because of her, too," I heard a girl say.

I turned around instinctively to see who it was and looked directly at a blonde girl who was talking to a brunette.

"Oh my god. Did she hear me? No. What am I saying? She couldn't have heard me," she said then walked away warily.

I looked away from her quickly when I realized what I was doing. She was too far away for any normal person to have heard her speak. But how could I not react to that? Did people know about me and Connor?

Before I could think about it for too long, I felt Aaron grab my hand again, which made me turn to him right away.

"I need to explain," he began.

"I already know," I stopped him.

"I don't think you do," he insisted.

"I know you slept with Amanda."

Aaron looked away from me quickly. "Ian told you."

"*You* should have told me."

"Why? Why would I hurt you like that? You didn't need to know. It was when you were—"

"Away. I know. But you knew I wasn't dead," I cut him off and looked directly into his eyes.

"Yes," he said sheepishly, "but you were with Connor, too."

I looked at him in disgust and spit out, "I never slept with him. And you need to keep your voice down. I already have enough problems as it is."

"You never slept with him?"

"Of course not," I said and started to walk away, but he chased me down the hall.

"I'm so sorry, Nina."

"Why would you think I slept with him?" I asked a little too loudly.

Aaron pulled me around the corner when people started to stare at us.

"I... I thought you... I don't know," he said nervously. "He's an angel," he whispered.

In that one second, I let myself look into his eyes, and that was all it took. I was so frustrated with him, but I was even more frustrated with myself. Even knowing that he had slept with Amanda, I still wanted to be with him. I couldn't help it. I looked away but then looked right back into his eyes. He was devastated.

"He's only half an angel," I said sheepishly.

Aaron came closer to me and smiled as he brushed my hair from my face.

"No," I said when I came to my senses. "I don't know why you even care. You are the one who doesn't want me."

"What are you talking about?"

I looked at him and rolled my eyes as I walked past him.

As I moved past a bulletin board, papers ripped off and started to fly around me. I turned back to see Aaron controlling them.

"Aaron, stop."

"Not until you talk to me," he insisted.

"Okay, okay," I acknowledged as I ran back to him and pushed his arms down.

"Why did you say I don't want to be with you? Did someone tell you that? Was it Connor?" he asked in rapid fire.

"No one had to tell me. And Connor? You wouldn't believe me if I told you."

He looked confused. "What do you mean?"

"It doesn't matter. Connor has nothing to do with this."

"Then who?"

I wasn't sure if he was just playing a game. I couldn't believe how he could forget. Just thinking about it made my heart hurt.

"Who?" he repeated.

"You didn't want to have sex with me last night," I said in a shy whisper.

He put his head down, now obviously realizing what I was talking about. "We were about to go into battle, but I regretted that the second I pulled away from you."

"You still have feelings for Amanda," I surmised.

He looked away and appeared to be gathering his thoughts before he turned back to me. "I'm not going to lie to you. There are still feelings there. We were together for a long time, but I'm not interested in her."

"You slept with her," I reminded him.

"I know," he said guiltily. "I was hurting, and she was there... and things just happened. I hurt her when I broke up with her. I didn't understand how much losing someone could hurt until I lost you."

"But you didn't lose me," I said.

"I wasn't sure what was going on. I thought that when you changed, you might forget about me or would be more interested in the bloodlust."

"That's vampires," I reminded him.

"Well, I didn't know that at the time."

As much as I didn't want to listen to his excuses, I had to admit some of them did make sense. When he'd left Amanda for me, theirs wasn't just a regular relationship. They had been promised to each other by their families. As outdated as that was, it was how the relationship had started. And vampires did have severe bloodlust for the first few years of their undead lives. He couldn't have known nyxlings wouldn't be the same.

"That doesn't explain why you didn't want to sleep with me."

"You had been gone a while, and I thought maybe..."

"Connor and I were having sex?" I asked incredulously.

He nodded then leaned back on the wall with a sigh.

I couldn't believe myself. The truth was that I *had* cheated on him, even if I hadn't slept with Connor. The worst part was that if Connor hadn't stopped it, I probably would have.

"Can we just forget about that entire night?" he asked, pulling me out of the depths of my thoughts.

"Okay," I answered as guilt seeped into me.

He smiled and kissed me deeply. "You will not regret it."

"I'm still going to stay with Becca."

"That's fine," he said then kissed me again.

I smiled as I watched him walk down the hall to his next class. The sense that things might be finally moving in the right direction brought a warm feeling to my heart.

However, a shadow of doubt lingered. Would he still want to be with me if he knew about the complex situation between Connor and me? Even though we hadn't slept together, if Aaron knew how I actually felt about Connor, things might be different.

Maybe that was why I had been so upset that Aaron still had feelings for Amanda. If he felt for her anything like what I felt for Connor, I wouldn't be able to trust him with her living so close to us.

Suddenly, the vivid image of me kissing Connor against the tree flashed through my mind and halted my steps. The memory of his tender lips pressed against mine overwhelmed me, and I closed my eyes to savor the moment. His glowing eyes and that heavenly smile etched in my memory appeared full force and intensified my longing for him.

It had only been a day, yet the ache of missing him cut me deep. I kicked myself for even thinking about him. I shook my head, determined to refocus as I continued walking to class and attempted to push him out of my mind.

The rest of the day went by quickly, and it was strangely normal. I let Becca take my car to go see Alan, and Aaron drove me to my house because I had never grabbed the suitcase I'd packed.

When we got to the house, I ran straight upstairs to grab the suitcase. Once in my bedroom, I saw that the window was open. I looked around but didn't see anything out of place.

I scanned the room again more slowly then noticed an envelope on the desk with my name on it. I picked it up and immediately noticed that it felt a little heavy. I flipped it over, but there was nothing else on it.

I heard Aaron coming up the stairs, so I quickly put it in my pocket and grabbed the suitcase off the bed then turned toward the door. He stopped in front of me and placed his hand on my stomach to stop me from walking out.

"We're alone," he said seductively.

"Yes, we are," I agreed with a smile.

He kissed me ardently, lifting me effortlessly before placing me on the bed. Swiftly, he unzipped my sweater. Removing it, his hands grazed my skin. Another passionate kiss followed, and he stepped back to pull his shirt over his head.

My fingers traced the contours of his abs as he leaned back over the bed and pressed me flat beneath him. The touch of his lips on my neck sent waves of pleasure through me and tempted my desires.

My urge to bite him lingered, but fear of losing control held me back. Thoughts of him and Amanda invaded my mind, but I pushed them aside as our passionate kissing continued.

Our hands explored each other's bodies with an intensity that heightened the sensations. He caressed my breasts over my shirt then provocatively pushed it up to reveal my stomach. Soft caresses followed, and he withdrew his kiss, fixing his gaze on me as he unzipped my pants, then his lips moved down to my stomach.

"I love your curves," he whispered in a deep voice as he continued to explore my body.

Nervous anticipation set in, but the desire to be with him overpowered my reservations. He lifted my shirt over my head, threw it to the side, then resumed kissing down to my neck. Pleasure and anticipation intertwined, creating a mind-blowing sensation.

Standing up, he unbuckled his belt and unzipped his pants, which revealed a seasoned confidence. As he undressed me, my thoughts raced with concerns about his past with Amanda.

Climbing back on top of me, he smiled and kissed me passionately, tugging at the waistband of my underwear.

The unsettling thought of him and Amanda together flashed through my thoughts again. My fear intensified as the idea of being with a man who harbored feelings for someone else gnawed at me.

Despite my love for Aaron, the fear of history repeating itself was palpable. If we succumbed to our passion, and he returned to Amanda, I couldn't bear the thought of becoming just a new chapter in his cycle of leaving.

"Wait. I can't," I whispered nervously.

"What? What's wrong?"

"I... I'm just not ready."

"What do you mean?"

I didn't want to tell him the full reason because I didn't know how he would react. I was sure Amanda wasn't the only girl he had been with, but sex was not just a physical act to me. I wanted to be very careful about who I gave my body to, so I gave him a half truth.

"I've never done it," I said vaguely.

"Done what?"

"Sex. I have never done it."

"Are you serious?" he asked then smiled.

"Yes," I answered and pushed against him playfully.

"But you are so..."

"What?"

"Hot," he giggled.

"What? Hot girls can't be virgins?" I laughed.

"No. I mean yes, they can, but... I just didn't think that *you* were one."

"Well, I am."

He smiled at me and kissed me again softly. "Then we can wait until you're ready," he said sweetly.

"Really?"

"Of course," he laughed.

"But other girls—"

"I don't want other girls. I just want you," he said then kissed my hand.

I smiled at him. I couldn't believe he was okay with my hesitation, especially with him being so experienced.

I heard my phone start to buzz on the desk, but I ignored it and took his face in my palms and kissed him deeply.

"Hey, hey, put your clothes back on now," he scolded lightheartedly.

I laughed and heard my phone buzz again.

"It's probably just Becca's mom wondering where I am," I said as he looked at the buzzing phone.

He grabbed it off the table and handed it to me. "It's your brother. He's called four times already. And... there's a text message," he explained, disheartened as he handed me the phone.

"What?"

I took it from him and read the text messages from Ian.

There has been an accident. It's Mom. It doesn't look good. Please call me.

# CHAPTER 25
## ASHES TO ASHES, DUST TO DUST

[**News Ancor**] Details are scarce at the moment, but investigators are working to gather more information. What we do know is that at 3:59 p.m., American Airlines Flight 1567 stalled and rolled onto its side during its descent into O'Hare International Airport. The plane quickly plunged and crashed into Lake Michigan. First responders are on the scene, undertaking exhaustive efforts to locate any survivors. Survivors will be transported to Weiss Memorial Hospital in Chicago. This heartbreaking incident casts a somber shadow over what was supposed to be a joyful holiday weekend. Our thoughts go out to all those affected by this unfortunate event. Now, back to you, Nicole.

I watched in horror as the news reporter spoke about the crash that she was standing only a few hundred feet away from.

Aaron put his arm around me as I sat on the couch and cried. When I'd spoken to Ian, he'd told me that he'd spoken to our dad earlier. Dad had been annoyed that he'd had to fly back home a day early for a meeting at work he couldn't miss. Mom had decided to stay for the last night to have dinner with a few old friends.

While Ian was on the phone listening to Dad complain, Dad had received another call. Ian waited, and when Dad got back on the line with him, he told Ian that the airline had sent automatic calls to the emergency contacts of those on Flight AA1567 to inform them of the crash.

"We have to go," I declared.

"I know," Aaron agreed.

"Now," I insisted.

"I'll drive," he offered.

Lost in my grief, I said, "I'm not going to drive."

"Okay, let's go," he responded with a smile.

"Are you sure?" I asked, knowing how disorienting it could be.

"Yes, but you are not carrying me like a baby," he chuckled.

"Okay. How do you want to do this then?" I laughed.

"Piggyback ride?" he suggested jokingly.

I smiled and turned my back to him then he jumped on.

"Hang on tight," I told him right before we blurred out the door.

I didn't run as fast as I could have because I didn't want Aaron to get sick. We also stopped a few times to lessen his dizziness. Plus, since the sun was still out, running like this made me feel worn down.

As we arrived on the scene, the sun was beginning to set. I saw ambulances waiting in the parking lot next to the beach and paramedics watching from the shore. Out in the water were three Coast Guard ships full of rescuers, some of whom wore SCUBA gear and were waiting on the deck to jump in.

Suddenly, the rescuers in the water started flocking back toward the boats with overwhelming fear painting their faces. I didn't understand the reason behind their terror. Panic seized me as I considered the possibility of a threat in the water, but to my knowledge, Lake Michigan only had fish in it.

As I stood with Aaron just a few feet from the police barrier, a sudden explosion coursed through the air.

"No!" I screamed as I rushed toward the barrier.

Aaron grabbed me by the waist as I tried to run past him then pulled me into him. I wanted to push him away, but I didn't want to hurt him, and I knew he was only trying to make sure I didn't expose myself and my extraordinary abilities.

A weight of despair pressed me to my knees, and Aaron, with his protective embrace, knelt beside me. Tears streamed down my face as I gazed helplessly at the Coast Guard's frantic efforts to quell the inferno that now engulfed the aircraft. Each flicker of the flames was a painful reminder that my mom was inside.

Even if I had exposed myself and attempted a desperate swim toward the wreckage, I knew there was little chance anyone had survived that explosion. As the harsh truth settled over me, I buried my face in Aaron's shoulder, seeking solace in his embrace.

My phone started to ring, but I didn't move. It stopped then started ringing again right away, so I pulled it from my pocket and saw it was Ian. I blankly watched his name blink on the screen then handed it to Aaron, reluctant to engage with anyone in my current state of despair. I knew that was selfish, but I didn't care.

Aaron's voice on the phone became part of the background noise drowned out by the sorrow that consumed me.

When he finished the call, he told me Alan would come pick us up and take us back to the house. I was thankful for that because I felt really weak and didn't think I could make the run back by myself let alone with someone on my back.

A while later, I slumped into the back seat of Alan's car, resting my head against the door and feeling too drained to face the reality awaiting me at home.

By the time we made it back to the house, it was dark. I found out that Ian and my dad had watched the explosion live on TV, so they already knew Mom was gone. Knowing I couldn't be selfish anymore, I went to sit with my brothers, and we cried.

For the next few days, Aaron and Lavinia helped our dad plan the funeral. My brothers and I were so thankful to them because it was difficult for us to do anything without breaking down. Lavinia even helped Ian write the eulogy.

For the first time I was annoyed about being a nyxling. I was so exhausted, and I hadn't fed or slept in days. There were no nighttime medications I could take to help me fall asleep, and I refused to take Aaron's blood because I just didn't want to feel good. Lavinia brought a few blood bags to the house, but I wasn't interested in those either.

"You have to feed," Lavinia said to me.

"I am not thirsty," I protested hollowly.

"It could be very dangerous if you don't feed. I don't know if it's the same for nyxlings, but when a vampire doesn't feed, our minds start decaying until we are mindlessly driven by hunger and essentially turn into zombies."

I didn't want to hurt anyone, so I took a cup from Lavinia and drank the entire thing. I smiled warmly at her then walked up to my room and laid down on the bed. As the blood coursed through me, I felt my body starting to feel stronger and my mind becoming less cloudy. Lavinia had been right. I'd needed that. It only took me moments to fall asleep after that.

The next day was Mom's funeral. We decided to have the service at 8 p.m. so Ian could attend. Lavinia bought a black dress for me and black suits for the rest of my family. I still wanted to be cautious about her, but she was being so good to us that it felt impossible. Although I would never forget what she had done, I was pretty sure I'd already forgiven her.

"Nina! Do you have your keys? Your car is behind Dad's," Zay yelled up to me from the bottom of the stairs.

I walked over to my jacket hanging on my computer chair and pulled out the keys, but I felt something else in there, too. It was the letter I had found a few days earlier. I'd completely forgotten about it.

I threw the keys down to Zay then went back into my room to open it. Inside I found two letters and a necklace. I examined the necklace closer and instantly knew what it was. It was the same one Connor had worn every day. I put it in my palm then placed it near my heart.

Hesitant to open the letters, I was afraid they were going to be from someone letting me know Connor hadn't made it. With that possibility, I started to cry again, but I stopped myself after a short while and looked back at the letters.

One was addressed to Ian and me and the other just to me. I read the one for both of us first.

Before I could think about how that letter made me feel, I moved on to the second one.

As I read the last line, a single tear fell onto the page. I folded it back up and put it in my desk drawer. I looked at the necklace in my hands. It was beautiful. Even though I knew it was possibly older than the Earth itself, the silver looked brand-new. I kissed it and put it around my neck then put on a black sweater and brushed my hair out.

I glanced at my reflection in the mirror, catching the gleam of the still unfamiliar color of my eyes. I smiled, thinking about how Becca had come through with a plausible—well, semi-plausible—explanation for the change: Waardenburg Syndrome.

Although the symptoms were not exactly the same as ours, our dad, as a doctor, had been able to manipulate the diagnosis to match. He had kept the fact that the syndrome was genetic but had added that since we hadn't been born with it, the cause was due to an infection. That also explained why the color of my eyes was gray and not blue like in most of the cases. He had named this form Waardenburg-2009.

As I stewed in my thoughts, I heard a knock at the door.

"Are you ready?" Aaron asked.

He looked down at the envelope in my hand. I smiled as I handed it to him.

"He's really gone?" he asked after he finished reading the letter to Ian and me.

"Sounds like it," I answered as I started walking toward the door.

"I'm sorry. I know you cared for him and—"

"I love *you*, Aaron," I cut him off then kissed him gently on the lips.

I knew that by not showing Aaron the other letter I was lying to him, but I thought it best that he didn't worry. The truth was that I didn't know if I would ever see Connor again. He said he would come back, but if his brother was that dangerous, I didn't think he would risk our safety.

When we walked into the living room, Ian and Becca were waiting for us. Everyone else had already left for the funeral home to help my dad with the arrangements. I was thankful when Aaron offered to drive because I didn't feel up to it.

When we pulled up to the funeral home, I couldn't even bring myself to step out of the car. Going into the building somehow felt like accepting the finality of my mom's death.

"I just need a minute," I muttered under my breath.

Everyone exited the car and went inside, but I remained in the front passenger seat, lost in contemplation about how we had arrived at this devastating point.

Despite supernatural occurrences in the past few months, my mom's life had been claimed by a tragically ordinary accident. I couldn't shake the haunting question about whether things would have been different if Ian and I hadn't enrolled at VP.

Hallowed Hills was home to so much that I cherished—my friends, my boyfriend—but none of it was worth the cost of my mom's life. I would have given anything to have her back.

The driver's side door opened, and Alan sat down next to me. I looked at him but didn't say anything. I had the feeling he was going to try to cheer me up by being his usual, sarcastic self, but I wasn't in the mood, so I just sat there staring out the window.

"I just want to be alone," I finally said after a few moments.

"You don't have to be by yourself to be alone," he responded with a sympathetic smile.

I looked at him and nodded. It was nice to have him there even if it was just to sit quietly next to me.

I watched as people started to arrive and walk toward the building. My mom had been a well-loved person. I could see my dad and brothers greeting everyone as they entered. I heard people ask where I was and my family telling them I was inside.

I watched the last person walk in, and I knew I couldn't just continue to sit there, but I was frozen. I looked over at the driver's side door when I heard it open. Alan exited the car then walked around to the passenger side.

When he opened my door, he squatted down beside me. "I know this is going to be hard, but you will regret not going. Trust me," he explained with a crooked smile.

With that, he put his hand out for me, and I took it.

We walked toward the funeral home, but I stopped and began to cry. Alan put his arms around me and pulled me into his chest.

After a few minutes I was able to collect myself. "Thank you," I whispered.

He nodded and gave me his arm; I wrapped my arm around his, and we went up the steps.

As we reached the imposing black doors, I took a deep breath before stepping inside. I didn't want to speak to anyone, so I stayed back. Aaron came up to me and gave me his arm, so I dropped Alan's and smiled before taking Aaron's.

I heard my dad speaking to the priest about getting the service going, and he asked everyone to take their seats while Aaron led me to mine. I could hear people whispering, but I didn't care to hear what they were saying. I was starting to realize that sometimes I had to ignore the voices because there were things I just didn't want to know.

The service was beautiful, and we listened to heartfelt words spoken about my mom. Ian delivered a moving eulogy that brought tears to everyone's eyes. As the service concluded, my family and I stood at the front next to the casket, expressing gratitude to those who'd attended.

Amidst the departing crowd, I observed a tall, striking man standing off to one side. His skin was tan. His dark hair was pulled back into a ponytail, and his gray suit accentuated his muscular physique beneath it. I was entranced by his presence when he turned and our eyes met, a sudden jolt of intensity passing between us.

Startled, I averted my gaze, but when I dared to look back again, he was leaving with the rest of the guests. As the crowd dispersed, I noticed Calix among them. I smiled at him as he waved and left with the others.

"Do you know him?" Alan asked as he and Aaron walked up to us.

"Not really. He just goes to our school."

"There's something off about him," he remarked with a hint of unease.

"Yes, there is," Aaron agreed.

"There is not. He's just new."

"Hmm, he smells... different," Alan said cryptically.

As I exchanged a puzzled glance with Aaron, a sense of foreboding washed over me. The unsettling notion that there may be more to our fellow classmate than met the eye lingered in the back of my mind. "Weirdo," I said instead, trying to lighten the mood.

"You're young. You will learn to recognize the scents of different creatures."

"Different creatures? You think he's some sort of creature?" Ian interjected, his voice tinged with a mixture of curiosity and apprehension as he voiced the unspoken question everyone was thinking.

"I don't know, but I'm going to find out," Alan announced as he started to walk away.

"Not now," I pleaded with him as I grabbed his arm.

A silent exchange passed between us, and we shared a wordless understanding in the depths of our gazes. I smiled at him shyly, and he reciprocated with a sweet smile of his own. He nodded then returned to his spot next to me.

I wasn't ready to join everyone for the burial, so I sat back down in one of the pews and watched Lavinia and Aaron help our dad with the hearse driver. I was thankful for that. Alan, Becca, and my brothers came to sit with me in the pew but didn't say anything. We just sat in silence.

"Help me," a haunting plea echoed through the air like some kind of mysterious summons that commanded immediate attention.

Ian, Alan, and I exchanged glances, and a shared sense of unease settled over us.

"What's wrong?" Zay asked, sensing the tension we were experiencing.

All three of us simultaneously turned toward the front door of the funeral home.

"Help me," the voice called again.

"Doesn't that sound like—"

"Mom," I interjected, cutting Ian off as a chilling realization dawned on me.

"What?" Zay asked in horror.

"Help me," the voice implored again. The desperate plea compelled me into action. Without hesitation, I stood, and the others followed me out of the building.

"Mom!" I yelled as I blurred toward the source of the mysterious plea.

Seconds later, Alan and Ian blurred up next to me. I listened for the voice again but didn't hear anything.

"Mom!" I shouted again.

"Nina," whispered the voice, distant yet somehow intimate.

We walked slowly into an adjacent field of wheat. The tall, overgrown plants enveloped us as we advanced, rustling in accompaniment of our journey. I heard the murmur of running water, which guided our path through the maze of vegetation.

We continued walking for a few more minutes before we arrived in a clearing within which was a small circular pond, no larger than six feet in diameter.

As we looked in, its depths held a substance, a profound black liquid that defied categorization. Too thick to be water, too thin to be oil, it broke all known laws of nature. As I leaned over to observe its peculiar properties, the liquid suddenly began draining away, leaving behind a gaping hole.

"Help me," my mom's voice echoed once more from an abyss deep within the Earth.

Continued in...

*Hart of the Night: Immortals*

# CHAPTER 26
## ABOUT THE AUTHOR

M.C. Ruskuls, a native of Naperville, Illinois, dives into the world of storytelling with the same tenacity she brings to the wrestling ring. Her journey as an independent professional wrestler, which began in 2013, has taken her across the heartlands of the Midwestern U.S. where she has faced challenges head-on. When she's not grappling with opponents in the ring, she's wrangling her energetic toddler and loyal German Shepherd.

Despite the ever-present demands of motherhood and canine companionship, Ruskuls carves out precious moments during naptime and late into the night to indulge in her true passion: writing. Raised in a household where science fiction and fantasy were as essential as air, she devoured novels and binge-watched superhero TV shows with her family, thereby fostering a love for imaginative worlds and heroic tales.

Drawing from her experiences in professional wrestling, Ruskuls infuses her writing with adrenaline-pumping action and larger-than-life characters. She doesn't boast any formal training in her writing; instead, she relies on her sheer dedication to crafting stories that captivate and entertain. With each word she pens, Ruskuls aims to transport readers to realms where heroes rise, villains fall, and the spirit of adventure reigns supreme.

# CHAPTER 27
## SNEAK PREVIEW

After their mother's death, the Harts' quest for truth spirals into the unknown. Nina encounters a captivating stranger tied to her past, whose charm lures her into a deadly web, unraveling a sinister plot threatening everyone she loves. Amidst the turmoil, divine players emerge with hidden agendas. What secrets still lie in the shadows? Discover the answers in Book 2: Hart of the Night: Immortals.

# CHAPTER 28
## THANK YOU FOR READING

Enjoyed *Hart of the Night: Bloodline*? Please consider leaving a review! Your feedback is invaluable and helps more readers discover the story. Don't forget to follow @mcruskuls on Facebook, Twitter, Instagram, and TikTok for exclusive updates and exciting content! Visit www.mcruskuls .com for information on current and upcoming novels.